AND ON
THE SEVENTH DAY

PAULO
COELHO

AND ON
THE SEVENTH DAY

HarperCollins*Publishers*

HarperCollins*Publishers*

This edition containing *By the River Piedra I Sat Down and Wept, Veronika Decides to Die*, and
The Devil and Miss Prym first published in Australia in 2004
by HarperCollins*Publishers* Pty Limited
ABN 36 009 913 517
A member of the HarperCollins*Publishers* (Australia) Pty Limited Group
www.harpercollins.com.au

By the River Piedra I Sat Down and Wept was first published in Brazil in 1994 under
the title *Na margem do rio Piedra eu sentei e chorei* by Editora Rocca Ltd, Rio de Janeiro
First published in Australia in 1996
by HarperCollins*Publishers*
Copyright © Paulo Coelho 1994
English translation by Alan R Clarke; copyright © HarperCollins*Publishers* 1996

Veronika Decides to Die was first published in English in the UK in 1999
by HarperCollins*Publishers*
First published in Australia in 1999
by HarperCollins*Publishers*
Copyright © Paulo Coelho 1998
English translation copyright © Margaret Jull Costa 1999

The Devil and Miss Prym was first published in English in the UK in 2001
by HarperCollins*Publishers*
First published in Australia in 2001
by HarperCollins*Publishers*
Copyright © Paulo Coelho 2001
English translation copyright © Amanda Hopkinson and Nick Caistor 2001

HarperCollins*Publishers*
25 Ryde Road, Pymble, Sydney, NSW 2073, Australia
31 View Road, Glenfield, Auckland 10, New Zealand

National Library of Australia Cataloguing-in-Publication data:

Coelho, Paulo.
    And on the seventh day.
    ISBN 0 7322 7875 9.
    I. Title. II. Title : Coelho, Paulo. Na magrem do rio Piedra eu sentai
    e chorei. English. III. Title : Coelho, Paulo. Veronika decide morrer. English.
    IV. Title : Coelho, Paulo. Demonio e a Stra. Prym. English.
869.3

Cover photo and design by Marcia Grace Designs
Internal design by Avril Makula
Typeset in Goudy 11.5/16
Printed and bound in Australia by Griffin Press on 70gsm Bulky Book Ivory

5 4 3 2 1   04 05 06 07

Contents

By the River Piedra
I Sat Down and Wept

For I. C. and S. B., whose loving communion made me see the feminine face of God;

for Monica Antunes, my companion from the beginning, who with her love and enthusiasm spreads the fire all over the world;

for Paulo Rocco, for the joy of the battles we have fought together and for the dignity of the battles we have fought between us;

and for Matthew Lore, for not having forgotten a sage quotation from the *I Ching*: 'Perseverance is favorable.'

Author's Note

A Spanish missionary was visiting an island when he came across three Aztec priests.

'How do you pray?' the missionary asked.

'We have only one prayer,' answered one of the Aztecs. 'We say, "God, you are three, we are three. Have pity on us."'

'A beautiful prayer,' said the missionary. 'But it is not exactly the one that God heeds. I'm going to teach you one that's much better.'

The padre taught them a Catholic prayer and then continued on his path of evangelism. Years later, when he was returning to Spain, his ship stopped again at the island. From the deck, the missionary saw the three priests on the shore and waved to them.

Just then, the three men began to walk across the water toward him.

'Padre! Padre!' one of them called, approaching the ship. 'Teach us again that prayer that God heeds. We've forgotten how it goes.'

'It doesn't matter,' responded the missionary, witnessing the miracle. And he promptly asked God's forgiveness for failing to recognize that He speaks all languages.

This story illustrates just what this book is about. Rarely do we realize that we are in the midst of the extraordinary. Miracles occur all around us, signs from God show us the way, angels plead to be heard, but we pay little attention to them because we have been taught that we must follow certain formulas and rules if we want to find God. We do not recognize that God is wherever we allow Him/Her to enter.

Traditional religious practices are important: they allow us to share with others the communal experience of adoration and prayer. But we must never forget that spiritual experience is above all a *practical* experience of love. And with love, there are no rules. Some may try to control their emotions and develop strategies for their behavior; others may turn to reading books of advice from 'experts' on relationships but this is all folly. The heart decides, and what it decides is all that really matters.

All of us have had this experience. At some point, we have each said through our tears, 'I'm suffering for a love that's not worth it.' We suffer because we feel we are giving more than we receive. We suffer because our love is going unrecognized. We suffer because we are unable to impose our own rules.

But ultimately there is no good reason for our suffering, for in every love lies the seed of our growth. The more we love, the closer we come to spiritual experience. Those who are truly enlightened, those whose souls are illuminated by love, have been able to overcome all of the inhibitions and preconceptions of their era. They have been able to sing, to laugh, and to pray out loud; they have danced and shared what Saint Paul called 'the madness of saintliness.' They have been joyful – because those who love conquer the world and have no fear of loss. True love is an act of total surrender.

This book is about the importance of that surrender. Pilar and her companion are fictitious, but they represent the many conflicts that beset us in our search for love. Sooner or later, we have to overcome our fears, because the spiritual path can only be traveled through the daily experience of love.

Thomas Merton once said that the spiritual life is essentially to love. One doesn't love in order to do what is good or to help or to protect someone. If we act that way, we are perceiving the other as a simple object, and we are seeing ourselves as wise and generous persons. This has nothing to do with love. To love is to be in communion with the other and to discover in that other the spark of God.

May Pilar's lament on the bank of the River Piedra guide us toward such communion.

Paulo Coelho

But wisdom is justified by all her children.

LUKE 7:35

By the River Piedra I sat down and wept. There is a legend that everything that falls into the waters of this river – leaves, insects, the feathers of birds – is transformed into the rocks that make the riverbed. If only I could tear out my heart and hurl it into the current, then my pain and longing would be over, and I could finally forget.

By the River Piedra I sat down and wept. The winter air chills the tears on my cheeks, and my tears fall into the cold waters that course past me. Somewhere, this river joins another, then another, until – far from my heart and sight – all of them merge with the sea.

May my tears run just as far, that my love might never know that one day I cried for him. May my tears run just as far, that I might forget the River Piedra, the monastery, the church in the Pyrenees, the mists, and the paths we walked together.

I shall forget the roads, the mountains, and the fields of my dreams – the dreams that will never come true.

I remember my 'magic moment' that instant when a 'yes' or a 'no' can change one's life forever. It seems so long ago now. It is hard to believe that it was only last week that I had found my love once again, and then lost him.

I am writing this story on the bank of the River Piedra. My hands are freezing, my legs are numb, and every minute I want to stop.

'Seek to live. Remembrance is for the old,' he said.

Perhaps love makes us old before our time – or young, if youth has passed. But how can I not recall those moments? That is why I write – to try to turn sadness into longing, solitude into remembrance. So that when I finish telling myself the story, I can toss it into the Piedra. That's what the woman who has given me shelter told me to do. Only then – in the words of one of the saints – will the water extinguish what the flames have written.

All love stories are the same.

WE HAD BEEN CHILDREN TOGETHER. Then he left, like so many young people who leave small towns. He said he was going to learn about the world, that his dreams lay beyond the fields of Soria.

Years passed with almost no news of him. Every now and then he would send me a letter, but he never returned to the paths and forests of our childhood.

When I finished school, I moved to Zaragoza, and there I found that he had been right. Soria was a small town, and as its only famous poet had said, roads are made to be traveled. I enrolled in the university and found a boyfriend. I began to study for a scholarship (I was working as a salesgirl to pay for my courses). But I lost the competition for the scholarship, and after that I left my boyfriend.

Then the letters from my childhood friend began to arrive more frequently – and I was envious of the stamps from so many different places. He seemed to know everything; he had sprouted wings, and now he roamed the world. Meanwhile, I was simply trying to put down roots.

Some of his letters, all mailed from the same place in France, spoke of God. In one, he wrote about wanting to enter a seminary and dedicate his life to prayer. I wrote him back, asking him to wait a bit, urging him to experience more of his freedom before committing himself to something so serious.

But after I reread my letter, I tore it up. Who was I to speak about freedom or commitment? Compared to him, I knew nothing about such things.

One day I learned that he had begun to give lectures. This surprised me; I thought he was too young to be able to teach anything to anyone. And then he wrote to me that he was going to speak to a small group in Madrid – and he asked me to come.

So I made the four-hour trip from Zaragoza to Madrid. I wanted to see him again; I wanted to hear his voice. I wanted to sit with him in a cafe and remember the old days, when we had thought the world was far too large for anyone ever to know it truly.

Saturday, December 4, 1993

The place where the conference was held was more formal than I had imagined it, and there were more people there than I had expected. How had all this come about?

He must be famous, I thought. He'd said nothing about this in his letters. I wanted to go up to the people in the audience and ask them why they were there, but I didn't have the nerve.

I was even more surprised when I saw him enter the room. He was quite different from the boy I had known – but of course, it had been twelve years; people change. Tonight his eyes were shining – he looked wonderful.

'He's giving us back what was ours,' said a woman seated next to me.

A strange thing to say.

'What is he giving back?' I asked.

'What was stolen from us. Religion.'

'No, no, he's not giving us anything back,' said a younger woman seated on my right. 'They can't return something that has always belonged to us.'

'Well, then, what are you doing here?' the first woman asked, irritated.

'I want to listen to him. I want to see how they think; they've already burned us at the stake once, and they may want to do it again.'

'He's just one voice,' said the woman. 'He's doing what he can.'

The young woman smiled sarcastically and turned away, putting an end to the conversation.

'He's taking a courageous position for a seminarian,' the other woman went on, looking to me for support.

I didn't understand any of this, and I said nothing. The woman finally gave up. The girl at my side winked at me, as if I were her ally.

But I was silent for a different reason. I was thinking, *Seminarian? It can't be! He would have told me.*

When he started to speak, I couldn't concentrate. I was sure he had spotted me in the audience, and I was trying to guess what he was thinking. How did I look to him? How different was the woman of twenty-nine from the girl of seventeen?

I noticed that his voice hadn't changed. But his words certainly had.

YOU HAVE TO TAKE RISKS, he said. *We will only understand the miracle of life fully when we allow the unexpected to happen.*

Every day, God gives us the sun – and also one moment in which we have the ability to change everything that makes us unhappy. Every day, we try to pretend that we haven't perceived that moment, that it doesn't exist – that today is the same as yesterday and will be the same as tomorrow. But if people really pay attention to their everyday lives, they will discover that magic moment. It may arrive in the instant when we are doing something mundane, like putting our front door key in the lock; it may lie hidden in the quiet that follows the lunch hour or in the thousand and one things that all seem the same to us. But that moment exists – a moment when all the power of the stars becomes a part of us and enables us to perform miracles.

Joy is sometimes a blessing, but it is often a conquest. Our magic moment helps us to change and sends us off in search of our dreams. Yes, we are going to suffer, we will have difficult times, and we will experience many disappointments – but all of this is transitory; it leaves no permanent mark. And one day we will look back with pride and faith at the journey we have taken.

Pitiful is the person who is afraid of taking risks. Perhaps this person will never be disappointed or disillusioned; perhaps she won't suffer the way people do when they have a dream to follow. But when that person looks back – and at some point everyone looks back – she will hear her heart saying, 'What have you done with the miracles that God planted in your days? What have you done with the talents God bestowed on you? You buried yourself in a cave because you were fearful of losing those talents. So this is your heritage: the certainty that you wasted your life.'

Pitiful are the people who must realize this. Because when they are finally able to believe in miracles, their life's magic moments will have already passed them by.

AFTER THE LECTURE, MEMBERS OF the audience rushed up to him. I waited, worried about what his first impression of me would be after so many years. I felt like a child – insecure, tense because I knew none of his new friends, and jealous that he was paying more attention to the others than to me.

When he finally came up to me, he blushed. Suddenly he was no longer a man with important things to say but was once again the boy who had hidden with me at the hermitage of San Saturio, telling me of his dream to travel the world (while our parents were calling the police, sure that we had drowned in the river).

'Pilar,' he said.

I kissed him. I could have complimented him on his presentation. I could have said I was tired of being around so many people. I could have made some humorous remark about our childhood or commented on how proud I was to see him there, so admired by others.

I could have explained that I had to run and catch the last bus back to Zaragoza.

I could have. What does this phrase mean? At any given moment in our lives, there are certain things that could have happened but didn't. The magic moments go unrecognized, and then suddenly, the hand of destiny changes everything.

That's what happened to me just then. In spite of all the things I could have done or said, I asked a question that has brought me, a week later, to this river and has caused me to write these very lines.

'Can we have coffee together?' I said.

And he, turning to me, accepted the hand offered by fate.

'I really need to talk to you. Tomorrow I have a lecture in Bilbao. I have a car. Come with me.'

'I have to get back to Zaragoza,' I answered, not realizing that this was my last chance.

Then I surprised myself – perhaps because in seeing him, I had become a child again . . . or perhaps because we are not the ones who write the best moments of our lives. I said, 'But they're about to celebrate the holiday of the Immaculate Conception in Bilbao. I can go there with you and then continue on to Zaragoza.'

Just then, it was on the tip of my tongue to ask him about his being a 'seminarian.' He must have read my expression, because he said quickly, 'Do you want to ask me something?'

'Yes. Before your lecture, a woman said that you were giving her back what had been hers. What did she mean?'

'Oh, that's nothing.'

'But it's important to me. I don't know anything about your life; I'm even surprised to see so many people here.'

He just laughed, and then he started to turn away to answer other people's questions.

'Wait,' I said, grabbing his arm. 'You didn't answer me.'

'I don't think it would interest you, Pilar.'

'I want to know anyway.'

Taking a deep breath, he led me to a corner of the room. 'All of the great religions – including Judaism, Catholicism, and Islam – are masculine. Men are in charge of the dogmas, men make the laws, and usually all the priests are men.'

'Is that what the woman meant?'

He hesitated before he answered. 'Yes. I have a different view of things: I believe in the feminine side of God.'

I sighed with relief. The woman was mistaken; he couldn't be a seminarian because seminarians don't have such different views of things.

'You've explained it very well,' I said.

THE GIRL WHO HAD WINKED at me was waiting at the door.

'I know that we belong to the same tradition,' she said. 'My name is Brida.'

'I don't know what you're talking about.'

'Of course you do,' she laughed.

She took my arm and led me out of the building before I could say anything more. It was a cold night, and I wasn't sure what I was going to do until we left for Bilbao the next morning.

'Where are we going?' I asked.

'To the statue of the Goddess.'

'But . . . I need to find an inexpensive hotel where I can stay for the night.'

'I'll show you one later.'

I wanted to go to some warm cafe where I could talk to her for a bit and learn as much as I could about him. But I didn't want to argue. While she guided me across the Paseo de Castellana, I looked around at Madrid; I hadn't been there in years.

In the middle of the avenue, she stopped and pointed to the sky. 'There She is.'

The moon shone brilliantly through the bare branches of the trees on either side of the road.

'Isn't that beautiful!' I exclaimed.

But she wasn't listening. She spread her arms in the form of a cross, turning her palms upward, and just stood there contemplating the moon.

What have I gotten myself into? I thought. *I came here to attend a conference, and now I wind up in the Paseo de Castellana with this crazy girl. And tomorrow I'm going to Bilbao!*

'O mirror of the Earth Goddess,' Brida was saying, her eyes closed. 'Teach us about our power and make men understand us. Rising, gleaming, waning, and reviving in the heavens, you show us the cycle of the seed and the fruit.'

She stretched her arms toward the night sky and held this position for some time. Several passersby looked at her and laughed, but she paid no attention; I was the one who was dying of embarrassment, standing there beside her.

'I needed to do that,' she said, after her long adoration of the moon, 'so that the Goddess would protect us.'

'What are you talking about?'

'The same thing that your friend was talking about, only with words that are true.'

I was sorry now that I hadn't paid closer attention to the lecture.

'We know the feminine side of God,' Brida continued as we started to walk on. 'We, the women, understand and love the Great Mother. We have paid for our wisdom with persecution and burnings at the stake, but we have survived. And now we understand Her mysteries.'

Burnings at the stake? She was talking about witches!

I looked more closely at the woman by my side. She was pretty, with hair that hung to the middle of her back.

'While men were going off to hunt, we remained in the caves, in the womb of the Mother, caring for our children. And it was there that the Great Mother taught us everything.'

'Men lived through movement, while we remained close to the womb of the Mother. This allowed us to see that seeds are turned into plants, and we told this to the men. We made the first bread, and we fed our people. We shaped the first cup so that we could drink. And we came to understand the cycle of creation, because our bodies repeat the rhythm of the moon.'

She stopped suddenly. 'There She is!'

I looked. There in the middle of the plaza, surrounded on all sides by traffic, was a fountain portraying a woman in a carriage drawn by lions.

'This is the Plaza Cybele,' I said, trying to show off my knowledge of Madrid. I had seen this fountain on dozens of postcards.

But the young woman wasn't listening. She was already in the middle of the street, trying to make her way through the traffic. 'Come on! Let's go over there!' she shouted, waving to me from the midst of the cars.

I decided to try to follow her, if only to get the name of a hotel. Her craziness was wearing me out; I needed to get some sleep.

We made it to the fountain at almost the same time; my heart was pounding, but she had a smile on her lips. 'Water!' she exclaimed. 'Water is Her manifestation.'

'Please, I need the name of an inexpensive hotel.'

She plunged her hands into the water. 'You should do this, too,' she said to me. 'Feel the water.'

'No! But I don't want to spoil your experience. I'm going to look for a hotel.'

'Just a minute.'

Brida took a small flute from her bag and began to play. To my surprise, the music had a hypnotic effect; the sounds of the traffic receded, and my racing heart began to slow down. I sat on the edge of the fountain, listening to the noise of the water and the sound of the flute, my eyes on the full moon gleaming above us. Somehow I was sensing – although I couldn't quite understand it – that the moon was a reflection of my womanhood.

I don't know how long she continued to play. When she stopped, she turned to the fountain. 'Cybele, manifestation of the Great Mother, who governs the harvests, sustains the cities, and returns to woman her role as priestess . . .'

'Who are you?' I asked. 'Why did you ask me to come with you?'

She turned to me. 'I am what you see me to be. I am a part of the religion of the earth.'

'What do you want from me?'

'I can read your eyes. I can read your heart. You are going to fall in love. And suffer.'

'I am?'

'You know what I'm talking about. I saw how he was looking at you. He loves you.'

This woman was really nuts!

'That's why I asked you to come with me – because he is important. Even though he says some silly things, at least he recognizes the Great Mother. Don't let him lose his way. Help him.'

'You don't know what you're talking about. You're dreaming!' And I turned and rushed back into the traffic, swearing I'd forget everything she had said.

Sunday, December 5, 1993

We stopped for a cup of coffee.

'Yes, life teaches us many things,' I said, trying to continue the conversation.

'It taught me that we can learn, and it taught me that we can change,' he replied, 'even when it seems impossible.'

Clearly he wanted to drop the subject. We had hardly spoken during the two-hour drive that had brought us to this roadside cafe.

In the beginning, I had tried to reminisce about our childhood adventures, but he'd shown only a polite interest. In fact, he hadn't even really been listening to me; he kept asking me questions about things I had already told him.

Something was wrong. Had time and distance taken him away from my world forever? *After all, he talks about 'magic moments,'* I reasoned. *Why would he care about an old friend's career? He lives in a different universe, where Soria is only a remote memory – a town frozen in time, his childhood friends still young boys and girls, the old folks still alive and doing the same things they'd been doing for so many years.*

I was beginning to regret my decision to come with him. So when he changed the subject again, I resolved not to insist any further.

The last two hours of the drive to Bilbao were torture. He was watching the road, I was looking out the window, and neither of us could hide the bad feelings that had arisen between us. The rental car didn't have a radio, so all we could do was endure the silence.

'Let's ask where the bus station is,' I suggested as soon as we left the highway. 'The buses leave from here regularly for Zaragoza.'

It was the hour of siesta, and there were few people in the streets. We passed one gentleman and then a couple of teenagers, but he didn't stop to ask them. 'Do you know where it is?' I spoke up, after some time had passed.

'Where what is?'

He still wasn't paying attention to what I said.

And then suddenly I understood what the silence was about. What did he have in common with a woman who had never ventured out into the world? How could he possibly be interested in spending time with someone who feared the unknown, who preferred a secure job and a conventional marriage to the life he led? Poor me, chattering away about friends from childhood and dusty memories of an insignificant village – those were the only things I could discuss.

When we seemed to have reached the center of town, I said, 'You can let me off here.' I was trying to sound casual, but I felt stupid, childish, and irritated.

He didn't stop the car.

'I have to catch the bus back to Zaragoza,' I insisted.

'I've never been here before,' he answered. 'I have no idea where my hotel is, I don't know where the conference is being held, and I don't know where the bus station is.'

'Don't worry, I'll be all right.'

He slowed down but kept on driving.

'I'd really like to . . . ,' he began. He tried again but still couldn't finish his thought.

I could imagine what he would like to do: thank me for the company, send greetings to his old friends – maybe that would break the tension.

'I would really like it if you went with me to the conference tonight,' he finally said.

I was shocked. Was he stalling for time so that he could make up for the awkward silence of our trip?

'I'd really like you to go with me,' he repeated.

Now, maybe I'm a girl from the farm with no great stories to tell. Maybe I lack the sophistication of women from the big city. Life in the country may not make a woman elegant or worldly, but it still teaches her how to listen to her heart and to trust her instincts.

To my surprise, my instincts told me that he meant what he said.

I sighed with relief. Of course I wasn't going to stay for any conference, but at least my friend seemed to be back. He was even inviting me along on his adventures, wanting to share his fears and triumphs with me.

'Thanks for the invitation,' I said, 'but I don't have enough money for a hotel, and I do need to get back to my studies.'

'I have some money. You can stay in my room. We'll ask for two beds.'

I noticed that he was beginning to perspire, despite the chill in the air. My heart sounded an alarm, and all the joy of the moment before turned into confusion.

Suddenly he stopped the car and looked directly into my eyes.

No one can lie, no one can hide anything, when he looks directly into someone's eyes. And any woman with the least bit of sensitivity can read the eyes of a man in love.

I thought immediately of what that weird young woman at the fountain had said. It wasn't possible – but it seemed to be true.

I had never dreamed that after all these years he would still remember. When we were children, we had walked through the world hand in hand. I had loved him – if a child can know what love means. But that was so many years ago – it was another life, a life whose innocence had opened my heart to all that was good.

And now we were responsible adults. We had put away childish things.

I looked into his eyes. I didn't want to – or wasn't able to – believe what I saw there.

'I just have this last conference, and then the holidays of the Immaculate Conception begin. I have to go up into the mountains; I want to show you something.'

This brilliant man who was able to speak of magic moments was now here with me, acting as awkward as could be. He was moving too fast, he was unsure of himself; the things he was proposing were confused. It was painful for me to see him this way.

I opened the door and got out, then leaned against the fender, looking at the nearly deserted street. I lit a cigarette. I could try to hide my thoughts, pretend that I didn't understand what he was saying; I could try to convince myself that this was just a suggestion made by one childhood friend to another. Maybe he'd been on the road too long and was beginning to get confused.

Maybe I was exaggerating.

He jumped out of the car and came to my side.

'I'd really like you to stay for the conference tonight,' he said again. 'But if you can't, I'll understand.'

There! The world made a complete turn and returned to where it belonged. It wasn't what I had been thinking; he was no longer insisting, he was ready to let me leave – a man in love doesn't act that way.

I felt both stupid and relieved. Yes, I could stay for at least one more day. We could have dinner together and get a little drunk – something we'd never done when we were younger. This would give me a chance to forget the stupid ideas I'd just had, and it would be a good opportunity to break the ice that had frozen us ever since we left Madrid.

One day wouldn't make any difference. And then at least I'd have a story to tell my friends.

'Separate beds,' I said, joking. 'And you pay for dinner, because I'm still a student. I'm broke.'

✳

We put our bags in the hotel room and came down to see where the conference was to be held. Since we were so early, we sat down in a cafe to wait.

'I want to give you something,' he said, handing me a small red pouch.

I opened it and found inside an old rusty medal, with Our Lady of Grace on one side and the Sacred Heart of Jesus on the other.

'That was yours,' he said, noticing my surprise. My heart began to sound the alarm again. 'One day – it was autumn, just like it is now, and we must have been ten – I was sitting with you in the plaza where the great oak stood.'

'I was going to tell you something, something I had rehearsed for weeks. But as soon as I began, you told me that you had lost your medal at the hermitage of San Saturio, and you asked me to see if I could find it there.'

I remembered. Oh, God, I remembered!

'I did find it. But when I returned to the plaza, I no longer had the courage to say what I had rehearsed. So I promised myself that I would return the medal to you only when I was able to complete the sentence that I'd begun that day almost twenty years ago. For a long time, I've tried to forget it, but it's always there. I can't live with it any longer.'

He put down his coffee, lit a cigarette, and looked at the ceiling for a long time. Then he turned to me. 'It's a very simple sentence,' he said. 'I love you.'

SOMETIMES AN UNCONTROLLABLE FEELING OF *sadness grips us*, he said. *We recognize that the magic moment of the day has passed and that we've done nothing about it. Life begins to conceal its magic and its art.*

We have to listen to the child we once were, the child who still exists inside us. That child understands magic moments. We can stifle its cries, but we cannot silence its voice.

The child we once were is still there. Blessed are the children, for theirs is the kingdom of heaven.

If we are not reborn – if we cannot learn to look at life with the innocence and the enthusiasm of childhood – it makes no sense to go on living.

There are many ways to commit suicide. Those who try to kill the body violate God's law. Those who try to kill the soul also violate God's law, even though their crime is less visible to others.

We have to pay attention to what the child in our heart tells us. We should not be embarrassed by this child. We must not allow this child to be scared because the child is alone and is almost never heard.

We must allow the child to take the reins of our lives. The child knows that each day is different from every other day.

We have to allow it to feel loved again. We must please this child – even if this means that we act in ways we are not used to, in ways that may seem foolish to others.

Remember that human wisdom is madness in the eyes of God.

But if we listen to the child who lives in our soul, our eyes will grow bright. If we do not lose contact with that child, we will not lose contact with life.

THE COLORS AROUND ME WERE growing vivid; I felt that I was speaking with more intensity and that my glass made a louder sound when I put it down on the table.

A group of about ten of us were having dinner together after the conference. Everyone was speaking at the same time, and I was smiling, for this night was special: it was the first night in many years that I had not planned.

What a joy!

When I'd decided to go to Madrid, I had been in control of my actions and my feelings. Now, suddenly, all that had changed. Here I was in a city where I'd never set foot before, even though it was only three hours from the place where I'd been born. I was sitting at a table where I knew only one person, and everyone was speaking to me as if they'd known me for years. I was amazed that I could enter into the conversation, that I could drink and enjoy myself with them.

I was there because suddenly life had presented me with Life. I felt no guilt, no fear, no embarrassment. As I listened to what he was saying – and felt myself growing closer to him – I was more and more convinced that he was right: there are moments when you have to take a risk, to do crazy things.

I spend day after day with my texts and notebooks, making this superhuman effort just to purchase my own servitude, I thought. *Why do I want that job? What does it offer me as a human being, as a woman?*

Nothing! I wasn't born to spend my life behind a desk, helping judges dispose of their cases.

No, I can't think that way about my life. I'm going to have to return to it this week. It must be the wine. After all, when all is said and done, if you don't work, you don't eat. This is all a dream. It's going to end.

But how long can I make the dream go on?

For the first time I considered going to the mountains with him for the next few days. After all, a week of holidays was about to begin.

'Who are you?' a woman at our table asked me.

'A childhood friend,' I answered.

'Was he doing these things when he was a child, too?'

'What things?'

The conversation at the table seemed to fade and then die out.

'You know: the miracles.'

'He could always speak well.' I didn't understand what she meant.

Everyone laughed, including him. I had no idea what was going on. But – maybe because of the wine – I felt relaxed, and for once I didn't feel like I had to be in control.

I looked around and then said something that I forgot the next moment. I was thinking about the upcoming holiday.

It was good to be here, meeting new people, talking about serious things but always with a touch of humor. I felt like I was really participating in the world. For at least this one night, I was no longer just seeing the real world through television or the newspapers. When I returned to Zaragoza, I'd have stories to tell. If I accepted his invitation for the holidays, I'd have whole years of memories to live on.

He was so right not to pay any attention to my remarks about Soria, I thought. And I began to feel sorry for myself; for so many years, my drawer full of memories had held the same old stories.

'Have some more wine,' a white-haired man said, filling my glass.

I drank it down. I kept thinking about how few things I would have had to tell my children and grandchildren if I hadn't come with him.

'I'm counting on our trip to France,' he said to me so that only I could hear.

The wine had freed my tongue. 'But only if you understand one thing.'

'What's that?'

'It's about what you said before the conference. At the cafe.'

'The medal?'

'No,' I said, looking into his eyes and doing everything I could to appear sober. 'What you said.'

'We'll talk about it later,' he said, quickly trying to change the subject.

He had said that he loved me. We hadn't had time to talk about it, but I knew I could convince him that it wasn't true.

'If you want me to take the trip with you, you have to listen to me,' I said.

'I don't want to talk about it here. We're having a good time.'

'You left Soria when you were very young,' I went on. 'I'm only a link to your past. I've reminded you of your roots, and that's what makes you think as you do. But that's all it is. There can't be any love involved.'

He listened but didn't answer. Someone asked him his opinion about something, and our conversation was interrupted.

At least I've explained how I feel, I thought. *The love he was talking about only exists in fairy tales.*

In real life, love has to be possible. Even if it is not returned right away, love can only survive when the hope exists that you will be able to win over the person you desire.

Anything else is fantasy.

From the other side of the table, as if he had guessed what I was thinking, he raised his glass in a toast. 'To love,' he said.

I could tell that he, too, was a little drunk. So I decided to take advantage of the opening: 'To those wise enough to understand that sometimes love is nothing more than the foolishness of childhood,' I said.

'The wise are wise only because they love. And the foolish are foolish only because they think they can understand love,' he answered.

The others at the table heard him, and in a moment an animated discussion about love was in full swing. Everyone had a strong opinion and was defending their position tooth and nail; it took more wine to calm things down. Finally someone said it was getting late and that the owner of the restaurant wanted to close.

'We have five days of vacation,' someone shouted from another table. 'If the owner wants to close, it's just because you were getting too serious.'

Everyone laughed – except me.

'Then where can we talk about serious things?' someone asked the drunk at the other table.

'In church!' said the drunk. And this time all of us laughed.

My friend stood up. I thought he was going to start a fight, because we were all acting like adolescents, and that's what adolescents do. Fighting is as much a part of being a teenager as the kisses, the secret embraces, the loud music, and the fast pace.

But instead he took my hand and moved toward the door. 'We should go,' he said. 'It's getting late.'

IT WAS RAINING IN BILBAO. Lovers need to know how to lose themselves and then how to find themselves again. He was able to do both well. Now he was happy, and as we returned to the hotel he sang:

Son los locos que inventaron el amor.

The song was right: it must have been the lunatics who invented love.

I was still feeling the effects of the wine, but I was struggling to think clearly. I had to stay in control of the situation if I wanted to make the trip with him.

But it will be easy to be in control because I'm not too emotional, I thought. *Anyone who can conquer her heart can conquer the world.*

Con un poema y un tromhón
a develarte el corazón

To lose my heart to you with a poem and a trombone. I wish I didn't have to control my heart. If I could surrender, even if only for a weekend, this rain falling on my face would feel different. If love were easy, I would be embracing him now, and the words of his song would be our story. If Zaragoza weren't waiting for me after the holidays, I'd want to stay drunk and be free to kiss him, caress him, say the things and hear the things that lovers say and do to each other.

But no! I can't. I don't want to.

Salgamos a volar, querida mia, *the song says.*

Yes, let's fly away. But under my conditions.

He still didn't know that I was going to say yes to his invitation. Why did I want to take this risk?

Because I was drunk, because I was tired of days that were all the same.

But this weariness will pass. I'm going to want to get back to Zaragoza, where I have chosen to live. My studies are waiting for me. The husband I'm still looking for is waiting for me – a husband who won't be as difficult to find.

An easier life waits for me, with children and grandchildren, with a clear budget and a yearly vacation. I don't know what his fears are, but I know my own. I don't need new fears – my own are enough.

I was sure I could never fall in love with someone like him. I knew him too well, all his weaknesses and fears. I just couldn't admire him as the others seemed to.

But love is much like a dam: if you allow a tiny crack to form through which only a trickle of water can pass, that trickle will quickly bring down the whole structure, and soon no one will be able to control the force of the current.

For when those walls come down, then love takes over, and it no longer matters what is possible or impossible; it doesn't even matter whether we can keep the loved one at our side. To love is to lose control.

No, no, I cannot allow such a crack to form. No matter how small.

'Hey, hold up a minute!'

He stopped singing immediately. Quick steps echoed on the damp pavement behind us.

'Let's get out of here,' he said, grabbing my arm.

'Wait!' a man shouted. 'I need to talk to you!'

But he moved ahead even more rapidly. 'This has nothing to do with us,' he said. 'Let's get to the hotel.'

Yet it did have to do with us – there was no one else on the street. My heart was beating fast, and the effects of the wine disappeared altogether. I remembered that Bilbao was in Basque country and that terrorist attacks were common. The man's footsteps came closer.

'Let's go,' he said, hurrying along.

But it was too late. A man's figure, soaked from head to foot, stepped in front of us.

'Stop, please!' the man said. 'For the love of God.'

I was frightened. I looked around frantically for a means of escape, hoping that by some miracle a police car would appear. Instinctively, I clutched at his arm – but he pulled away.

'Please!' said the man. 'I heard that you were in the city. I need your help. It's my son.' The man knelt on the pavement and began to weep. 'Please,' he said, 'please!'

My friend gasped for breath; I watched as he lowered his head and closed his eyes. For a few minutes the silence was broken only by the sound of the rain and the sobs of the man kneeling on the sidewalk.

'Go to the hotel, Pilar,' he said finally. 'Get some sleep. I won't be back until dawn.'

Monday, December 6, 1993

Love is a trap. When it appears, we see only its light, not its shadows.

'Look at the land around here!' he said. 'Let's lie down on the ground and feel the planet's heart beating!'

'But I'll get my coat dirty, and it's the only one I have with me.'

We were driving through hills of olive groves. After yesterday's rain in Bilbao, the morning sun made me sleepy. I hadn't brought sunglasses – I hadn't brought anything, since I'd expected to return to Zaragoza two days ago. I'd had to sleep in a shirt he loaned me, and I'd bought a T-shirt at a shop near the hotel in Bilbao so that at least I could wash the one I was wearing.

'You must be sick of seeing me in the same clothes every day,' I said, trying to make a joke about something trivial to see if that would make all this seem real.

'I'm glad you're here.'

He hadn't mentioned love again since he had given me the medal, but he had been in a good mood; he seemed to be eighteen again. Now he walked along beside me bathed in the clear morning light.

'What do you have to do over there?' I asked, pointing toward the peaks of the Pyrenees on the horizon.

'Beyond those mountains lies France,' he answered with a smile.

'I know – I studied geography, too, you know. I'm just curious about why we have to go there.'

He paused, smiling to himself. 'So you can take a look at a house you might be interested in.'

'If you're thinking about becoming a real estate agent, forget it. I don't have any money.'

It didn't matter to me whether we visited a village in Navarra or went all the way to France. I just didn't want to spend the holidays in Zaragoza.

You see? I heard my brain say to my heart. *You're happy that you've accepted his invitation. You've changed – you just haven't recognized it yet.*

No, I hadn't changed at all. I was just relaxing a little.

'Look at the stones on the ground.'

They were rounded, with no sharp edges. They looked like pebbles from the sea. But the sea had never been here in the fields of Navarra.

'The feet of laborers, pilgrims, and explorers smoothed these stones,' he said. 'The stones were changed – and the travelers were too.'

'Has traveling taught you all the things you know?'

'No. I learned from the miracles of revelation.'

I didn't understand, but I didn't pursue it. For now, I was content to bask in the beauty of the sun, the fields, and the mountains.

'Where are we going now?' I asked.

'Nowhere. Let's just enjoy the morning, the sun, and the countryside. We have a long trip ahead of us.' He hesitated for a moment and then asked, 'Do you still have the medal?'

'Sure, I've kept it,' I said, and began to walk faster. I didn't want to talk about the medal – I didn't want to talk about anything that might ruin the happiness and freedom of our morning together.

A VILLAGE APPEARED. LIKE MOST medieval cities, it was situated atop a mountain peak; even from a distance, I could see the tower of a church and the ruins of a castle.

'Let's drive to that village,' I suggested.

Although he seemed reluctant, he agreed. I could see a chapel along the road, and I wanted to stop and go in. I didn't pray anymore, but the silence of churches always attracted me.

Don't feel guilty, I was saying to myself. *If he's in love, that's his problem.* He had asked about the medal. I knew that he was hoping we'd get back to our conversation at the cafe. But I was afraid of hearing something I didn't want to hear. *I won't get into it, I won't bring up the subject.*

But what if he really did love me? What if he thought that we could transform this love into something deeper?

Ridiculous, I thought to myself. *There's nothing deeper than love. In fairy tales, the princesses kiss the frogs, and the frogs become princes. In real life, the princesses kiss princes, and the princes turn into frogs.*

After driving for another half hour, we reached the chapel. An old man was seated on the steps. He was the first person we'd seen since our drive began.

It was the end of fall, and, in keeping with tradition, the fields had been returned once more to the Lord, who would fertilize the land with his blessings and allow human beings to harvest his sustenance by the sweat of their brows.

'Hello,' he said to the man.

'How are you?'

'What is the name of this village?'

'San Martin de Unx.'

'Unx?' I said. 'It sounds like the name of a gnome.'

The old man didn't understand the joke. Disappointed, I walked toward the entrance to the chapel.

'You can't go in,' warned the old man. 'It closed at noon. If you like, you can come back at four this afternoon.'

The door was open and I could look inside, although it was so bright out that I couldn't see clearly.

'Just for a minute?' I asked. 'I'd like to say a prayer.'

'I'm very sorry. It's already closed.'

He was listening to my conversation with the old man but didn't say anything.

'All right, then, let's leave,' I said. 'There's no point in arguing.'

He continued to look at me, his gaze empty, distant. 'Don't you want to see the chapel?' he asked.

I could see he didn't approve of my decision. *He thinks I'm weak, cowardly, unable to fight for what I want. Even without a kiss, the princess is transformed into a frog.*

'Remember yesterday?' I said. 'You ended our conversation in the bar because you didn't want to argue with me. Now when I do the same thing, you criticize me.'

The old man watched our discussion impassively. He was probably happy that something was actually happening, there in a place where all the mornings, all the afternoons, and all the nights were the same.

'The door to the church is open,' he said, speaking to the old man. 'If you want some money, we can give you some. But she wants to see the church.'

'It's too late.'

'Fine. We'll go in anyway.' He took my arm and we went in.

My heart was pounding. The old man could get nasty, call the police, ruin the trip.

'Why are you doing this?'

'Because you wanted to see the chapel.'

I was so nervous I couldn't even focus on what was inside. The argument and my attitude had ruined our perfect morning.

I listened carefully for any sounds from outside. *The old man might call the village police,* I thought. *Trespassers in the chapel! Thieves! They're breaking the law!* The old man had said the chapel was closed, that visiting hours were over. *He's a poor old man, unable to keep us from going in. And the police will be tough on us because we offended a feeble old man.*

I stayed inside the chapel just long enough to show that I'd really wanted to see it. As soon as enough time had passed for an imaginary Ave Maria, I said, 'Let's go.'

'Don't be frightened, Pilar. Don't just fall into playing a role.'

I didn't want my problem with the old man to become a problem with him, so I tried to stay calm. 'I don't know what you mean by "playing a role."'

'Some people always have to be doing battle with someone, sometimes even with themselves, battling with their own lives. So they begin to create a kind of play in their head, and they write the script based on their frustrations.'

'I know a lot of people like that. I know just what you mean.'

'But the worst part is that they cannot present the play by themselves,' he continued. 'So they begin to invite other actors to join in.'

'That's what that fellow outside was doing. He wanted revenge for something, and he chose us to play a part. If we had accepted his restrictions, we'd be regretting it now. We would have been defeated. We would have agreed to participate in his miserable life and in his frustrations.'

'The man's aggression was easy to see, so it was easy for us to refuse the role he wanted us to play. But other people also "invite" us to behave like victims, when they complain about the unfairness of life, for example, and ask us to agree, to offer advice, to participate.'

He looked into my eyes. 'Be careful. When you join in that game, you always wind up losing.'

He was right. But I still wasn't happy about being inside the chapel. 'OK, but I've already said my prayer. I've done what I wanted to do. Let's go.'

The contrast between the darkness inside the chapel and the strong sunlight blinded me for a few moments. When my eyes adjusted, I saw that the old man was no longer there.

'Let's have some lunch,' he said, walking in the direction of the village.

I DRANK TWO GLASSES OF wine at lunch. I'd never done that in my life.

He was speaking to the waiter, who told him that there were several Roman ruins in the area. I was trying to listen to their conversation, but I was having trouble stifling my bad mood.

The princess turned into a frog. So what? Who do I have to prove anything to? I wasn't looking for anything – not for a man and certainly not for love.

I knew it, I said to myself. *I knew he was going to turn my world upside down. My brain warned me, but my heart didn't want to take its advice.*

I've paid a considerable price for the little I have gained. I've been forced to deny myself many things I've wanted, to abandon so many roads that were open to me. I've sacrificed my dreams in the name of a larger dream – a peaceful soul. I didn't want to give up that peace.

'You're tense,' he said, breaking off his conversation with the waiter.

'Yes, I am. I think that old man went for the police. I think this is a small place, and they know where we are. I think this boldness of yours about having lunch here could wind up ruining our holiday.'

He twirled his glass of water. Surely he knew that this was not the problem – that I was actually ashamed.

Why do we always do this? Why do we notice the speck in our eye but not the mountains, the fields, the olive groves?

'Listen, that's not going to happen,' he said. 'The old man has gone home and has already forgotten the whole thing. Trust me.'

That's not why I'm so tense, you idiot.

'Listen to your heart more,' he went on.

'That's just it! I *am* listening to it,' I said. 'And I feel that we should leave. I'm not enjoying this place.'

'You shouldn't drink during the day. It doesn't help anything.'

Up to that point, I'd controlled myself. Now it was time to say what I thought.

'You think you know everything,' I said, 'that you know all about magic moments, the inner child . . . I don't know what you're doing here with me.'

He laughed. 'I admire you. And I admire the battle you're waging with your heart.'

'What battle?'

'Never mind,' he said.

But I knew what he was talking about.

'Don't kid yourself,' I said. 'We can talk about it if you like. You're mistaken about my feelings.'

He stopped fooling with his glass and looked at me. 'No, I'm not mistaken. I know you don't love me.'

This confused me even more.

'But I'm going to fight for your love,' he continued. 'There are some things in life that are worth fighting for to the end.'

I was speechless.

'You are worth it,' he said.

I turned away, trying to pretend that I was interested in the restaurant's décor. I had been feeling like a frog, and suddenly I was a princess again.

I want to believe what you're saying, I thought to myself. *It won't change anything, but at least I won't feel so weak, so incapable.*

'I apologize for my outburst,' I said.

He smiled, signaled to the waiter, and paid the check.

On the way back to the car, I became confused again. Maybe it was the sun – but no, it was autumn, and the sun was weak. Perhaps the old man – but he disappeared a while ago.

All this was so new to me. Life takes us by surprise and orders us to move toward the unknown – even when we don't want to and when we think we don't need to.

I tried to concentrate on the scenery, but I couldn't focus on the olive groves, the village atop the mountain, the chapel with the old man at the gate. All of it was so unfamiliar.

I remembered how much I'd drunk the day before and the song he had sung:

Las tardecitas de Buenos Aires tienen este no sé . . .
¿Qué sé yo?
Viste, salí de tu casa, por Arenales . . .

Why sing of the nights of Buenos Aires, when we were in Bilbao? I didn't live on a street called Arenales. What had gotten into him?

'What was that song you were singing yesterday?' I asked.

'*Balada para un loco,*' he said. 'Why do you ask about it now?'

'I don't know.'

But I had a reason: I knew he'd sung the song as a kind of snare. He'd made me memorize the words, just as I would memorize course work for an examination. He could have sung a song I was familiar with – but he'd chosen one I'd never heard before.

It was a trap. Later, if I heard the song played on the radio or at a club, I'd think of him, of Bilbao, and of a time in my life when autumn turned to spring. I'd recall the excitement, the adventure, and the child who was reborn out of God knows where.

That's what he was thinking. He was wise, experienced; he knew how to woo the woman he wanted.

I'm going crazy, I told myself. *I must be an alcoholic, drinking so much two days in a row. He knows all the tricks. He's controlling me, leading me along with his sweetness.*

'I admire the battle you are waging with your heart,' he had said at the restaurant.

But he was wrong. Because I had fought with my heart and defeated it long ago. I was certainly not going to become passionate about something that was impossible. I knew my limits; I knew how much suffering I could bear.

'Say something,' I demanded, as we walked back to the car.

'What?'

'Anything. Talk to me.'

So he began to tell me about the visions of the Virgin Mary at

Fátima. I don't know why he came up with that, but the story of the three shepherds who had spoken to the Virgin distracted me.

My heart relaxed. *Yes, I know my limits, and I know how to stay in control.*

WE ARRIVED AT NIGHT IN a fog so dense we could hardly see where we were. I could make out only a small plaza, a lamppost, some medieval houses barely illuminated by the yellow light, and a well.

'The fog!' he exclaimed.

I couldn't understand why he was so excited.

'We're in Saint-Savin,' he explained.

The name meant nothing to me. But we were in France, and that in itself thrilled me.

'Why this place?' I asked.

'Because the house I want you to see is here,' he answered, laughing. 'Also, I promised that I would come back here on the day of the Immaculate Conception.'

'Here?'

'Well, near here.'

He stopped the car. When we stepped out, he took my hand, and we began to walk through the fog.

'This place became a part of my life quite unexpectedly,' he said.

You too? I thought.

'When I first came here, I thought I was lost. But I wasn't – actually, I was just rediscovering it.'

'You talk in riddles sometimes,' I said.

'This is where I realized how much I needed you in my life.'

I looked away; I couldn't understand him. 'But what does that have to do with losing your way?'

'Let's find someone who'll rent us a room, because the two hotels in this village are only open during the summer. Then we'll have dinner at a good restaurant – no tension, no fear of the police, no need to think about running back to the car! And when the wine loosens our tongues, we'll talk about many things.'

We both laughed. I already felt more relaxed. During the drive here, I had looked back over the wild things I'd been thinking. And as we crossed over the top of the mountains that separate France from Spain, I'd asked God to cleanse my soul of tension and fear.

I was tired of playing the child and acting the way many of my friends did – the ones who are afraid that love is impossible without even knowing what love is. If I stayed like that, I would miss out on everything good that these few days with him might offer.

Careful, I thought. *Watch out for the break in the dam. If that break occurs, nothing in the world will be able to stop it.*

'May the Virgin protect us from here on,' he said.

I remained silent.

'Why didn't you say "amen"?' he asked.

'Because I don't think that's important anymore. There was a time when religion was a part of my life, but that time has passed.'

He turned around and began to walk back to the car. 'I still pray,' I went on. 'I prayed as we were crossing the Pyrenees. But it's something automatic, and I'm not even sure I still believe in it.'

'Why?'

'Because I've suffered, and God didn't listen to my prayers. Because many times in my life I have tried to love with all my heart, and my love has wound up being trampled or betrayed. If God is love, he should have cared more about my feelings.'

'God is love. But the one who understands this best is the Virgin.'

I burst out laughing. When I turned to look at him, I saw that he was serious – this was not a joke.

'The Virgin understands the mystery of total surrender,' he went on. 'And having loved and suffered, she freed us from pain. In the same way that Jesus freed us from sin.'

'Jesus was the son of God. They say that the Virgin was merely a woman who happened to receive him into her womb,' I said. I was trying to make up for my laughter and let him know that I respected his faith.

He opened the car door and took out our bags. When I tried to take mine from his hand, he smiled. 'Let me carry your bag.'

No one's done that for me in a long time, I thought.

We knocked on the door of the first house, but the woman said she didn't rent rooms. At the second door, no one answered. At the third, a kind old man greeted us – but when we looked at the room, there was only a double bed. I turned it down.

'Maybe we should head for a larger city,' I suggested as we left.

'We'll find a room,' he said. 'Do you know the exercise of the Other? It's part of a story written a hundred years ago, whose author . . .'

'Forget the author, and tell me the story,' I interrupted. We were once more walking along the only street in Saint-Savin.

A MAN RUNS INTO AN old friend who had somehow never been able to make it in life. 'I should give him some money,' he thinks. But instead he learns that his old friend has grown rich and is actually seeking him out to repay the debts he had run up over the years.

They go to a bar they used to frequent together, and the friend buys drinks for everyone there. When they ask him how he became so successful, he answers that until only a few days ago, he had been living the role of the 'Other.'

'What is the Other?' they ask.

'The Other is the one who taught me what I should be like, but not what I am. The Other believes that it is our obligation to spend our entire life thinking about how to get our hands on as much money as possible so that we will not die of hunger when we are old. So we think so much about money and our plans for acquiring it that we discover we are alive only when our days on earth are practically done. And then it's too late.'

'And you? Who are you?'

'I am just like everyone else who listens to their heart: a person who is enchanted by the mystery of life. Who is open to miracles, who experiences joy and enthusiasm for what they do. It's just that the Other, afraid of disappointment, kept me from taking action.'

'But there is suffering in life,' one of the listeners said.

'And there are defeats. No one can avoid them. But it's better to lose some of the battles in the struggle for your dreams than to be defeated without ever even knowing what you're fighting for.'

'That's it?' another listener asked.

'Yes, that's it. When I learned this, I resolved to become the person I had always wanted to be. The Other stood there in the corner of my room, watching me, but I will never let the Other into myself again – even though it has already tried to frighten me, warning me that it's risky not to think about the future.'

'From the moment that I ousted the Other from my life, the Divine Energy began to perform its miracles.'

IN SPITE OF THE FACT that my friend had long ago expelled the Other from his life, he still wasn't having much luck finding us lodging for the night. But I knew he hadn't told me that story for his own sake – he had told it for mine. He seemed to be talking about my fears, my insecurity, and my unwillingness to see what was wonderful because tomorrow it might disappear and then I would suffer.

The gods throw the dice, and they don't ask whether we want to be in the game or not. They don't care if when you go, you leave behind a lover, a home, a career, or a dream. The gods don't care whether you have it all, whether it seems that your every desire can be met through hard work and persistence. The gods don't want to know about your plans and your hopes. Somewhere they're throwing the dice – and you are chosen. From then on, winning or losing is only a question of luck.

The gods throw the dice, freeing love from its cage. And love can create or destroy – depending on the direction of the wind when it is set free.

For the moment, the wind was blowing in his favor. But the wind is as capricious as the gods – and deep inside myself, I had begun to feel some gusts.

AT LAST, AS IF FATE wanted to show me that the story of the Other was true – and the universe always conspires to help the dreamer – we found a house to stay in, with a room with separate beds. My first move was to bathe, wash my clothes, and put on the shirt I had bought. I felt refreshed, and this made me feel more secure.

After having dinner with the couple who owned the house – the restaurants were also closed during the autumn and winter – he asked for a bottle of wine, promising to replace it the next day. We put on our coats, borrowed two glasses, and went out.

'Let's sit on the edge of the well,' I suggested.

And there we sat, drinking to keep the cold and the tension away.

'It looks like the Other has gotten to you,' I joked. 'Your good mood seems to have disappeared.'

He laughed. 'I knew we were going to find a room, and we did. The universe always helps us fight for our dreams, no matter how foolish they may be. Our dreams are our own, and only we can know the effort required to keep them alive.'

In the fog, which hung yellow under the glow of the street lamp, we couldn't see even as far as the other side of the plaza.

I took a deep breath. We couldn't avoid the subject any longer.

'We have to talk about love,' I said. 'You know how I've been these last few days. If it had been up to me, the subject would never have come up. But ever since you brought it up, I haven't been able to stop thinking about it.'

'It's risky, falling in love.'

'I know that,' I answered. 'I've been in love before. It's like a narcotic. At first it brings the euphoria of complete surrender. The next day, you want more. You're not addicted yet, but you like the sensation, and you think you can still control things. You think about the person you love for two minutes, and forget them for three hours.'

'But then you get used to that person, and you begin to be completely dependent on them. Now you think about him for three hours and forget him for two minutes. If he's not there, you feel like an addict who can't get a fix. And just as addicts steal and humiliate themselves to get what they need, you're willing to do anything for love.'

'What a horrible way to put it,' he said.

It really was a horrible way to put it; my analogy didn't go with the romance of the evening – the wine, the well, and the medieval houses in the plaza. But it was true. If he was going to base so many of his actions on love, he needed to know what the risks were.

'So we should love only those who can stay near us,' I said.

He looked out at the fog. Now he no longer seemed interested in whether we negotiated the dangerous waters of a conversation about love. I was being tough, but there was no other way.

Subject closed, I thought. *Our being together for these three days has been enough to change his mind.* My pride was a bit wounded, but my heart was relieved. *Do I really want this?* I asked myself. I realized that I was already beginning to sense the storms brought on by the winds of love. I had already begun to feel the break in the dam.

We drank for some time without bringing up anything serious. We talked about the couple who owned the house and the saint for whom the town had been named. He told me some of the legends about the church across the square, which I could barely see in the fog.

'You're upset,' he said at one point.

Yes, my mind was wandering. I wished I were there with someone who could bring peace to my heart – someone with whom I could spend a little time without being afraid that I would lose him the next day. With that reassurance, the time would pass more slowly. We could be silent for a while because we'd know we had the rest of our lives together for conversation. I wouldn't have to worry about serious matters, about difficult decisions and hard words.

WE SAT THERE IN SILENCE – and that in itself was a sign. For the first time, we had nothing to say, although I only noticed this when he stood up to go find us another bottle of wine.

Silence. Then I heard the sound of his footsteps returning to the well where we'd been sitting for more than an hour, drinking and staring at the fog.

This was the first time we'd been silent for so long. It was not the awkward silence of the trip from Madrid to Bilbao. And not the silence of my fearful heart when we were in the chapel near San Martin de Unx.

This was a silence that spoke for itself. A silence that said we no longer needed to explain things to each other.

The sound of his footsteps halted. He was looking at me – and what he saw must have been beautiful: a woman seated on the edge of a well, on a foggy night, in the light of the street lamp.

The ancient houses, the eleventh-century church, and the silence.

The second bottle of wine was half empty when I decided to speak.

'This morning, I convinced myself that I was an alcoholic. I've been drinking from morning to night. In these past three days, I've drunk more than in the entire past year.'

He reached out and stroked my hair without saying anything. I absorbed his touch without trying to pull away.

'Tell me about your life since I last saw you,' I asked.

'There are no great mysteries to tell. My path is always there, and I do everything I can to follow it in a dignified way.'

'What is your path?'

'The path of someone seeking love.'

He hesitated for a moment, fiddling with the near-empty bottle.

'And love's path is really complicated,' he concluded.

'Because on that path we can go either to heaven or to hell?' I wasn't sure whether he was referring to us or not.

He didn't respond. Perhaps he was still deep in the ocean of silence, but the wine had loosened my tongue again, and I had to speak.

'You said that something here in this city altered your course.'

'Yes, I think it did. I'm still not absolutely sure, and that's why I wanted to bring you here.'

'Is this some kind of test?'

'No. It's a surrender. So that She will help me to make the right decision.'

'Who will?'

'The Virgin.'

The Virgin! I should have known. I was surprised that all his years of travel, of learning, of new horizons hadn't freed him from the Catholicism of his childhood. In at least this respect, my friends and I had come a long way – we no longer lived under the weight of guilt and sin.

'I'm surprised that after all you've been through, you still keep the faith.'

'I haven't kept it. I lost it and recovered it.'

'But a faith in virgins? In impossible things and in fantasies? Haven't you had an active sex life?'

'Well, normal. I've been in love with many women.'

To my surprise, I felt a stab of jealousy. But my inner battle seemed already to have subsided, and I didn't want to start it up again.

'Why is she "The Virgin"? Why isn't She presented to us as a normal woman, like any other?'

He drained the few drops remaining in the bottle and asked if I wanted him to go for another. I said no.

'What I want is an answer from you. Every time we start to speak about certain things, you try to talk about something else.'

'She *was* normal. She had already had other children. The Bible tells us that Jesus had two brothers. Virginity, as it relates to Jesus, is based on a different thing: Mary initiated a new generation of grace.

A new era began. She is the cosmic bride, Earth, which opens to the heavens and allows itself to be fertilized.'

'Because of the courage She showed in accepting her destiny, She allowed God to come down to earth – and She was transformed into the Great Mother.'

I didn't understand exactly what he was telling me, and he could see that.

'She is the feminine face of God. She has her own divinity.'

He spoke with great emotion; in fact, his words almost sounded forced, as if he felt he was committing a sin.

'A goddess?' I asked.

I waited for him to explain, but he couldn't say anything more. I thought about his Catholicism and about how what he had just said seemed blasphemous.

'Who is the Virgin? What is the Goddess?'

'It's not easy to explain,' he said, clearly growing more and more uncomfortable. 'I have some written material with me. If you want, you can read it.'

'I don't want to read right now; I want you to explain it to me,' I insisted.

He looked around for the wine bottle, but it was empty. Neither of us could remember why we had come to the well in the first place. Something important was in the air – as if what he was saying were part of a miracle.

'Go on,' I urged him.

'Her symbol is water – like the fog all around us. The Goddess uses water as the means to manifest Herself.'

The mist suddenly seemed to take on a life of its own, becoming sacred – even though I still didn't understand what he was trying to say.

'I don't want to talk to you about history. If you want to learn about the history, you can read the books I brought with me. But you should know that this woman – the Goddess, the Virgin Mary, the

Shechinah, the Great Mother, Isis, Sofia, slave and mistress – is present in every religion on the face of the earth. She had been forgotten, prohibited, and disguised, but Her cult has continued from millennium to millennium and continues to survive today.'

'One of the faces of God is the face of a woman.'

I studied his face. His eyes were gleaming, and he was staring into the fog that enveloped us. I could see that I no longer needed to prompt him.

'She is present in the first chapter of the Bible when the spirit of God hovered over the waters, and He placed them below and above the stars. It was the mystic marriage of earth and heaven. She is present in the final chapter of the Bible, when

the Spirit and the bride say, "Come!"
And let him who hears say, "Come!"

And let him who thirsts come.
Whoever desires, let him take the
water of life freely.'

'Why is water the symbol of the feminine face of God?'

'I don't know. But She normally chooses that medium to manifest Herself. Maybe because She is the source of life; we are generated in water, and for nine months we live in it. Water is the symbol of the power of woman, the power that no man – no matter how enlightened or perfect he may be – can capture.'

He paused for a moment and then began again.

'In every religion and in every tradition, She manifests Herself in one form or another – She always manifests Herself. Since I am a Catholic, I perceive Her as the Virgin Mary.'

He took me by the hand, and in less than five minutes, we had walked out of Saint-Savin. We passed a column by the side of the road that had something strange at the top: it was a cross with an image of the Virgin in the place where Jesus ought to have been.

Now the darkness and the mist completely enveloped us. I began to imagine I was immersed in water, in the maternal womb – where time and thought do not exist. Everything he had been saying to me was beginning to make sense. I remembered the woman at the conference. And then I thought of the girl who had led me to the plaza. She too had said that water was the symbol of the Goddess.

'TWENTY KILOMETERS FROM HERE THERE'S a grotto,' he was telling me. 'On the eleventh of February, 1858, a young girl was baling hay near the grotto with two other children. She was a fragile, asthmatic girl who lived in miserable poverty. On that winter's day, she was afraid of crossing a small stream, because if she got wet she might fall ill. And her parents needed the little money she made as a shepherd.

'A woman dressed in white, with two golden roses on her feet, appeared. The woman treated the child as if she were a princess, asked if she might return to that place a certain number of times, and then vanished. The two other girls, who were entranced by what had happened, quickly spread the story.

'This brought on a long ordeal for the girl. She was imprisoned, and the authorities demanded that she deny the whole story. Others offered her money to get her to ask the apparition for special favors. Within days, her family began to be insulted in the plaza by people who thought that the girl had invented the story in order to get attention.

'The girl, whose name was Bernadette, had no understanding of what she had seen. She referred to the lady who had appeared as "That," and her parents, concerned as they were, went to the village priest for assistance.

'The Priest suggested that when the apparition next appeared, Bernadette should ask the woman's name.

'Bernadette did as she was asked, but received only a smile in response. "That" appeared before her a total of eighteen times and, for the most part, said nothing. During one of her appearances, though, she asked the girl to kiss the ground. Without understanding why, Bernadette did as she was asked. During another visitation, she asked the girl to dig a hole in the floor of the grotto. Bernadette obeyed, and there immediately appeared a hole filled with filthy water, because swine were kept there.

'"Drink the water," the woman said.

'The water was so dirty that although Bernadette cupped it in her hands, she threw it away three times, afraid to bring it to her mouth.

Finally she did, despite her repugnance. In the place where she had dug, more water began to come forth. A man who was blind in one eye applied several drops of the water to his face and recovered his vision. A woman, desperate because her new-born child appeared to be dying, dipped the child in the spring – on a day when the temperature had fallen below zero. And the child was cured.

'Little by little, the word spread, and thousands of people began to come to the place. The girl repeatedly asked the woman her name, but the woman merely smiled.

'Until one day, "That" turned to Bernadette, and said, "I am the Immaculate Conception."

'Satisfied at last, the girl ran to tell the parish priest.

' "That cannot be," he said. "No one can be the tree and the fruit at the same time, my child. Go there, and throw holy water on her."

'As far as the priest was concerned, only God could have existed from the very beginning – and God, as far as anyone could tell, was a man.'

He paused for a long time.

'Bernadette threw holy water on "That," and the apparition smiled tenderly, nothing more.

'On the sixteenth of July, the woman appeared for the last time. Shortly after, Bernadette entered a convent, not knowing that she had changed forever the destiny of that small village near the grotto. The spring continued to flow, and miracles followed, one after the other.

'The story spread, first throughout France and later the world. The city grew and was transformed. Businesses sprang up everywhere. Hotels opened. Bernadette died and was buried in a place far from there, never knowing what had occurred.

'Some people who wanted to put the church in a bad light – and who knew that the Vatican was now acknowledging apparitions – began to invent false miracles that were later unmasked. The church reacted strongly: from a certain date on, it would accept as miracles only those phenomena that passed a rigorous series of examinations performed by medical and scientific commissions.

'But the water still flows, and the cures continue.'

I heard something nearby; it frightened me, but he didn't seemed to notice. The fog now had a life and a story of its own. I was thinking about everything he had told me, and I wondered how he knew all of this.

I thought about the feminine face of God. The man at my side had a soul filled with conflict. A short time ago, he had written to me that he wanted to enter a Catholic seminary, yet now he was thinking that God has a feminine face.

He was silent. I still felt as if I were in the womb of the Earth Mother, beyond time and place.

'There were two important things that Bernadette didn't know,' he finally said. 'The first was that prior to the arrival of the Christian religion in these parts, these mountains were inhabited by Celts – and the Goddess was their principal object of devotion. Generations and generations had understood the feminine face of God and shared in Her love and Her glory.'

'And the second thing?'

'The second was that a short time before Bernadette experienced her visions, the authorities at the Vatican had met in secret. Virtually no one knew what had occurred at those meetings – and there's no question but that the priest in the small village didn't have the slightest idea. The highest council of the Catholic Church was deciding whether they should ratify the dogma regarding the Immaculate Conception.

'The dogma wound up being ratified, through the papal bull known as *Ineffabilis Deus*. But the general public never knew exactly what this meant.'

'And what do you have to do with all this?' I asked.

'I am Her disciple. I have learned through Her.' He seemed to be saying that She was the source of all his knowledge.

'You have seen Her?'

'Yes.'

WE RETURNED TO THE PLAZA and walked toward the church. I saw the well in the lamplight, with the bottle of wine and two glasses on its wall. *A couple of sweethearts must have been here,* I think. *Silent, allowing their hearts to speak to each other. And after their hearts had said all they had to say, they began to share the great mysteries.*

I felt that I was facing something quite serious and that I needed to learn everything I could from my experiences. For a few moments, I thought about my studies, about Zaragoza, and about the man I was hoping to find in my life – but all that seemed far away, clouded by the mists over Saint-Savin.

'Why did you tell me the story of Bernadette?' I asked.

'I don't know why exactly,' he answered, without looking at me directly. 'Maybe because we're not too far from Lourdes. Maybe because the day after tomorrow is the day of the Immaculate Conception. Or maybe it was because I wanted to show you that my world is not so solitary and mad as it may appear. There are others who are part of that world, and they believe in what they say.'

'I never said that your world is mad. Maybe it's mine that's crazy. I mean, here I am, spending the most crucial time of my life concentrating on textbooks and courses that won't help me at all to escape from the place I already know too well.'

I sensed that he was relieved that I understood him. I expected him to say something more about the Goddess, but instead he turned to me and said, 'Let's get some sleep. We've had a lot to drink.'

Tuesday, December 7, 1993

He went straight to sleep, but I was awake for a long time, thinking about the fog, the wine, and our conversation. I read the manuscript he gave me, and what was in it thrilled me: God – if God really existed – was both Father and Mother.

Later, I turned out the light and lay there thinking. When we were quiet with each other, I was able to see how close I felt to him.

Neither of us had said anything. Love doesn't need to be discussed; it has its own voice and speaks for itself. That night, by the well, the silence had allowed our hearts to approach each other and get to know each other better. My heart had listened closely to what his had said, and now it was content.

Before I feel asleep, I decided I would do what he called the 'exercise of the Other.'

I am here in this room, I thought, *far from everything familiar to me, talking about things that have never interested me and sleeping in a city where I've never set foot on before. I can pretend – at least for a few minutes – that I am different.*

I began to imagine how I would like to be living right at that moment. I wanted to be happy, curious, joyful – living every moment intensely, drinking the water of life thirstily. Believing again in my dreams. Able to fight for what I wanted.

Loving a man who loved me.

Yes, that was the woman I wanted to be – the woman who was suddenly presenting herself and becoming me.

I felt that my soul was bathed in the light of a god – or of a goddess – in whom I had lost faith. And I felt that at that moment, the Other left my body and was standing in the corner of that small room.

I observed the woman I had been up until then: weak but trying to give the impression of strength. Fearful of everything but telling herself it wasn't fear – it was the wisdom of someone who knew what reality was. Putting up shutters in front of windows to keep the joy of the sun from entering – just so the sun's rays wouldn't fade my old furniture.

I looked at the Other, there in the corner of the room – fragile, exhausted, disillusioned. Controlling and enslaving what should really be free: her emotions. Trying to judge her future loves by the rules of her past suffering.

But love is always new. Regardless of whether we love once, twice, or a dozen times in our life, we always face a brand-new situation. Love can consign us to hell or to paradise, but it always takes us somewhere. We simply have to accept it, because it is what nourishes our existence. If we reject it, we die of hunger, because we lack the courage to stretch out a hand and pluck the fruit from the branches of the tree of life. We have to take love where we find it, even if that means hours, days, weeks of disappointment and sadness.

The moment we begin to seek love, love begins to seek us.

And to save us.

When the Other left me, my heart once again began to speak to me. It told me that the breach in the dike had allowed the waters to pour through, that the wind was blowing in all directions at once, and that it was happy because I was once again willing to listen to what it had to say.

My heart told me that I was in love. And I fell asleep with a smile on my lips.

WHEN I AWOKE, THE WINDOW was open and he was gazing at the mountains in the distance. I watched him without saying anything, ready to close my eyes if he turned toward me.

As if he knew, he turned and looked at me.

'Good morning,' he said.

'Good morning. Close the window – it's so cold.'

The Other had appeared with no warning. It was still trying to change the direction of the wind, to detect shortcomings, to say, No, that's impossible. But it knew it was too late.

'I have to get dressed,' I said.

'I'll wait for you downstairs.'

I got up, banished the Other from my thoughts, opened the window again, and let the sun in. Its light bathed everything – the mountains with their snow-covered peaks, the ground blanketed in dry leaves, and the river, which I could hear but not see.

The sun shone on me, warming my nude body. I was no longer cold – I was consumed by a heat, the heat of a spark becoming a flame, the flame becoming a bonfire, the bonfire becoming an inferno. I knew.

I wanted this.

I also knew that from this moment on I was going to experience heaven and hell, joy and pain, dreams and hopelessness; that I would no longer be capable of containing the winds that blew from the hidden corners of my soul. I knew that from this moment on love would be my guide – and that it had waited to lead me ever since childhood, when I had felt love for the first time. The truth is, I had never forgotten love, even when it had deemed me unworthy of fighting for it. But love had been difficult, and I had been reluctant to cross its frontiers.

I recalled the plaza in Soria and the moment when I had asked him to find the medal I had lost. I had known what he was going to tell me, and I hadn't wanted to hear it, because he was the type who would someday go off in search of wealth, adventure, and dreams. I needed a love that was possible.

I realized that I had known nothing of love before. When I saw him at the conference and accepted his invitation, I'd thought that I, as a mature woman, would be able to control the heart of the girl who had been looking for so long for her prince. Then he had spoken about the child in all of us – and I'd heard again the voice of the child I had been, of the princess who was fearful of loving and losing.

For four days, I had tried to ignore my heart's voice, but it had grown louder and louder, and the Other had become desperate. In the furthest corner of my soul, my true self still existed and I still believed in my dreams. Before the Other could say a word, I had accepted the ride with him. I had accepted the invitation to travel with him and to take the risks involved.

And because of that – because of that small part of me that had survived – love had finally found me, after it had looked for me everywhere. Love had found me, despite the barricade that the Other had built across a quiet street in Zaragoza, a barricade of preconceived ideas, stubborn opinions, and textbooks.

I opened the window and my heart. The sun flooded the room, and love inundated my soul.

WE WANDERED FOR HOURS, THROUGH the snow and along the roads. We breakfasted in a village whose name I never found out but in whose central plaza a dramatic fountain sculpture displayed a serpent and a dove combined into a single fabulous creature.

He smiled when he saw it. 'It's a sign – masculine and feminine joined in a single figure.'

'I'd never thought before about what you told me yesterday,' I said. 'But it makes sense.'

'"And God created man and woman,"' he quoted from Genesis, 'because that was his image and simulacrum: man and woman.'

I noted a new gleam in his eye. He was happy and laughed at every silly thing. He fell into easy conversation with the few people we met along the way – workers dressed in gray on their way to the fields, adventurers in colorful gear, preparing to climb a mountain peak. I said little – my French is awful – but my soul rejoiced at seeing him this way.

His joy made everyone who spoke with him smile. Perhaps his heart had spoken to him, and now he knew that I loved him – even though I was still behaving like just an old friend.

'You seem happier,' I said at one point.

'Because I've always dreamed of being here with you, walking through these mountains and harvesting the "golden fruits of the sun."'

The golden fruits of the sun – a verse written ages ago, repeated by him now, at just the right moment.

'There's another reason you're happy,' I said, as we left the small village with the strange statue.

'What's that?'

'You know that I'm happy. You're responsible for my being here today, climbing the mountains of truth, far from my mountains of notebooks and texts. You're making me happy. And happiness is something that multiplies when it is divided.'

'Did you do the exercise of the Other?'

'Yes. How did you know?'

'Because you've changed too. And because we always learn that exercise at the right time.'

The Other pursued me all through the morning. Every minute, though, its voice grew fainter, and its image seemed to dissolve. It reminded me of those vampire films where the monster crumbles into dust.

We passed another column with an image of the Virgin on the cross.

'What are you thinking about?' he asked me.

'About vampires. Those creatures of the night, locked inside themselves, desperately seeking company. Incapable of loving.'

'That's why legend has it that only a stake through the heart can kill them; when that happens, the heart bursts, freeing the energy of love and destroying the evil.'

'I never thought of that before. But it makes sense.'

I had succeeded in burying the stake. My heart, freed of all its curses, was aware of everything. The Other no longer had a place to call its own.

A thousand times I wanted to take his hand, and a thousand times I stopped myself. I was still confused – I wanted to tell him I loved him, but I didn't know how to begin.

We talked about the mountains and the rivers. We were lost in a forest for almost an hour, but eventually we found the path again. We ate sandwiches and drank melted snow. When the sun began to set, we decided to return to Saint-Savin.

THE SOUND OF OUR FOOTSTEPS echoed from the stone walls. At the entrance to the church, I instinctively dipped my hand in the font of holy water and made the sign of the cross. I recalled that water was the symbol of the Goddess.

'Let's go in,' he suggested.

We walked through the dark, empty building. Saint Savin, a hermit who had lived at the start of the first millennium, was buried below the main altar. The walls of the place were crumbling and had clearly been reconstructed several times.

Some places are like that: they can suffer through wars, persecutions, and indifference, but they still remain sacred. Finally someone comes along, senses that something is missing, and rebuilds them.

I noticed an image of the crucified Christ that gave me a funny feeling – I had the impression that his head was moving, following me.

'Let's stop here.'

We were before an altar of Our Lady.

'Look at the image.'

Mary, with her son in her lap. The infant Jesus pointing to the heavens.

'Look more carefully,' he said.

I studied the details of the wooden carving: the gilt paint, the pedestal, the perfection with which the artist had traced the folds of the robe. But it was when I focused on the finger of the child Jesus that I understood what he meant.

Although Mary held him in her arms, it was Jesus who was supporting her. The child's arm, raised to the sky, appeared to be lifting the Virgin toward heaven, back to the place of Her Groom's abode.

'The artist who created this more than six hundred years ago knew what he wanted to convey,' he commented.

Footsteps sounded on the wooden floor. A woman entered and lit a candle in front of the main altar.

We remained silent for a while, respecting her moment of prayer.

Love never comes just a little at a time, I thought, as I watched him, absorbed in contemplation of the Virgin. The previous day, the world had made sense, even without love's presence. But now we needed each other in order to see the true brilliance of things.

When the woman had gone, he spoke again. 'The artist knew the Great Mother, the Goddess, and the sympathetic face of God. You've asked me a question that up until now I haven't been able to answer directly. It was "Where did you learn all this?"'

Yes, I had asked him that, and he had already answered me. But I didn't say so.

'Well, I learned in the same way that this artist did: I accepted love from on high. I allowed myself to be guided,' he went on. 'You must remember the letter I wrote you, when I spoke of wanting to enter a monastery. I never told you, but I did in fact do that.'

I immediately remembered the conversation we'd had before the conference in Bilbao. My heart began to beat faster, and I tried to fix my gaze on the Virgin. She was smiling.

It can't be, I thought. *You entered and then you left. Please, tell me that you left the monastery.*

'I had already lived some pretty wild years,' he said, not guessing my thoughts this time. 'I got to see other peoples and other lands. I had already looked for God in the four corners of the earth. I had fallen in love with other women and worked in a number of different jobs.'

Another stab. I would have to be careful that the Other didn't return. I kept my gaze on the Virgin's smile.

'The mysteries of life fascinated me, and I wanted to understand them better. I looked for signs that would tell me that someone knew something. I went to India and to Egypt. I sat with masters of magic and of meditation. And finally I discovered what I was looking for: that truth resides where there is faith.'

Truth resides where there is faith! I looked around again at the interior of the church – the worn stones, fallen and replaced so many times. What had made human beings so insistent? What had caused them to work so hard at rebuilding this small temple in such a remote spot, hidden in the mountains?

Faith.

'The Buddhists were right, the Hindus were right, the Muslims were right, and so were the Jews. Whenever someone follows the path to faith – sincerely follows it – he or she is able to unite with God and to perform miracles.

'But it wasn't enough simply to know that – you have to make a choice. I chose the Catholic Church because I was raised in it, and my childhood had been impregnated with its mysteries. If I had been born Jewish, I would have chosen Judaism. God is the same, even though He has a thousand names; it is up to us to select a name for Him.'

Once again, steps sounded in the church.

A MAN APPROACHED AND STARED at us. Then he turned to the center altar and reached for the two candelabra. He must have been the one responsible for guarding the church.

I remembered the watchman at the other chapel, the man who wouldn't allow us to enter. But this man said nothing.

'I have a meeting tonight,' he said when the man left.

'Please, go on with what you were saying. Don't change the subject.'

'I entered a monastery close to here. For four years, I studied everything I could. During that time, I made contact with the Clarifieds and the Charismatics, the sects that have been trying to open doors that have been closed for so long to certain spiritual experiences. I discovered that God was not the ogre that had frightened me as a child. There was a movement afoot for a return to the original innocence of Christianity.'

'You mean that after two thousand years, they finally understood that it was time to allow Jesus to become a part of the church?' I said with some sarcasm.

'You may think you're joking, but that was exactly it. I began to study with one of the superiors at the monastery. He taught me that we have to accept the fire of revelation, the Holy Spirit.'

The Virgin continued to smile, and the infant Jesus kept his joyful expression, but my heart stopped when he said that. I too had believed in that once – but time, age, and the feeling that I was a logical and practical person had distanced me from religion. I realized how much I wanted to recover my childhood faith, when I had believed in angels and miracles. But I couldn't possibly bring it back simply through an act of will.

'The superior told me that if I believed that I knew, then I would in fact eventually know,' he continued. 'I began to talk to myself when I was in my cell. I prayed that the Holy Spirit would manifest itself and teach me what I needed to know. Little by little, I discovered that as I talked to myself, a wiser voice was saying things for me.'

'That's happened to me, too,' I interrupted him.

He waited for me to go on. But I couldn't say anything else.

'I'm listening,' he said.

Something had stopped my tongue. He was speaking so beautifully, and I couldn't express myself nearly as well.

'The Other wants to come back,' he said, as if he had guessed what I was thinking. 'The Other is always afraid of saying something that might sound silly.'

'Yes,' I said, struggling to overcome my fear. 'OK, sometimes when I'm talking with someone and get excited about what I'm saying, I find myself saying things I've never said before. It seems almost as if I'm "channeling" an intelligence that isn't mine – one that understands life much better than me. But this is rare. In most conversations I prefer to listen. I always feel as if I'm learning something new, even though I wind up forgetting it all.'

'We are our own greatest surprise,' he said. 'Faith as tiny as a grain of sand allows us to move mountains. That's what I've learned. And now, my own words sometimes surprise me.'

'The apostles were fishermen, illiterate and ignorant. But they accepted the flame that fell from the heavens. They were not ashamed of their own ignorance; they had faith in the Holy Spirit. This gift is there for anyone who will accept it. One has only to believe, accept, and be willing to make mistakes.'

The Virgin smiled down on me. She had every reason to cry – but She was joyful.

'Go on.'

'That's all,' he answered. 'Accept the gift. And then the gift manifests itself.'

'It doesn't work that way.'

'Didn't you understand me?'

'I understand. But I'm like everyone else: I'm scared. It might work for you or for my neighbor, but never for me.'

'That will change someday – when you begin to see that we are really just like that child there.'

'But until then, we'll all go on thinking we've come close to the light, when actually we can't even light our own flame.'

He didn't answer.

'You didn't finish your story about the seminary,' I said.

'I'm still there.'

Before I could react, he stood up and walked to the center of the church.

I stayed where I was. My head was spinning. *Still in the seminary?*

Better not to think about it. Love had flooded my soul, and there was no way I could control it. There was only one recourse: the Other, with whom I had been harsh because I was weak, and cold because I was afraid – but I no longer wanted the Other. I could no longer look at life through its eyes.

A sharp, sustained sound like that of an immense flute interrupted my thoughts. My heart jumped.

The sound came again. And again. I looked behind me and saw a wooden staircase that led up to a crude platform, which didn't seem to fit with the frozen beauty of the church. On the platform was an ancient organ.

And there he was. I couldn't see his face because the lighting was bad – but I knew he was up there.

I stood up, and he called to me.

'Pilar!' he said, his voice full of emotion. 'Stay where you are.'

I obeyed.

'May the Great Mother inspire me,' he said. 'May this music be my prayer for the day.'

And he began to play the Ave Maria. It must have been about six in the evening, time for the Angelus – a time when light and darkness merge. The sound of the organ echoed through the empty church, blending in my mind with the stones and the images laden with history and with faith. I closed my eyes and let the music flow through me, cleansing my soul of all fear and sin and reminding me that I am always better than I think and stronger than I believe.

For the first time since I had abandoned the path of faith, I felt a strong desire to pray. Although I was seated in a pew, my soul was kneeling at the feet of the Lady before me, the woman who had said,

'Yes,'

when She could have said 'no.' The angel would have sought out someone else, and there would have been no sin in the eyes of the Lord, because God knows His children's weakness.

But She had said,

'Thy will be done,'

even though She sensed that She was receiving, along with the words of the angel, all the pain and suffering of Her destiny; even though Her heart's eyes could see Her beloved son leaving the house, could see the people who would follow Him and then deny Him; but

'Thy will be done,'

even when, at the most sacred moment in a woman's life, She had to lie down with the animals in a stable to give birth, because that was what the Scriptures required;

'Thy will be done,'

even when, in agony, She looked through the streets for Her son and found Him at the temple. And He asked that She not interfere because He had other obligations and tasks to perform;

'Thy will be done,'

even when She knew that She would search for Him for the rest of Her days, Her heart filled with pain, fearing every moment for His life, knowing that He was being persecuted and threatened;

'Thy will be done,'

even when, finding Him in the crowd, She was unable to draw near Him;

'Thy will be done,'

even when She asked someone to tell Him that She was there and the son sent back the response, 'My mother and my brothers are those who are here with me';

'Thy will be done,'

even when at the end, after everyone had fled, only She, another woman, and one of them stood at the foot of the cross, bearing the laughter of His enemies and the cowardice of His friends;

'*Thy will be done.*'

Thy will be done, my Lord. Because you know the weakness in the heart of your children, and you assign each of them only the burden they can bear. May you understand my love – because it is the only thing I have that is really mine, the only thing that I will be able to take with me into the next life. Please allow it to be courageous and pure; please make it capable of surviving the snares of the world.

The organ stopped, and the sun went into hiding behind the mountains – as if both were ruled by the same Hand. The music had been his prayer, and his prayer had been heard. I opened my eyes and found the church in complete darkness, except for the solitary candle that illuminated the image of the Virgin.

I heard his footsteps again, returning to where I sat. The light of that single candle gleamed on my tears, and my smile – a smile that wasn't perhaps as beautiful as the Virgin's – showed that my heart was alive.

He looked at me, and I at him. My hand reached out for his and found it. Now it was his heart that was beating faster – I could almost hear it in the silence.

But my soul was serene, and my heart at peace.

I held his hand, and he embraced me. We stood there at the feet of the Virgin for I don't know how long. Time had stopped.

She looked down at us. The adolescent girl who had said 'yes' to her destiny. The woman who had agreed to carry the son of God in Her womb and the love of God in Her heart. She understood.

I didn't want to ask for anything. That afternoon in the church had made the entire journey worthwhile. Those four days with him had made up for an entire year in which so little had happened.

We left the church hand in hand and walked back toward our room. My head was spinning – seminary, Great Mother, the meeting he had later that night.

I realized then that we both wanted to unite our souls under one destiny – but the seminary and Zaragoza stood in the way. My heart felt squeezed. I looked around at the medieval homes and the well where we had sat the previous night. I recalled the silence and the sadness of the Other, the woman I had once been.

God, I am trying to recover my faith. Please don't abandon me in the middle of this adventure, I prayed, pushing my fears aside.

HE SLEPT A LITTLE, BUT I stayed awake, looking out the darkened window. Later, we got up and dined with the family – they never spoke at the table. He asked for a key to the house.

'We'll be home late tonight,' he said to the woman.

'Young people should enjoy themselves,' she answered, 'and take advantage of the holidays as best they can.'

'I have to ask you something,' I said, when we were back in the car. 'I've been trying to avoid it, but I have to ask.'

'The seminary,' he said.

That's right. I don't understand. Even though it's no longer important, I thought.

'I have always loved you,' he began. 'I kept the medal, thinking that someday I would give it to you and that I'd have the courage to tell you that I love you. Every road I traveled led back to you. I wrote the letters to you and opened every letter of yours afraid that you would tell me you had found someone.

'Then I was called to the spiritual life. Or rather, I accepted the call, because it had been with me since childhood – just as it was for you. I discovered that God was extremely important to my life and that I couldn't be happy if I didn't accept my vocation. The face of Christ was there in the face of every poor soul I met on my travels, and I couldn't deny it.'

He paused, and I decided not to push him.

Twenty minutes later, he stopped the car and we got out.

'This is Lourdes,' he said. 'You should see it during the summer.'

What I saw now were deserted streets, closed shops, and hotels with bars across their entrances.

'Six million people come here in the summer,' he went on enthusiastically.

'It looks like a ghost town to me.'

We crossed a bridge and arrived at an enormous iron gate with angels on either side. One side of the gate was standing open, and we passed through it.

'Go on with what you were saying,' I said, in spite of my decision not to pursue it. 'Tell me about the face of Christ on the people you met.'

I could see that he didn't want to continue the conversation. Perhaps this wasn't the right time or place. But having begun, he had to complete it.

We were walking down a broad avenue, bordered on both sides by snow-covered fields. At its end, I could see the silhouette of a cathedral.

'Go on,' I repeated.

'You already know. I entered the seminary. During the first year, I asked that God help me to transform my love for you into a love for all people. In the second year, I sensed that God had heard me. By the third year, even though my longing for you was still strong, I became certain that my love was turning toward charity, prayer, and helping the needy.'

'Then why did you seek me out? Why rekindle the flame in me? Why did you tell me about the exercise of the Other and force me to see how shallow my life is?' I sounded confused and tremulous. From one minute to the next, I could see him drawing closer to the seminary and further from me. 'Why did you come back? Why wait until today to tell me this very story, when you can see that I am beginning to love you?'

He did not answer immediately. Then he said, 'You'll think it's stupid.'

'I won't. I'm not worried anymore about seeming ridiculous. You've taught me that.'

'Two months ago, my superior asked me to accompany him to the house of a woman who had died and left all her wealth to the seminary. She lived in Saint-Savin, and my superior had to prepare an inventory of what was there.'

We were approaching the cathedral at the end of the avenue. My intuition told me that as soon as we reached it, any conversation we were having would be interrupted.

'Don't stop,' I said. 'I deserve an explanation.'

'I remember the moment I stepped into that house. The windows looked out on the Pyrenees, and the whole scene was filled with the brightness of the sun, intensified by the snow's glare. I began to make a list of the things in the house, but after just a few minutes, I had to stop.

'I had discovered that the woman's taste was exactly the same as mine. She owned records that I would have purchased, the same music that I would have enjoyed listening to as I looked out on that beautiful landscape. Her bookshelves were filled with books I had already read and others that I would have loved to read. Looking at the furnishings, the paintings, and all her other possessions, I felt as if I had chosen them myself.

'From that day on, I couldn't forget that house. Every time I went to the chapel to pray, I realized that my renunciation had not been total. I imagined myself there with you, looking out at the snow on the mountaintops, a fire blazing in the hearth. I pictured our children running around the house and playing in the fields around Saint-Savin.'

Although I had never been near the house, I knew exactly what it looked like. And I hoped he'd say nothing else so that I could fantasize.

But he went on.

'For the past two weeks, I haven't been able to stand the sadness in my soul. I went to my superior and told him what was happening to me. I told him about my love for you and what had begun when we were taking the inventory.'

A light rain began to fall. I bowed my head and gathered the front of my coat. I suddenly didn't want to hear the rest of the story.

'So my superior said, "There are many ways to serve our Lord. If you feel that's your destiny, go in search of it. Only a man who is happy can create happiness in others."'

'"I don't know if that's my destiny," I told my superior. "Peace came into my heart when I entered this seminary."

'"Well, then, go there and resolve any doubts you may have," he said. "Remain out there in the world, or come back to the seminary. But you have to be committed to the place you choose. A divided kingdom cannot defend itself from its adversaries. A divided person cannot face life in a dignified way."'

He pulled something from his pocket and handed it to me. It was a key.

'The superior loaned me the key to the house. He said that he would hold off for a while on selling the possessions. I know that he wants me to return to the seminary. But he was the one who arranged the presentation in Madrid – so that we could meet.'

I looked at the key in my hand and smiled. In my heart, bells were ringing, and the heavens had opened to me. He could serve God in a different way – by my side. Because I was going to fight for that to happen.

I put the key in my bag.

THE BASILICA LOOMED IN FRONT of us. Before I could say anything, someone spotted him and came toward us. The light rain continued, and I had no idea how long we would be there; I couldn't forget that I had only one set of clothes, and I didn't want them to get soaked.

I concentrated on that problem. I didn't want to think about the house – that was a matter suspended between heaven and earth, awaiting the hand of destiny.

He introduced me to several people who had gathered around. They asked where we were staying, and when he said Saint-Savin, one of them told us the story of the hermit saint who was buried there. It was Saint Savin who had discovered the well in the middle of the plaza and the original mission of the village had been to create a refuge for religious persons who had left the city and come to the mountains in search of God.

'They are still living there,' another said.

I didn't know if the story was true, nor did I have any idea who 'they' were.

Other people began to arrive, and the group began to move toward the entrance of the grotto. An older man tried to tell me something in French. When he saw that I didn't understand, he switched to an awkward Spanish.

'You are with a very special man,' he said. 'A man who performs miracles.'

I said nothing but remembered that night in Bilbao when a desperate man had come looking for him. He had told me nothing about where he had gone, and I hadn't asked. Right now, I preferred to think about the house, which I could picture perfectly – its books, its records, its view, its furniture.

Somewhere in the world, a home awaited us. A place where we could care for daughters or sons who would come home from school, fill the house with joy, and never pick up after themselves.

We walked in silence through the rain until finally we reached the place where the visions of Mary had occurred. It was exactly as I had imagined: the grotto, the statue of Our Lady, and the fountain – protected by glass – where the miracle of the water had taken place. Some pilgrims were praying; others were seated silently inside the grotto, their eyes closed. A river ran past the entrance, and the sound of the water made me feel at peace. As soon as I saw the image, I said a quick prayer, asking the Virgin to help me – my heart needed no more suffering.

If pain must come, may it come quickly. Because I have a life to live, and I need to live it in the best way possible. If he has to make a choice, may he make it now. Then I will either wait for him or forget him.

Waiting is painful. Forgetting is painful. But not knowing which to do is the worst kind of suffering.

In some corner of my heart, I felt that she had heard my plea.

Wednesday, December 8, 1993

By the time the cathedral's clock struck midnight, the group around us had grown considerably. We were almost a hundred people – some of them priests and nuns – standing in the rain, gazing at the statue.

'Hail, Our Lady of the Immaculate Conception,' someone close to me said, as soon as the tolling of the bells ceased.

'Hail,' everyone answered, with some applause.

A guard immediately came forward and asked that we be quiet. We were bothering the other pilgrims.

'But we've come a long way,' said one of the men in our group.

'So have they,' answered the guard, pointing to the others who were praying in the rain. 'And they are praying silently.'

I wanted to be alone with him, far from this place, holding his hand and telling him how I felt. We needed to talk more about the house, about our plans, about love. I wanted to reassure him, to make clear how strong my feelings were, and to let him know that his dream could come true – because I would be at his side, helping him.

The guard retreated, and one of the priests began to recite the rosary in a low voice. When we reached the creed that closes the series of prayers, everyone remained silent, their eyes closed.

'Who are these people?' I asked.

'Charismatics,' he answered.

I had heard of them before but didn't know exactly what their name meant. He could see that I didn't understand.

'These are people who accept the fire of the Holy Spirit,' he said, 'the fire that Jesus left but that is used by so few people to light their candles. These people are very close to the original truth of Christianity, when everyone was capable of performing miracles.

'They are guided by the Woman Dressed by the Sun,' he said, pointing with his eyes to the Virgin.

The group began to chant quietly, as if in response to an invisible command.

'You're shivering from the cold. You don't have to take part in this,' he said.

'Are you going to stay?'

'Yes. This is my life.'

'Then I'm going to participate,' I answered, even though I would have preferred to be far from there. 'If this is your world, I want to learn to be a part of it.'

The group continued to sing. I closed my eyes and tried to follow the words, even though I couldn't speak French. I repeated the words without understanding them. But their sound helped the time to pass more quickly.

It would end soon. And we could return to Saint-Savin, just the two of us.

I went on singing mechanically – but little by little, l began to feel the music taking hold of me, as if it had a life of its own. It was hypnotizing. The cold seemed less bitter, and the rain no longer bothered me. The music made me feel better. It transported me back to a time when God had felt closer to me and had helped me.

Just as I was about to surrender completely to the music, it stopped.

I opened my eyes. This time, instead of a guard, there was a priest. He approached one of the other priests in our group. They whispered to one another for a few moments, and the padre left.

Our priest turned to us. 'We have to say our prayers on the other side of the river,' he said.

SILENTLY, WE WALKED ACROSS THE bridge directly in front of the grotto and moved to the other bank. It was a prettier place, on the bank of the river, surrounded by trees and an open field. The river now separated us from the grotto. From there, we could clearly see the illuminated image, and we could sing loudly without disturbing others' prayers.

The people around me began to sing louder, raising their faces to the sky and smiling as the raindrops coursed down their cheeks. Some raised their arms, and soon everyone joined in, waving their arms from side to side in rhythm to the music.

I wanted to give in to the moment, but at the same time I wanted to pay close attention to what they were doing. One priest near me was singing in Spanish, and I tried to repeat the words. They were invocations to the Holy Spirit and the Virgin, requesting their presence and asking that they rain down their blessings and their powers on each of us.

'May the gift of tongues befall us,' said another priest, repeating the phrase in Spanish, Italian, and French.

What happened next was incomprehensible. Each of the many people present began to speak a language that was different from any I had ever heard. It was more sound than speech, with words that seemed to come straight from the soul, making no sense at all. I recalled our conversation in the church, when he had spoken about revelations, saying that all wisdom was the result of listening to one's own soul. *Perhaps this is the language of the angels*, I thought, trying to mimic what they were doing – and feeling ridiculous.

Everyone was looking at the statue of the Virgin on the other side of the river; they all seemed to be in a trance. I looked around for him and found him standing at some distance from me. His hands were raised to the heavens and he was speaking rapidly, as if in conversation with Her. He was smiling and nodding his head as if in agreement; occasionally he looked surprised.

This is his world, I thought.

The whole scene began to scare me. The man I wanted at my side was telling me that God is also female, he was speaking an incomprehensible language, he was in a trance, and he seemed closer to the angels than to me. The house in the mountains began to seem less real, as if it were part of a world that he had already left behind. All of our days together – starting with the conference in Madrid – seemed to be part of a dream, a voyage beyond the space and time of my life. At the same time, though, the dream had the flavor of the world, of romance, and of new adventures. I had tried to resist; now I knew how easily love could set fire to the heart. I had tried to stay unreceptive to all of this in the beginning; now I felt that since I had loved before, I would know how to handle it.

I looked around again, and it dawned on me that this was not the Catholicism I had been taught at school. And this was not the way I had pictured the man in my life.

A man in my life! How strange! I said to myself, surprised at the thought.

There on the bank of the river, looking across at the grotto, I felt both fear and jealousy. Fear because it was all new to me, and what is new has always scared me. Jealousy because, bit by bit, I could see that his love was greater than I'd thought and spread over places where I'd never set foot.

Forgive me, Our Lady. Forgive me if I'm being selfish or smallminded, competing with you for this man's love.

But what if his vocation wasn't to be with me but was to retreat from the world, locking himself in a seminary and conversing with angels? How long would he resist before he fled from our house to return to his true path? Or even if he never went back to the seminary, what price would I have to pay to keep him from returning to that path?

Everyone there, except me, seemed to be concentrating on what they were doing. I was staring at him, and he was speaking the language of the angels.

Suddenly, fear and jealousy were replaced by calm and solitude. The angels had someone to talk with, and I was alone.

I had no idea what pushed me into trying to speak that strange language. Perhaps it was my strong need to connect with him, to tell him what I was feeling. Perhaps I needed to let my soul speak to me – my heart had so many doubts and needed so many answers.

I didn't know exactly what to do, and I felt ridiculous. But all around me were men and women of all ages, priests and laypeople, novices and nuns, students and old-timers. They gave me the courage to ask the Holy Spirit for the strength to overcome my fear.

Try, I said to myself. *All you have to do is open your mouth and have the courage to say things you don't understand. Try!*

I prayed that this night – the night following a day that had been so long that I couldn't even remember how it had begun – would be an epiphany. A new beginning for me.

God must have heard me. The words began to come more easily – and little by little they lost their everyday meanings. My embarrassment diminished, my confidence grew, and the words began to flow freely. Although I understood nothing of what I was saying, it all made sense to my soul.

Simply having the courage to say senseless things made me euphoric. I was free, with no need to seek or to give explanations for what I was doing. This freedom lifted me to the heavens – where a greater love, one that forgives everything and never allows you to feel abandoned, once again enveloped me.

It feels as if my faith is coming back, I thought, surprised at the miracles that love can perform. I sensed that the Virgin was holding me in her lap, covering me and warming me with her mantle. The strange words flew more rapidly from my lips.

Without realizing it, I began to cry. Joy flooded my heart – a joy that overpowered my fears and was stronger than my attempts to control every second of my life.

I realized that my tears were a gift; at school, the sisters had taught me that the saints wept with ecstasy. I opened my eyes, gazed at the darkness of the heavens, and felt my tears blending with the raindrops. The earth was alive and the drops from above brought the miracles of heaven with them. We were all a part of that same miracle.

How wonderful that God may be a woman, I said to myself, as the others continued to chant. *If that's true, then it was certainly God's feminine face that taught us how to love.*

'Let us pray in tents of eight,' said the priest in Spanish, Italian, and French.

Once again, I was confused. What was happening? Someone came over to me and put his arm around my shoulders. Another person did the same on my other side. We formed a circle of eight people, arms around each other's shoulders. Then we leaned forward, our heads touching.

We looked like a human tent. The rain fell harder, but no one cared. The position we had taken concentrated all our energies and heat.

'May the Immaculate Conception help my child find his way,' said the man embracing me from the right. 'Please, let's say an Ave Maria for my child.'

'Amen,' everyone said. And we eight prayed an Ave Maria.

'May the Immaculate Conception enlighten me and arouse in me the gift of curing,' said a woman from our circle. 'Let us say an Ave Maria.'

Again, all of us said 'Amen' and we prayed. Each person made a petition, and everyone participated in the prayers. I was surprised at myself, because I was praying like a child – and like a child, I believed that our prayers would be answered.

The group fell silent for a fraction of a second. I realized that it was my turn to make a petition. Under any other circumstances, I would have died of embarrassment and been unable to say a word. But I felt a presence and that presence gave me confidence.

'May the Immaculate Conception teach me to love as she loves,' I finally said. 'May that love grow in me and in the man to whom it is dedicated. Let us say an Ave Maria.'

We prayed together, and again I felt a sense of freedom. For years, I had fought against my heart, because I was afraid of sadness, suffering, and abandonment. But now I knew that true love was above all that and that it would be better to die than to fail to love.

I had thought that only others had the courage to love. But now I discovered that I too was capable of loving. Even if loving meant leaving, or solitude, or sorrow, love was worth every penny of its price.

I have to stop thinking of these things. I have to concentrate on the ritual.

The priest leading the group asked that we disband the tents and pray for the sick. Everyone continued to pray, sing, and dance in the rain, adoring God and the Virgin Mary. Now and then, people went back to speaking strange languages, waving their arms, and pointing to the sky.

'Someone here . . . someone who has a sick daughter-in-law . . . must know that she is being cured,' cried one woman.

The prayers resumed, along with chants of joy. From time to time we would hear the voice of this woman again.

'Someone in this group who lost her mother recently must have faith and know that she is in the glory of heaven.'

Later, he would tell me that she had the gift of prophecy, that certain individuals can sense what is happening at some distant place or what will happen in the future.

Secretly, I too believed in the power of that voice that was speaking of miracles. I hoped that voice would. speak of the love between two of those present. I hoped to hear that voice proclaim that this love was blessed by all the angels and saints – and by God and by the Goddess.

I'M NOT SURE HOW LONG the ritual lasted. People continued to speak in tongues and to chant; they danced with their arms held up to the sky, prayed for the people around them, and petitioned for miracles.

Finally, the priest who was conducting the ceremony said, 'Let us chant a prayer for all of those here who are participating for the first time in a Charismatic renewal.'

Apparently I was not the only one. That made me feel better.

Everyone chanted a prayer. This time I just listened, asking that favors be granted to me.

I needed many.

'Let us receive the blessing,' said the priest.

The crowd turned toward the illuminated grotto across the river. The priest said several prayers and blessed us all. Then everyone kissed, wished each other a 'Happy Day of the Immaculate Conception,' and went their separate ways.

He came to me. His expression was happier than usual.

'You're soaked,' he said.

'So are you!' I laughed.

We walked back to the car and drove to Saint-Savin. I'd been so eager for this moment to arrive but now that it was here, I didn't know what to say. I couldn't even bring myself to talk about the house in the mountains, the ritual, the strange languages, or the tent prayers.

He was living in two worlds. Somewhere, those two worlds intersected – and I had to find where that was.

But at that moment, words were useless. Love can only be found through the act of loving.

'I've only got one sweater left,' he said when we reached the room. 'You can have it. I'll buy another for myself tomorrow.'

'We'll put our wet things on the heater. They'll be dry by tomorrow. Anyway, I've got the blouse that I washed yesterday.'

Neither of us said anything for a few minutes.

Clothing. Nakedness. Cold.

Finally, he took another shirt out of his bag. 'You can sleep in this,' he said.

'Great,' I answered.

I turned out the light. In the dark, I took off my wet clothes, spread them over the heater, and turned it to high.

By the light from the lamppost outside the window, he must have been able to make out my silhouette and known that I was naked. I slipped the shirt on and crawled under the covers.

'I love you,' I heard him say.

'I'm learning how to love you.'

He lit a cigarette. 'Do you think the right moment will come?' he asked.

I knew what he meant. I got up and sat on the edge of his bed.

The light from his cigarette illuminated our faces. He took my hand and we sat there for some time. I ran my fingers through his hair.

'You shouldn't have asked,' I said. 'Love doesn't ask many questions, because if we stop to think we become fearful. It's an inexplicable fear; it's difficult even to describe it. Maybe it's the fear of being scorned, of not being accepted, or of breaking the spell. It's ridiculous, but that's the way it is. That's why you don't ask – you act. As you've said many times, you have to take risks.'

'I know. I've never asked before.'

'You already have my heart,' I told him. 'Tomorrow you may go away, but we will always remember the miracle of these few days. I think that God, in Her infinite wisdom, conceals hell in the midst of paradise – so that we will always be alert, so that we won't forget the pain as we experience the joy of compassion.'

He took my face in his hands. 'You learn quickly,' he said.

I had surprised myself. But sometimes if you think you know something, you do wind up understanding it.

'I hope you won't think I'm being difficult,' I said. 'I have been with many men. I've made love to some I've barely known.'

'Same here,' he said.

He was trying to sound natural, but from his touch, I could tell that he hadn't wanted to hear this from me.

'But since this morning, I feel as if I'm rediscovering love. Don't try to understand it, because only a woman would know what I mean. And it takes time.'

He caressed my face. Then I kissed him lightly on the lips and returned to my bed.

I wasn't sure why I did. Was I trying to bind him even closer to me, or was I trying to set him free? In any case, it had been a long day, and I was too tired to think about it.

That was a night of great peace. At one point, I seemed to be awake even though I was still sleeping. A feminine presence cradled me in Her lap; I felt as if I had known Her a long time. I felt protected and loved.

I woke at seven, dying of the heat. I remembered having turned the heater to high in order to dry my clothes. It was still dark, and I tried to get up without making a sound so that I wouldn't disturb him.

But as soon as I stood, I could see that he wasn't there.

I started to panic. The Other immediately awoke and said to me, 'See? You agreed, and he disappeared. Like all men do.'

My panic was increasing by the minute, but I didn't want to lose control. 'I'm still here,' the Other said. 'You allowed the wind to change direction. You opened the door, and now love is flooding your life. If we act quickly, we'll be able to regain control.'

I had to be practical, to take precautions.

'He's gone,' said the Other. 'You have to get away from this place in the middle of nowhere. Your life in Zaragoza is still intact; get back there quickly before you lose everything you've worked so hard to gain.'

He must have had some good reason, I thought.

'Men always have their reasons,' said the Other. 'But the fact is that they always wind up leaving.'

Well, then, I had to figure out how to get back to Spain. I had to keep my wits about me.

'Let's start with the practical problem: money,' the Other said.

I didn't have a cent. I would have to go downstairs, call my parents collect, and wait for them to wire me the money for a ticket home.

But it was a holiday, and the money wouldn't arrive until the next day. How would I eat? How would I explain to the owners of the house that they would have to wait for several days for their payment? 'Better not to say anything,' said the Other.

Right, she was the experienced one. She knew how to handle situations like this. She wasn't the impassioned girl who loses control of herself. She was the woman who always knew what she wanted in life. I should simply stay on there, as if he were expected to return. And when the money arrived, I would pay the bill and leave.

'Very good,' said the Other. 'You're getting back to how you were before. Don't be sad. One of these days, you'll find another man – one you can love without taking so many risks.'

I gathered my clothes from the heater. They were dry. I needed to find out which of the surrounding villages had a bank, make a phone call, take steps. If I thought carefully about all of that, there wouldn't be time for crying or regrets.

Then I saw his note:

> *I've gone to the seminary. Pack up your things, because we're going back to Spain tonight. I'll be back by late afternoon. I love you.*

I clutched the note to my breast, feeling miserable and relieved at the same time. I noticed that the Other had retreated.

I loved him. With every minute that passed, my love was growing and transforming me. I once again had faith in the future, and little by little, I was recovering my faith in God. All because of love.

I will not talk to my own darkness anymore, I promised myself, closing the door on the Other. *A fall from the third floor hurts as much as a fall from the hundredth.*

If I have to fall, may it be from a high place.

'DON'T GO OUT HUNGRY AGAIN,' said the woman.

'I didn't realize you spoke Spanish,' I answered, surprised.

'The border isn't far from here. Tourists come to Lourdes in the summer. If I couldn't speak Spanish, I couldn't rent rooms.'

She made me some toast and coffee. I was already trying to prepare myself to make it through the day – each hour was going to seem like a year. I hoped that this snack would distract me for a while.

'How long have you two been married?' she asked.

'He was the first person I ever loved,' I said. That was enough.

'Do you see those peaks out there?' the woman continued. 'The first love of my life died up in those mountains.'

'But you found someone else.'

'Yes, I did. And I found happiness again. Fate is strange: almost no one I know married the first love of their lives. Those who did are always telling me that they missed something important, that they didn't experience all that they might have.'

She stopped talking suddenly. 'I'm sorry,' she said. 'I didn't mean to offend you.'

'I'm not offended.'

'I always look at that well there in the plaza. And I think to myself that before, no one knew where there was water. Then Saint Savin decided to dig and found it. If he hadn't done that, this village would be down there by the river.'

'But what does that have to do with love?' I asked.

'That well brought many people here, with their hopes and dreams and conflicts. Someone dared to look for water, water was found, and people gathered where it flowed. I think that when we look for love courageously, it reveals itself, and we wind up attracting even more love. If one person really wants us, everyone does. But if we're alone, we become even more alone. Life is strange.'

'Have you ever heard of the book called the *I Ching*?' I asked her.

'No, I haven't.'

'It says that a city can be moved but not a well. It's around the well that lovers find each other, satisfy their thirst, build their homes, and raise their children. But if one of them decides to leave, the well cannot go with them. Love remains there, abandoned – even though it is filled with the same pure water as before.'

'You speak like a mature woman who has already suffered a great deal, my dear,' she said.

'No. I've always been frightened. I've never dug a well. But I'm trying to do that now, and I don't want to forget what the risks are.'

I felt something in the pocket of my bag pressing at me. When I realized what it was, my heart went cold. I quickly finished my coffee.

The key. I had the key.

'There was a woman in this city who died and left everything to the seminary at Tarbes,' I said. 'Do you know where her house is?'

The woman opened the door and showed me. It was one of the medieval houses on the plaza. The back of the house looked out over the valley toward the mountains in the distance.

'Two priests went through the house about two months ago,' she said. 'And . . .' She stopped, looking at me doubtfully. 'And one of them looked a lot like your husband.'

'It was,' I answered. The woman stood in her doorway, puzzled, as I quickly left. I felt a burst of energy, happy that I had allowed the child in me to pull a prank.

I soon stood in front of the house, not knowing what to do. The mist was everywhere, and I felt as if I were in a gray dream where strange figures might appear and take me away to places even more peculiar.

I toyed nervously with the key.

With the mist as thick as it was, it would be impossible to see the mountains from the window. The house would be dark; there would be no sun shining through the curtains. The house would seem sad without him at my side.

I looked at my watch. Nine in the morning.

I had to do something – something that would make the time pass, that would help me wait.

Wait. This was the first lesson I had learned about love. The day drags along, you make thousands of plans, you imagine every possible conversation, you promise to change your behavior in certain ways – and you feel more and more anxious until your loved one arrives. But by then, you don't know what to say. The hours of waiting have been transformed into tension, the tension has become fear, and the fear makes you embarrassed about showing affection.

I didn't know whether I should go in. I remembered our conversation of the previous day – the house was the symbol of a dream.

But I couldn't spend the whole day just standing there. I gathered up my courage, grasped the key firmly, and walked to the door.

'PILAR!'

The voice, with a strong French accent, came from the midst of the fog. I was more surprised than frightened. I thought it might be the owner of the house where we had rented the room – although I didn't recall having told him my name.

'Pilar!' I heard again, nearer this time.

I looked back at the plaza shrouded in mist. A figure was approaching, walking hurriedly. Perhaps the ghosts that I had imagined in the fog were becoming a reality.

'Wait,' the figure said. 'I want to talk to you.'

When he had come closer, I could see that it was a priest. He looked like a caricature of the country padre: short, on the heavy side, with sparse white hair on a nearly bald head.

'Hola,' he said, holding out his hand and smiling.

I answered him, a bit astonished.

'Too bad the fog is hiding everything,' he said, looking toward the house. 'Since Saint-Savin is in the mountains, the view from this house is beautiful; you can see the valley down below and the snow-covered peaks. But you probably already knew that.'

I decided that this must be the superior from the monastery.

'What are you doing here?' I asked. 'And how do you know my name?'

'Do you want to go in?' he said, trying to change the subject.

'No! I'd like you to answer my questions.'

Rubbing his hands together to warm them, he sat down on the curb. I sat down next to him. The fog was growing thicker by the minute. The church was already hidden from sight, and it was only sixty feet away from us.

All I could see was the well. I remembered what the young woman in Madrid had said.

'She is present,' I said.

'Who?'

'The Goddess,' I answered. 'She is this mist.'

'So, he must have talked to you about that,' he laughed. 'Well, I prefer to refer to Her as the Virgin Mary. That's what I'm used to.'

'What are you doing here? How do you know my name?' I repeated.

'I came here because I wanted to see you two. A member of the Charismatic group last night told me you were both staying in Saint-Savin. And it's a small place.'

'He went to the seminary.'

The padre's smile disappeared, and he shook his head. 'Too bad,' he said, as if speaking to himself.

'You mean, too bad he went to the seminary?'

'No, he's not there. I've just come from the seminary.'

For a moment, I couldn't say anything. I thought back to the feeling I'd had when I woke up: the money, the arrangements I needed to make, the call to my parents, the ticket. But I'd made a vow, and I wasn't going to break it.

A priest was sitting beside me. As a child, I used to tell everything to our priest.

'I'm exhausted,' I said, breaking the silence. 'Less than a week ago, I finally learned who I am and what I want in life. Now I feel like I've been caught in a storm that's tossing me around, and I can't seem to do anything about it.'

'Resist your doubts,' the padre said. 'It's important.'

His advice surprised me.

'Don't be frightened,' he continued, as if he knew what I was feeling. 'I know that the church is in need of new priests, and he would be an excellent one. But the price he would have to pay would be very high.'

'Where is he? Did he leave me here to return to Spain?'

'To Spain? There's nothing for him to do in Spain,' said the priest. 'His home is at the monastery, only a few kilometers from here. He's not there. But I know where we can find him.'

His words brought back some of my joy and courage – at least he hadn't gone away.

But the priest was no longer smiling. 'Don't let that encourage you,' he went on, again reading my mind. 'It would be better if he *had* gone back to Spain.'

He stood and asked me to go with him. We could see only a few yards in front of us, but he seemed to know where he was going. We left Saint-Savin by the same road along which, two nights before – or could it have been five years before? – I had heard the story of Bernadette.

'Where are we going?' I asked.

'To find him,' he answered.

'Padre, you've confused me,' I said, as we walked along together. 'You seemed sad when you said he wasn't at the seminary.'

'Tell me what you know about the religious life, my child.'

'Very little. Only that the priests take a vow of poverty, chastity, and obedience.' I wondered whether I should go on and decided that I would. 'And that they judge the sins of others, even though they may commit the same sins themselves. That they know all there is to know about marriage and love, but they never marry. That they threaten us with the fires of hell for mistakes that they themselves make. And they present God to us as a vengeful being who blames man for the death of His only Son.'

The padre laughed. 'You've had an excellent Catholic education,' he said. 'But I'm not asking you about Catholicism. I'm asking about the spiritual life.'

I didn't respond for a moment. 'I'm not sure. There are people who leave everything behind and go in search of God.'

'And do they find Him?'

'Well, you would know the answer to that, Padre. I have no idea.'

The padre noticed that I was beginning to gasp with exertion, and he slowed his pace.

'You had that wrong,' he said. 'A person who goes in search of God is wasting his time. He can walk a thousand roads and join many religions and sects – but he'll never find God that way.

'God is here, right now, at our side. We can see Him in this mist, in the around we're walking on, even in my shoes. His angels keep watch while we sleep and help us in our work. In order to find God, you have only to look around.

'But meeting Him is not easy. The more God asks us to participate in His mysteries, the more disoriented we become, because He asks us constantly to follow our dreams and our hearts. And that's difficult to do when we're used to living in a different way.

'Finally we discover, to our surprise, that God wants us to be happy, because He is the father.'

'And the mother,' I said.

The fog was beginning to clear. I could see a small farmhouse where a woman was gathering hay.

'Yes, and the mother,' he said. 'In order to have a spiritual life, you need not enter a seminary, or fast, or abstain, or take a vow of chastity. All you have to do is have faith and accept God. From then on, each of us becomes a part of His path. We become a vehicle for His miracles.'

'He has already told me about you,' I interrupted, 'and he has taught me these ideas.'

'I hope that you accept God's gifts,' he answered. 'Because it hasn't always been that way, as history teaches us. Osiris was drawn and quartered in Egypt. The Greek gods battled because of the mortals on earth. The Aztecs expelled Quetzalcoatl. The Viking gods witnessed the burning of Valhalla because of a woman. Jesus was crucified. Why?'

I didn't have an answer.

'Because God came to earth to demonstrate His power to us. We are a part of His dream, and He wants His dream to be a happy one. Thus, if we acknowledge that God created us for happiness, then we have to assume that everything that leads to sadness and defeat is our own doing. That's the reason we always kill God, whether on the cross, by fire, through exile, or simply in our hearts.'

'But those who understand Him . . .'

'They are the ones who transform the world – while making great sacrifices.'

The woman carrying the hay saw the priest and came running in our direction. 'Padre, thank you!' she said, kissing his hands. 'The young man cured my husband!'

'It was the Virgin who cured your husband,' he said. 'The lad is only an instrument.'

'It was he. Come in, please.'

I recalled the previous night. When we arrived at the cathedral, a man had told me I was with a man who performed miracles.

'We're in a hurry,' the padre said.

'No! No, we're not,' I said, in my halting French. 'I'm cold, and I'd like some coffee.'

The woman took me by the hand, and we entered the house. It was simple but comfortable: stone walls, wood floors, and bare rafters. Seated in front of the fireplace was a man of about sixty. As soon as he saw the padre, he stood to kiss his hand.

'Don't get up,' said the priest. 'You still need to convalesce a bit.'

'I've already gained twenty-five pounds,' he answered. 'But I'm still not able to be of much help to my wife.'

'Not to worry. Before long, you'll be better than ever.'

'Where is the young man?' the husband asked.

'I saw him heading toward where he always goes,' the wife said. 'Only today, he went by car'

The padre eyed me but didn't say anything.

'Give us your blessing, Père,' the woman asked. 'His power . . .'

'The Virgin's power,' the priest corrected.

'The Virgin Mother's power is also your power, Père It was you who brought it here.'

This time, he didn't look my way.

'Pray for my husband, Père,' the woman insisted.

The priest took a deep breath. 'Stand in front me,' he said to the man.

The old man did as he was told. The padre closed his eyes and said an Ave Maria. Then he invoked the Holy Spirit, asking that it be present and help the man.

He suddenly began to speak rapidly. It sounded like a prayer of exorcism, although I couldn't understand what he was saying. His hands touched the man's shoulders and then slid down his arms to his fingertips. He repeated this gesture several times.

The fire began to crackle loudly in the fireplace. This may have been a coincidence, yet it seemed that the priest was entering into territory I knew nothing about – and that he was affecting the very elements.

Every snap of the fire startled the woman and me, but the padre paid no attention to it; he was completely involved in his task – an instrument of the Virgin, as he had said. He was speaking a strange language, and the words came forth at great speed. He was no longer moving his hands; they simply rested on the man's shoulders.

The ritual stopped as quickly as it had started. The padre turned and gave a conventional blessing, making the sign of the cross with his right hand. 'May God be ever here in this house,' he said.

And turning to me, he asked that we continue our walk.

'But you haven't had coffee,' the woman said, as she saw that we were about to leave.

'If I have coffee now, I won't be able to sleep,' the padre answered.

The woman laughed and murmured something like 'It's still morning.' But we were already on our way.

'Padre, the woman spoke of a young man who cured her husband. Was it he?'

'Yes, it was.'

I began to feel uneasy. I remembered the day before, and Bilbao, and the conference in Madrid, and people speaking of miracles, and the presence that I had sensed as we embraced and prayed.

I was in love with a man who was capable of performing cures. A man who could help others, bring relief to suffering, give health to the sick and hope to their loved ones. Was I distracting him from his mission just because it was at odds with my image of a house with white curtains, cherished records, and favorite books?

'Don't blame yourself, my child,' the padre said.

'You're reading my mind.'

'Yes, I am,' the padre said. 'I have that gift too, and I try to be worthy of it. The Virgin taught me to penetrate the turmoil of human emotions in order to control them as well as possible.'

'Do you perform miracles, too?'

'I am not able to cure. But I have one of the gifts of the Holy Spirit.'

'So you can read my heart, Padre. And you know I love him, with a love that is growing every minute. We discovered the world together, and together we remain in it. He has been present every day of my life – whether I wanted him there or not.'

What could I say to this priest who was walking beside me? He would never understand that I had had other men, that I had been in love, and that if I had married, I would be happy. Even as a child, I had found and forgotten love in the plaza of Soria.

But the way things looked now, I hadn't forgotten that first love very well. It had taken only three days for all of it to come rushing back.

'I have a right to be happy, Padre. I've recovered what was lost, and I don't want to lose it again. I'm going to fight for my happiness. If I give up the fight, I will also be renouncing my spiritual life. As you said, I would be putting God aside, along with my power and my strength as a woman. I'm going to fight for him, Padre.'

I knew what that man was doing here. He had come to convince me to leave him, because he had a more important mission to accomplish.

No, I couldn't believe that the padre walking at my side wanted us to marry and live in a house like the one in Saint-Savin. The priest had said that to trick me. He wanted me to lower my defenses and then – with a smile – he would convince me of the opposite.

He read my thoughts without saying a word. Or perhaps he was trying to fool me. Maybe he didn't know what others were thinking.

The fog was dissipating rapidly, and I could now see the path, the mountain peak, the fields, and the snow-covered trees. My emotions were becoming clearer, as well.

Damn! If it's true that he can read someone's thoughts, then let him read mine and know everything! Let him know that yesterday he wanted to make love to me – that I refused and that now I regret it.

Yesterday I had thought that if he had to leave, I would still at least have the memory of my childhood friend. But that was nonsense. Even though he hadn't entered me, something even more profound had, and it had touched my heart.

'Padre, I love him,' I repeated.

'So do I. And love always causes stupidity. In my case, it requires that I try to keep him from his destiny.'

'That won't be easy, Padre. And it won't be easy in my case, either. Yesterday, during the prayers at the grotto, I discovered that I too can bring forth these gifts that you were talking about. And I'm going to use them to keep him with me.'

'Good luck,' said the padre, with a smile. 'I hope you can.'

He stopped and took a rosary from his pocket. Holding it, he looked into my eyes. 'Jesus said that we should not take oaths, and I am not doing so. But I'm telling you, in the presence of all that is sacred to me, that I would not like him to adopt the conventional religious life. I would not like to see him ordained a priest. He can serve God in other ways – at your side.'

It was hard for me to believe that he was telling me the truth. But he was.

'He's up there,' the padre said.

I turned. I could see a car parked a bit further ahead – the same car we had driven from Spain.

'He always comes on foot,' he said, smiling. 'This time he wanted to give us the impression that he'd traveled a long way.'

THE SNOW WAS SOAKING MY sneakers. But the padre was wearing only open sandals with woolen socks. I decided not to complain – if he could stand it, so could I. We began to hike toward the top of the mountains.

'How long will it take us?'

'Half an hour at the most.'

'Where are we going?'

'To meet with him. And others.'

I could see that he didn't want to say any more. Maybe he needed all of his energy for climbing. We walked along in silence – the fog had by now disappeared almost completely, and the yellow disk of the sun was coming into view.

For the first time I had a view of the entire valley; there was a river running through it, some scattered villages, and Saint-Savin, looking as though it were pasted against the slope of the mountain. I could make out the tower of the church, a cemetery I had not noticed before, and the medieval houses looking down on the river.

A bit below us, at a point we had already passed, a shepherd was tending his flock of sheep.

'I'm tired,' the padre said. 'Let's stop for a while.'

We brushed the snow from the top of a boulder and rested against it. He was perspiring – and his feet must have been frozen.

'May Santiago preserve my strength, because I still want to walk his path one more time,' said the padre, turning to me.

I didn't understand his comment, so I decided to change the subject. 'There are footsteps in the snow.'

'Some are those of hunters. Others are of men and women who want to relive a tradition.'

'Which tradition?'

'The same as that of Saint Savin. Retreat from the world, come to these mountains, and contemplate the glory of God.'

'Padre, there's something I need to understand. Until yesterday, I was with a man who couldn't choose between the religious life and marriage. Today, I learn that this same man performs miracles.'

'We all perform miracles,' he said. 'Jesus said, "If our faith is the size of a mustard seed, we will say to the mountain, 'Move!' And it will move."'

'I don't want a lesson in religion, Padre. I'm in love with a man, and I want to know more about him, understand him, help him. I don't care what everyone else can do or can't do.'

The padre took a deep breath. He hesitated for a moment and then said, 'A scientist who studied monkeys on an island in Indonesia was able to teach a certain one to wash bananas in the river before eating them. Cleansed of sand and dirt, the food was more flavorful. The scientist – who did this only because he was studying the learning capacity of monkeys – did not imagine what would eventually happen. So he was surprised to see that the other monkeys on the island began to imitate the first one.

'And then, one day, when a certain number of monkeys had learned to wash their bananas, the monkeys on all of the other islands in the archipelago began to do the same thing. What was most surprising, though, was that the other monkeys learned to do so without having had any contact with the island where the experiment had been conducted.'

He stopped. 'Do you understand?'

'No,' I answered.

'There are several similar scientific studies. The most common explanation is that when a certain number of people evolve, the entire human race begins to evolve. We don't know how many people are needed – but we know that's how it works.'

'Like the story of the Immaculate Conception,' I said. 'The vision appeared for the wise men at the Vatican and for the simple farmer.'

'The world itself has a soul, and at a certain moment, that soul acts on everyone and everything at the same time.'

'A feminine soul.'

He laughed, without saying just what he was laughing about.

'By the way, the dogma of the Immaculate Conception was not just a Vatican matter,' he said. 'Eight million people signed a petition to the pope, asking that it be recognized. The signatures came from all over the world.'

'Is that the first step, Padre?'

'What do you mean?'

'The first step toward having Our Lady recognized as the incarnation of the feminine face of God? After all, we already accept the fact that Jesus was the incarnation of His masculine side.'

'And so . . . ?'

'How much time must pass before we accept a Holy Trinity that includes a woman? The Trinity of the Holy Spirit, the Mother, and the Son?'

'Let's move on. It's too cold for us to stand here,' he said. 'A little while ago, you noticed my sandals.'

'Have you been reading my mind?' I asked.

'I'm going to tell you part of the story of the founding of our religious order,' he said. 'We are barefoot Carmelites, according to the rules established by Saint Teresa of Avila. The sandals are a part of the story, for if one can dominate the body, one can dominate the spirit.

'Teresa was a beautiful woman, placed by her father in a convent so that she would receive a pure education. One day, when she was walking along a corridor, she began to speak with Jesus. Her ecstasies were so strong and deep that she surrendered totally to them, and in a short time, her life had been completely changed. She felt that the Carmelite convents had become nothing more than marriage brokerages, and she decided to create an order that would once again follow the original teachings of Christ and the Carmelites.

'Saint Teresa had to conquer herself, and she had to confront the great powers of her day – the church and the state. But she was determined to press on, because she was convinced that she had a mission to perform.

'One day – just when Teresa felt her soul to be weakening – a woman in tattered clothing appeared at the house where she was staying. The woman wanted to speak with Teresa, no matter what. The owner of the house offered the woman some alms, but the woman refused them; she would not go away until she had spoken with Teresa.

'For three days, the woman waited outside the house, without eating or drinking. Finally Teresa, out of sympathy, bade the woman come in.

'"No," said the owner of the house. "The woman is mad."

'"If I were to listen to everyone, I'd wind up thinking that I'm the crazy one," Teresa answered. "It may be that this woman has the same kind of madness as I: that of Christ on the cross."'

'Saint Teresa spoke with Christ,' I said.

'Yes,' he answered. 'But to get back to our story: the woman was brought to Teresa. She said that her name was María de Jesus Yepes and that she was from Granada. She was a Carmelite novice, and the Virgin had appeared and asked that she found a convent that followed the primitive rules of the order.'

Like Saint Teresa, I thought.

'María de Jesus left the convent on the day of her vision and began walking barefoot to Rome. Her pilgrimage lasted two years – and for that entire period, she slept outdoors, in the heat and the cold, living on alms and the charity of others. It was a miracle that she made it. But it was an even greater miracle that she was received by Pope Pius IV. Because the pope, just like María de Jesus, Teresa, and many others, was thinking of the same thing,' he finished.

Just as Bernadette had known nothing of the Vatican's decision and the monkeys from the other islands couldn't have known about the experiment that was being conducted, so María de Jesus and Teresa knew nothing of what the other was planning.

Something was beginning to make sense to me.

We were now walking through a forest. With the fog all but gone, the highest tree branches, covered with snow, were receiving the first rays of the sun.

'I think I know where you're going with this, Padre.'

'Yes. The world is at a point when many people are receiving the same order: "Follow your dreams, transform your life, take the path that leads to God. Perform your miracles. Cure. Make prophecies. Listen to your guardian angel. Transform yourself. Be a warrior, and be happy as you wage the good fight. Take risks."'

Sunshine was everywhere. The snow was glistening, and the glare hurt my eyes. Yet at the same time, it seemed to support what the priest was saying.

'And what does all this have to do with him?'

'I've told you the heroic side of the story. But you don't know anything about the soul of these heroes.'

He paused.

'The suffering,' he picked up again. 'At moments of transformation, martyrs are born. Before a person can follow his dream, others have to make sacrifices. They have to confront ridicule, persecution, and attempts to discredit what they are trying to do.'

'It was the church that burned the witches at the stake, Padre.'

'Right. And Rome threw the Christians to the lions. But those who died at the stake or in the sand of the arena rose quickly to eternal glory – they were better off.

'Nowadays, warriors of the light confront something worse than the honorable death of the martyrs. They are consumed, bit by bit, by shame and humiliation. That's how it was with Saint Teresa – who suffered for the rest of her life. That's how it was for María de Jesus, too. And for the happy children who saw Our Lady in Fátima, Portugal – well, Jacinta and Francisco died just a few months later; Lucia entered a convent from which she never emerged.'

'But that's not how it was for Bernadette.'

'Yes, it was. She had to live through prison, humiliation, and discredit. He must have described that to you. He must have told you the words of the visitation.'

'Some of them.'

'In the visitations at Lourdes, the phrases uttered by Our Lady wouldn't fill half a page of a notebook, but one of the things the Virgin said clearly to the girl was "*I do not promise you happiness in this world.*" Why did she warn Bernadette? Because she knew the pain that awaited Bernadette if she accepted her mission.'

I looked at the sun, the snow, and the bare branches of the trees.

'He is a revolutionary,' he continued, sounding humble. 'He has the power, and he converses with Our Lady. If he is able to concentrate his forces well, he can be one of the leaders in the spiritual transformation of the human race. This is a critical point in the history of the world.

'But if he chooses this path, he is going to go through a great deal of suffering. His revelations have come to him before their time. I know the human soul well enough to know what he can expect.'

The padre turned to me and held me by the shoulders. 'Please,' he said. 'Keep him from the suffering and tragedy that lie in store for him. He will not be able to survive them.'

'I understand your love for him, Padre.'

He shook his head. 'No, no. You don't understand anything. You are still too young to know the evils of the world. At this point, you see yourself as a revolutionary too. You want to change the world with him, open new paths, see the story of your love for each other become legend – a story passed down through the generations. You still think that love can conquer all.'

'Well, can't it?'

'Yes, it can. But it conquers at the right time – after the celestial battles have ended.'

'But I love him. I don't have to wait for the celestial battles to end for my love to win out.'

He gazed into the distance.

'On the banks of the rivers of Babylon, we sat down and wept,' he said, as if talking to himself. 'On the willows there, we hung up our harps.'

'How sad,' I answered.

'Those are the first lines of one of the psalms. It tells of exile and of those who want to return to the promised land but cannot. And that exile is still going to last for a long time. What can I do to try to prevent the suffering of someone who wants to return to paradise before it is time to do so?'

'Nothing, Padre. Absolutely nothing.'

'THERE HE IS,' SAID THE padre.

I saw him. He was about two hundred yards from me, kneeling in the snow. He was shirtless, and even from that distance, I could see that his skin was red with the cold.

His head was bowed and his hands joined in prayer. I don't know if I was influenced by the ritual I had attended the night before or by the woman who had been gathering hay, but I felt that I was looking at someone with an incredible spiritual force. Someone who was no longer of this world – who lived in communion with God and with the enlightened spirits of heaven. The brilliance of the snow seemed to strengthen this perception.

'At this moment, there are others like him,' said the priest. 'In constant adoration, communing with God and the Virgin. Hearing the angels, the saints, the prophecies and words of wisdom, and transmitting all of that to a small gathering of the faithful. As long as they continue in this way, there won't be a problem.

'But he is not going to remain here. He is going to travel the world, preaching the concept of the Great Mother. The church is not yet ready for that. And the world has stones at hand to hurl at those who must introduce the subject.'

'And it has flowers to throw on those who come afterward.'

'Yes. But that's not what will happen to him.'

The priest began to approach him.

'Where are you going?'

'To bring him out of his trance. To tell him how much I like you. To say that I give my blessing to your union. I want to do that here, in this place, which for him is sacred.'

I began to feel sick with an inexplicable fear.

'I have to think, Padre. I don't know if this is right.'

'It's not right,' he answered. 'Many parents make mistakes with their children, thinking they know what's best for them. I'm not his father, and I know I'm doing the wrong thing. But I have to fulfill my destiny.'

I was feeling more and more anxious.

'Let's not disturb him,' I said. 'Let him finish his contemplation.'

'He shouldn't be here. He should be with you.'

'Maybe he's communicating with the Virgin.'

'He may be. But even so, we have to go to him. If I approach him with you at my side, he will know that I have told you everything. He knows what I think.'

'Today is the day of the Immaculate Conception,' I insisted. 'A very special day for him. I saw his happiness last night at the grotto.'

'The Immaculate Conception is special for all of us,' the padre answered. 'But now I'm the one who doesn't want to discuss religion. Let's go to him.'

'Why now, Padre? Why at this moment?'

'Because I know that he is deciding his future. And he may make the wrong choice.'

I turned away and began to walk down the same path we had just come up. The padre followed me.

'What are you doing? Don't you see that you're the only one who can save him? Don't you see that he loves you and would give up everything for you?'

I hurried my steps, and it was difficult for him to keep up. Yet he fought to stay at my side.

'At this very moment, he is making his decision! He may be deciding to leave you! Fight for the person you love!'

But I didn't stop. I walked as fast as I could, trying to escape the mountains, the priest, and the choices behind me. I knew that the man who was rushing along behind me was reading my thoughts and that he understood that it was useless to try to make me go back. Yet he insisted; he argued and struggled to the end.

Finally, we reached the boulder where we had rested a half hour earlier. Exhausted, I threw myself down.

I tried to relax. I wanted to run from there, to be alone, to have time to think.

The padre appeared a few minutes later, as exhausted as I was.

'Do you see these mountains surrounding us?' he started in. 'They don't pray; they are already a part of God's prayers. They have found their place in the world and here they will stay. They were here before people looked to the heavens, heard thunder, and wondered who had created all of this. We are born, we suffer, we die, and the mountains endure.

'There is some point at which we have to wonder whether all our effort is worth it. Why not try to be like those mountains – wise, ancient, and in their place; Why risk everything to transform a half-dozen people who will immediately forget what they've been taught and move on to the next adventure? Why not wait until a certain number of monkeys learn, and then the knowledge will spread, with no suffering, to all the other islands?'

'Is that what you really think, Padre?'

He was silent for a few moments.

'Are you reading my thoughts now?'

'No. But if that's the way you feel, you wouldn't have chosen the religious life.'

'I've tried many times to understand my fate,' he said. 'But I haven't yet. I accepted that I was to be a part of God's army, and everything I've done has been in an attempt to explain to people why there is misery, pain, and injustice. I ask them to be good Christians, and they ask me, "How can I believe in God when there is so much suffering in the world?"

'And I try to explain something that has no explanation. I try to tell them that there is a plan, a battle among the angels, and that we are all involved in the battle. I try to say that when a certain number of people have enough faith to change the scenario, all of the others – everywhere on the planet – will benefit. But they don't believe me. They do nothing.'

'They are like the mountains,' I said. 'The mountains are beautiful. Anyone who beholds them has to think about the grandness of creation. They are living proof of the love that God feels for us, but their fate is merely to give testimony. They are not like the rivers, which move and transform what is around them.'

'Yes. But why not be like the mountains?'

'Maybe because the fate of mountains is terrible,' I answered. 'They are destined to look out at the same scene forever.'

The padre said nothing.

'I was studying to become a mountain,' I continued. 'I had put everything in its proper place. I was going to take a job with the state, marry, and teach the religion of my parents to my children, even though I no longer accepted it. But now I have decided to leave all that behind me in order to be with the man I love. And it's a good thing I decided not to be a mountain – I wouldn't have lasted very long.'

'You say some very wise things.'

'I'm surprising myself. Before, all I could talk about was my childhood.'

I stood and started back down the trail. The padre seemed to respect my silence and did not try to speak to me until we reached the road.

I took his hands and kissed them. 'I'm going to say good-bye. But I want you to know that I understand you and your love for him.'

The padre smiled and gave me his blessing. 'And I understand your love for him, too,' he said.

I spent the rest of the day walking through the valley. I played in the snow, visited a village near Saint-Savin, had a sandwich, and watched some boys playing soccer.

At the church in the village, I lit a candle. I closed my eyes and repeated the invocations I had learned the previous night. Then, concentrating on a crucifix that hung behind the altar, I began to speak in tongues. Bit by bit, the gift took over. It was easier than I had thought.

Perhaps this all seems silly – murmuring things, saying words that have no meaning, that don't help us in our reasoning. But when we do this, the Holy Spirit is conversing with our souls, saying things the soul needs to hear.

When I felt that I was sufficiently purified, I closed my eyes and prayed.

Our Lady, give me back, my faith. May I also serve as an instrument of your work. Give me the opportunity to learn through my love, because love has never kept anyone away from their dreams.

May I be a companion and ally of the man I love. May we accomplish everything we have to accomplish – together.

When I returned to Saint-Savin, night had almost fallen. The car was parked in front of the house where we were staying.

'Where have you been?' he asked.

'Walking and praying,' I answered.

He embraced me.

'At first, I was afraid you had gone away. You are the most precious thing I have on this earth.'

'And you are for me,' I answered.

IT WAS LATE WHEN WE stopped in a small village near San Martin de Unx. Crossing the Pyrenees had taken longer than we'd thought because of the rain and snow of the previous day.

'We need to find someplace that's open,' he said, climbing out of the car. 'I'm hungry.'

I didn't move.

'Come on,' he insisted, opening my door.

'I want to ask you a question – a question I haven't asked since we found each other again.'

He became serious, and I laughed at his concern.

'Is it an important question?'

'Very important,' I answered, trying to look serious. 'It's the following: where are we going?'

We both laughed.

'To Zaragoza,' he said, relieved.

I jumped out of the car, and we went looking for a restaurant that was open. It was going to be almost impossible at that hour of the night.

No, it's not impossible. The Other is no longer with me. Miracles do happen, I said to myself. 'When do you have to be in Barcelona?' I asked him. He'd told me he had another conference there.

He didn't answer, and his expression turned serious.

I shouldn't ask such questions, I thought. *He may think I'm trying to control his life.*

We walked along without speaking. In the village plaza, there was an illuminated sign: *Mesón el Sol.*

'It's open – let's have something to eat' was all he said.

The red peppers with anchovies were arranged on the plate in the shape of a star. On the side, some *manchego* cheese, in slices that were almost transparent. In the center of the table, a lighted candle and a half-full bottle of Rioja wine.

'This was a medieval wine cellar,' our waiter told us.

There was no one in the place at that time of night. He went off to make a telephone call. When he came back to the table, I wanted to ask him whom he had called – but this time I controlled myself.

'We're open until two-thirty in the morning,' the man said. 'So if you like, we can bring you some more ham, cheese, and wine, and you can go out in the plaza. The wine will keep you warm.'

'We won't be here that long,' he answered. 'We have to get to Zaragoza before dawn.'

The man returned to the bar, and we refilled our glasses. I felt the same sense of lightness I had experienced in Bilbao – the smooth inebriation that helps us to say and hear things that are difficult.

'You're tired of driving, and we've been drinking,' I said. 'Wouldn't it be better to stay the night? I saw an inn as we were driving.'

He nodded in agreement.

'Look at this table,' he said. 'The Japanese call it *shibumi*, the true sophistication of simple things. Instead, people fill their bank accounts with money and travel to expensive places in order to feel they're sophisticated.'

I had some more wine.

The inn. Another night at his side.

'It's strange to hear a seminarian speak of sophistication,' I said, trying to focus on something else.

'I learned about it at the seminary. The closer we get to God through our faith, the simpler He becomes. And the simpler He becomes, the greater is His presence.

'Christ learned about his mission while he was cutting wood and making chairs, beds, and cabinets. He came as a carpenter to show us that – no matter what we do – everything can lead us to the experience of God's love.'

He stopped suddenly.

'But I don't want to talk about that,' he said. 'I want to talk about the other kind of love.'

He reached out to caress my face. The wine made things easier for him. And for me.

'Why did you stop so suddenly? Why don't you want to talk about God and the Virgin and the spiritual world?'

'I want to talk about the other kind of love,' he said again. 'The love that a man and a woman share, and in which there are also miracles.'

I took his hands. He might know of the great mysteries of the Goddess, but he didn't know any more than I did about love – even though he had traveled much more than I had.

We held hands for a long time. I could see in his eyes the deep fears that true love tests us with. I could see that he was remembering the rejection of the night before, as well as the long time we had been separated, and his years in the monastery, searching for a world where such anxieties didn't intrude.

I could see in his eyes the thousands of times that he had imagined this moment and the scenes he had constructed about us. I wanted to say that yes, he was welcome, that my heart had won the battle. I wanted to tell him how much I loved him and how badly I wanted him at that moment.

But I was silent. I witnessed, as if in a dream, his inner conflict. I could see that he was wondering whether I'd reject him again, that he was thinking about his fear of losing me, and about the hard words he had heard at other, similar times – because we all have such experiences, and they leave scars.

His eyes gleamed. He was ready to surmount any barrier.

I took one of my hands from his and placed my glass of wine at the edge of the table.

'It's going to fall,' he said.

'Exactly. I want you to tip it over the edge.'

'Break the glass?'

Yes, break the glass. A simple gesture, but one that brings up fears we can't really understand. What's wrong with breaking an inexpensive glass, when everyone has done so unintentionally at some time in their life?

'Break the glass?' he repeated. 'Why?'

'Well, I could give you lots of reasons,' I answered. 'But actually, just to break it.'

'For you?'

'No, of course not.'

He eyed the glass on the edge of the table – worried that it might fall.

It's a rite of passage, I wanted to say. It's something prohibited. Glasses are not purposely broken. In a restaurant or in our home, we're careful not to place glasses by the edge of a table. Our universe requires that we avoid letting glasses fall to the floor.

But when we break them by accident, we realize that it's not very serious. The waiter says, 'It's nothing,' and when has anyone been charged for a broken glass? Breaking glasses is part of life and does no damage to us, to the restaurant, or to anyone else.

I bumped the table. The glass shook but didn't fall.

'Careful!' he said, instinctively.

'Break the glass,' I insisted.

Break the glass, I thought to myself, *because it's a symbolic gesture. Try to understand that I have broken things within myself that were much more important than a glass, and I'm happy I did. Resolve your own internal battle, and break the glass.*

Our parents taught us to be careful with glasses and with our bodies. They taught us that the passions of childhood are impossible, that we should not flee from priests, that people cannot perform miracles, and that no one leaves on a journey without knowing where they are going.

Break the glass, please – and free us from all these damned rules, from needing to find an explanation for everything, from doing only what others approve of.

'Break the glass,' I said again.

He stared at me. Then, slowly, he slid his hand along the tablecloth to the glass. And with a sudden movement, he pushed it to the floor.

The sound of the breaking glass caught the waiter's attention. Rather than apologize for having broken the glass, he looked at me, smiling – and I smiled back.

'Doesn't matter,' shouted the waiter.

But he wasn't listening. He had stood, seized my hair in his hands, and was kissing me.

I clutched at his hair, too, and squeezed him with all my strength, biting his lips and feeling his tongue move in my mouth. This was the kiss I had waited for so long – a kiss born by the rivers of our childhood, when we didn't yet know what love meant. A kiss that had been suspended in the air as we grew, that had traveled the world in the souvenir of a medal, and that had remained hidden behind piles of books. A kiss that had been lost so many times and now was found. In the moment of that kiss were years or searching, disillusionment, and impossible dreams.

I kissed him hard. The few people there in the bar must have been thinking that all they were seeing was just a kiss. They didn't know that this kiss stood for my whole life – and his life, as well. The life of anyone who has waited, dreamed, and searched for their true path.

The moment of that kiss contained every happy moment I had ever lived.

HE TOOK OFF MY CLOTHES and entered me with strength, with fear, and with great desire. I ran my hands over his face, heard his moans, and thanked God that he was there inside me, making me feel as if it were the first time.

We made love all night long – our lovemaking blended with our sleeping and dreaming. I felt him inside me and embraced him to make sure that this was really happening, to make sure that he wouldn't disappear, like the knights who had once inhabited this old castle-hotel. The silent walls of stone seemed to be telling stories of damsels in distress, of fallen tears and endless days at the window, looking to the horizon, looking for a sign of hope.

But I would never go through that, I promised myself. I would never lose him. He would always be with me – because I had heard the tongues of the Holy Spirit as I looked at a crucifix behind an altar, and they had said that I would not be committing a sin.

I would be his companion, and together we would tame a world that was going to be created anew. We would talk about the Great Mother, we would fight at the side of Michael the Archangel, and we would experience together the agony and the ecstasy of pioneers. That's what the tongues had said to me – and because I had recovered my faith, I knew they were telling the truth.

Thursday, December 9, 1993

I awoke with his arm across my breast. It was already midmorning, and the bells of a nearby church were tolling.

He kissed me. His hands once again caressed my body.

'We have to go,' he said. 'The holiday ends today, and the roads will be jammed.'

'I don't want to go back to Zaragoza,' I answered. 'I want to go straight to where you're going. The bank will be open soon, and I can use my bank card to get some money and buy some clothes.'

'You told me you didn't have much money.'

'There are things I can do. I need to break with my past once and for all. If we go back to Zaragoza, I might begin to think I'm making a mistake, that the exam period is almost here and we can stand to be separated for two months until my exams are over. And then if I pass my exams, I won't want to leave Zaragoza. No, no, I can't go back. I need to burn the bridges that connect me with the woman I was.'

'Barcelona,' he said to himself.

'What?'

'Nothing. Let's move on.'

'But you have a presentation to make.'

'But that's two days from now,' he said. His voice sounded different. 'Let's go somewhere else. I don't want to go straight to Barcelona.'

I got out of bed. I didn't want to focus on problems. As always after a first night of love with someone, I had awakened with a certain sense of ceremony and embarrassment.

I went to the window, opened the curtains, and looked down on the narrow street. The balconies of the houses were draped with drying laundry. The church bells were ringing.

'I've got an idea,' I said. 'Let's go to a place we shared as children. I've never been back there.'

'Where?'

'The monastery at Piedra.'

As we left the hotel, the bells were still sounding, and he suggested that we go into a church nearby.

'That's all we've done,' I said. 'Churches, prayers, rituals.'

'We made love,' he said. 'We've gotten drunk three times. We've walked in the mountains. We've struck a good balance between rigor and compassion.'

I'd said something thoughtless. I had to get used to this new life.

'I'm sorry,' I said.

'Let's just go in for a few minutes. The bells are a sign.'

He was right, but I wouldn't know that until the next day.

Afterward, without really understanding the meaning of the sign we had witnessed in the church, we got the car and drove for four hours to get to the monastery at Piedra.

THE ROOF HAD FALLEN IN, and the heads were missing from the few images that were still there – all except for one.

I looked around. In the past, this place must have sheltered strong-willed people, who'd seen to it that every stone was cleaned and that each pew was occupied by one of the powerful individuals of the time.

But all I saw now were ruins. When we had played here as children, we'd pretended these ruins were castles. In those castles I had looked for my enchanted prince.

For centuries, the monks of the monastery at Piedra had kept this small piece of paradise to themselves. Situation on a valley floor, it enjoyed a plentiful supply of what the neighboring villages had to beg for – water. Here the River Piedra broke up into dozens of waterfalls, streams, and lakes, creating luxuriant vegetation all around.

Yet one had only to walk a few hundred yards to leave the canyon and find aridity and desolation. The river itself once again became a narrow thread of water as if it had exhausted all of its youth and energy in crossing the valley.

The monks knew all this, and they charged dearly for the water they supplied to their neighbors. An untold number of battles between the priests and the villagers marked the history of the monastery.

During one of the many wars that shook Spain, the monastery at Piedra had been turned into a barracks. Horses rode through the central nave of the church, and soldiers slept in its pews, telling ribald stories there and making love with women from the neighboring villages.

Revenge – although delayed – finally came. The monastery was sacked and destroyed.

The monks were never able to reconstruct their paradise. In one of the many legal battles that followed, someone said that the inhabitants of the nearby villages had carried out a sentence pronounced by God. Christ had said, 'Give drink to those who thirst,' and the priests had paid no heed. For this, God had expelled those who had regarded themselves as nature's masters.

And it was perhaps for this reason that although much of the monastery had been rebuilt and made into a hotel, the main church remained in ruins. The descendants of the local villagers had never forgotten the high price that their parents had paid for something that nature provides freely.

'Which statue is that? The only one with its head?' I asked him.

'Saint Teresa of Avila,' he answered. 'She is powerful. And even with the thirst for vengeance that the wars brought about, no one dared to touch her.'

He took my hand, and we left the church. We walked along the broad corridors of the monastery, climbed the wooden staircases, and marveled at the butterflies in the inner gardens. I recalled every detail of that monastery because I had been there as a girl, and the old memories seemed more vivid than what I was seeing now.

Memories. The months and years leading up to that week seemed to be part of some other incarnation of mine – an era to which I never wanted to return, because it hadn't been touched by the hand of love. I felt as if I had lived the same day over and over for years on end, waking up every morning in the same way, repeating the same words, and dreaming the same dreams.

I remembered my parents, my grandparents, and many of my old friends. I recalled how much time I had spent fighting for something I didn't even want.

Why had I done that? I could think of no explanation. Maybe because I had been too lazy to think of other avenues to follow. Maybe because I had been afraid of what others would think. Maybe because it was hard work to be different. Perhaps because a human being is condemned to repeat the steps taken by the previous generation until – and I was thinking of the padre – a certain number of people begin to behave in a different fashion.

Then the world changes, and we change with it.

But I didn't want to be that way anymore. Fate had returned to me what had been mine and now offered me the chance to change myself and the world.

I thought again of the mountain climbers we had met as we traveled. They were young and wore brightly colored clothing so as to be easily spotted should they become lost in the snow. They knew the right path to follow to the peaks.

The heights were already festooned with aluminum pins; all they had to do was attach their lines to them, and they could climb safely. They were there for a holiday adventure, and on Monday they would return to their jobs with the feeling that they had challenged nature – and won.

But this wasn't really true. The adventurous ones were those who had climbed there first, the ones who had found the routes to the top. Some, who had fallen to their death on the rocks, had never even made it halfway up. Others had lost fingers and toes to frostbite.

Many were never seen again. But one day, some of them had made it to the summit.

And their eyes were the first to take in that view, and their hearts beat with joy. They had accepted the risks and could now honor – with their conquest – all of those who had died trying.

There were probably some people down below who thought, 'There's nothing up there. Just a view. What's so great about that?'

But the first climber knew what was great about it: the acceptance of the challenge of going forward. He knew that no single day is the same as any other and that each morning brings its own special miracle, its *magic moment* in which ancient universes are destroyed and new stars are created.

The first one who climbed those mountains must have asked, looking down at the tiny houses with their smoking chimneys, 'All of their days must seem the same. What's so great about that?'

Now all the mountains had been conquered and astronauts had walked in space. There were no more islands on earth – no matter how small – left to be discovered. But there were still great adventures of the spirit, and one of them was being offered to me now.

It was a blessing. The padre didn't understand anything. These pains are not the kind that hurt.

Fortunate are those who take the first steps. Someday people will realize that men and women are capable of speaking the language of the angels – that all of us are possessed of the gifts of the Holy Spirit and that we can perform miracles, cure, prophesy, and understand.

WE SPENT THE AFTERNOON WALKING along the canyon, reminiscing about our childhood. It was the first time he had done so; during our trip to Bilbao, he had seemed to have lost all interest in Soria.

Now, though, he asked me about each of our mutual friends, wanting to know whether they were happy and what they were doing with their lives.

Finally, we arrived at the largest waterfall of the Piedra, where a number of small, scattered streams come together and the water is thrown to the rocks below from a height of almost one hundred feet. We stood at the edge of the waterfall, listening to its deafening roar and gazing at the rainbow in its mist.

'The Horse's Tail,' I said, surprised that I still remembered this name from so long ago.

'I remember . . . ,' he began.

'Yes! I know what you're going to say!'

Of course I knew! The waterfall concealed a gigantic grotto. When we were children, returning from our first visit to the monastery at Piedra, we had talked about that place for days.

'The cavern,' he said. 'Let's go there.'

It was impossible to pass through the torrent of water. But ancient monks had constructed a tunnel that started at the highest point of the falls and descended through the earth to a place at the rear of the grotto.

It wasn't difficult to find the entrance. During the summer, there may even have been lights showing the way, but now the tunnel was completely dark.

'Is this the right way?' I asked.

'Yes. Trust me.'

We began to descend through the hole at the side of the falls. Although we were in complete darkness, we knew where we were going – and he asked me again to trust him.

Thank you, Lord, I was thinking, as we went deeper and deeper into the earth, *because I was a lost sheep, and you brought me back*.

Because my life was dead, and you revived it. Because love wasn't alive in my heart, and you gave me back that gift.

I held on to his shoulder. My loved one guided my steps through the darkness, knowing that we would see the light again and that it would bring us joy. Perhaps in our future there would be moments when the situation was reversed – when I would guide him with the same love and certainty until we reached a safe place and could rest together.

We walked slowly, and it seemed as if we would never stop descending. Maybe this was another rite of passage, marking the end of an era in which there had been no light in my life. As I walked through the tunnel, I was remembering how much time I had wasted in one place, trying to put down roots in soil where nothing could grow any longer.

But God was good and had given me back my lost enthusiasm, directing me toward the adventures I had always dreamed about. And toward the man who – without my knowing it – had waited for me all my life. I felt no remorse over the fact that he was leaving the seminary – there were many ways to serve God, as the padre had said, and our love only multiplied the number of them. Starting now, I would also have the chance to serve and help – all because of him.

We would go out into the world, bringing comfort to others and to each other.

Thank you, Lord, for helping me to serve. Teach me to be worthy of that. Give me the strength to be a part of his mission, to walk with him on this earth, and to develop my spiritual life anew. May all our days be as these have been – going from place to place, curing the sick, comforting those in sorrow, speaking of the Great Mother's love for all of us.

SUDDENLY, THE SOUND OF WATER could be heard again and light flooded our path. The dark tunnel was transformed into one of the most beautiful spectacles on earth. We were in an immense cavern, the size of a cathedral. Three of its walls were of stone, and the fourth was the Horse's Tail, with its water falling into the emerald-green lake at our feet.

The rays of the setting sun passed through the waterfall, and the moist walls glittered.

We leaned back against the stone wall, saying nothing.

When we were children, this place was a pirates' hideout, where the treasures of our childhood imagination were kept. Now, it was the miracle of Mother Earth; I knew she was there and felt myself to be in her womb. She was protecting us with her walls of stone and washing away our sins with her purifying water.

'Thank you,' I said in a loud voice.

'Whom are you thanking?'

'Her. And you, because you were an instrument in restoring my faith.'

He walked to the edge of the water. Looking out, he smiled. 'Come over here,' he said.

I joined him.

'I want to tell you something you don't know about yet,' he said.

His words worried me a little. But he looked calm and happy, and that reassured me.

'Every person on earth has a gift,' he began. 'In some, the gift manifests itself spontaneously; others have to work to discover what it is. I worked with my gift during the four years I was at the seminary.'

Now I would have to 'play a role,' as he had taught me when the old man had barred us from the church. I would have to feign that I knew nothing. *There's nothing wrong with doing this,* I told myself. *This is a not a script based on frustration but on happiness.*

'What did you do at the seminary?' I asked, trying to stall for time in order to play my role better.

'That doesn't matter,' he said. 'The fact is that I developed a gift. I am able to cure, when God so wills it.'

'That's wonderful,' I answered, acting surprised. 'We won't have to spend money on doctors!'

He didn't laugh. I felt like an idiot.

'I developed my gift through the Charismatic practices that you saw,' he went on. 'In the beginning, I was surprised. I would pray, asking that the Holy Spirit appear, and then, through the laying on of my hands, I would restore many of the sick to good health. My reputation began to spread, and every day people lined up at the gates of the seminary, seeking my help. In every infected, smelly laceration, I saw the wounds of Jesus.'

'I'm so proud of you,' I said.

'Many of the people at the monastery opposed me, but my superior gave me his complete support.'

'We'll continue this work. We'll go out together into the world. I will clean and bathe the wounds, and you will bless them, and God will demonstrate His miracles.'

He looked away from me, out at the lake. There seemed to be a presence in the cavern similar to the one I had sensed that night in Saint-Savin when we had gotten drunk at the well in the plaza.

'I've already told you this, but I'll say it again,' he continued. 'One night I awoke, and my room was completely bright. I saw the face of the Great Mother; I saw Her loving look. After that, She began to appear to me from time to time. I cannot make it happen, but every once in a while, She appears.

'By the time of my first vision, I was already aware of the work being done by the true revolutionaries of the church. I knew that my mission on earth, in addition to curing, was to smooth the way for this new acceptance of God as a woman. The feminine principle, the column of Misericordia, would be rebuilt – and the temple of wisdom would be reconstructed in the hearts of all people.'

I was staring at him. His face, which had grown tense, now relaxed again.

'This carried a price – which I was willing to pay.'

He stopped, as if not knowing how to go on with his story.

'What do you mean when you say you were willing?' I asked.

'The path of the Goddess can only be opened through words and miracles. But that's not the way the world works. It's going to be very hard – tears, lack of understanding, suffering.'

That padre, I thought to myself. *He tried to put fear in his heart. But I shall be his comfort.*

'The path isn't about pain; it's about the glory of serving,' I answered.

'Most human beings still cannot trust love.'

I felt that he was trying to tell me something but couldn't. I wanted to help him.

'I've been thinking about that,' I broke in. 'The first man who climbed the highest peak in the Pyrenees must have felt that a life without that kind of adventure would lack grace.'

'What do you mean when you use the word grace?' he asked me, and I could see that he was feeling tense again. 'One of the names of the Great Mother is Our Lady of the Graces. Her generous hands heap Her blessings on those who know how to receive them. We can never judge the lives of others, because each person knows only their own pain and renunciation. It's one thing to feel that you are on the right path, but it's another to think that yours is the only path.

'Jesus said, "The house of my Father has many mansions." A gift is a grace, or a mercy. But it is also a mercy to know how to live a life of dignity, love, and work. Mary had a husband on earth who tried to demonstrate the value of anonymous work. Although he was not heard from very much, he was the one who provided the roof over their heads and the food for their mouths, who allowed his wife and son to do all that they did. His work was as important as theirs, even though no one ever gave him much credit.'

I didn't say anything, and he took my hand. 'Forgive me for my intolerance.'

I kissed his hand and put it to my cheek.

'This is what I'm trying to explain to you,' he said, smiling again. 'I realized, from the moment I found you again, that I couldn't cause you to suffer because of my mission.'

I began to feel worried.

'Yesterday I lied to you. It was the first and last lie I've ever told you,' he continued. 'The truth is that instead of going to the monastery, I went up on the mountain and conversed with the Great Mother. I said to Her that if She wanted, I would leave you and continue along my path. I would go back to the gate where the sick gathered, to the visits in the middle of the night, to the lack of understanding of those who would deny the idea of faith, and to the cynical attitude of those who cannot believe that love is a savior. If She were to ask me, I would give up what I want most in the world: you.'

I thought again of the padre. He had been right. A choice had been made that morning.

'But,' he continued, 'if it were possible to resolve this awful predicament in my life, I would promise to serve the world through my love for you.'

'What are you saying?' I asked, frightened now.

He seemed not to hear me.

'It's not necessary to move mountains in order to prove one's faith,' he said. 'I was ready to face the suffering alone and not share it. If I had continued along that path, we would never have our house with the white curtains and the view of the mountains.'

'I don't care about that house! I didn't even want to go in!' I said, trying not to shout. 'I want to go with you, to be with you in your struggle. I want to be one of those who does something for the first time. Don't you understand? You've given me back my faith!'

The last rays of the sun illuminated the walls of the cavern. But I couldn't see its beauty.

God hides the fires of hell within paradise.

'You're the one who doesn't understand,' he said, and I could see his eyes begging me to comprehend. 'You don't see the risks.'

'But you were willing to accept those risks!'

'I *am* willing. But they are *my* risks.'

I wanted to interrupt him, but he wasn't listening.

'So yesterday, I asked a miracle of the Virgin,' he continued. 'I asked that She take away my gift.'

I couldn't believe what I was hearing.

'I have a little money and all the experience that years of traveling have given me. We'll buy a house, I'll get a job, and I'll serve God as Saint Joseph did, with the humility of an anonymous person. I don't need miracles in my life anymore to keep the faith. I need you.'

My legs were growing weak, and I felt as if I might faint.

'And just as I was asking that the Virgin take away my gift, I began to speak in tongues,' he went on. 'The tongues told me, "Place your hands on the earth. Your gift will leave you and return to the Mother's breast."'

I was in a panic. 'You didn't . . .'

'Yes. I did as the inspiration of the Holy Spirit bade. The fog lifted, and the sun shone on the mountains. I felt that the Virgin understood – because She had also loved so greatly.'

'But She followed Her man! She accepted the path taken by Her son!'

'We don't have Her strength, Pilar. My gift will be passed on to someone else – such gifts are never wasted.

'Yesterday, from that bar, I phoned Barcelona and canceled my presentation. Let's go to Zaragoza – you know the people there, and it's a good place for us to start. I'll get a job easily.'

I could no longer think.

'Pilar!' he said.

But I was already climbing back through the tunnel – this time without a friendly shoulder to lean on – pursued by the multitude of the sick who would die, the families that would suffer, the miracles that would never be performed, the smiles that would no longer grace the world, and the mountains that would remain in place.

I saw nothing – only the darkness that engulfed me.

Friday, December 10, 1993

On the bank of the River Piedra I sat down and wept. My memory of that night is confused and vague. I know that I almost died, but I can't remember his face nor where he took me.

I'd like to be able to remember all of it – so that I could expel it from my heart. But I can't. It all seems like a dream, from the moment when I came out of that dark tunnel into a world where darkness had already fallen.

There was not a star in the sky. I remember vaguely walking back to the car, retrieving my small bag, and beginning to wander at random. I must have walked to the road, trying to hitch a ride to Zaragoza – with no success. I wound up returning to the gardens at the monastery.

The sound of water was everywhere – there were waterfalls on all sides, and I felt the presence of the Great Mother following me wherever I walked. Yes, She had loved the world; She loved it as much as God did – because She had also given Her son to be sacrificed by men. But did She understand a woman's love for a man?

She may have suffered because of love, but it was a different kind of love. Her Groom knew everything and performed miracles. Her husband on earth was a humble laborer who believed everything his dreams told him. She never knew what it was to abandon a man or to be abandoned by one. When Joseph considered expelling Her from their home because She was pregnant, Her Groom in heaven immediately sent an angel to keep that from happening.

Her son left Her. But children always leave their parents. It's easy to suffer because you love a person, or the world, or your son. That's the kind of suffering that you accept as a part of life; it's a noble, grand sort of suffering. It's easy to suffer for a cause or a mission; this ennobles the heart of the person suffering.

But how to explain suffering because of a man? It's not explainable. With that kind of suffering, a person feels as if they're in hell, because there is no nobility, no greatness – only misery.

That night, I slept on the frozen ground, and the cold anesthetized me. I thought I might die without a covering – but where could I find one? Everything that was most important in my life had been given so generously to me in the course of one week – and had been taken from me in a minute, without my having a chance to say a thing.

My body was trembling from the cold, but I hardly noticed. At some point, the trembling would stop. My body's energy would be exhausted from trying to provide me with heat and would be unable to do anything more. It would resume its customary state of relaxation and death would take me in its arms.

I shook for another hour. And then peace came.

Before I closed my eyes, I began to hear my mother's voice. She was telling a story she had often told me when I was a child, not realizing it was a story about me.

'A boy and a girl were insanely in love with each other,' my mother's voice was saying. 'They decided to become engaged. And that's when presents are always exchanged.

'The boy was poor – his only worthwhile possession was a watch he'd inherited from his grandfather. Thinking about his sweetheart's lovely hair, he decided to sell the watch in order to buy her a silver barrette.

'The girl had no money herself to buy him a present. She went to the shop of the most successful merchant in the town and sold him her hair. With the money, she bought a gold watchband for her lover.

'When they met on the day of the engagement party, she gave him the wristband for a watch he had sold, and he gave her the barrette for the hair she no longer had.'

I WAS AWAKENED BY A man shaking me.

'Drink this!' he was saying. 'Drink this quickly!'

I had no idea what was happening nor the strength to resist. He opened my mouth and forced me to drink a hot liquid. I noticed that he was in his shirtsleeves and that he had given me a wrap.

'Drink more!' he insisted.

Without knowing what I was doing, I obeyed. Then I closed my eyes.

I awoke in the convent, and a woman was tending me.

'You almost died,' she said. 'If it weren't for the watchman, you wouldn't be here.'

I stood up dizzily. Parts of the previous day came back to me, and I wished that the watchman had never passed my way.

But apparently this was not the time for me to die. I was to go on living.

The woman led me to the kitchen and prepared some coffee, biscuits, and bread for me. She asked me no questions, and I explained nothing. When I had finished eating, she gave me my bag.

'See if everything's still there,' she said.

'I'm sure it is. I didn't really have anything much.'

'You have your life, my child. A long life. Take better care of it.'

'There's a city near here where there's a church,' I said, wanting to cry. 'Yesterday, before I came here, I went into that church with . . .'

I couldn't explain.

'. . . with a friend from my childhood. I had already had enough of the churches around here, but the bells were ringing, and he said it was a sign – that we should go in.'

The woman refilled my cup, poured some coffee for herself, and sat down to hear my story.

'We entered the church,' I continued. 'There was no one there, and it was dark. I tried to look for the sign, but I saw only the same old altars and the same old saints. Suddenly, we heard a movement above, where the organ was.

'It was a group of boys with guitars, who began to tune their instruments. We decided to sit and listen to the music for a while before continuing our trip. Shortly a man came in and sat down next to us. He was happy and shouted to the boys to play a *paso doble*.'

'Bullfight music?' the woman said. 'I hope they didn't do that!'

'They didn't. But they laughed and played a flamenco melody instead. My friend and I felt as if heaven had descended on us; the church, the surrounding darkness, the sound of the guitars, and the man's delight – it was all a miracle.

'Little by little, the church began to fill. The boys continued to play the flamenco, and everyone who came in smiled, infected by the joy of the musicians.

'My friend asked if I wanted to attend the mass that was about to begin. I said no – we had a long ride ahead of us. So we decided to leave – but before we did, we thanked God for yet another beautiful moment in our lives.

'As we arrived at the gate, we saw that many people – perhaps the entire population of the town – were walking to the church. I thought it must have been the last completely Catholic town in Spain – maybe because the crowds seemed to be having so much fun.

'As we got into the car, we saw a funeral procession approaching. Someone had died; it was a mass for the dead. As soon as the cortege reached the gates of the church, the musicians stopped the flamenco music and began to play a dirge.'

'May God have mercy on that soul,' said the woman, crossing herself.

'May He have mercy,' I said, repeating her gesture. 'But our having gone into that church really had been a sign – that every story has a sad ending.'

The woman said nothing. Then she left the room and returned immediately with a pen and paper.

'Let's go outside,' she said.

We went out together, and the sun was rising.

'Take a deep breath,' she said. 'Let this new morning enter your lungs and course through your veins. From what I can see, your loss yesterday was not an accident.'

I didn't answer.

'You also didn't really understand the story you told me, about the sign in the church,' she went on. 'You saw only the sadness of the procession at the end. You forgot the happy moments you spent inside. You forgot the feeling that heaven had descended on you and how good it was to be experiencing all of that with your . . .'

She stopped and smiled.

'. . . childhood friend,' she said, winking. 'Jesus said, "Let the dead bury the dead" because he knew that there is no such thing as death. Life existed before we were born and will continue to exist after we leave this world.'

My eyes filled with tears.

'It's the same with love,' she went on. 'It existed before and will go on forever.'

'You seem to know everything about my life,' I said.

'All love stories have much in common. I went through the same thing at one point in my life. But that's not what I remember. What I remember is that love returned in the form of another man, new hopes, and new dreams.'

She held out the pen and paper to me.

'Write down everything you're feeling. Take it out of your soul, put it on the paper, and then throw it away. Legend says that the River Piedra is so cold that anything that falls into it – leaves, insects, the feathers of birds – is turned to stone. Maybe it would be a good idea to toss your suffering into its waters.'

I took the pages. She kissed me, and said I could come back for lunch if I wanted to.

'Don't forget!' she shouted as she walked away. 'Love perseveres. It's men who change.'

I smiled, and she waved good-bye.

I looked out at the river for some time. And I cried until there were no more tears.

Then I began to write.

Epilogue

I wrote for an entire day, and then another, and another. Every morning, I went to the bank of the River Piedra. Every afternoon, the woman came, took me by the arm, and led me back to the old convent.

She washed my clothes, made me dinner, chatted about trivial things, and sent me to bed.

One morning, when I had almost finished the manuscript, I heard the sound of a car. My heart leaped, but didn't want to believe it. I felt free again, ready to return to the world and be a part of it once again.

The worst had passed, although the sadness remained

But my heart was right. Even without raising my eyes from my work, I felt his presence and heard his footsteps.

'Pilar,' he said, sitting down next to me.

I went on writing, without answering. I couldn't pull my thoughts together. My heart was jumping, trying to free itself from my breast and run to him. But I wouldn't allow it.

He sat there looking at the river, while I went on writing. The entire morning passed that way – without a word – and I recalled the silence of a night near a well when I'd suddenly realized that I loved him.

When my hand could write no longer, I stopped. Then he spoke.

'It was dark when I came up out of the cavern. I couldn't find you, so I went to Zaragoza. I even went to Soria. I looked everywhere for you. Then I decided to return to the monastery at Piedra to see if there was any sign of you, and I met a woman. She showed me where you were, and she said you had been waiting for me.'

My eyes filled with tears.

'I am going to sit here with you by the river. If you go home to sleep, I will sleep in front of your house. And if you go away, I will follow you – until you tell me to go away. Then I'll leave. But I have to love you for the rest of my life.'

I could no longer hold back the tears, and he began to weep as well.

'I want to tell you something . . . ,' he started to say.

'Don't say a thing. Read this.' I handed him the pages.

I GAZED AT THE RIVER Piedra all afternoon.

The woman brought us sandwiches and wine, commented on the weather, and left us alone. Every once in a while, he paused in his reading and stared out into space, absorbed in his thoughts.

At one point I went for a walk in the woods, past the small waterfalls, through the landscape that was so laden with stories and meanings for me. When the sun began to set, I went back to the place where I had left him.

'Thank you' was what he said as he gave the papers back to me. 'And forgive me.'

On the bank of the River Piedra, I sat down and wept.

'Your love has saved me and returned me to my dream,' he continued.

I said nothing.

'Do you know Psalm 137?' he asked.

I shook my head. I was afraid to speak.

'On the banks of the rivers of Babylon . . .'

'Yes, yes, I know it,' I said, feeling myself coming back to life, little by little. 'It talks about exile. It talks about people who hand up their harps because they cannot play the music their hearts desire.'

'But after the psalmist cries with longing for the land of his dreams, he promises himself,

> If I forget you, O Jerusalem,
> let my right hand forget its skill.
> Let my tongue cling to the roof of my mouth,
> if I do not exalt Jerusalem.'

I smiled again.

'I had forgotten, and you brought it back to me.'

'Do you think your gift has returned?' I asked.

'I don't know. But the Goddess has always given me a second chance in life. And She is giving me that with you. She will help me to find my path again.'

'Our path.'

'Yes, ours.'

He took my hands and lifted me to my feet.

'Go and get your things,' he said. 'Dreams mean work.'

Veronika Decides
to Die

*Behold I give unto you power to tread
on serpents … and nothing shall by
any means hurt you.*

LUKE 10:19

For S.T. de L, who began to help me
without my realising it.

On 11 November 1997, Veronika decided that the moment to kill herself had – at last! – arrived. She carefully cleaned the room that she rented in a convent, turned off the heating, brushed her teeth and lay down.

She picked up the four packs of sleeping pills from her bedside table. Instead of crushing them and mixing them with water, she decided to take them one by one, because there is always a gap between intention and action, and she wanted to feel free to turn back half way. However, with each pill she swallowed, she felt more convinced: after five minutes the packs were empty.

Since she didn't know exactly how long it would take her to lose consciousness, she had placed on the bed that month's issue of a French magazine, *Homme*, which had just arrived in the library where she worked. She had no particular interest in computer science, but, as she leafed through the magazine, she came across an article about a computer game (one of those CD-Roms), created by Paulo Coelho, a Brazilian writer she had happened to meet at a lecture in the café at the Grand Union Hotel. They had exchanged a few words and she had ended up being invited by his publisher to join them for supper. There were a lot of people there, though, and they hadn't had a chance to talk in depth about anything.

The fact that she had met the author, however, led her to think that he was part of her world, and that reading an article about his work could help pass the time. While she was waiting for death, Veronika started reading about computer science, a subject in which she was not in the least bit interested, but then that was in keeping with what she had done all her life, always looking for the easy option, for whatever was nearest to hand. Like that magazine, for example.

To her surprise, though, the first line of text shook her out of her natural passivity (the tranquillizers had not yet dissolved in her stomach, but Veronika was, by nature, passive), and, for the first time in her life, it made her ponder the truth of a saying that was very fashionable amongst her friends: 'nothing in this world happens by chance'.

Why that first line, at precisely the moment when she had begun to die? What was the hidden message she saw before her, assuming there are such things as hidden messages rather than mere coincidences.

Underneath an illustration of the computer game, the journalist began his article by asking: 'Where is Slovenia?'

'Honestly,' she thought, 'no one ever knows where Slovenia is.'

But Slovenia existed nonetheless, and it was outside, inside, in the mountains around her and in the square she was looking out at: Slovenia was her country.

She put the magazine to one side, there was no point now in getting indignant with a world that knew absolutely nothing about the Slovenes; her nation's honour no longer concerned her. It was time to feel proud of herself, to recognise that she had been able to do this, that she had finally had the courage and was leaving this life: what joy! Also she was doing it as she had always dreamed she would – by taking sleeping pills, which leave no mark.

Veronika had been trying to get hold of the pills for nearly six months. Thinking that she would never manage it, she had even considered slashing her wrists. It didn't matter that the room would end up awash with blood, and the nuns would be left feeling confused and troubled, for suicide demands that people think of themselves first and of others later. She was prepared to do all she could so that her death would cause as little upset as possible, but if slashing her wrists was the only way, then she had no option – and the nuns could clean up the room and quickly forget the whole story, otherwise they would find it hard to rent out the room again. We may live at the end of the twentieth century, but people still believe in ghosts.

Obviously she could have thrown herself off one of the few tall buildings in Ljubljana, but what about the further suffering caused to her parents by a fall from such a height? Apart from the shock of learning that their daughter had died, they would also have to identify a disfigured corpse; no, that was a worse solution than bleeding to death, because it would leave indelible marks on two people who only wanted the best for her.

'They would get used to their daughter's death eventually. But it must be impossible to forget a shattered skull.'

Shooting, jumping off a high building, hanging, none of these options suited her feminine nature. Women, when they kill themselves, choose far more romantic methods – like slashing their wrists or taking an overdose of sleeping pills. Abandoned princesses and Hollywood actresses have provided numerous examples of this.

Veronika knew that life was always a matter of waiting for the right moment to act. And so it proved. In response to her complaints that she could no longer sleep at night, two friends of hers managed to get hold of two packs each of a powerful drug, used by musicians at a local nightclub. Veronika left the four packs on her bedside table for a week, courting approaching death and saying goodbye – entirely unsentimentally – to what people called Life.

Now she was there, glad she had gone all the way, and bored because she didn't know what to do with the little time that remained to her.

She thought again about the absurd question she had just read. How could an article about computers begin with such an idiotic opening line: 'Where is Slovenia?'

Having nothing more interesting to do, she decided to read the whole article and she learned that the said computer game had been made in Slovenia – that strange country that no one seemed quite able to place, except the people who lived there – because it was a cheap source of labour. A few months before, when the product was launched, the French manufacturer had given a party for journalists from all over the world in a castle in Vled.

Veronika remembered reading something about the party, which had been quite an event in the city, not just because the castle had been redecorated in order to match as closely as possible the medieval atmosphere of the CD-Rom, but because of the controversy in the local press: journalists from Germany, France, Britain, Italy and Spain had been invited, but not a single Slovene.

Homme's correspondent – who was visiting Slovenia for the first time, doubtless with all expenses paid, and determined to spend his visit chatting up other journalists, making supposedly interesting comments and enjoying the free food and drink at the castle – had decided to begin his article with a joke which must have appealed to the sophisticated intellectuals of his country. He had probably told his fellow journalists on the magazine various untrue stories about local customs too, and said how badly Slovene women dress.

That *was* his problem. Veronika was dying, and she had other concerns, such as wondering if there was life after death, or when her body would be found. Nevertheless – or perhaps precisely because of the important decision she had taken – the article bothered her.

She looked out of the convent window that gave on to the small square in Ljubljana. 'If they don't know where Slovenia is, then Ljubljana must be a myth,' she thought. Like Atlantis or Lemuria, or the other lost continents that fill men's imaginations. No one, anywhere in the world, would begin an article asking where Mount Everest was, even if they had never been there. Yet, in the middle of Europe, a journalist on an important magazine felt no shame at asking such a question, because he knew that most of his readers would not know where Slovenia was, still less its capital, Ljubljana.

It was then that Veronika found a way of passing the time, now that ten minutes had gone by and she had still not noticed any bodily changes. The final act of her life would be to write a letter to the magazine, explaining that Slovenia was one of the five republics into which the former Yugoslavia had been divided.

The letter would be her suicide note. She would give no explanation of the real reasons for her death.

When they found her body, they would conclude that she had killed herself because a magazine did not know where her country was. She laughed to think of the controversy in the newspapers, with some for and some against her suicide committed in honour of her country's cause. And she was shocked by how quickly she could change her mind, since only moments before she had thought exactly the opposite, that the world and other geographical problems were no longer her concern.

She wrote the letter. That moment of good humour almost made her have second thoughts about the need to die, but she had already taken the pills, it was too late to turn back.

Anyway, she had had such moments before and, besides, she was not killing herself because she was a sad, embittered woman, constantly depressed. She had spent many afternoons walking gaily along the streets of Ljubljana or gazing – from the window in her convent room – at the snow falling on the small square with its statue of the poet. Once, for almost a month, she had felt as if she were walking on air, all because a complete stranger, in the middle of that very square, had given her a flower.

She believed herself to be completely normal. Two very simple reasons lay behind her decision to die, and she was sure that, were she to leave a note explaining, many people would agree with her.

The first reason: everything in her life was the same and, once her youth was gone, it would be downhill all the way, with old age beginning to leave irreversible marks, the onset of illness, the departure of friends. She would gain nothing by continuing to live; indeed, the likelihood of suffering only increased.

The second reason was more philosophical: Veronika read the newspapers, watched TV, and she was aware of what was going on in the world. Everything was wrong, and she had no way of putting things right – that gave her a sense of complete powerlessness.

In a short while, though, she would have the final experience of her life, which promised to be very different: death. She wrote the letter to the magazine, then abandoned the topic, and concentrated on more pressing matters, more appropriate to what she was living, or, rather, dying, through at that moment.

She tried to imagine what it would be like to die, but failed to reach any conclusion.

Besides, there was no point worrying about that, for in a few minutes' time she would know.

How many minutes?

She had no idea. But she relished the thought that she was about to find out the answer to the question that everyone asked themselves: does God exist?

Unlike many people, this had not been the great inner debate of her life. Under the old Communist regime, the official line in schools had been that life ended with death and she had got used to the idea. On the other hand, her parents' generation and her grandparents' generation still went to church, said prayers and went on pilgrimages, and were utterly convinced that God listened to what they said.

At twenty-four, having experienced everything she could experience – and that was no small achievement – Veronika was almost certain that everything ended with death. That is why she had chosen suicide: freedom at last. Eternal oblivion.

In her heart of hearts, though, there was still a doubt: what if God did exist? Thousands of years of civilization had made of suicide a taboo, an affront to all religious codes: man struggles to survive, not to succumb. The human race must procreate. Society needs workers. A couple has to have a reason to stay together, even when love has ceased to exist, and a country needs soldiers, politicians and artists.

'If God exists, and I truly don't believe he does, he will know that there are limits to human understanding. He was the one who created this confusion in which there is poverty, injustice, greed and loneliness. He doubtless had the best of intentions, but the results have proved disastrous; if God exists, He will be generous with those creatures who chose to leave this Earth early, and He might even apologise for having made us spend time here.'

To hell with taboos and superstitions. Her devout mother would say: God knows the past, the present and the future. In that case, He had placed her in this world in the full knowledge that she would end up killing herself, and He would not be shocked by her actions.

Veronika began to feel a slight nausea, which became rapidly more intense.

In a few moments, she would no longer be able to concentrate on the square outside her window. She knew it was winter, it must have been about four o'clock in the afternoon, and the sun was setting fast. She knew that other people would go on living. At that moment, a young man passed her window and saw her, utterly unaware that she was about to die. A group of Bolivian musicians (where is Bolivia? why don't magazine articles ask that?) were playing in front of the statue of France Prešeren, the great Slovenian poet, who had made such a profound impact on the soul of his people.

Would she live to hear the end of that music drifting up from the square? It would be a beautiful memory of this life: the late afternoon, a melody recounting the dreams of a country on the other side of the world, the warm cosy room, the handsome young man passing by, full of life, who had decided to stop and was now standing looking up at her. She realised that the pills were beginning to take effect and that he was the last person who would see her.

He smiled. She returned his smile – she had nothing to lose. He waved; she decided to pretend she was looking at something else, the young man was going too far. Disconcerted, he continued on his way, forgetting that face at the window for ever.

But Veronika was glad to have felt desired by somebody one last time. She wasn't killing herself because of a lack of love. It wasn't because she felt unloved by her family, or had money problems or an incurable disease.

Veronika had decided to die on that lovely Ljubljana afternoon, with Bolivian musicians playing in the square, with a young man passing by her window, and she was happy with what her eyes could see and her ears hear. She was even happier that she would not have to go on seeing those same things for another thirty, forty or fifty years, because they would lose all their originality and be transformed into the tragedy of a life in which everything repeats itself and where one day is exactly like another.

Her stomach was beginning to churn now and she was feeling very ill indeed. 'It's odd, I thought an overdose of tranquillizers would send me straight to sleep.' What she was experiencing, though, was a strange buzzing in her ears and a desire to vomit.

'If I throw up, I won't die.'

She decided not to think about the stabbing pains in her stomach and tried to concentrate on the rapidly falling night, on the Bolivians, on the people who were starting to shut up their shops and go home. The noise in her ears was becoming more and more strident and, for the first time since she had taken the pills, Veronika felt fear, a terrible fear of the unknown.

It did not last long. Soon afterwards, she lost consciousness.

When she opened her eyes, Veronika did not think 'this must be heaven'. Heaven would never use a fluorescent tube to light a room, and the pain – which started a fraction of a second later – was typical of the Earth. Ah, that Earth pain – unique, unmistakable.

She tried to move and the pain increased. A series of bright dots appeared, but, even so, Veronika knew that those dots were not the stars of Paradise, but the consequences of the intense pain she was feeling.

'She's coming round,' she heard a woman say. 'You've landed slap bang in hell, so you'd better make the most of it.'

No, it couldn't be true, that voice was deceiving her. It wasn't hell, because she felt really cold and she was aware of plastic tubes coming out of her nose and mouth. One of the tubes – the one stuck down her throat – made her feel as if she were choking.

She made as if to remove it, but her arms were strapped down.

'I'm joking, it's not really hell,' the voice went on. 'It's worse than hell, not that I've ever actually been there. You're in Villete.'

Despite the pain and the feeling of choking, Veronika realised at once what had happened. She had tried to kill herself and someone had arrived in time to save her. It could have been one of the nuns, a friend who had decided to drop by unannounced, someone delivering something she had forgotten she had ordered. The fact is, she had survived, and she was in Villete.

Villete, the famous and much-feared lunatic asylum, which had been in existence since 1991, the year of the country's independence. At that time, believing that the partitioning of the former Yugoslavia would be achieved through peaceful means (after all, Slovenia had only experienced eleven days of war), a group of European businessmen had obtained permission to set up a hospital for mental patients in an old barracks, abandoned because of high maintenance costs.

Shortly afterwards, however, the wars commenced: first in Croatia, then in Bosnia. The businessmen were worried. The money for the investment came from capitalists scattered all round the globe, from people whose names they didn't even know, so there was no possibility of sitting down in front of them, offering a few excuses and asking them to be patient. They resolved the problem by adopting practices which were far from commendable in a psychiatric hospital, and for the young nation that had just emerged from a benign communism, Villete came to symbolise all the worst aspects of capitalism: to be admitted to the hospital, all you needed was money.

There was no shortage of people who, in their desire to get rid of some family member because of arguments over an inheritance (or over that person's embarrassing behaviour), were willing to pay large sums of money to obtain a medical report that would allow the internment of their problematic children or parents. Others, fleeing from debts or trying to justify certain attitudes that could otherwise result in long prison sentences, spent a brief time in the asylum and then simply left without paying any penalty or undergoing any judicial process.

Villete was the place from which no one had ever escaped, where genuine madmen – sent there by the courts or by other hospitals – mingled with those merely accused of madness or those pretending to be mad. The result was utter confusion, and the press were constantly publishing tales of ill-treatment and abuse, although they had never been given permission to visit Villete and actually see what was happening. The government was investigating the complaints, but could get no proof; the shareholders threatened to spread the word that foreign investment was difficult in Slovenia, and so the institution managed to remain afloat, indeed, it went from strength to strength.

'My aunt killed herself a few months ago,' the female voice continued. 'For almost eight years she was too afraid to even leave her room, eating, getting fat, smoking, taking tranquillisers and sleeping most of the time. She had two daughters and a husband who loved her.'

Veronika tried to move her head in the direction of the voice, but failed.

'I only saw her fight back once, when her husband took a lover. Then she kicked up a fuss, lost a few pounds, smashed some glasses and – for weeks on end – kept the rest of the whole neighbourhood awake with her shouting. Absurd though it may seem, I think that was the happiest time of her life. She was fighting for something, she felt alive and capable of responding to the challenges facing her.'

'What's all that got to do with me?' thought Veronika, unable to say anything. 'I'm not your aunt and I haven't got a husband.'

'In the end, her husband got rid of his lover,' said the woman, 'and gradually, my aunt returned to her former passivity. One day, she phoned to say that she wanted to change her life: she'd given up smoking. That same week, after increasing the number of tranquillisers she was taking because she'd stopped smoking, she told everyone that she wanted to kill herself.

'No one believed her. Then, one morning, she left a message on my answerphone, saying goodbye, and she gassed herself. I listened to that message several times: I had never heard her sound so calm, so resigned to her fate. She said she was neither happy nor unhappy, and that was why she couldn't go on.'

Veronika felt sorry for the woman telling the story, for she seemed to be doing so in an attempt to understand her aunt's death. In a world where everyone struggles to survive whatever the cost, how could one judge those people who decide to die?

No one can judge. Each person knows the extent of their own suffering, or the total absence of meaning in their lives. Veronika wanted to explain that, but instead she choked on the tube in her mouth and the woman hurried to her aid.

She saw the woman bending over her bound body, which was full of tubes and protected against her will, her freely expressed desire to destroy it. She moved her head from side to side, pleading with her eyes for them to remove the tubes and let her die in peace.

'You're upset,' said the woman. 'I don't know if you're sorry for what you did or if you still want to die; that doesn't interest me. What interests me is doing my job. If the patient gets agitated, the regulations say I must give them a sedative.'

Veronika stopped struggling, but the nurse was already injecting something into her arm. Soon afterwards, she was back in a strange dreamless world, where the only thing she could remember was the face of the woman she had just seen: green eyes, brown hair, and a very distant air, the air of someone doing things because she has to do them, never questioning why the rules say this or that.

P aulo Coelho heard about Veronika's story three months later when he was having supper in an Algerian restaurant in Paris with a Slovenian friend, also called Veronika, who happened to be the daughter of the doctor in charge at Villete.

Later, when he decided to write a book about the subject, he considered changing his friend's name in order not to confuse the reader. He thought of calling her Blaska or Edwina or Marietzja, or some other Slovenian name, but he ended up keeping the real names. When he referred to his friend Veronika, he would call her his friend, Veronika. When he referred to the other Veronika, there would be no need to describe her at all, because she would be the central character in the book, and people would get irritated if they were always having to read 'Veronika the mad woman,' or 'Veronika the one who tried to commit suicide'. Besides, both he and his friend Veronika would only take up a very brief part of the book, this part.

His friend Veronika was horrified at what her father had done, especially bearing in mind that he was the director of an institution seeking respectability and was himself working on a thesis that would be judged by the conventional academic community.

'Do you know where the word "asylum" comes from?' she was saying. 'It dates back to the Middle Ages, from a person's right to seek refuge in churches and other holy places. The right of asylum is something any civilised person can understand. So how could my father, the director of an asylum, treat someone like that?'

Paulo Coelho wanted to know all the details of what had happened, because he had a genuine reason for finding out about Veronika's story.

The reason was the following: he himself had been admitted into an asylum or, rather, mental hospital as they were better known. And this had happened not once, but three times, in 1965, 1966 and 1967. The place where he had been interned was the Dr Eiras Sanatorium in Rio de Janeiro.

Precisely why he had been admitted into hospital was something which, even today, he found odd; perhaps his parents were confused by his unusual behaviour, half-shy, half-extrovert, and by his desire to be an 'artist', something that everyone in the family considered a perfect recipe for ending up as a social outcast and dying in poverty.

When he thought about it – and, it must be said, he rarely did – he considered the real madman to have been the doctor who had agreed to admit him for the flimsiest of reasons (as in any family, the tendency is always to place the blame on others, and to state adamantly that the parents didn't know what they were doing when they took that drastic decision).

Paulo laughed when he learned of the strange letter to the newspapers that Veronika had left behind, complaining that an important French magazine didn't even know where Slovenia was.

'No one would kill themselves over something like that.'

'That's why the letter had no effect,' said his friend Veronika, embarrassed. 'Yesterday, when I checked in at the hotel, the receptionist thought Slovenia was a town in Germany.'

He knew the feeling, for many foreigners believed the Argentine city of Buenos Aires to be the capital of Brazil.

But apart from having foreigners blithely compliment him on the beauty of his country's capital city (which was to be found in the neighbouring country of Argentina), Paulo Coelho shared with Veronika the fact just mentioned, but which is worth restating: he too had been admitted into a mental hospital, and, as his first wife had once remarked, 'should never have been let out'.

But he was let out. And when he left the sanatorium for the last time, determined never to go back, he had made two promises: (a) that he would one day write about the subject and (b) that he would wait until both his parents were dead before touching publicly on the issue, because he didn't want to hurt them, since both had spent many years of their lives blaming themselves for what they had done.

His mother had died in 1993, but his father, who had turned eighty-four in 1997, was still alive and in full possession of his mental faculties and his health, despite having emphysema of the lungs (even though he'd never smoked) and despite living entirely off frozen food because he couldn't get a housekeeper who could put up with his eccentricities.

So, when Paulo Coelho heard Veronika's story, he discovered a way of talking about the issue without breaking his promises. Even though he had never considered suicide, he had an intimate knowledge of the world of the mental hospital – the treatments, the relationships between doctors and patients, the comforts and anxieties of living in a place like that.

So let us allow Paulo Coelho and his friend Veronika to leave this book for good and let us get on with the story.

Veronika didn't know how long she had slept. She remembered waking up at one point – still with the life-giving tubes in her mouth and nose – and hearing a voice say:

'Do you want me to masturbate you?'

But now, looking round the room with her eyes wide open, she didn't know if that had been real or an hallucination. Apart from that one memory, she could remember nothing, absolutely nothing.

The tubes had been taken out, but she still had needles stuck all over her body, wires connected to the area around her heart and her head, and her arms were still strapped down. She was naked, covered only by a sheet, and she felt cold, but she was determined not to complain. The small area surrounded by green curtains was filled by the bed she was lying on, the machinery of the Intensive Care Unit and a white chair on which a nurse was sitting reading a book.

This time, the woman had dark eyes and brown hair. Even so, Veronika was not sure if it was the same person she had talked to hours – or was it days? – ago.

'Can you unstrap my arms?'

The nurse looked up, said a brusque 'No', and went back to her book.

I'm alive, thought Veronika. Everything's going to start all over again. I'll have to stay in here for a while, until they realise that I'm perfectly normal. Then they'll let me out, and I'll see the streets of Ljubljana again, its main square, the bridges, the people going to and from work.

Since people always tend to help others – just so that they can feel they are better than they really are – they'll give me my job back at the library. In time, I'll start frequenting the same bars and nightclubs, I'll talk to my friends about the injustices and problems of the world, I'll go to the cinema, take walks around the lake.

Since I only took sleeping pills, I'm not disfigured in any way: I'm still young, pretty, intelligent, I won't have any difficulty in getting boyfriends, I never did. I'll make love with them in their houses, or in the woods, I'll feel a certain degree of pleasure, but the moment I reach orgasm, the feeling of emptiness will return. We won't have much to talk about, and both he and I will know it. The time will come to make our excuses – 'It's late', or 'I have to get up early tomorrow' – and we'll part as quickly as possible, avoiding looking each other in the eye.

I'll go back to my rented room in the convent. I'll try and read a book, turn on the TV to see the same old programmes, set the alarm clock to wake up at exactly the same time I woke up the day before and mechanically repeat my tasks at the library. I'll eat a sandwich in the park opposite the theatre, sitting on the same bench, along with other people who also choose the same benches on which to sit and have their lunch, people who all have the same vacant look, but pretend to be pondering extremely important matters.

Then I'll go back to work, I'll listen to the gossip about who's going out with whom, who's suffering from what, how such and such a person was in tears about her husband, and I'll be left with the feeling that I'm privileged: I'm pretty, I have a job, I can have any boyfriend I choose. So I'll go back to the bars at the end of the day, and the whole thing will start again.

My mother, who must be out of her mind with worry over my suicide attempt, will recover from the shock and will keep asking me what I'm going to do with my life, why I'm not the same as everyone else, things really aren't as complicated as I think they are. 'Look at me, for example, I've been married to your father for years, and I've tried to give you the best possible upbringing and set you the best possible example.'

One day, I'll get tired of hearing her constantly repeating the same things, and to please her I'll marry a man whom I oblige myself to love. He and I will end up finding a way of dreaming of a future together: a house in the country, children, our children's future. We'll make love often in the first year, less in the second, and after the third year, people perhaps think about sex only once a fortnight and transform that thought into action only once a month. Even worse, we'll barely talk. I'll force myself to accept the situation, and I'll wonder what's wrong with me, because he no longer takes any interest in me, ignores me, and does nothing but talk about his friends, as if they were his real world.

When the marriage is just about to fall apart, I'll get pregnant. We'll have a child, feel closer to each other for a while, and then the situation will go back to what it was before.

I'll begin to put on weight like the aunt that nurse was talking about yesterday – or was it days ago, I don't really know. And I'll start to go on diets, systematically defeated each day, each week, by the weight that keeps creeping up regardless of the controls I put on it. At that point, I'll take those magic pills that stop you feeling depressed, then I'll have a few more children, conceived during nights of love that pass all too quickly. I'll tell everyone that the children are my reason for living, when in reality my life is their reason for living.

People will always consider us a happy couple, and no one will know how much solitude, bitterness and resignation lies beneath the surface happiness.

Until one day, when my husband takes a lover for the first time, and I will perhaps kick up a fuss like the nurse's aunt, or think again of killing myself. By then, though, I'll be too old and cowardly, with two or three children who need my help, and I'll have to bring them up and help them find a place in the world before I can just abandon everything. I won't commit suicide: I'll make a scene, I'll threaten to leave and take the children with me. Like all men, my husband will back down, he'll tell me he loves me and that it won't happen again. It won't even occur to him that, if I really did decide to leave, my only option would be to go back to my parents' house and stay there for the rest of my life, forced to listen to my mother going on and on all day about how I lost my one opportunity for being happy, that he was a wonderful husband despite his peccadillos, that my children will be traumatised by the separation.

Two or three years later, another woman will appear in his life. I'll find out – because I saw them, or because someone told me – but this time I'll pretend I don't know. I used up all my energy fighting against that other lover, I've no energy left, it's best to accept life as it really is, and not as I imagined it to be. My mother was right.

He will continue being a considerate husband, I will continue working at the library, eating my sandwiches in the square opposite the theatre, reading books I never quite manage to finish, watching television programmes that are the same as they were ten, twenty, fifty years ago.

Except that I'll eat my sandwiches with a sense of guilt, because I'm getting fatter; and I won't go to bars any more, because I have a husband expecting me to come home and look after the children.

After that, it's a matter of waiting for the children to grow up and of spending all day thinking about suicide, without the courage to do anything about it. One fine day, I'll reach the conclusion that that's what life is like, there's no point worrying about it, nothing will change. And I'll accept it.

✳

Veronika brought her interior monologue to a close and made a promise to herself: she would not leave Villete alive. It was best to put an end to everything now, while she was still brave and healthy enough to die.

She fell asleep and woke up several times, noticing that the number of machines around her was diminishing, the warmth of her body was growing, and the nurses' faces kept changing; but there was always someone beside her. Through the green curtain she heard the sound of someone crying, groans or voices whispering in calm, technical tones. From time to time, a distant machine would buzz and she would hear hurried footsteps along the corridor. Then the voices would lose their calm, technical tone and become tense, issuing rapid orders.

In one of her lucid moments, a nurse asked her:

'Don't you want to know how you are?'

'I already know,' replied Veronika. 'And it's nothing to do with what you can see happening in my body, it's what's happening in my soul.'

The nurse tried to continue the conversation, but Veronika pretended to be asleep.

When she opened her eyes again, she realised that she had been moved; she was in what looked like a large ward. She still had a drip in her arm, but all the other wires and needles had been removed.

A tall doctor, wearing the traditional white coat, in sharp contrast to the artificial black of his dyed hair and beard, was standing at the foot of her bed. Beside him, a young junior doctor holding a clipboard was taking notes.

'How long have I been here?' she asked, noticing that she spoke with some difficulty, slurring her words slightly.

'You've been in this ward for two weeks, after five days spent in the Intensive Care Unit,' replied the older man. 'And just be grateful that you're still here.'

The younger man seemed surprised, as if that final remark did not quite fit the facts. Veronika noticed his reaction at once, and her instincts were alerted: had she been here longer? Was she still in some danger? She began to pay attention to each gesture, each movement the two men made; she knew it was pointless asking questions, they would never tell her the truth, but if she was clever, she could find out what was going on.

'Tell me your name, address, marital status and date of birth,' the older man said. Veronika knew her name, her marital status and her date of birth, but she realised there were blanks in her memory: she couldn't quite remember her address.

The doctor shone a light in her eyes and examined them for a long time, in silence. The young man did the same thing. They exchanged glances, which meant absolutely nothing.

'Did you say to the night nurse that we couldn't see into your soul?' asked the younger man.

Veronika couldn't remember. She was having difficulty knowing who she was and what she was doing there.

'You have been kept in an artificially induced sleep with tranquillisers, and that might affect your memory a bit, but please try to answer all our questions.'

And the doctors began an absurd questionnaire, wanting to know the names of the principal Ljubljana newspapers, the name of the poet whose statue was in the main square (ah, that she would never forget, every Slovene has the image of Prešeren engraved on his or her soul), the colour of her mother's hair, the names of her colleagues at work, the titles of the most popular books at the library.

To begin with, Veronika considered not replying – her memory was still confused – but as the questionnaire continued, she began reconstructing what she'd forgotten. At one point, she remembered that she was now in a mental hospital, and that the mad were not obliged to be coherent; but, for her own good, and to keep the doctors by her side, in order to see if she could find out something more about her state, she began making a mental effort. As she recited the names and facts, she was recovering not only her memory, but also her personality, her desires, her way of seeing life. The idea of suicide, which, that morning, appeared buried beneath several layers of sedatives, resurfaced.

'Fine,' said the older man, at the end of the questionnaire.

'How much longer must I stay here?'

The younger man lowered his eyes, and she felt as if everything were hanging in the air, as if, once that question was answered, a new chapter of her life would be written, and no one would be able to change it.

'You can tell her,' said the older man. 'A lot of other patients have already heard the rumours, and she'll find out in the end anyway; it's impossible to keep secrets round here.'

'Well, you decided your own fate,' sighed the young man, weighing each word. 'So you had better know the consequence of your actions: during the coma brought on by the pills you took, your heart was irreversibly damaged. There was a necrosis of the ventricle. . . '

'Put it in layman's terms,' said the older man. 'Get straight to the point.'

'Your heart was irreversibly damaged and soon it will stop beating altogether.'

'What does that mean?' she asked, frightened.

'If your heart stops beating, that means only one thing, death. I don't know what your religious beliefs are, but. . . '

'When will my heart stop beating?' asked Veronika, interrupting him.

'Within five days, a week at most.'

Veronika realised that behind his professional appearance and behaviour, behind the concerned manner, the young man was taking immense pleasure in what he was saying, as if she deserved the punishment, and would serve as an example to all the others.

During her life, Veronika noticed that a lot of people she knew would talk about the horrors in other people's lives as if they were genuinely concerned to help them, but the truth was that they took pleasure in the suffering of others, because that made them believe they were happy and that life had been generous with them. She hated that kind of person and she wasn't going to give the young man an opportunity to take advantage of her state, in order to mask his own frustrations.

She kept her eyes fixed on his and, smiling, said:

'So I succeeded then.'

'Yes,' came the reply. But any pleasure he had taken in giving her the tragic news had vanished.

During the night, however, she began to feel afraid. It was one thing to die quickly after taking some pills, it was quite another to wait five days or a week for death to come, when she had already been through so much.

She had always spent her life waiting for something: for her father to come back from work, for the letter from a lover that never arrived, for her end-of-year exams, for the train, the bus, the phone call, the holiday, the end of the holidays. Now she was going to have to wait for death, which had made an appointment with her.

'This could only happen to me. Normally, people die on precisely the day they least expect.'

She had to get out of there and get some more pills. If she couldn't, and the only solution was to jump from a high building in Ljubljana, that's what she'd do; she had tried to save her parents any unnecessary suffering, but now she had no option.

She looked about her. All the beds were occupied by sleeping people, some of whom were snoring loudly. There were bars on the windows. At the end of the ward, there was a small bright light that filled the place with strange shadows and meant that the ward could be kept under constant vigilance. Near the light, a woman was reading a book.

'These nurses must be very cultivated, they spend their whole lives reading.'

Veronika's bed was the farthest from the door; between her and the woman there were nearly twenty other beds. She got up with difficulty because, if she was to believe what the doctor had said, she hadn't walked for nearly three weeks. The nurse looked up and saw the girl approaching, dragging her drip-feed with her.

'I want to go to the toilet,' she whispered, afraid of waking the other mad women.

The woman gestured vaguely towards the door. Veronika's mind was working fast, looking everywhere for an escape route, a crack, a way out. 'It has to be quick, while they think I'm still too frail, incapable of acting.'

She peered about her. The toilet was a cubicle with no door. If she wanted to get out of there, she would have to grab the nurse and overcome her in order to get the key from her, but she was too weak for that.

'Is this a prison?' she asked the nurse, who had stopped reading and was now watching her every movement.

'No, it's a mental hospital.'

'But I'm not mad.'

The woman laughed.

'That's what they all say.'

'All right then, I am mad, but what does that mean?'

The woman told Veronika not to stay too long on her feet, and sent her back to her bed.

'What does it mean to be mad?' insisted Veronika.

'Ask the doctor tomorrow. But go to sleep now, otherwise I'll have to give you a sedative, whether you want it or not.'

Veronika obeyed. On her way back, she heard someone whispering from one of the beds:

'Don't you know what it means to be mad?'

For a moment, she considered ignoring the voice: she didn't want to make friends, to develop a social circle, to create allies for a great mass revolt. She had only one fixed idea: death. If she really couldn't escape, she would find some way to kill herself right there, as soon as possible.

But the woman asked her the same question she had asked the nurse.

'Don't you know what it means to be mad?'

'Who are you?'

'My name is Zedka. Go to your bed. Then, when the nurse thinks you're asleep, crawl back over here.'

Veronika returned to her bed, and waited for the nurse to resume her reading. What did it mean to be mad? She hadn't the slightest idea, because the word was used in a completely anarchic way: people would say, for example, that certain sportsmen were mad because they wanted to break records, or that artists were mad, because they led such strange, insecure lives, different from the lives of normal people. On the other hand, Veronika had often seen thinly clad people walking the streets of Ljubljana in winter, pushing supermarket trolleys full of plastic bags and rags, and proclaiming the end of the world.

She didn't feel sleepy. According to the doctor, she had slept for almost a week, too long for someone who was used to a life without great emotions, but with rigid timetables for rest. What did it mean to be mad? Perhaps she should ask one of the mad.

Veronika crouched down, pulled the needle out of her arm and went over to Zedka's bed, trying to ignore her churning stomach. She didn't know if the feeling of nausea was because of her weakened heart or the effort she was having to make.

'I don't know what it means to be mad,' whispered Veronika. 'But I'm not. I'm just a failed suicide.'

'Anyone who lives in their own world is mad. Like schizophrenics, psychopaths, maniacs. I mean people who are different from others.'

'Like you?'

'On the other hand,' Zedka continued, pretending not to have heard the remark, 'you have Einstein, saying that there was no time or space, just a combination of the two. Or Columbus, insisting that on the other side of the world lay not an abyss but a continent. Or Edmund Hillary, convinced that a man could reach the top of Everest. Or the Beatles, who created an entirely different sort of music and dressed like people from another time. Those people – and thousands of others – all lived in their own world.'

'This madwoman talks a lot of sense,' thought Veronika, remembering stories her mother used to tell her about saints who swore they had spoken to Jesus or the Virgin Mary. Did *they* live in a world apart?

'I once saw a woman wearing a low-cut dress; she had a glazed look in her eyes and she was walking the streets of Ljubljana when it was five degrees below zero. I thought she must be drunk and I went to help her, but she refused my offer to lend her my jacket. Perhaps in her world it was summer and her body was warmed by the desire of the person waiting for her. Even if that person only existed in her delirium, she had the right to live and die as she wanted, don't you think?'

Veronika didn't know what to say, but the madwoman's words made sense to her. Who knows, perhaps she was the woman who had been seen half-naked walking the streets of Ljubljana?

'I'm going to tell you a story,' said Zedka. 'A powerful wizard, who wanted to destroy an entire kingdom, placed a magic potion in the well from which all the inhabitants drank. Whoever drank that water would go mad.

'The following morning, the whole population drank from the well and they all went mad, apart from the king and his family, who had a well set aside for them alone, and which the magician had not managed to poison. The king was worried and tried to control the population by issuing a series of edicts governing security and public health. The policemen and the inspectors, however, had also drunk the poisoned water and they thought the king's decisions were absurd and resolved to take no notice of them.

'When the inhabitants of the kingdom heard these decrees, they became convinced that the king had gone mad and was now giving nonsensical orders. They marched on the castle and called for his abdication.

'In despair, the king prepared to step down from the throne, but the queen stopped him, saying: "Let us go and drink from the communal well. Then, we will be the same as them."

'And that was what they did: the king and the queen drank the water of madness and immediately began talking nonsense. Their subjects repented at once; now that the king was displaying such wisdom, why not allow him to continue ruling the country?

'The country continued to live in peace, although its inhabitants behaved very differently from those of its neighbours. And the king was able to govern until the end of his days.'

Veronika laughed.

'You don't seem mad at all,' she said.

'But I am, although I'm undergoing a cure, because my problem is that I lack a particular chemical. However, while I hope that the chemical gets rid of my chronic depression, I want to continue being mad, living my life the way I dream it, and not the way other people want it to be. Do you know what exists out there, beyond the walls of Villete?'

'People who have all drunk from the same well.'

'Exactly,' said Zedka. 'They think they're normal, because they all do the same thing. Well, I'm going to pretend that I have drunk from the same well as them.'

'I already did that, and that's precisely my problem. I've never been depressed, never felt great joy or sadness, at least none that lasted. I have the same problems as everyone else.'

For a while, Zedka said nothing, then:

'They told us you're going to die.'

Veronika hesitated for a moment. Could she trust this woman? She needed to take the risk.

'Yes, within about five or six days. I keep wondering if there's a way of dying sooner. If you, or someone else, could get me some more pills, I'm sure my heart wouldn't survive this time. You must understand how awful it is to have to wait for death, you must help me.'

Before Zedka could reply, the nurse appeared with an injection.

'I can give you the injection myself,' she said, 'or, depending on how you feel about it, I can ask the guards outside to help me.'

'Don't waste your energy,' said Zedka to Veronika. 'Save your strength, if you want to get what you asked me.'

Veronika got up, went back to her bed and allowed the nurse to do her work.

It was her first normal day in a mental hospital. She left the ward, had some breakfast in the large refectory where men and women were eating together. She noticed how different it was to the way these places were usually depicted in films – hysterical scenes, shouting, people making demented gestures – everything seemed wrapped in an aura of oppressive silence; it seemed that no one wanted to share their inner world with strangers.

After breakfast (which wasn't bad at all, no one could blame Villete's terrible reputation on the meals), they all went out to take the sun. In fact, there wasn't any sun – the temperature was below zero and the garden was covered in snow.

'I'm not here to preserve my life, but to lose it,' said Veronika to one of the nurses.

'You must still go out and take the sun.'

'You're the ones who are mad; there isn't any sun.'

'But there is light, and that helps to calm the patients. Unfortunately, our winter lasts a long time, if it didn't, we'd have a lot less work.'

It was useless arguing; she went out and walked a little, looking about her and surreptitiously seeking some way of escaping. The wall was high, as required by the builders of the old type of barracks, but the watchtowers for the sentries were empty. The garden was surrounded by military-looking buildings, which now housed the male and female wards, the administrative offices and the employees' rooms. After a first, rapid inspection, she noticed that the only place that was really guarded was the main gate, where everyone who entered and left had their papers checked by two guards.

Everything seemed to be falling into place in her mind again. In order to exercise her memory, she began trying to remember small things, like the place where she used to leave the key to her room, the record she'd just bought, the last book she was asked for at the library.

'I'm Zedka,' said a woman, approaching.

The previous night, Veronika hadn't been able to see her face, she had been crouched down beside the bed all the time they were talking. Zedka must have been about thirty-five and seemed absolutely normal.

'I hope the injection didn't bother you too much. After a while, the body gets habituated, and the sedatives lose their effect.'

'I'm fine.'

'About our conversation last night, do you remember what you asked me?'

'Of course I do.'

Zedka took her by the arm, and they began to walk along together, amongst the many leafless trees in the courtyard. Beyond the walls, you could see the mountains disappearing into the clouds.

'It's cold, but a lovely morning all the same,' said Zedka. 'Oddly enough, I never used to suffer from depression on cold, grey, cloudy days like this. I felt as if nature was in harmony with me, that it reflected my soul. On the other hand, when the sun appeared, the children would come out to play in the streets, and everyone was happy that it was such a lovely day, and then I would feel terrible, as if that display of exuberance in which I could not participate was somehow unfair.'

Delicately, Veronika detached herself from the woman. She didn't like physical contact.

'You didn't finish what you were saying. You were saying something about what I asked you last night.'

'There's a group of people here, men and women who could have left, who could be back home, but who don't want to leave. There are many reasons for this: Villete isn't as bad as people say, although it's far from being a five-star hotel. Here inside, everyone can say what they like, do what they want, without being criticised, after all, they're in a mental hospital. Then, when there are government inspections, these men and women behave like dangerous maniacs, because some are here at the State's expense. The doctors know this, but there must be some order from the owners which allows the situation to continue, because there are more vacancies than there are patients.'

'Could they get hold of some pills for me?'

'Try and contact them, they call their group the Fraternity.'

Zedka pointed to a woman with white hair, who was talking animatedly with some younger women.

'Her name is Mari, she belongs to the Fraternity. Ask her.'

Veronika started walking towards Mari, but Zedka stopped her:

'No, not now, she's having fun. She's not going to stop something which gives her pleasure, just to be nice to a complete stranger. If she should react badly, you'll never have another chance to approach her. The "mad" always believe in first impressions.'

Veronika laughed at the way Zedka said the word 'mad', but she was worried too, because everything here seemed so normal, so nice. After so many years of going straight from work to a bar, from that bar to the bed of some lover, from his bed to her room, from her room to her mother's house, she was now experiencing something she had never dreamed of: a mental hospital, madness, an insane asylum, where people were not ashamed to say they were mad, where no one stopped doing something they were enjoying just to be nice to others.

She began to doubt that Zedka was serious, or if it wasn't just a way by which mental patients could pretend that the world they lived in was better than that of others. But what did it matter? She was experiencing something interesting, different, totally unexpected: imagine a place where people pretend to be mad in order to do exactly what they want.

At that precise moment, Veronika's heart turned over. She suddenly remembered what the doctor had said and she felt frightened.

'I want to walk alone for a bit,' she said to Zedka. After all, she was 'mad' too, and she no longer had to worry about pleasing anyone.

The woman moved off, and Veronika stood looking at the mountains beyond the walls of Villete. A faint desire to live seemed about to surface, but Veronika determinedly pushed it away.

'I must get hold of those pills as soon as possible.'

She reflected on her situation there; it was far from ideal. Even if they allowed her to do all the mad things she wanted to do, she wouldn't know where to start.

She had never done anything mad.

After some time in the garden, everyone went back to the refectory and had lunch. Immediately afterwards, the nurses led both men and women to a huge lounge divided up into lots of different areas; there were tables, chairs, sofas, a piano, a television and large windows through which you could see the grey sky and the low clouds. None of the windows had bars on them, because the room opened onto the garden. The doors were closed because of the cold, but all you had to do was turn the handle, and you could go outside again and walk once more amongst the trees.

Most people went and sat down in front of the television. Others stared into space, others talked in low voices to themselves, but who has not done the same at some moment in their lives? Veronika noticed that the older woman, Mari, was now with a larger group, in one of the corners of the vast room. Some other patients were walking nearby and Veronika tried to join them in order to eavesdrop on what the group members were saying.

She tried to disguise her intentions as best she could, but whenever she came close, they all fell silent and turned as one to look at her.

'What do you want?' said an elderly man, who seemed to be the leader of the Fraternity (if such a group really existed, and Zedka was not actually madder than she seemed).

'Nothing, I was just passing.'

They exchanged glances, and made a few mad gestures with their heads. One said to the other: 'She was just passing.' The other repeated the remark more loudly this time and soon they were all shouting the same words.

Veronika didn't know what to do and stood there paralysed with fear. A burly, shifty-looking male nurse came over, wanting to know what was going on.

'Nothing,' said one member of the group. 'She was just passing. She's standing right there, but she's still just passing.'

The whole group fell about laughing. Veronika assumed an ironic air, smiled, turned and moved off, so that no one would notice that her eyes were filling with tears. She went straight out into the garden, without bothering to put on a coat or jacket. A nurse tried to convince her to come back in, but another appeared soon after and whispered something in his ear, and the two of them left her in peace, in the cold. There was no point taking care of the health of someone who was condemned to die.

She was confused, tense, irritated with herself. She had never allowed herself to be provoked; she had learned from early on that, whenever a new situation presented itself, you had to remain cool and distant. Those mad people, however, had managed to make her feel shame, fear, rage, a desire to murder them all, to wound them with words she hadn't dared to utter.

Perhaps the pills or the treatment they had administered to get her out of her coma had transformed her into a frail woman, incapable of fending for herself. She had confronted far worse situations in her adolescence, and yet for the first time, she had been unable to hold back her tears. She needed to get back to the person she used to be, someone able to respond with irony, to pretend that the insults didn't bother her because she was better than all of them. Who, in that group, had had the courage to desire death? Who amongst them could teach her about life when they were all huddled behind the walls of Villete? She would never want to depend on their help for anything, even if she had to wait five or six days to die.

'One day's already gone. There are only another four or five left.'

She walked a little, letting the freezing cold enter her body and calm the blood that was flowing too fast, her heart that was beating too hard.

'Honestly, here I am, with my days literally numbered, giving importance to remarks made by people I've never even seen before, people who soon I'll never see again. And yet I suffer and get upset, I want to attack and defend. Why waste my time?'

But she *was* wasting the little time left to her, fighting for her tiny bit of space in that strange community where you had to put up a fight if you didn't want others imposing their rules on you.

'I can't believe it, I never used to be like this. I never used to fight over stupid things.'

She stopped in the middle of the icy garden. It was precisely because she had found everything so stupid that she had ended up accepting what life had naturally imposed on her. In adolescence, she thought it was too early to choose; now, in youth, she was convinced it was too late to change.

And what had she spent all her energies on until then? On trying to ensure that her life continued exactly as it always had. She had given up many of her desires so that her parents would continue to love her as they had when she was a child, even though she knew that real love changes and grows with time and discovers new ways of expressing itself. One day, when she had listened to her mother telling her, in tears, that her marriage was over, Veronika had sought out her father; she had cried, threatened and finally extracted a promise from him that he would not leave home, never imagining the high price her parents would have to pay for this.

When she decided to get a job, she rejected a tempting offer from a company that had just been set up in her recently created country in favour of a job at the public library, where you didn't earn much money, but where you were secure. She went to work every day, always keeping to the same timetable, always making sure she wasn't perceived as a threat by her superiors; she was contented, she didn't struggle and so she didn't grow: all she wanted was her salary at the end of the month.

She rented the room in the convent because the nuns required all tenants to be back at a certain hour, and then they locked the door: anyone still outside after that had to sleep in the street. She always had a genuine excuse to give boyfriends, so as not to have to spend the night in hotel rooms or strange beds.

When she used to dream of getting married, she imagined herself in a little house outside Ljubljana, with a man quite different from her father, a man who earned enough to support his family, one who would be contented just to be with her in a house with an open fire and to look out at the snow-covered mountains.

She had taught herself to give men a precise amount of pleasure, never more, never less, only what was necessary. She didn't get angry with anyone, because that would mean having to react, having to do battle with the enemy, and then having to face unforeseen consequences, such as vengeance.

When she had achieved almost everything she wanted in life, she had reached the conclusion that her existence had no meaning, because every day was the same. And she had decided to die.

✳

Veronika went back in and walked over to the group gathered in one corner of the room. The people were talking animatedly, but fell silent as soon as she approached.

She went straight over to the oldest man, who seemed to be the leader. Before anyone could stop her, she gave him a resounding slap in the face.

'Aren't you going to react?' she asked out loud, so that everyone in the room could hear her. 'Aren't you going to do something?'

'No,' the man said and passed a hand over his face. A little thread of blood ran from his nose. 'You won't be troubling us for very long.'

She left the lounge and went triumphantly back to her ward. She had done something that she had never done in her entire life.

Three days had passed since the incident with the group that Zedka called the Fraternity. Veronika regretted that slap, not because she was afraid of the man's reaction, but because she had done something different. If she wasn't careful, she might end up convinced that life was worth living, and that would cause her pointless pain, since she would soon have to leave this world anyway.

Her only option was to keep away from everything and everyone, to try to be in every way as she had been before, to obey Villete's rules and regulations. She adapted herself to the routine imposed by the hospital: rising early, having breakfast, going for a walk in the garden, having lunch, going to the lounge, for another walk in the garden, then supper, television and bed.

Before Veronika went to sleep, a nurse always appeared with medication. All the other women took pills, Veronika was the only one who was given an injection. She never complained, she just wanted to know why she was given so many sedatives, since she had never had any problems sleeping. They explained that the injection was not a sedative, but medication for her heart.

And so, by falling in with that routine, her days in the hospital all began to seem the same. When the days are all the same, they pass more quickly; in another two or three days she would no longer have to brush her teeth or comb her hair. Veronika noticed her heart growing rapidly weaker: she became easily out of breath, she got pains in her chest, she had no appetite, and the slightest effort made her dizzy.

After the incident with the Fraternity, she had sometimes thought: 'If I had a choice, if I had understood earlier that the reason my days were all the same was because I wanted them like that, perhaps. . . '

But the reply was always the same: 'There is no perhaps, because there is no choice.' And her inner peace returned, because everything had already been decided.

During this period, she formed a relationship with Zedka (not a friendship, because friendship requires a lot of time spent together, and that wouldn't be possible). They used to play cards – which helps the time pass more rapidly – and sometimes they would walk together, in silence, in the garden.

On one particular morning, immediately after breakfast, they all went out to take the sun, as the regulations demanded. A nurse, however, asked Zedka to go back to the ward, because it was her treatment day.

Veronika, who was having breakfast with her, heard the request.

'What treatment's that?'

'It's an old treatment, from the sixties, but the doctors think it might hasten my recovery. Do you want to come and watch?'

'You said you were depressed. Isn't taking the medication enough to replace the chemical you're lacking?'

'Do you want to watch?' insisted Zedka.

She was going to step outside the routine, thought Veronika. She was going to discover new things, when she didn't need to learn anything more – all she needed was patience. But her curiosity got the better of her and she nodded.

'This isn't a show, you know,' said the nurse.

'She's going to die. She's hardly seen anything. Let her come with us.'

Veronika watched the woman, still smiling, being strapped to the bed.

'Tell her what's going on,' said Zedka to the male nurse. 'Otherwise she'll be frightened.'

He turned and showed her the syringe. He seemed pleased to be treated like a doctor, explaining to a younger doctor the correct procedures and the proper treatments.

'This syringe contains a dose of insulin,' he said, speaking in a grave, technical tone of voice. 'It's used by diabetics to combat high blood glucose. However, when the dose is much larger than normal, the consequent drop in blood glucose provokes a state of coma.'

He tapped the needle lightly, to get rid of any air, and then stuck it in a vein in Zedka's right foot.

'That's what's going to happen now. She's going to enter a state of induced coma. Don't be frightened if her eyes go glazed, and don't expect her to recognise you when she's under the effects of the medication.'

'That's awful, inhuman. People struggle to get out of a coma not to go into one.'

'People struggle to live, not to commit suicide,' replied the nurse, but Veronika ignored the remark. 'And a state of coma allows the organism to rest; its functions are all drastically reduced and any existing tension disappears.'

While he was talking, he was injecting the liquid, and Zedka's eyes were growing dull.

'Don't worry,' Veronika was saying to her. 'You're absolutely normal, the story you told me about the king. . . '

'Don't waste your time. She can't hear you any more.'

The woman on the bed, who a few minutes before had seemed so lucid and full of life, now had her eyes fixed on some point in the distance, and there was liquid bubbling from one corner of her mouth.

'What did you do?' she shouted at the nurse.

'Just my job.'

Veronika started calling to Zedka, shouting, threatening that she would go to the police, the press, the human rights organisations.

'Calm down. You may be in a mental hospital, but you still have to abide by certain rules.'

She saw that the man was utterly serious and she was afraid. But since she had nothing to lose, she went on shouting.

From where she was, Zedka could see the ward and the beds, all empty except for one, to which her body was strapped, and beside which a girl was standing, staring in horror. The girl didn't know that the person in the bed was still alive with all her biological functions working perfectly, but that her soul was flying, almost touching the ceiling, experiencing a sense of profound peace.

Zedka was making an astral journey, something that had been a surprise during her first experience of insulin shock. She hadn't mentioned it to anyone, she was only there to be cured of depression and, as soon as she was in a fit state, she hoped to leave that place for ever. If she started telling them that she had left her body, they would think she was madder than when she had entered Villete. However, as soon as she had returned to her body, she began reading up on both subjects: insulin shock and that strange feeling of floating in space.

There wasn't much written about the treatment. It had been used for the first time around 1930, but had been completely banned in psychiatric hospitals, because of the possibility of irreversible damage to the patient. During one such session, she had visited Dr Igor's office in her astral form, at precisely the moment when he was discussing the subject with one of the owners of the hospital. 'It's a crime,' Dr Igor was saying. 'Yes, but it's cheap and it's quick!' replied the other man. 'Anyway, who's interested in the rights of the mad? No one's going to complain.'

Even so, some doctors still considered it a quick way of treating depression. Zedka had sought out and borrowed everything that had been written about insulin shock, especially first-hand reports by patients who had experienced it. The story was always the same: horrors and more horrors, not one of them had experienced anything resembling what she was living through at that moment.

She concluded – quite rightly – that there was no relationship between insulin and the feeling that her consciousness was leaving her body. On the contrary, the tendency with that kind of treatment was to diminish the patient's mental capacity.

She started researching into the existence of the soul, read a few books on occultism, and then, one day, she stumbled on a vast literature that described exactly what she was experiencing: it was called 'astral travel' and many people had already had the same experience. Some had merely set out to describe what they had felt, while others had developed techniques to provoke it. Zedka now knew those techniques by heart and she used them every night to go wherever she wished.

The descriptions of those experiences and visions varied, but they all had certain points in common: the strange, irritating noise that preceded the separation of the body from the spirit, followed by a shock, a rapid loss of consciousness, and then the peace and joy of floating in the air, attached to the body by a silvery cord, a cord that could be stretched indefinitely, although there were legends (in books, of course) that said the person would die if they allowed that silver thread to break.

Her experience, however, showed that she could go as far as she wanted and the cord never broke. But, generally speaking, the books had been very useful in teaching her how to get more and more out of her astral travelling. She had learned, for example, that when she wanted to move from one place to another, she had to concentrate on projecting herself into space, imagining where exactly she wanted to go. Unlike the routes followed by planes – which leave from one place and fly the necessary distance to reach another – an astral journey was made through mysterious tunnels. You imagined yourself in a place, you entered the appropriate tunnel at a terrifying speed, and the other place would appear.

It was through books too that she had lost her fear of the creatures inhabiting space. Today there was no one else in the ward, but the first time she had left her body, she had found a lot of people watching her, amused by her look of surprise.

Her first reaction was to assume that these were dead people, ghosts haunting the hospital. Then, with the help of books and of her own experience, she realised that, although there were a few disembodied spirits wandering about there, amongst them were people as alive as she was, who had either developed the technique of leaving their bodies, or who were not even aware of what was happening to them because, in some other part of the world, they were sleeping deeply, while their spirits roamed freely abroad.

Today – knowing that this was her last astral journey on insulin, because she had just been to visit Dr Igor's office and overheard him saying he was ready to release her – she decided to remain inside Villete. From the moment she went out through the main gate, she would never again return, not even in spirit, and she wanted to say goodbye.

To say goodbye. That was the really difficult part: once in a mental hospital, a person grows used to the freedom that exists in the world of madness and becomes addicted to it. You no longer have to take on responsibilities, to struggle to earn your daily bread, to be bothered with repetitive, mundane tasks. You could spend hours looking at a picture or making absurd doodles. Everything is tolerated because, after all, the person is mentally ill. As she herself had had occasion to observe, most of the inmates showed a marked improvement once they entered the hospital: they no longer had to hide their symptoms, and the 'family' atmosphere helped them to accept their own neuroses and psychoses.

At the beginning, Zedka had been fascinated by Villete and had even considered joining the Fraternity once she was cured. But she realised that if she was sensible, she could continue doing everything she enjoyed doing outside, as long as she dealt with the challenges of daily life. As someone had said, all you had to do was to keep your madness under control. You could cry, get worried or angry like any other normal human being, as long as you remembered that, up above, your spirit was laughing out loud at all those thorny situations.

She would soon be back home, with her children and her husband, and that part of her life also had its charms. Of course it would be difficult to find work; after all, in a small town like Ljubljana news travels fast, and her internment in Villete was already common knowledge to many people. But her husband earned enough to keep the family, and she could use her free time to continue making her astral journeys, though not under the dangerous influence of insulin.

There was only one thing she did not want to experience again, the reason that had brought her to Villete.

Depression.

The doctors said that a recently discovered substance, serotonin, was one of the compounds responsible for how human beings felt. A lack of serotonin impaired one's capacity to concentrate at work, to sleep, to eat and to enjoy life's pleasures. When this substance was completely absent, the person experienced despair, pessimism, a sense of futility, terrible tiredness, anxiety, difficulties in making decisions, and would end up sinking into permanent gloom, which would lead either to complete apathy or to suicide.

Other more conservative doctors said that any drastic change in life could trigger depression – moving to another country, losing a loved one, divorce, an increase in the demands of work or family. Some modern studies, based on the number of internments in winter and summer, pointed to the lack of sunlight as one of the causes of depression.

In Zedka's case, however, the reasons were simpler than anyone suspected: a man hidden in her past, or rather, the fantasy she had built up about a man she had known a long time ago.

It was so stupid. Plunging into depression and madness all because of a man whose current whereabouts she didn't even know, but with whom she had fallen hopelessly in love in her youth, since, like every normal young girl, Zedka had needed to experience the Impossible Love.

However, unlike her friends, who only dreamed of the Impossible Love, Zedka had decided to go further; she had actually tried to realise that dream. He lived on the other side of the ocean and she sold up everything to go and join him. He was married, but she accepted her role as mistress, plotting secretly to make him her husband. He barely had enough time for himself, but she resigned herself to spending days and nights in a cheap hotel room, waiting for his rare telephone calls.

Despite her determination to put up with everything in the name of love, the relationship did not work out. He never said anything directly, but one day Zedka realised that she was no longer welcome and she returned to Slovenia.

She spent a few months barely eating and remembering every second they had spent together, reviewing again and again their moments of joy and pleasure in bed, trying to fix on something that would allow her to believe in the future of that relationship. Her friends were worried about the state she was in, but something in Zedka's heart told her it was just a passing phase; personal growth has its price, and she was paying it without complaint. And so it was: one morning she woke up with an immense will to live; for the first time in ages, she ate heartily and then went out and found a job. She found not only a job, but also the attentions of a handsome, intelligent young man, much sought after by other women. A year later, she was married to him.

She aroused both the envy and the applause of her girlfriends. The two of them went to live in a comfortable house, with a garden that looked over the river that flows through Ljubljana. They had children and took trips to Austria or Italy during the summer.

When Slovenia decided to separate from Yugoslavia, he was called up into the army. Zedka was a Serb – that is, the enemy – and her life seemed on the point of collapse. In the ten tense days that followed, with the troops prepared for confrontation, and no one knowing quite what the result of the declaration of independence would be and how much blood would have to be spilt because of it, Zedka realised how much she loved him. She spent the whole time praying to a God who, until then, had seemed remote, but who now seemed her only hope. She promised the saints and angels anything as long as she could have her husband back.

And so it was. He came back, the children were able to go to schools where they taught the Slovene language, and the threat of war shifted to the neighbouring republic of Croatia.

Three years had passed. Yugoslavia's war with Croatia moved to Bosnia, and reports began to circulate of massacres committed by the Serbs. Zedka thought it unjust to label a whole nation as criminals because of the folly of a few madmen. Her life took on a meaning she had never expected: she defended her people with pride and courage, writing in newspapers, appearing on television, organising conferences. None of this bore any fruit, and even today, foreigners still believe all the Serbs were responsible for those atrocities, but Zedka knew she had done her duty, and that she could not abandon her brothers and sisters at such a difficult time. She could count on the support of her Slovene husband, of her children, and of people who were not manipulated by the propaganda machines of either side.

✳

One evening, she walked past the statue of Prešeren, the great Slovene poet, and she began to think about his life. When he was thirty-four, he went into a church and saw an adolescent girl, Julia Primic, with whom he fell passionately in love. Like the ancient minstrels, he began to write her poems, in the hope of one day marrying her.

It turned out that Julia was the daughter of an upper middle-class family and, apart from that chance sighting inside the church, Prešeren never again managed to get near her. But that encounter inspired his finest poetry and created a whole legend around his name. In the small central square of Ljubljana, the statue of the poet stares fixedly at something. If you follow his gaze, you will see, on the other side of the square, the face of a woman carved into the stone of one of the houses. That was where Julia had lived. Even after death, Prešeren gazes for all eternity on his Impossible Love.

And what if he had fought a little harder?

Zedka's heart started beating fast, perhaps it was a presentiment of something bad, an accident involving one of her children. She raced back home only to find them watching television and eating popcorn.

That sadness, however, did not pass. Zedka lay down and slept for nearly twelve hours and, when she woke, she didn't feel like getting up. Prešeren story had brought back to her the image of her first lover, who had never again contacted her.

And Zedka asked herself: did I fight hard enough? Should I have accepted my role as mistress, rather than wanting things to go as I expected them to? Did I fight for my first love with the same energy with which I fought for my people?

Zedka persuaded herself that she had, but the sadness would not go away. What once had seemed to her a Paradise – the house near the river, the husband whom she loved, the children eating popcorn in front of the television – was gradually transformed into a hell.

Today, after many astral journeys and many encounters with highly evolved beings, Zedka knew that this was all nonsense. She had used her Impossible Love as an excuse, a pretext for breaking the ties with the life she led, and which was far from being the life she really expected for herself.

But twelve months earlier, the situation had been quite different: she began frantically looking for that distant lover, she spent a fortune on international phone calls, but he no longer lived in the same city, and it was impossible to find him. She sent letters by express mail, which were always returned. She phoned all his friends, but no one had any idea what had happened to him.

Her husband was completely unaware of what was going on, and that infuriated her, because he should at least have suspected something, made a scene, complained, threatened to put her out in the street. She became convinced that the international telephone operators, the postman and all her girlfriends had been bribed by him to pretend indifference. She sold the jewellery that had been given to her when she married and bought a plane ticket to the other side of the ocean, until someone managed to convince her that America was a very large place and there was no point going there if you didn't know quite what you were looking for.

One evening, she lay down, suffering for love as she had never suffered before, not even when she had come back to the awful day-to-day life of Ljubljana. She spent that night and the following two days in her room. On the third day, her husband – so kind, so concerned about her – called a doctor. Did he really not know that Zedka was trying to get in touch with the other man, to commit adultery, to exchange her life as a respected wife for life as someone's secret mistress, to leave Ljubljana, her home, her children for ever?

The doctor arrived. She became hysterical and locked the door, and only opened it again when the doctor had left. A week later, she no longer had sufficient strength of will to get out of bed and began to use the bed as a toilet. She did not think any more, her head was completely taken up by fragmentary memories of the man who, she was convinced, was also unsuccessfully looking for her.

Her infuriatingly generous husband changed the sheets, smoothed her hair, said that it would all be all right in the end. The children no longer came into her bedroom, ever since she had slapped one of them for no reason, and then knelt down, kissed his feet, begging forgiveness, tearing her nightdress into shreds in order to show her despair and repentance.

After another week, in which she spat out the food offered to her, drifted in and out of reality several times, spent whole nights awake and whole days asleep, two men came into her room without knocking. One of them held her down while the other gave her an injection, and she woke up in Villete.

'Depression,' she heard the doctor say to her husband. 'Sometimes it's provoked by the most banal things, for example, the lack of a chemical substance, serotonin, in the organism.'

From the ceiling in the ward, Zedka watched the nurse approaching, syringe in hand. The girl was still standing there, trying to talk to her body, terrified by her vacant gaze. For some moments, Zedka considered the possibility of telling her about everything that was happening, but then she changed her mind; people never learn anything by being told, they have to find out for themselves.

The nurse placed the needle in Zedka's arm and injected her with glucose. As if grabbed by an enormous arm, her spirit left the ceiling, sped through a dark tunnel and returned to her body.

'Hello, Veronika.'

The girl looked frightened.

'Are you all right?'

'Yes, I'm fine. Fortunately, I've managed to survive this dangerous treatment, but it won't be repeated.'

'How do you know? Here no one respects the patient's wishes.'

Zedka knew because, during her astral journey, she had gone to Dr Igor's office.

'I can't explain why, I just know. Do you remember the first question I ever asked you?'

'Yes, you asked me if I knew what being mad meant?'

'Exactly. This time I'm not going to tell you a story. Madness is the inability to communicate your ideas. It's as if you were in a foreign country, able to see and understand everything that's going on around you, but incapable of explaining what you need to know or of being helped, because you don't understand the language they speak there.'

'We've all felt that.'

'And all of us, one way or another, are mad.'

Outside the barred window, the sky was thick with stars, and the moon, in its first quarter, was rising behind the mountains. Poets loved the full moon, they wrote thousands of poems about it, but it was the new moon that Veronika loved best because there was still room for it to grow, to expand, to fill the whole of its surface with light before its inevitable decline.

She felt like going over to the piano in the lounge, and celebrating that night with a lovely sonata she had learned at school. Looking up at the sky, she had an indescribable sense of well-being, as if the infinite nature of the universe had revealed her own eternity to her. However, she was separated from her desire by a steel door and a woman who was always endlessly reading a book. Besides, no one played the piano at that hour of night, she would wake up the whole neighbourhood.

Veronika laughed. The 'neighbourhood' were the wards full of mad people, and those mad people were, in turn, full of drugs to make them sleep.

Her sense of well-being continued though. She got up and went over to Zedka's bed, but she was sound asleep too, perhaps recovering from the horrible experience she had been through.

'Go back to bed,' said the nurse. 'Good girls should be dreaming of angels or lovers.'

'Don't treat me like a child. I'm not some tame mad woman who's afraid of everything, I'm raving, hysterical, I don't even respect my own life, or the lives of others. Anyway, today I'm in a bad way. I've looked at the moon and I need to talk to someone.'

The nurse looked at her, surprised by her reaction.

'Are you afraid of me?' asked Veronika. 'In a couple of days' time I'll be dead, what have I got to lose?'

'Why don't you go for a walk, dear, and let me finish my book?'

'Because this is a prison and there's a prison warder pretending to read a book, just to make others think she's an intelligent woman. The fact is, though, that she's watching every movement in the ward, and she guards the keys to the door as if they were a treasure. It's doubtless all in the regulations and so she must obey, because that way she can pretend to an authority she doesn't have in her everyday life, with her husband and children.'

Veronika was trembling, without quite knowing why.

'Keys?' said the nurse. 'The door is always open. You don't think I'd stay locked up in here with a load of mental patients, do you?'

What does she mean the door's open? A few days ago I wanted to get out of here, and this woman even went with me to the toilet. What is she talking about?

'Don't take me too seriously,' said the nurse. 'The fact is we don't need a lot of security here, because of the sedatives we dole out. You're shivering, are you cold?'

'I don't know. I think it must be something to do with my heart.'

'If you like, you can go for a walk.'

'What I'd really like is to play the piano.'

'The lounge is quite separate, so your piano playing won't disturb anyone. Do what you like.'

Veronika's trembling changed into low, timid, suppressed sobs. She knelt down, lay her head on the woman's lap and cried and cried.

The nurse put down the book, and stroked Veronika's hair, allowing that wave of sadness and tears its natural expression. There they sat, for almost half an hour, one crying, the other consoling, though neither knew why or what.

The sobbing finally ceased. The nurse helped her up, took her by the arm and led her to the door.

'I've got a daughter your age. When you were first admitted, full of drips and tubes, I kept wondering why a pretty young girl, with her whole life ahead of her, should want to kill herself. Then all kinds of rumours started flying around: about the letter that you left behind, which I never believed could be the real motive, and how you didn't have long to live because of some incurable heart problem. I couldn't get the image of my own daughter out of my head: what if she decided to do something like that? Why do certain people try to go against the natural order of things, which is to fight for survival whatever happens?'

'That's why I was crying,' said Veronika. 'When I took the pills, I wanted to kill someone I hated. I didn't know that other Veronikas existed inside me, Veronikas that I could love.'

'What makes a person hate themselves?'

'Cowardice perhaps. Or the eternal fear of being wrong, of not doing what others expect. A few moments ago I was happy, I forgot I was under sentence of death; then, when I remembered the situation I'm in, I felt frightened.'

The nurse opened the door and Veronika went out.

How could she ask me that? What does she want, to understand why I was crying? Doesn't she realise I'm a perfectly normal person, with the same desires and fears as everyone else, and that a question like that, now that it's all too late, could throw me into panic?

As she was walking down the corridors, lit by the same faint light as in the ward, Veronika realised that it *was* too late: she could no longer control her fear.

'I must get a grip on myself. I'm the kind of person who sticks to any decision she makes, who always sees things through.'

It's true that in her life she had seen many things through to their ultimate conclusions, but only unimportant things, like prolonging a quarrel that could easily have been resolved with an apology, or not phoning a man she was in love with, simply because she thought the relationship would lead nowhere. She was intransigent about the easy things, as if trying to prove to herself how strong and indifferent she was, when, in fact, she was just a fragile woman, who had never been an outstanding student, never excelled at school sports and had never succeeded in keeping the peace at home.

She had overcome her minor defects, only to be defeated by matters of fundamental importance. She had managed to appear utterly independent, when she was, in fact, desperately in need of company. When she entered a room, everyone would turn to look at her, but she almost always ended the night alone, in the convent, watching a TV that she hadn't even bothered to have properly tuned in. She gave all her friends the impression that she was a woman to be envied, and she expended most of her energy in trying to behave in accordance with the image she had created of herself.

Because of that, she had never had enough energy to be herself, a person who, like everyone else in the world, needed other people in order to be happy. But other people were so difficult. They reacted in unpredictable ways, they surrounded themselves with defensive walls, they behaved just as she did, pretending they didn't care about anything. When someone more open to life appeared, they either rejected them outright, or made them suffer, considering them inferior, 'ingenuous'.

She may have impressed a lot of people with her strength and determination, but where had it left her? In the void. Utterly alone. In Villete. In the anteroom of death.

Veronika's remorse over her attempted suicide resurfaced, and she firmly pushed it away again. Now she was feeling something she had never allowed herself to feel: hatred.

Hatred. Something almost as physical as walls, pianos or nurses; she could almost touch the destructive energy leaking out of her body. She allowed the feeling to emerge, regardless of whether it was good or bad, she was sick of self-control, of masks, of appropriate behaviour. Veronika wanted to spend her remaining two or three days of life behaving as inappropriately as she could.

She had begun by slapping an old man in the face, she had burst into tears in front of a nurse, she had refused to be nice and to talk to the others when what she really wanted was to be alone, and now she was free enough to feel hatred, although intelligent enough not to smash everything around her and risk spending what remained of her life under sedation and in a bed in a ward.

At that moment, she hated everything: herself, the world, the chair in front of her, the broken radiator in one of the corridors, people who were perfect, criminals. She was in a mental hospital and so could allow herself to feel things that people usually hide from themselves, because we are all brought up only to love, to accept, to look for ways round things, to avoid conflict. Veronika hated everything, but mainly she hated the way she had lived her life, never bothering to discover the hundreds of other Veronikas who lived inside her and who were interesting, mad, curious, brave, bold.

Then she started to feel hatred for the person she loved most in the world: her mother. A wonderful wife who worked all day and washed the dishes at night, sacrificing her own life so that her daughter would have a good education, know how to play the piano and the violin, dress like a princess, have the latest trainers and jeans, while she mended the same old dress she had worn for years.

'How can I hate someone who only ever gave me love?' thought Veronika, confused, trying to check her feelings. But it was too late, her hatred had been unleashed, she had opened the door to her personal hell. She hated the love she had been given, because it had asked for nothing in return, which was absurd, unreal, against the laws of nature.

That love asking for nothing in return had managed to fill her with guilt, with a desire to fulfil another's expectations, even if that meant giving up everything she had dreamed of for herself. It was a love that for years had tried to hide from her the difficulties and the corruption that existed in the world, ignoring the fact that, one day, she would have to find this out, and would then be defenceless against them.

And her father? She hated her father too, because, unlike her mother, who worked all the time, he knew how to live, he took her to bars and to the theatre, they had fun together, and when he was still young, she had loved him secretly, not the way one loves a father, but as a man. She hated him because he had always been so charming and so open with everyone except her mother, the only person who really deserved such treatment.

She hated everything. The library with its pile of books full of explanations about life, the school that had forced her to spend whole evenings learning algebra, even though she didn't know a single person, apart from teachers and mathematicians, who needed algebra in order to be happy. Why did they make them learn so much algebra or geometry or any of that mountain of other useless things?

Veronika pushed open the door to the lounge, went over to the piano, opened the lid, and, summoning up all her strength, pounded on the keys. A mad, cacophonous, jangled chord echoed round the empty room, bounced off the walls and returned to her in the guise of a shrill sound that seemed to tear at her soul. Yet it was an accurate portrait of her soul at that moment.

She pounded on the keys again, and again the dissonant notes reverberated about her.

'I'm mad. I'm allowed to do this. I can hate, I can pound away at the piano. Since when have mental patients known how to play notes in the right order?'

She pounded the piano again, once, twice, ten, twenty times, and each time she did it, her hatred seemed to diminish, until it passed away completely.

Then, once more, a deep peace flooded through her and Veronika again looked out at the starry sky and at the new moon, her favourite, filling the room she was in with gentle light. The impression returned of Infinity and Eternity walking hand in hand; you only had to look for one of them, for example, the limitless universe, to feel the presence of the other, Time that never ends, that never passes, that remains in the Present, where all of life's secrets lie. As she had been walking from the ward to that room, she had felt such pure hatred that now she had no more rancour left in her heart. She had finally allowed her negative feelings to surface, feelings that had been repressed for years in her soul. She had actually *felt* them, and they were no longer necessary, they could leave.

She sat on in silence, enjoying the present moment, letting love fill up the empty space left behind by hatred. When she felt the moment had come, she turned to the moon and played a sonata in homage to it, knowing that the moon was listening and would feel proud, and that this would provoke the jealousy of the stars. Then she played music for the stars, for the garden, for the mountains that she could not see in the darkness, but which she knew were there.

While she was playing that music for the garden, another mad person appeared, Eduard, a schizophrenic who was beyond all cure. She was not frightened by his presence; on the contrary, she smiled, and to her surprise, he smiled back.

The music could even penetrate his remote world, more distant than the moon itself; it could even perform miracles.

'I must buy a new key ring,' thought Dr Igor, as he opened the door to his small consulting room in Villete. The old one was falling to pieces and a small decorative metal shield had just fallen to the floor.

Dr Igor bent down and picked it up. What should he do with that shield bearing the Ljubljana coat of arms? He might as well throw it away, although he could have it mended and ask them to make a new leather strap, or else he could give it to his nephew to play with. Both alternatives seemed equally absurd. A key ring doesn't cost very much and his nephew had no interest in shields; he spent all his time watching television, or playing with electronic toys imported from Italy. Dr Igor still could not bring himself to throw it out, however, so he put it back in his pocket; he would decide what to do with it later on.

That was why he was the director of the hospital and not a patient, because he thought a lot before making any decisions.

He turned on the light; as winter advanced, dawn came ever later. Moving house, getting divorced and the absence of light were the main reasons for the increase in the number of cases of depression. Dr Igor was hoping that spring would arrive early and solve half his problems.

He looked at his diary for the day. He needed to find some way to prevent Eduard from dying of hunger; his schizophrenia made him unpredictable, and now he had stopped eating. Dr Igor had already prescribed intravenous feeding, but he couldn't keep that up for ever. Eduard was a strong young man of twenty-eight, but even with a drip, he would eventually waste away, becoming more and more skeletal.

What would Eduard's father think? He was one of the young Slovene republic's best-known ambassadors. He had been one of the people behind the delicate negotiations with Yugoslavia in the early 1990s. He, after all, had managed to work for years for the Belgrade government, surviving his detractors, who accused him of working for the enemy, and he was still in the diplomatic corps, except, this time, he represented a different country. He was a powerful and influential man, feared by everyone.

Dr Igor felt momentarily worried, just as before he had been worried about the shield on his key ring, but he immediately dismissed the thought. As far as the ambassador was concerned, it didn't matter whether his son looked well or not; he had no intention of taking him to official functions or having him accompany him to the various places in the world where he was sent as a government representative. Eduard was in Villete, and there he would stay forever, or at least as long as his father continued earning his nice, fat salary.

Dr Igor decided to stop the intravenous feeding, and allow Eduard to waste away a little more, until he himself felt like eating. If the situation got worse, he would write a report and pass responsibility on to the council of doctors who administered Villete. 'The best way to avoid trouble is to share responsibility,' his father had taught him. He had been a doctor too, and although he had had various deaths on his hands, he had never had any problem with the authorities.

Once Dr Igor had ordered Eduard's treatment to stop, he moved on to the next case. According to the report, Zedka Mendel had completed her course of treatment and could be allowed to leave. Dr Igor wanted to see for himself. There was nothing a doctor dreaded more than getting complaints from the families of patients who had been in Villete, which was what nearly always happened, for it was rare for a patient to readjust successfully to normal life after a period spent in a mental hospital.

It wasn't the fault of the hospital, nor of any of the hospitals scattered round the world; the problem of readjustment was exactly the same everywhere. Just as prison never corrects the prisoner – it only teaches him to commit more crimes – so hospitals merely got patients used to a completely unreal world, where everything was allowed and where no one had to take responsibility for their actions.

There was only one way out: to discover a cure for insanity. And Dr Igor was engaged heart and soul on just that, developing a thesis that would revolutionise the psychiatric world. In mental hospitals, temporary patients who lived alongside incurable patients began a process of social degeneration which, once started, was impossible to stop. Zedka Mendel would come back to hospital eventually, this time of her own volition, complaining of non-existent ailments, simply in order to be close to people who seemed to understand her better than those in the outside world.

If, however, he could find a way of combating Vitriol, the poison which Dr Igor believed to be the cause of madness, his name would go down in history and people would finally know where Slovenia was. That week, he had been given a heaven-sent opportunity in the shape of a would-be suicide; he was not going to lose this opportunity for all the money in the world.

Dr Igor felt happy. Although he was obliged for economic reasons to accept treatments, like insulin shock for example, that had long ago been condemned by the medical profession, the same economic reasons lay behind Villete's instigation of a new psychiatric treatment. As well as having the time and the staff to carry out his researches into Vitriol, he also had the owners' permission to allow the group calling itself the Fraternity to remain in the hospital. The shareholders in the institution tolerated – note that word well, not encouraged, but tolerated – a longer period of internment than was strictly necessary. They argued that, for humanitarian reasons, they should give the recently-cured the option of deciding for themselves when would be the best moment for them to rejoin the world, and that had led to a group of people deciding to stay in Villete, as if at a select hotel, or a club for those with similar interests and views. Thus Dr Igor managed to keep the mad and the sane in the same place, allowing the latter to have a positive influence on the former. To prevent things from degenerating and to stop the mad having a negative effect on those who had been cured, every member of the Fraternity had to leave the hospital at least once a day.

Dr Igor knew that the reasons given by the shareholders for allowing the presence of healthy people in the hospital – 'humanitarian reasons' they said – were just an excuse. They were afraid that Ljubljana, Slovenia's small but charming capital, did not have a sufficient number of wealthy mad people to sustain this expensive, modern building. Besides, the public health system ran a number of first-class mental hospitals of its own, and that left Villete at a disadvantage in the mental health market.

When the shareholders had converted the old barracks into a hospital, their target market had been the men and women likely to be affected by the war with Yugoslavia. The war, however, had been brief. The shareholders had felt certain that war would return, but it didn't.

Moreover, recent research had shown that whilst wars did have their psychological victims, they were far fewer than, say, the victims of stress, tedium, congenital illness, loneliness and rejection. When a community had a major problem to face, for example, war, hyperinflation or plague, there was a slight increase in the number of suicides, but a marked decline in cases of depression, paranoia and psychosis. These returned to their normal levels as soon as that problem had been overcome, indicating, or so Dr Igor thought, that people only allow themselves the luxury of being mad when they are in a position to do so.

He had before him another recent survey, this time from Canada, which an American newspaper had recently voted the country with the highest standard of living. Dr Igor read:

According to *Statistics Canada*, 40% of people between 15 and 34, 33% of people between 35 and 54 and 20% of people between 55 and 64 have already had some kind of mental illness. It is thought that one in every five individuals suffers some form of psychiatric disorder and one in every eight Canadians will be hospitalised at least once in their lifetime because of mental disturbances.

'They've got a bigger market there than we have,' he thought. 'The happier people can be, the unhappier they are.'

Dr Igor analysed a few more cases, thinking carefully about those he should share with the council and those he should resolve alone. By the time he had finished, day had broken, and he turned off the light.

He immediately ordered his first appointment to be shown in: the mother of the patient who had tried to commit suicide.

'I'm Veronika's mother. How is my daughter?'

Dr Igor wondered if he should tell her the truth and save her any unpleasant surprises – after all, he had a daughter with the same name – but he decided it was best to say nothing.

'We don't yet know,' he lied. 'We need another week.'

'I've no idea why Veronika did it,' said the woman tearfully. 'We've always been loving parents, we sacrificed everything to give her the best possible upbringing. Although my husband and I have had our ups and downs, we've kept the family together, as an example of perseverance in adversity. She's got a good job, she's nice-looking, and yet. . . '

'. . . and yet she tried to kill herself,' said Dr Igor. 'There's no reason to be surprised, that's the way it is. People just can't cope with happiness. If you like, I could show you the statistics for Canada.'

'Canada?'

The woman seemed startled. Dr Igor saw that he had managed to distract her and went on.

'Look, you haven't come here to find out how your daughter is, but to apologise for the fact that she tried to commit suicide. How old is she?'

'Twenty-four.'

'So she's a mature, experienced woman who knows what she wants and is perfectly capable of making her own choices. What has that got to do with your marriage or with the sacrifices that you and your husband made? How long has she lived on her own?'

'Six years.'

'You see? She's fundamentally independent. But, because of what a certain Austrian doctor – Dr Sigmund Freud, I'm sure you've heard of him – wrote about unhealthy relationships between parents and children, people today still blame themselves for everything. Do you imagine that Indians believe that the son-turned-murderer is a victim of his parents' upbringing? Tell me.'

'I haven't the faintest idea,' replied the woman, who couldn't get over her bewilderment at the doctor's behaviour. Perhaps he was influenced by his patients.

'Well, I'll tell you,' said Dr Igor. 'The Indians believe the murderer to be guilty, not society, not his parents, not his ancestors. Do the Japanese commit suicide because a son of theirs decides to take drugs and go out and shoot people? The reply is the same: no! And, as we all know, the Japanese will commit suicide at the drop of a hat. The other day, I read that a young Japanese man killed himself because he had failed his university entrance exams.'

'Do you think I could talk to my daughter?' asked the woman, who was not interested in the Japanese, the Indians or the Canadians.

'Yes, yes, in a moment,' said Dr Igor, slightly annoyed by the interruption. 'But first, I want you to understand one thing: apart from certain grave pathological cases, people only go mad when they try to escape from routine. Do you understand?'

'I do,' she replied. 'And if you think that I won't be capable of looking after her, you can rest assured, I've *never* tried to change my life.'

'Good.' Dr Igor seemed relieved. 'Can you imagine a world in which, for example, we were not obliged to repeat the same thing every day of our lives? If, for example, we all decided to eat only when we were hungry, what would housewives and restaurants do?'

'It would be more normal to eat only when we were hungry,' thought the woman, but she said nothing, afraid that he might not let her speak to Veronika.

'Well, it would cause tremendous confusion,' she said at last. 'I'm a housewife myself, and I know what I'm talking about.'

'So we have breakfast, lunch and supper. We have to wake up at a certain hour every day and rest once a week. Christmas exists so that we can give each other presents, Easter so that we can spend a few days at the lake. How would you like it if your husband were gripped by a sudden, passionate impulse and decided he wanted to make love in the living room?'

The woman thought: 'What *is* the man talking about? I came here to see my daughter.'

'I would find it very sad,' she said, carefully, hoping she was giving the right answer.

'Excellent,' roared Dr Igor. 'The bedroom is the correct place for making love. To make love anywhere else would set a bad example and promote the spread of anarchy.'

'Can I see my daughter?' said the woman.

Dr Igor gave up. This peasant would never understand what he was talking about; she wasn't interested in discussing madness from a philosophical point of view, even though she knew her daughter had made a serious suicide attempt and had been in a coma.

He rang the bell and his secretary appeared.

'Call the young woman who tried to commit suicide,' he said. 'The one who wrote the letter to the newspapers, saying that she was killing herself in order to put Slovenia on the map.'

'I don't want to see her. I've cut all my links with the outside world.'

It had been hard to say that in the lounge, with everyone else there. But the nurse hadn't been exactly discreet either, and had announced in a loud voice that her mother was waiting to see her, as if it were a matter of general interest.

She didn't want to see her mother; it would only upset both of them. It was best that her mother should think of her as dead. Veronika had always hated goodbyes.

The man disappeared whence he had come, and she went back to looking at the mountains. After a week, the sun had finally returned, something she had known would happen the previous night, because the moon had told her while she was playing the piano.

'No, that's crazy, I'm losing my grip. Planets don't talk, or only to self-styled astrologers. If the moon spoke to anyone, it was to that schizophrenic.'

The very moment she thought this, she noticed a sharp pain in her chest, and her arm went numb. Veronika felt her head spinning. A heart attack!

She entered a kind of euphoric state, as if death had freed her from the fear of dying. So, it was all over. She might still experience some pain, but what were five minutes of agony in exchange for an eternity of peace? The only possible response was to close her eyes: in films, the thing she most hated to see was dead people with staring eyes.

But the heart attack was different from what she had imagined; her breathing became laboured, and Veronika was horrified to realise that she was about to experience the worst of her fears: suffocation. She was going to die as if she were being buried alive, or had suddenly been plunged into the depths of the sea.

She stumbled, fell, felt a sharp blow on her face, continued making heroic efforts to breathe, but the air wouldn't go in. Worst of all, death did not come. She was entirely conscious of what was going on around her, she could still see colours and shapes, although she had difficulty in hearing what others were saying; the cries and exclamations seemed distant, as if coming from another world. Apart from this, everything else was real; the air wouldn't enter her lungs, it would simply not obey the commands of her lungs and her muscles, and still she did not lose consciousness.

She felt someone touch her and turn her over, but now she had lost control of her eye movements, and her eyes were flickering wildly, sending hundreds of different images to her brain, combining the feeling of suffocation with a sense of complete visual confusion.

After a while, the images became distant too, and just when the agony reached its peak, the air finally rushed into her lungs, making a tremendous noise that left everyone in the room paralysed with fear.

Veronika began to vomit copiously. Once the near-tragedy had passed, some of the mad people there began to laugh, and she felt humiliated, lost, paralysed.

A nurse came running in and gave her an injection in her arm.

'It's all right, calm down, it's over now.'

'I didn't die!' she started shouting, crawling towards the other patients, smearing the floor and the furniture with her vomit. 'I'm still in this bloody hospital, forced to live with you lot, living a thousand deaths every day, every night, and not one of you feels an ounce of pity for me.'

She rounded on the nurse, grabbed the syringe from his hand and threw it out into the garden.

'And what do you want? Why don't you just inject me with poison, since I'm already condemned to die? How can you be so heartless?'

Unable to control herself any longer, she sat down on the floor again and started crying uncontrollably, shouting, sobbing loudly, while some of the patients laughed and made remarks about her filthy clothes.

'Give her a sedative,' said a doctor, hurrying in. 'Get this situation under control.'

The nurse, however, was frozen to the spot. The doctor went out again and returned with two more male nurses and another syringe. The men grabbed the hysterical girl struggling in the middle of the room, while the doctor injected the last drop of sedative into a vein in her vomit-smeared arm.

She was in Dr Igor's consulting room, lying on an immaculate white bed with clean sheets on it.

He was listening to her heart. She was pretending that she was still asleep, but something inside her must have changed, judging by the doctor's muttered words:

'Don't you worry. In your state of health, you could live to be a hundred.'

Veronika opened her eyes. Someone had taken her clothes off. Who? Dr Igor? Did that mean he had seen her naked? Her brain wasn't working properly.

'What did you say?'

'I said not to worry.'

'No, you said I could live to be a hundred.'

The doctor went over to his desk.

'You said I could live to be a hundred,' Veronika repeated.

'Nothing is certain in medicine,' said Dr Igor, trying to cover up. 'Everything's possible.'

'How's my heart?'

'The same.'

She didn't need to hear any more. When faced with a serious case, doctors always say: 'You'll live to be a hundred', or 'There's nothing seriously wrong with you,' or 'You have the heart and blood pressure of a young girl,' or even 'We need to redo the tests.' They're probably afraid the patient will go berserk in the consulting room.

She tried to get up, but couldn't; the whole room started to turn.

'Just lie down for a bit longer, until you feel better. You're not bothering me.'

Oh good, thought Veronika. But what if I was?

Being an experienced physician, Dr Igor remained silent for some time, pretending to be reading the papers on his desk. When we're with another person, and they say nothing, the situation becomes irritating, tense, unbearable. Dr Igor was hoping that the girl would start talking so that he could collect more data for his thesis on madness and the cure he was developing.

But Veronika didn't say a word. 'She may still be suffering from a high level of Vitriol poisoning,' thought Dr Igor, and decided to break the silence, which was becoming tense, irritating, unbearable.

'So you like to play the piano,' he said, trying to sound as nonchalant as possible.

'And the mad enjoy it too. Yesterday there was a guy listening who was utterly transfixed.'

'Yes, Eduard. He mentioned to someone how much he'd enjoyed it. Who knows, he might start eating normally again.'

'A schizophrenic liking music? And he mentioned it to someone else?'

'Yes. And I imagine you have no idea what you're talking about.'

The doctor – who looked more like a patient, with his dyed black hair – was right. Veronika had often heard the word 'schizophrenic', but she had no idea what it meant.

'Is there a cure, then?' she asked, hoping to find out more about schizophrenics.

'It can be controlled. We still don't really know what goes on in the world of madness. Everything's still so new, and the treatments change every decade or so. A schizophrenic is a person who already has a natural tendency to absent himself from this world, until some factor, sometimes serious, sometimes superficial, depending on the individual circumstances, forces him to create his own reality. It can develop into a state of complete alienation, what we call catatonia, but people do occasionally recover, at least enough to allow the patient to work and lead a near-normal life. It all depends on one thing, environment.'

'You say they create their own reality,' said Veronika, 'but what is reality?'

'It's whatever the majority deems it to be. It's not necessarily the best or the most logical, but it's the one that has become adapted to the desires of society as a whole. You see this thing I've got round my neck?'

'You mean your tie?'

'Exactly. Your answer is the logical, coherent answer an absolutely normal person would give: it's a tie! A madman, however, would say that what I have round my neck is a ridiculous, useless bit of coloured cloth tied in a very complicated way, which makes it harder to get air into your lungs and difficult to turn your neck. I have to be careful when I'm anywhere near a fan, or I could be strangled by this bit of cloth.

'If a mad person were to ask me what this tie is for, I would have to say, absolutely nothing. It's not even purely decorative, since nowadays it's become a symbol of slavery, power, aloofness. The only really useful function a tie serves is the sense of relief when you get home and take it off; you feel as if you've freed yourself from something, though quite what you don't know.

'But does that sense of relief justify the existence of ties? No. Nevertheless, if I were to ask a madman and a normal person what this is, the sane person would say: a tie. It doesn't matter who's correct, what matters is who's right.'

'So just because I gave the right name to a bit of coloured cloth you conclude that I'm not mad.'

No, you're not mad, thought Dr Igor, who was an authority on the subject, with various diplomas hung on the walls of his consulting room. Attempting to take your own life was something proper to a human being; he knew a lot of people who were doing just that, and yet they lived outside the hospital, feigning innocence and normality, merely because they had not chosen the scandalous route of suicide. They were killing themselves gradually, poisoning themselves with what Dr Igor called Vitriol.

Vitriol was a toxic substance, whose symptoms he had identified in his conversations with the men and women he had met. Now he was writing a thesis on the subject, which he would submit to the Slovenian Academy of Sciences for their scrutiny. It was the most important step in the field of insanity since Dr Pinel had ordered that patients should be unshackled, astonishing the medical world with the idea that some of them might even be cured.

As with the libido – the chemical reaction responsible for sexual desire which Dr Freud had identified, but which no laboratory had ever managed to isolate – Vitriol was released by the human organism whenever a person found him or herself in a frightening situation, although it had yet to be picked up in any spectrographic tests. It was easily recognised, though, by its taste, which was neither sweet nor savoury – a bitter taste. Dr Igor, the as yet unrecognised discoverer of this fatal substance, had given it the name of a poison much favoured in the past by emperors, kings and lovers of all kinds whenever they needed to rid themselves of some obstructive person.

A golden age, the age of kings and emperors, when you could live and die romantically. The murderer would invite his or her victim to partake of a magnificent supper, the servant would pour them drinks served in two exquisite glasses, and one of the drinks would be laced with Vitriol. Imagine the excitement aroused by each gesture the victim made, picking up the glass, saying a few tender or aggressive words, drinking as if the glass contained some delicious beverage, giving his host one last startled look, then falling to the floor.

But this poison, which was now very expensive and difficult to obtain, had been replaced by more reliable methods of extermination – revolvers, bacteria, etc. Dr Igor, a natural romantic, had rescued this name from obscurity and given it to the disease of the soul he had managed to diagnose, and whose discovery would soon amaze the world.

It was odd that no one had ever described Vitriol as a mortal poison, although most of the people affected could identify its taste, and they referred to the process of poisoning as Bitterness. To a greater or lesser degree, everyone had some Bitterness in their organism, just as we are all carriers of the tuberculosis bacillus. But these two illnesses only attack when the patient is debilitated; in the case of Bitterness, the right conditions for the disease occur when the person becomes afraid of so-called 'reality'.

Certain people, in their eagerness to construct a world which no external threat can penetrate, build exaggeratedly high defences against the outside world, against new people, new places, different experiences, and leave their inner world stripped bare. It is there that Bitterness begins its irrevocable work.

The will was the main target of Bitterness (or Vitriol, as Dr Igor preferred to call it). The people attacked by this malaise began to lose all desire, and, within a few years, they became unable to leave their world, where they had spent enormous reserves of energy constructing high walls in order to make reality what they wanted it to be.

In order to avoid external attack, they had also deliberately limited internal growth. They continued going to work, watching television, having children, complaining about the traffic, but these things happened automatically, unaccompanied by any particular emotion, because, after all, everything was under control.

The great problem with poisoning by Bitterness was that the passions – hatred, love, despair, enthusiasm, curiosity – also ceased to manifest themselves. After a while, the embittered person felt no desire at all. They lacked the will either to live or to die, that was the problem.

That is why embittered people find heroes and madmen a perennial source of fascination, for they have no fear of life or death. Both heroes and madmen are indifferent to danger and will forge ahead regardless of what other people say. The madman committed suicide, the hero offered himself up to martyrdom in the name of a cause, but both would die, and the embittered would spend many nights and days remarking on the absurdity and the glory of both. It was the only moment when the embittered person had the energy to clamber up his defensive walls and peer over at the world outside, but then his hands and feet would grow tired and he would return to daily life.

The chronically embittered person only noticed his illness once a week, on Sunday afternoons. Then, with no work or routine to relieve the symptoms, he would feel that something was very wrong, since he found the peace of those endless afternoons infernal and felt only a keen sense of constant irritation.

Monday would arrive, however, and the embittered man would immediately forget his symptoms, although he would curse the fact that he never had time to rest and would complain that the weekends always passed far too quickly.

From the social point of view, the only advantage of the disease was that it had become the norm, and internment was no longer necessary, except in cases where the poisoning was so serious that the patient's behaviour began to affect others. Most embittered people, though, could continue to live outside, constituting no threat to society or to others, since, because of the high walls with which they had surrounded themselves, they were totally isolated from the world, even though they appeared to participate in it.

Dr Sigmund Freud had discovered the libido and a cure for the problems it caused, in the form of psychoanalysis. Apart from discovering the existence of Vitriol, Dr Igor needed to prove that a cure for it was also possible. He wanted to leave his mark on the history of medicine, although he had no illusions about the difficulties he would face when it came to publishing his ideas, for 'normal' people were contented with their lives and would never admit to the existence of such an illness, whilst the 'sick' fed a gigantic industry of mental hospitals, laboratories, congresses, etc.

'I know the world will not recognise my efforts,' he said to himself, proud of being misunderstood. After all, that was the price every genius had to pay.

'Is there anything wrong, doctor?' asked the girl. 'You seem to have drifted off into the world of your patients.'

Dr Igor ignored the disrespectful comment.

'You can go now,' he said.

Veronika didn't know if it was day or night. Dr Igor had the light on, but then he did every morning. It was only when she reached the corridor and saw the moon that she realised she had slept far longer than she had thought.

On the way to the ward, she noticed a framed photograph on the wall: it was of the main square in Ljubljana, before the statue of the poet Prešeren had been put up; it showed couples strolling, probably on a Sunday.

She looked at the date on the photograph: the summer of 1910.

The summer of 1910. There were all those people, whose children and grandchildren had already died, frozen in one particular moment of their lives. The women wore voluminous dresses and the men were all wearing hat, jacket, gaiters, tie (or that coloured piece of cloth as the mad call it) and carrying an umbrella under one arm.

And how hot would it have been then? The temperature must have been what it would be today in summer, thirty-five degrees in the shade. If an Englishman turned up in clothing more suited to the heat – in Bermuda shorts and shirtsleeves – what would those people think?

'He must be mad.'

She had understood perfectly what Dr Igor meant, just as she understood that, although she had always felt loved and protected, there had been one missing element that would have transformed that love into a blessing: she should have allowed herself to be a little madder.

Her parents would still have loved her, but, afraid of hurting them, she had not dared to pay the price of her dream, the dream that was buried in the depths of her memory, although sometimes it was awoken by a concert or by a beautiful record she happened to hear. Whenever her dream was awoken, though, the feeling of frustration was so intense that she immediately sent it back to sleep again.

Veronika had known since childhood that her true vocation was to be a pianist.

This was something she had felt ever since her first lesson, at twelve. Her teacher had recognised her talent too and had encouraged her to become a professional. However, whenever she had felt pleased about a competition she had just won and said to her mother that she intended giving up everything and dedicating herself to the piano, her mother would look at her fondly and say: 'No one makes a living playing the piano, my love.'

'But you were the one who wanted me to have lessons.'

'To develop your artistic gifts, that's all. A husband likes that kind of thing in a wife; he can show you off at parties. Forget about being a pianist, and go and study law, that's the profession of the future.'

Veronika did as her mother asked, sure that her mother had enough experience of life to understand reality. She finished her studies, went to university, got a good degree, but ended up working as a librarian.

'I should have been madder.' But, as doubtless happens with most people, she had found this out too late.

She was about to continue on her way, when someone took her by the arm. The powerful sedative was still flowing in her veins; that's why she didn't react when Eduard, the schizophrenic, delicately began to lead her in a different direction – towards the lounge.

✳

The moon was still new and Veronika had already sat down at the piano – in response to Eduard's silent request – when she heard a voice coming from the refectory, someone speaking with a foreign accent which Veronika could not remember having heard in Villete before.

'I don't want to play the piano just now, Eduard. I want to know what's going on in the world, what they're talking about over there, who that man is.'

Eduard smiled, perhaps not understanding a word she was saying, but she remembered what Dr Igor had said: schizophrenics could move in and out of their separate realities.

'I'm going to die,' she went on, hoping that her words were making sense to him. 'Today, death brushed my face with its wing and will probably be knocking at my door if not tomorrow, then soon afterwards. It's not a good idea for you to get used to listening to the piano every night.

'No one should let themselves get used to anything, Eduard. Look at me, I was beginning to enjoy the sun again, the mountains, even life's problems, I was beginning to accept that the meaninglessness of life was no one's fault but mine. I wanted to see the main square in Ljubljana again, to feel hatred and love, despair and tedium, all those simple, foolish things that make up everyday life, but which give pleasure to your existence. If one day I could get out of here, I would allow myself to be mad, because everyone is, indeed, the maddest are the ones who don't know they're mad, but keep repeating what others tell them to.

'But none of that's possible, do you see? In the same way, you can't spend the whole day waiting for night to come and for one of the patients to play the piano, because soon that will end. My world and yours are about to come to an end.'

She got up, tenderly touched the boy's face and then went to the refectory.

✳

When she opened the door, she came upon an unusual scene; the tables and chairs had been pushed back against the walls, forming a large central space. There, sitting on the floor, were the members of the Fraternity, listening to a man in a suit and tie.

'. . . then they invited Nasrudin, the great master of the Sufi tradition, to give a lecture,' he was saying.

When the door opened, everyone in the room looked at Veronika. The man in the suit turned to her.

'Sit down.'

She sat down on the floor, next to Mari, the white-haired woman who had been so aggressive on their first encounter. To Veronika's surprise, Mari gave her a welcoming smile.

The man in the suit went on:

'Nasrudin arranged to give a lecture at two o'clock in the afternoon, and it looked set to be a great success: the thousand seats were completely sold out and more than seven hundred people were left outside, watching the lecture on closed-circuit television.

'At two o'clock precisely, an assistant of Nasrudin's came in, saying that, for unavoidable reasons, the lecture would begin late. Some got up indignantly, asked for their money back and left. Even so, a lot of people remained both inside and outside the lecture hall.

'By four in the afternoon, the Sufi master had still not appeared and people gradually began to leave the place, picking up their money at the box office. The working day was coming to an end, it was time to go home. When it was six o'clock, the original one thousand seven hundred spectators had dwindled to less than a hundred.

'At that moment, Nasrudin came in. He appeared to be extremely drunk and began to flirt with a beautiful young woman sitting in the front row.

'Astonished, the people who had remained behind began to feel indignant. How could the man behave like that after making them wait four solid hours? There were some disapproving murmurs, but the

Sufi master ignored them. He went on, in a loud voice, to say how sexy the young woman was, and invited her to go with him to France.'

Some teacher, thought Veronika. Just as well I've never believed in such things.

'After cursing the people who were complaining, Nasrudin tried to get up, but fell heavily to the floor. Disgusted, more people decided to leave, saying it was pure charlatanism, that they would denounce the degrading spectacle to the press.

'Only nine people remained. As soon as the final group of outraged spectators had left, Nasrudin got up; he was completely sober, his eyes glowed, and he had about him an air of great authority and wisdom. "Those of you who stayed are the ones who will hear me," he said. "You have passed through the two hardest tests on the spiritual road: the patience to wait for the right moment and the courage not to be disappointed with what you encounter. It is you I will teach."

'And Nasrudin shared with them some of the Sufi techniques.'

The man paused and took a strange flute out of his pocket.

'Let's take a short break now, and then we'll do our meditation.'

The members of the group stood up. Veronika didn't know what to do.

'You get up too,' said Mari, grabbing her hand. 'We've got a five-minute break.'

'I'll leave, I don't want to be in the way.'

Mari led her to one corner.

'Haven't you learned anything, not even with the approach of death? Stop thinking all the time that you're in the way, that you're bothering the person next to you. If people don't like it, they can complain. And if they don't have the courage to complain, that's their problem.'

'That day, when I came over to you, I was doing something I'd never dared to do before.'

'And you allowed yourself to be cowed by a joke made by a mad person. Why didn't you just stick to your guns? What did you have to lose?'

'My dignity, by being where I wasn't welcome.'

'What's dignity? It's wanting everyone to think you're good, well-behaved, full of love for your fellow man. Have some respect for nature, watch a few films about animals and see how they fight for their own space. We all heartily approved of that slap of yours.'

Veronika did not have any more time to spend fighting for space, and so she changed the subject and asked who the man in the suit was.

'You're improving,' laughed Mari. 'You now ask questions without worrying about whether you're being indiscreet or not. He's a Sufi master.'

'What does Sufi mean?'

'Wool.'

Veronika didn't understand. Wool?

'Sufism is the spiritual tradition of the dervishes. Its teachers never strive to show how wise they are, and their disciples go into a trance by performing a kind of whirling dance.'

'What's the point of that?'

'I'm not quite sure, but our group has resolved to investigate all prohibited experiences. All my life, the government taught us that the only purpose of searching for a spiritual meaning to life was to make people forget about their real problems. Now tell me this: wouldn't you say that trying to understand life was a real problem?'

Yes, it was, although Veronika wasn't sure any more what the word 'real' meant.

The man in the suit – a Sufi master, according to Mari – asked them all to sit in a circle. From a vase he removed all the flowers but one, a single red rose, and this he placed in the centre of the group.

'You see how far we've come,' said Veronika to Mari. 'Some madman decided it was possible to grow flowers in winter, and nowadays, throughout Europe, we have roses all year round. Do you think even a Sufi master, with all his knowledge, could do that?'

Mari seemed to guess her thoughts.

'Save your criticisms for later.'

'I'll try to, although all I have is the present, and a very brief one too it seems.'

'That's all anyone has, and it's always very brief, although, of course, some people believe they have a past where they can accumulate things and a future where they will accumulate still more. By the way, speaking of the present moment, do you masturbate a lot?'

Although still under the effects of the sedative she had been given, Veronika was immediately reminded of the first words she had heard in Villete.

'When I was first brought here and was still full of tubes from the artificial respirator, I clearly heard someone asking me if I wanted to be masturbated. What *is* all that about? Why do you people spend your time thinking about such things?'

'It's the same outside; it's just that here we don't need to hide the fact.'

'Was it you who asked me?'

'No, but I think that, as far as pleasure is concerned, you do need to discover how far you can go. Next time, with a little patience, you might be able to take your partner there too, instead of waiting to be guided by him. Even if you have only got two days to live, I don't think you should leave this life without knowing how far you can go.'

'Only if my partner is the schizophrenic who's right now waiting to hear me play the piano again.'

'He's certainly nice-looking.'

The man in the suit interrupted their conversation with a call for silence. He told everyone to concentrate on the rose and to empty their minds.

✳

'The thoughts will come back, but try to push them to one side. You have two choices: to control your mind or to let your mind control you. You're already familiar with the latter experience, allowing yourself to be swept along by fears, neuroses, insecurity, for we all have self-destructive tendencies.

'Don't confuse madness with a loss of control. Remember that in the Sufi tradition, the master – Nasrudin – is the one everyone calls the madman. And it is precisely because his fellow citizens consider him mad that Nasrudin can say whatever he thinks and do whatever he wants. So it was with court jesters in the Middle Ages; they could alert the king to dangers that the ministers would not dare to comment upon, because they were afraid of losing their positions.

'That's how it should be with you; stay mad, but behave like normal people. Run the risk of being different, but learn to do so without attracting attention. Concentrate on this flower and allow the real "I" to reveal itself.'

'What is the real "I"?' asked Veronika. Perhaps everyone else there knew, but what did it matter: she must learn to care less about annoying others.

The man seemed surprised by the interruption, but he answered her question.

'It's what you are, not what others make of you.'

Veronika decided to do the exercise, concentrating as hard as she could on discovering who she was. During those days in Villete, she had felt things she had never before felt with such intensity – hatred, love, fear, curiosity, a desire to live. Perhaps Mari was right: did she really know what it meant to have an orgasm? Or had she only gone as far as men had wanted to take her?

The man started playing the flute. Gradually the music calmed her soul, and she managed to concentrate on the rose. It might have been the effect of the sedative, but the fact was that since she had left Dr Igor's consulting room, she had felt extremely well.

She knew she was going to die soon, why be afraid? It wouldn't help at all, it wouldn't avoid the fatal heart attack; the best plan would be to enjoy the days and hours that remained to her, doing things she had never done before.

The music was soft, and the dim light in the refectory created an almost religious atmosphere. Religion: why didn't she try going deep inside herself and see what remained of her beliefs and her faith?

The music, however, was leading her elsewhere: empty your mind, stop thinking about anything, simply BE. Veronika gave herself up to the experience; she stared at the rose, saw who she was, liked what she saw and felt only regret that she had been so hasty.

W hen the meditation was over and the Sufi master had left, Mari stayed on for a while in the refectory, talking to the other members of the Fraternity. Veronika said she was tired and left at once; after all, the sedative she had been given that morning had been strong enough to knock out a horse, and yet she had still had strength enough to remain awake all that time.

'That's youth for you; it sets its own limits without even asking if the body can take it. Yet the body always does.'

Mari wasn't tired; she had slept until late, then decided to go for a walk in Ljubljana – Dr Igor required that the members of the Fraternity left Villete every day. She had gone to the cinema and fallen asleep again in her seat, watching a deeply boring film about marital conflict. Was there no other subject? Why always repeat the same stories – husband with lover, husband with wife and sick child, husband with wife, lover and sick child? There were more important things in the world to talk about.

The conversation in the refectory did not last long; the meditation had left the group members feeling relaxed and they were all ready to go back to their wards, apart from Mari, who instead went out into the garden. On the way, she passed the lounge and saw that the young woman had not yet managed to get to bed. She was playing for

Eduard the schizophrenic, who had perhaps been waiting all that time by the piano. Like children, the mad will not budge until their desires have been satisfied.

The air was icy. Mari came back in, grabbed a coat and went out again. Outside, far from the eyes of everyone, she lit a cigarette. She smoked slowly and guiltlessly, thinking about the young woman, the piano music she could hear and life outside the walls of Villete, which was becoming unbearably difficult for everyone.

In Mari's view, this difficulty was due not to chaos or disorganisation or anarchy, but to an excess of order. Society had more and more rules, and laws that contradicted the rules, and new rules that contradicted the laws. People felt too frightened to take even a step outside the invisible regulations that guided everyone's lives.

Mari knew what she was talking about; until her illness had brought her to Villete, she had spent forty years of her life working as a lawyer. She had lost her innocent vision of Justice early on in her career, and had come to understand that the laws had not been created to resolve problems, but in order to prolong quarrels indefinitely.

It was a shame that Allah, Jehovah, God – it didn't matter what name you gave him – did not live in the world today, because if He did, we would still be in Paradise, while He would be mired in appeals, requests, demands, injunctions, preliminary verdicts, and would have to justify to innumerable tribunals His decision to expel Adam and Eve from Paradise for breaking an arbitrary rule with no foundation in law: Of the tree of the knowledge of good and evil thou shalt not eat.

If He had not wanted that to happen, why did He put the tree in the midst of the garden and not outside the walls of Paradise? If she were called upon to defend the couple, Mari would undoubtedly accuse God of administrative negligence, because, as well as planting the tree in the wrong place, He had failed to surround it with warnings and barriers, had failed to adopt even minimal security arrangements, and had thus exposed everyone to danger.

Mari could also accuse him of inducement to criminal activity, for He had pointed out to Adam and Eve the exact place where the tree was to be found. If He had said nothing, generation upon generation would have passed on this earth without anyone taking the slightest interest in the forbidden fruit, since the tree was presumably in a forest full of similar trees, and therefore of no particular value.

But God had proceeded quite differently. He had devised a rule and then found a way of persuading someone to break it, merely in order to invent Punishment. He knew that Adam and Eve would become bored with perfection and would, sooner or later, test His patience. He set a trap, perhaps because He, Almighty God, was also bored with everything going so smoothly: if Eve had not eaten the apple, nothing of any interest would have happened in the last few billion years.

When the law was broken, God – the Omnipotent Judge – even pretended to pursue them, as if He did not already know every possible hiding place. With the angels looking on, amused by the game (life must have been very dreary for them since Lucifer left Heaven), He began to walk about the garden. Mari thought what a wonderful scene in a suspense movie that episode from the Bible would make: God's footsteps, the couple exchanging frightened glances, the feet suddenly stopping by their hiding place.

'Where art thou?' asked God.

'I heard thy voice in the garden, and I was afraid, because I was naked; and I hid myself,' Adam replied, without knowing that by making this statement, he had confessed himself guilty of a crime.

So, by means of a simple trick, pretending not to know where Adam was nor why he had run away, God got what He wanted. Even so, in order to leave no doubts amongst the audience of angels who were intently watching the episode, He decided to go further.

'Who told thee that thou was naked?' asked God, knowing that this question could have only one possible response: because I ate of the tree of the knowledge of good and evil.

With that question, God demonstrated to his angels that He was a just god, and that his condemnation of the couple was based on solid evidence. From then on, it wasn't a matter of whether it was the woman's fault or of their asking for forgiveness: God needed an example, so that no other being, earthly or heavenly, would ever again dare to go against His decisions.

God expelled the couple, and their children paid for the crime too (as still happens with the children of criminals) and thus the judiciary system was invented: the law, the transgression of the law (no matter how illogical or absurd), judgement (in which the more experienced triumphs over the ingenuous) and punishment.

Since all of humanity was condemned with no right of appeal, humankind decided to create a defence mechanism, against the eventuality of God deciding to wield His arbitrary power again. However, millennia of study resulted in so many legal measures that, ultimately, we went too far, and justice became a tangle of clauses, jurisprudence and contradictory texts that no one could quite understand.

So much so that, when God had a change of heart and sent His Son to save the world, what happened? He fell into the hands of the very justice He had invented.

The tangle of laws created such confusion that the Son ended up nailed to a cross. It was no simple trial; he was passed from Ananias to Caiphas, from the priest to Pilate, who alleged that there were insufficient laws in the Roman code. From Pilate to Herod, who, in turn, alleged that the Jewish code did not permit the death sentence. From Herod back to Pilate again, who, looking for a way out, offered the people a juridical deal: he had the Son beaten and then displayed to the people with his wounds, but it didn't work.

Like prosecutors nowadays, Pilate decided to save himself at the expense of the condemned man: he offered to exchange Jesus for Barabbas, knowing that, by then, justice had become a grand spectacle requiring a denouement: the death of the prisoner.

Finally, Pilate used the article of law that gave the judge, and not the person being judged, the benefit of the doubt. He washed his hands, which means: 'I'm not quite sure either way.' It was just another ruse to preserve the Roman juridical system without injuring relations with local magistrates, and even transferring the weight of the decision onto the people, just in case the sentence should cause any problems, and some inspector from the imperial capital came to see for himself what was going on.

Justice. Law. Although both were vital in order to protect the innocent, they did not always work to everyone's liking. Mari was glad to be far from all that confusion, although tonight, listening to the piano, she was not quite so sure that Villete was the right place for her.

'If I were to decide once and for all to leave here, I wouldn't go back to the law. I'm not going to spend my time with mad people who think they're normal and important, but whose sole function in life is to make everything more difficult for others. I'll be a seamstress, an embroiderer, I'll sell fruit outside the Municipal Theatre. I've already made my contribution to the futile madness of the law.'

In Villete you were allowed to smoke, but not to stub your cigarette out on the lawn. With great pleasure, she did what was forbidden, because the great advantage of being there was not having to respect the rules and not even having to put up with any major consequences if you broke them.

She went over to the door. The guard – there was always a guard there, after all, that was the law – nodded to her and opened the door.

'I'm not going out,' she said.

'Lovely piano music,' said the guard. 'I've listened to it nearly every night.'

'It won't last much longer,' she said and walked rapidly away so as not to have to explain.

She remembered what she had read in the young girl's eyes the moment she had come into the refectory: fear.

Fear. Veronika might feel insecurity, shyness, shame, constraint, but why fear? That was only justifiable when confronted by a real threat: ferocious animals, armed attackers, earthquakes, but not a group of people gathered together in a refectory.

'But human beings are like that,' she said. 'We've replaced nearly all our emotions with fear.'

And Mari knew what she was talking about, because that was what had brought her to Villete: panic attacks.

In her room Mari had a veritable library of articles on the subject. Now people talked about it openly, and she had recently seen a German television programme in which people discussed their experiences. In that same programme, a survey revealed that a significant percentage of the population suffers from panic attacks, although most of those affected tried to hide the symptoms, for fear of being considered mad.

But at the time when Mari had her first attack, none of this was known. 'It was absolute hell,' she thought, lighting another cigarette.

The piano was still playing, the girl seemed to have enough energy to play all night.

A lot of the inmates had been affected by the young woman's arrival in the hospital, Mari amongst them. At first, she had tried to avoid her, afraid to awaken the young woman's desire to live; since there was no escape, it was better that she should keep on wanting to die. Dr Igor had let it be known that, even though she would continue to be given daily injections, her physical condition would visibly deteriorate and there would be no way of saving her.

The inmates had understood the message and kept their distance from the condemned woman. However, without anyone knowing quite why, Veronika had begun fighting for her life, and the only two people who approached her were Zedka, who would be leaving tomorrow and didn't talk that much anyway, and Eduard.

Mari needed to have a word with Eduard; he always respected her opinions. Did he not realise he was drawing Veronika back into the world, and that that was the worst thing he could do to someone with no hope of salvation?

She considered a thousand ways of explaining the situation to him, but all of them would only make him feel guilty, and that she would never do. Mari thought a little and decided to let things run their normal course. She was no longer a lawyer and she did not want to set a bad example by creating new behaviour laws in a place where anarchy should reign.

But the presence of the young woman had touched a lot of people there, and some were ready to rethink their lives. At one of the meetings with the Fraternity, someone had tried to explain what was happening. Deaths in Villete tended to happen suddenly, without giving anyone time to think about it, or after a long illness, when death is always a blessing.

The young woman's case, though, was dramatic because she was so young and because she now wanted to live again, something they all knew to be impossible. Some people asked themselves 'What if that happened to me? I do have a chance to live. Am I making good use of it?'

Some were not bothered with finding an answer; they had long ago given up and now formed part of a world in which neither life nor death, space or time existed. Others, however, were being forced to think hard, and Mari was one of them.

Veronika stopped playing for a moment and looked out at Mari in the garden. She was wearing only a light jacket against the cold night air; did she want to die?

'No, I was the one who wanted to die.'

She turned back to the piano. In the last days of her life, she had finally realised her grand dream: to play with heart and soul, for as long as she wanted and whenever the mood took her. It didn't matter to her that her only audience was a young schizophrenic; he seemed to understand the music, and that was what mattered.

Mari had never wanted to kill herself. On the contrary, five years before, in the same cinema she had visited today, she had watched, horrified, a film about poverty in El Salvador and thought how important her life was. At that time – with her children grown up and making their way in their own professions – she had decided to give up the tedious, unending job of being a lawyer in order to dedicate the rest of her days to working for some humanitarian organisation. The rumours of civil war in the country were growing all the time, but Mari didn't believe them. It was impossible that, at the end of the twentieth century, the European Community would allow a new war at their gates.

On the other side of the world, however, there was no shortage of tragedies, and one of those tragedies was El Salvador's, where starving children were forced to live on the streets and turn to prostitution.

'It's terrible,' she said to her husband, who was sitting in the seat next to her.

He nodded.

Mari had been putting off the decision for a long time, but perhaps now was the moment to talk to him. They had been given all the good things that life could possibly offer them: a home, work, good children, modest comforts, interests and culture. Why not do something for others for a change? Mari had contacts in the Red

Cross and she knew that volunteers were desperately needed in many parts of the world.

She was tired of struggling with bureaucracy and law suits, unable to help people who had spent years of their lives trying to resolve problems not of their own making. Working with the Red Cross, though, she would see immediate results.

She decided that, when they left the cinema, she would invite her husband for a coffee so that they could discuss the idea.

Just as a Salvadorean government official appeared on screen to offer a bored excuse for some new injustice, Mari suddenly noticed her heart beating faster.

She told herself it was nothing. Perhaps the stuffy atmosphere in the cinema was getting to her; if the symptoms persisted she would go out to the foyer to get a breath of fresh air.

But events took on their own momentum; her heart began beating faster and faster, and she broke out in a cold sweat.

She felt afraid and tried hard to concentrate on the film, in an attempt to dispel any negative thoughts, but realised she could no longer follow what was happening on the screen. Mari could see the images and the subtitles, but she seemed to have entered a completely different reality, where everything going on around her seemed strange and out of kilter, as if taking place in a world she did not know.

'I don't feel well,' she said to her husband.

She had put off making that remark as long as possible, because it meant admitting that there was something wrong, but she could not hold out any longer.

'Let's go outside,' he said.

When he took his wife's hand to help her to her feet, he noticed it was ice cold.

'I don't think I can get that far. Please, tell me what's happening to me.'

Her husband felt afraid too. Sweat was pouring down Mari's face and there was a strange light in her eyes.

'Keep calm. I'll go out and call a doctor.'

She was gripped by despair. What he said made absolute sense, but everything – the cinema, the semi-darkness, the people sitting side by side staring up at the brilliant screen – all of it seemed so threatening. She was certain she was alive, she could even touch the life around her as if it were something solid. And that had never happened to her before.

'On no account leave me here alone. I'll get up and go out with you, but take it slowly.'

They both made their apologies to the people in the same row as them, and began walking to the exit at the back of the cinema. Mari's heart was now beating furiously, and she was certain, absolutely certain, that she would never get out of that place. Everything she did, every gesture she made – placing one foot in front of the other, saying 'excuse me', holding on to her husband's arm, breathing in and out – seemed terrifyingly conscious and deliberate.

She had never felt so frightened in her life.

'I'm going to die right here in this cinema.'

And she was convinced she knew what was happening, because many years before, a friend of hers had died in a cinema of a cerebral aneurism.

Cerebral aneurisms are like time bombs. They are tiny varicose veins that form along the arteries – like the ballooning you get on worn tyres – and they can remain there undetected during a whole lifetime. No one knows if they've got an aneurism, unless it's discovered accidentally, for example, after a brain scan carried out for other reasons, or at the moment when it actually ruptures, flooding everything with blood, leaving the person in an immediate state of coma, usually followed shortly by death.

While she was walking down the aisle of the dark cinema, Mari remembered the friend she had lost. The strangest thing, though, was the effect this ruptured aneurism was having on her perception. She seemed to have been transported to a different planet, seeing each familiar thing as if for the first time.

And then there was the terrifying, inexplicable fear, the sheer panic of being alone on that other planet. Death.

'I must stop thinking. I'll pretend that everything's all right and then everything will be.'

She tried to act naturally and, for a few seconds, the sense of oddness diminished. The two minutes that elapsed between first feeling the palpitations and reaching the exit with her husband were the most terrifying two minutes of her life.

When they reached the brightly-lit foyer, however, everything seemed to start up again. The colours were so garish, the noises from the street seemed to rush in on her from all sides, and everything seemed utterly unreal. She started to notice certain details for the first time, for example, the clarity of vision that covers only the small area on which we fix our gaze, while the rest remains completely unfocused.

There was more. She knew that everything she could see around her was just a scene created by electrical impulses inside her brain, using light impulses that passed through a gelatinous organ called the eye.

No, she must stop thinking. That way madness lay.

By then, her fear of an aneurism had passed; she had managed to get out of the cinema and was still alive. The friend who had died, on the other hand, never even had time to leave her seat.

'I'll call an ambulance,' said her husband, when he saw his wife's ashen face and bloodless lips.

'Call a taxi,' she said, hearing the sounds leaving her mouth, conscious of the vibration of each vocal cord.

Going to hospital would mean accepting that she really was seriously ill and Mari was determined to do her utmost to restore everything to normality.

They left the foyer, and the icy cold air seemed to have a positive effect; Mari recovered some control over herself, although the inexplicable feelings of panic and terror persisted. While her husband was desperately trying to find a taxi, which were scarce at that time of day, she sat down on the kerb and tried not to look at her surroundings: the children playing, the buses passing, the music coming from a nearby funfair, all seemed absolutely surreal, frightening, alien.

Finally, a taxi appeared.

'To the hospital,' said her husband, helping his wife in.

'Please, let's just go home,' she said. She didn't want any more strange places, she was desperately in need of familiar, ordinary things that might diminish the fear she was feeling.

While the taxi was driving them home, her heart rate gradually slowed and her temperature began to return to normal.

'I'm beginning to feel better,' she said to her husband. 'It must have been something I ate.'

When they reached home, the world again seemed exactly as it had been since her childhood. When she saw her husband go over to the phone, she asked him what he was doing.

'I'm going to call a doctor.'

'There's no need. Look at me, I'm fine.'

The colour had returned to her cheeks, her heart was beating normally and the uncontrollable fear had vanished.

Mari slept heavily that night and woke convinced that someone must have put some drug in the coffee they had drunk before they went into the cinema. It was a dangerous prank, and she was fully prepared, at the end of the afternoon, to call the prosecutor and go to the bar to try and find the person responsible.

She went to work, read through several pending law suits and tried to occupy herself with various other tasks, for the experience of the previous day had left a residue of fear, and she wanted to prove to herself that it would never happen again.

She discussed the film on El Salvador with one of her colleagues and mentioned in passing that she was fed up with doing the same thing every day.

'Perhaps it's time I retired.'

'You're one of the best lawyers we've got,' said the colleague. 'Besides, law is one of the few professions where age is in your favour. Why not take a long holiday instead? I'm sure you'd come back to work with renewed energy.'

'I want to do something completely different with my life. I want to have an adventure, help other people, do something I've never done before.'

The conversation ended there. She went down to the square, had lunch in a more expensive restaurant than the one she normally went to, and returned to the office early. That moment marked the beginning of her withdrawal.

The rest of the employees had still not come back, and Mari took the opportunity to look over the work still on her desk. She opened the drawer to take out the pencil which she always kept in the same place and she couldn't find it. For a fraction of a second, it occurred to her that her failure to put the pencil back in its proper place was an indication that she was perhaps behaving oddly.

That was enough to make her heart start pounding again, and the terror of the previous night returned in force.

Mari was frozen to the spot. The sun was coming in through the shutters, lending a brighter, more aggressive tone to everything about her, but she again had the feeling that she was about to die at any minute. It was all so strange; what was she doing in that office?

'I don't believe in you, God, but please, help me.'

Again she broke out in a cold sweat and realised that she was unable to control her fear. If someone came in at that moment, they would notice her frightened eyes and she would be lost.

'Cold air.'

The cold air had made her feel better the previous night, but how could she get as far as the street? Once more she was noticing each detail of what was happening to her – her breathing rate (there were moments when she felt that if she did not make a special effort to inhale and exhale, her body would be incapable of doing so itself), the movement of her head (the images succeeded each other as if there were television cameras whirring inside it), her heart beating faster and faster, her body bathed in a cold, sticky sweat.

And then the terror, an awful, inexplicable fear of doing anything, of taking a single step, of leaving the chair she was sitting in.

'It will pass.'

It had passed last time, but now she was at work, what could she do? She looked at the clock and it seemed to her an absurd mechanism, two needles turning on the same axis, indicating a measurement of time that no one had ever explained: why twelve and not ten, like all our other measurements?

'I mustn't think about these things, they make me crazy.'

Crazy. Perhaps that was the right word to describe what was wrong with her. Summoning all her willpower, she got to her feet and made her way to the toilets. Fortunately, the office was still empty and, in a minute that seemed to last an eternity, she managed to reach them. She splashed her face with water, and the feeling of strangeness diminished, although the fear remained.

'It will pass,' she said to herself. 'Yesterday it did.'

She remembered that, the day before, the whole thing had lasted about thirty minutes. She locked herself in one of the toilets, sat on the toilet seat and put her head between her knees. That position, however, seemed only to amplify the sound of her heart beating and Mari immediately sat up again.

'It will pass.'

She stayed there, thinking that she no longer knew who she was, that she was hopelessly lost. She heard the sound of people coming in and out of the toilets, taps being turned on and off, pointless conversations about banal subjects. More than once someone tried to open the door of the cubicle where she was sitting, but she said something in a murmur and no one insisted. The noise of toilets flushing was like some horrendous force of nature, capable of demolishing an entire building and sweeping everyone down into hell.

But, as she had foreseen, the fear passed away and her heartbeat returned to normal. It was just as well that her secretary was incompetent enough not even to notice her absence, otherwise the whole office would have been in the toilets asking if she was all right.

When she saw that she had regained control of herself, Mari opened the cubicle door, again splashed her face with water for a long time and went back to the office.

'You haven't got any make-up on,' said a trainee. 'Do you want to borrow some of mine?'

Mari didn't even bother to reply. She went into the office, picked up her handbag and her personal belongings, and told her secretary that she would be spending the rest of the day at home.

'But you've got loads of appointments,' protested her secretary.

'You don't give orders, you receive them. Do exactly as I say, and cancel the appointments.'

The secretary stared at this woman with whom she had been working for nearly three years, and who had never once been rude to her before. Something must be seriously wrong with her, perhaps someone had told her that her husband was at home with his lover, and she wanted to catch them in *flagrante*.

'She's a good lawyer, she knows what she's doing,' said the girl to herself. Doubtless tomorrow she would come and apologise to her.

There was no tomorrow. That night, Mari had a long conversation with her husband and described all the symptoms she had experienced. Together, they reached the conclusion that the palpitations, the cold sweats, the feelings of displacement, impotence, lack of control, could all be summed up in one word: fear. Together, husband and wife pondered what was happening. He thought it might be a brain tumour, but he didn't say anything. She thought she was having premonitions of some terrible event, but she didn't say anything either. They tried to find some common ground for discussion, like logical, reasonable, mature people.

'Perhaps you'd better have some tests done.'

Mari agreed, on one condition, that no one, not even their children, should know anything about it.

The next day she applied for and was given thirty days' unpaid leave from the office. Her husband thought of taking her to Austria where there were many eminent specialists in disorders of the brain, but she refused to leave the house; the attacks were becoming more frequent and lasted longer.

With great difficulty, with Mari dosed up on tranquillisers, the two of them managed to get as far as a hospital in Ljubljana where Mari underwent a vast range of tests. Nothing unusual was found, not even an aneurism – a source of consolation to Mari for the rest of her life.

The panic attacks continued however. While her husband did the shopping and the cooking, Mari obsessively cleaned the house every day, just to keep her mind fixed on other things. She started reading all the psychiatry books she could find, only immediately to put them down again because she seemed to recognise her own malaise in each of the illnesses they described.

The worst of it was that, although the attacks were no longer a novelty, she still felt the same intense fear and sense of alienation from reality, the same loss of self-control. In addition, she started to feel guilty about her husband, obliged to do his own job as well as all the housework, cleaning apart.

As time passed, and the situation remained unresolved, Mari began to feel and express a deep irritation. The slightest thing made her lose her temper and start shouting, then sob hysterically.

*

After her thirty days' leave was over, one of Mari's colleagues turned up at the house. He had phoned every day, but Mari either didn't answer the phone or else asked her husband to say she was busy. That afternoon, he simply stood there ringing the bell until she opened the front door.

Mari had had a quiet morning. She made some tea and they talked about the office, and he asked her when she would be coming back to work.

'Never.'

He remembered their conversation about El Salvador.

'You've always worked hard, and you have the right to choose what you want to do,' he said, with no rancour in his voice. 'But I think that, in cases such as these, work is the best therapy. Do some travelling, see the world, go wherever you think you might be useful, but the doors of the office are always open, awaiting your return.'

When she heard this, Mari burst into tears, which she often did now, with great ease.

Her colleague waited for her to calm down. Like a good lawyer, he didn't ask anything; he knew he had more chance of getting a reply to his silence than to any question.

And so it was. Mari told him the whole story, from what had happened in the cinema to her recent hysterical attacks on her husband, who had given her so much support.

'I'm mad,' she said.

'Possibly,' he replied, with an all-knowing air, but with real tenderness in his voice. 'In that case, you have two options: either get some treatment or continue being ill.'

'There isn't any treatment for what I'm feeling. I'm still in full possession of all my mental faculties and I'm worried because this situation has gone on now for such a long time. I don't have any of the classic symptoms of madness, like withdrawal from reality, apathy or uncontrolled aggression, just fear.'

'That's what all mad people say, that they're perfectly normal.'

The two of them laughed and she made some more tea. They talked about the weather, the success of Slovenian independence, the growing tensions between Croatia and Yugoslavia. Mari watched TV all day and was very well informed.

Before saying goodbye, her colleague touched on the subject again.

'They've just opened a new hospital in the city,' he said, 'backed by foreign money and offering first-class treatment.'

'Treatment for what?'

'Imbalances, shall we say. And excessive fear is definitely an imbalance.'

Mari promised to think about it, but she still made no real decision. She continued to have panic attacks for another month, until she realised that not only her personal life but her marriage was on the point of collapse. Again she asked for some tranquillisers and again she managed to set foot outside the house, for only the second time in sixty days.

She took a taxi and went to the new hospital. On the way, the driver asked if she was going to visit someone.

'They say it's very comfortable, but apparently they've got some real nutters in there too, and part of the treatment includes electric shocks.'

'I'm going to visit someone,' said Mari.

It took only an hour of conversation for Mari's two months of suffering to come to an end. The director of the hospital – a tall man with dyed hair, who answered to the name of Dr Igor – explained that it was merely a panic disorder, a recently recognised illness in the annals of world psychiatry.

'That doesn't mean it's a new illness,' he explained, taking care to make himself clear.

'What happens is that the people affected by it tend to hide, afraid they'll be mistaken for mad people. It's just a chemical imbalance in the body, as is depression.'

Dr Igor wrote her a prescription and told her to go back home.

'I don't want to go back now,' said Mari. 'Even after all you've told me, I won't have the courage to go out into the street. My marriage has become a hell, and my husband needs time to recover from these months he's spent looking after me.'

As always happened in such cases – because the share-holders wanted to keep the hospital working at full capacity – Dr Igor accepted her as a patient, although making it absolutely clear that it wasn't necessary.

Mari received the necessary medication, along with the appropriate psychiatric treatment, and the symptoms diminished and finally disappeared altogether.

During that time, however, the story of her internment in the hospital went the rounds of the small city of Ljubljana. Her colleague, a friend of many years, and companion of who knows how many moments of joy and trepidation, came to visit her in Villete. He complimented her on her courage in following his advice and getting help, but he then went on to explain the real reason for his visit:

'Perhaps it really is time you retired.'

Mari knew what lay behind those words: no one was going to entrust their affairs to a lawyer who had been a mental patient.

'You said that work was the best therapy. I need to come back, even if only for a short time.'

She waited for a response, but he said nothing. Mari went on:

'You were the one who suggested I get treatment. When I was considering retirement, my idea was to leave on a high note, fulfilled, having made a free, spontaneous decision. I don't want to leave my job just like that, defeated. At least give me a chance to win back my self-esteem, and then I'll ask to retire.'

The lawyer cleared his throat.

'I suggested you get treatment, I didn't say anything about going into hospital.'

'But it was a question of survival. I was too afraid to go out into the street, my marriage was falling apart.'

Mari knew she was wasting her words. Nothing she could say would persuade him; after all, it was the prestige of the office that was at risk. Even so, she tried once more.

'Inside here, I've lived with two sorts of people: those who have no chance of ever going back into society and those who are completely cured, but who prefer to pretend to be mad rather than face up to life's responsibilities. I want and need to learn to like myself again, I have to convince myself that I'm capable of making my own decisions. I can't be pushed into decisions not of my own making.'

'We're allowed to make a lot of mistakes in our lives,' said her colleague, 'except the mistake that destroys us.'

There was no point in continuing the conversation; in his opinion, Mari had committed a fatal error.

Two days later, she received a visit from another lawyer, this time from a different practice, her now ex-colleagues' greatest rival. Mari cheered up; perhaps he knew she was free to take up a new post, and there was a chance she could regain her place in the world.

The lawyer came into the visiting room, sat down opposite her, smiled, asked if she was feeling better and then took various papers out of his briefcase.

'I'm here at your husband's request,' he said.

'This is an application for divorce. Obviously, though, he'll continue to pay all your hospital bills for as long as you remain in here.'

This time Mari did not attempt to argue. She signed everything, even though she knew that, in accordance with the law she had studied and practised, she could prolong the quarrel indefinitely. She then went straight to see Dr Igor and told him that her symptoms had returned.

Dr Igor knew she was lying, but he nevertheless extended her internment for an indefinite period.

V eronika decided she would have to go to bed, but Eduard was
still standing by the piano.

'I'm tired, Eduard. I need to sleep.'

She would like to continue playing for him, dredging up from
her anaesthetised memory all the sonatas, requiems and adagios
she used to know, because he knew how to admire without
appearing to demand anything of her. But her body could take no
more.

He was so good-looking. If only he would take one step outside his
world and see her as a woman, then her last nights on this earth
might be the most beautiful of her entire life: Eduard was the only
one capable of understanding that Veronika was an artist. Through
the pure emotion of a sonata or a minuet she had forged a bond with
this man such as she had never known with anyone else.

Eduard was the ideal man, sensitive, educated; a man who had
destroyed an indifferent world in order to recreate it again in his
head, this time with new colours, new characters, new stories. And
this new world included a woman, a piano and a moon that was
continuing to grow.

'I could fall in love right now and give everything I have to you,'
she said, knowing that he couldn't understand her. 'All you ask from
me is a little music, but I am much more than I ever thought I was,

and I would like to share other things with you that I have only just begun to understand.'

Eduard smiled. Had he understood? Veronika felt afraid – all the manuals of good behaviour say that you should never speak of love so directly, and never to a man you barely know. But she decided to continue, because she had nothing to lose.

'You're the only man on the face of the Earth with whom I could fall in love, Eduard, for the simple reason that, when I die, you will not miss me. I don't know what a schizophrenic feels, but I'm sure they never miss anyone.

'Perhaps, to begin with, you'll miss the fact that there's no more night music, but the moon will still rise, there'll be someone willing to play sonatas for you, especially in a hospital, where each and every one of us is a "lunatic".'

She didn't quite know what the relationship was between mad people and the moon, but it must be a strong one, if they used a word like that to describe the mad.

'And I won't miss you either, Eduard, because I will be dead, far from here. And since I'm not afraid of losing you, I don't care what you think or don't think about me. Tonight I played for you like a woman in love. It was wonderful. It was the best moment of my entire life.'

She looked at Mari outside in the garden. She remembered her words. And again she looked at the man standing in front of her.

Veronika took off her sweater and moved closer to Eduard. If she was going to do something, let it be now. Mari would put up with the cold out there for a long time and only then would she come back in.

He stepped back. The question in his eyes was this: when was she going to play the piano again? When would she play a new piece of music to fill his soul with the same colour, pain, suffering and joy of those mad composers who had leapt the generations with their work?

'The woman outside told me to masturbate and to find out how far I could go. Could I really go farther than I've ever been before?'

She took his hand and tried to pull him towards the sofa, but Eduard politely declined. He preferred to remain standing where he was, beside the piano, waiting patiently for her to play again.

Veronika was disconcerted at first and then realised that she had nothing to lose. She was dead, what was the point of continuing to feed the fears or preconceptions that had always limited her life? She took off her blouse, her trousers, her bra, her pants, and stood before him naked.

Eduard laughed. She didn't know why, she merely noted that he had laughed. Delicately, she took his hand and placed it on her genitals; his hand remained there, immobile. Veronika gave up the idea and removed his hand.

Something was exciting her far more than any physical contact with this man: the fact that she could do whatever she wanted, that there were no limits. Apart from the woman outside, who might come back in at any moment, nobody else would be awake.

Her blood began to race, and the cold – which she had felt when she took off her clothes – was fading. Veronika and Eduard were both standing up, face to face, she naked, he fully clothed. Veronika slid her own hand down to her genitals and started to masturbate; she had done it before, either alone or with certain partners, but never in a situation like this, where the man showed no apparent interest in what was happening.

And this was exciting, very exciting. Standing up, legs apart, Veronika was touching her genitals, her breasts, her hair, surrendering herself as she had never done before, not because she wanted to see Eduard leave his distant world, but because this was something she had never experienced before.

She started talking, saying unthinkable things, things that her parents, her friends, her ancestors would have considered absolute filth. Her first orgasm came and she bit her lips so as not to cry out with pleasure.

Eduard was looking at her. There was a different light in his eyes, as if he understood, even if it was only the energy, heat, sweat and smell that her body gave off. Veronika was still not satisfied. She knelt down and started masturbating again.

She wanted to die of orgasmic pleasure, thinking about and realising everything that had always been forbidden to her: she begged him to touch her, to force her, to use her in any way he wanted. She wished Zedka was there too, because a woman knows how to touch another woman's body better than any man, because she already knows all its secrets.

On her knees before Eduard, who remained standing, she felt possessed, touched, and she used coarse words to describe what she wanted him to do to her. Another orgasm came, stronger than ever, as if everything around her were about to explode. She remembered the heart attack she had had that morning, but what did that matter, she would die in one great explosion of pleasure. She was tempted to touch Eduard – he was there before her – but she did not want to risk spoiling the moment. She was going far, very far, just as Mari had said.

She imagined herself both queen and slave, dominatrix and victim. In her imagination, she was making love with men of all skin colours – white, black, yellow – with homosexuals and beggars. She was anyone's and anyone could do anything to her. She had one, two, three orgasms one after the other. She imagined everything she had never imagined before and she gave herself to all that was most base and most pure. At last, unable to contain herself any longer, she cried out with pleasure, with the pain of all those orgasms, all those men and women who had entered and left her body through the doors of her mind.

She lay down on the ground and stayed there, drenched in sweat, her soul full of peace. She had concealed her hidden desires even from herself, unable to say why, but she needed no answer. It was enough that she had done what she had done: she had surrendered herself.

Gradually, the universe returned to its proper place and Veronika stood up. Eduard had not moved in all that time, but there seemed to be something different about him: there was a tenderness in his eyes, a very human tenderness.

'It was so good that I can see love in everything, even in the eyes of a schizophrenic.'

She was beginning to put her clothes back on, when she felt a third presence in the room.

Mari was there. Veronika didn't know when she had come in or what she had heard or seen, but even so she felt no shame or fear. She merely looked at her distantly, as one does at someone who has come too close.

'I did as you suggested,' she said. 'And I went a long, long way.'

Mari said nothing; she had just been reliving certain vital moments of her past life, and she was feeling slightly uneasy. Perhaps it was time to return to the world, to face up to things out there, to say that everyone could be a member of a great Fraternity, even if they had never been in a mental hospital.

Like this young girl, for example, whose only reason for being in Villete was because she had made an attempt on her own life. She had never known panic, depression, mystical visions, psychoses – the limits to which the mind can take us. Although she had known many men, she had never experienced the most hidden part of her own desires, and the result was that half of her life had been unknown to her. If only everyone could know and live with their inner madness. Would the world be a worse place for it? No, people would be fairer and happier.

'Why did I never do that before?'

'He wants you to play more music,' said Mari, looking at Eduard. 'I think he deserves it.'

'I will, but answer my question first: why did I never do that before? If I'm free, if I can think whatever I choose to think, why have I always avoided imagining forbidden situations?'

'Forbidden? Listen, I was a lawyer and I know the law. I was also a Catholic and I used to know whole sections of the Bible by heart. What do you mean by "forbidden"?'

Mari went over to her and helped her on with her sweater.

'Look me in the eye and never forget what I'm about to tell you. There are only two prohibitions, one according to man's law, the other according to God's. Never force a sexual relationship on anyone, because that is considered to be rape. And never have sexual relations with children, because that is the worst of all sins. Apart from that, you're free. There's always someone who wants exactly what you want.'

Mari didn't have the patience to teach important things to someone who was about to die. With a smile, she said good night and left the room.

Eduard didn't move; he was waiting for the music. Veronika needed to reward him for the immense pleasure he had given her, merely by staying with her and witnessing her madness without horror or repulsion. She sat down at the piano and started to play again.

Her soul was light, and not even the fear of death tormented her now. She had experienced what she had always kept hidden from herself. She had experienced the pleasures of virgin and prostitute, of slave and queen, albeit more slave than queen.

That night, as if by a miracle, all the songs she had known returned to her memory, and she played in order to give Eduard as much pleasure as she herself had experienced.

When he turned on the light, Dr Igor was surprised to see the young woman sitting in the waiting room outside his office.

'It's still very early. And I'm completely booked up all day.'

'I know it's early,' she said. 'And the day hasn't yet begun. I just need to talk for a while, only a short while. I need your help.'

She had dark shadows under her eyes and her hair was dull, the typical symptoms of someone who has spent the whole night awake.

Dr Igor decided to show her into his room.

He asked her to sit down, while he turned on the light and opened the curtains. It would be dawn in less than an hour, and then he would be able to save on electricity; the shareholders were very hot on expenses, however insignificant.

He glanced rapidly through his diary: Zedka had had her last insulin shock and had reacted positively, that is, she had managed to survive that inhuman treatment. Just as well, in this particular case, that Dr Igor had demanded that the hospital council sign a declaration taking full responsibility for the consequences.

He started reading some reports. Two or three patients had behaved aggressively during the night, amongst them, according to the nurses' report, Eduard. He had gone back to his ward at about four in the morning and had refused to take his sleeping tablets. Dr Igor would have to act. However liberal Villete might be inside, it was necessary to preserve its image as a harsh, conservative institution.

'I've got something very important to ask you,' said Veronika.

But Dr Igor ignored her. Picking up his stethoscope, he began to listen to her heart and lungs. He tested her reflexes and examined the back of her retina with a small torch. He saw that there were now almost no signs of Vitriol poisoning, or Bitterness as some preferred to call it.

He immediately went to the phone and asked the nurse to bring in some medication with a complicated name.

'It seems you didn't have your injection last night,' he said.

'But I'm feeling much better.'

'I just have to look at your face: dark shadows under the eyes, tiredness, the lack of immediate reflexes. If you want to make the most of the little time left to you, please do as I say.'

'That's exactly why I'm here. I want to make the most of that little time, but in my own way. How much time have I actually got?'

Dr Igor peered at her over the top of his glasses.

'You can tell me,' she said. 'I'm not afraid or indifferent or anything. I want to live, but I know that's not enough, and I'm resigned to my fate.'

'What is it you want then?'

The nurse came in with the injection. Dr Igor nodded and the nurse gently rolled up the sleeve of Veronika's sweater.

'How much time have I got left?' said Veronika again, while the nurse gave her the injection.

'Twenty-four hours, perhaps less.'

She looked down, and bit her lip, but managed to maintain her composure.

'I want to ask two favours. First, that you give me some medication, an injection or whatever, so that I can stay awake and enjoy every moment that remains of my life. I'm very tired, but I don't want to sleep. I've got a lot to do, things that I always postponed for some future date, in the days when I thought life would last for ever. Things I'd lost interest in, when I started to believe that life wasn't worth living.'

'And what's the second favour?'

'I want to leave here so that I can die outside. I need to visit Ljubljana castle. It's always been there and I've never even had the curiosity to go and see it close up. I need to talk to the woman who sells chestnuts in winter and flowers in the spring. We passed each other so often, and I never once asked her how she was. And I want to go out without a jacket and walk in the snow, I want to find out what extreme cold feels like, I, who was always so well wrapped up, so afraid of catching a cold.

'In short, Dr Igor, I want to feel the rain on my face, to smile at any man I feel attracted to, to accept all the coffees men might buy for me. I want to kiss my mother, tell her I love her, weep in her lap, unashamed of showing my feelings, because they were always there even though I hid them.

'I might go into a church and look at those images that never meant anything to me and see if they say something to me now. If an interesting man invites me out to a club, I'll accept, and I'll dance all night until I drop. Then I'll go to bed with him, but not the way I used to go to bed with other men, trying to stay in control, pretending things I didn't feel. I want to give myself to one man, to the city, to life and, finally, to death.'

When Veronika had finished speaking, there was a heavy silence. Doctor and patient looked each other in the eye, absorbed, perhaps distracted by all the many possibilities that a mere twenty-four hours could offer.

'I'm going to give you some stimulants, but I don't recommend you take them,' Dr Igor said at last. 'They'll keep you awake, but they'll also take away the peace you need in order to experience everything you want to experience.'

Veronika was starting to feel ill; whenever she was given that injection, something bad always happened inside her body.

'You're looking very pale. Perhaps you'd better go to bed, and we'll talk again tomorrow.'

Once more she felt like crying, but she remained in control.

'There won't be a tomorrow, as you well know. I'm tired, Dr Igor, very tired. That's why I asked for the tablets. I spent all night awake, half-desperate, half-resigned. I could succumb to another hysterical attack of fear, as happened yesterday, but what's the point? If I've still got twenty-four hours of life left, and there are so many experiences waiting for me, I decided it would be better to put aside despair.

'Please, Dr Igor, let me live a little of the time remaining to me, because we both know that tomorrow will be too late.'

'Go and sleep,' said the doctor, 'and come back here at midday. Then we'll speak again.'

Veronika saw there was no way out.

'I'll go and sleep and then I'll come back, but could I just talk to you for a few more minutes?'

'It'll have to be a few. I'm very busy today.'

'I'll come straight to the point. Last night, for the first time, I masturbated in a completely uninhibited way. I thought all the things I'd never dared to think, I took pleasure in things that before frightened or repelled me.'

Dr Igor assumed his most professional air. He didn't know where this conversation might lead and he didn't want any problems with his superiors.

'I discovered that I'm a pervert, doctor. I want to know if that played some part in my attempted suicide. There are so many things I didn't know about myself.'

'I just have to give her an answer,' he thought. 'There's no need to call in the nurse to witness the conversation, and avoid any future law suits for sexual abuse.'

'We all want different things,' he replied. 'And our partners do too. What's wrong with that?'

'You tell me.'

'There's everything wrong with it. Because when everyone dreams, but only a few realise their dreams, that makes cowards of us all.'

'Even if those few are right?'

'The person who's right is just the person who's strongest. In this case, paradoxically, it's the cowards who are the brave ones, and they manage to impose their ideas on everyone else.'

Dr Igor didn't want to go any further.

'Now, please, go and rest a little; I have other patients to see. If you do as I say, I'll see what can be done about your second request.'

Veronika left the room. The doctor's next patient was Zedka, who was due to be discharged, but Dr Igor asked her to wait a little; he needed to take a few notes on the conversation he had just had.

In his dissertation about Vitriol, he would have to include a long chapter on sex. After all, so many neuroses and psychoses had their origins in sex. He believed that fantasies were electrical impulses from the brain, which, if not realised, released their energy into other areas.

During his medical studies, Dr Igor had read an interesting treatise on sexual dissidence: sadism, masochism, homosexuality, coprophagy, coprolalia, voyeurism, the list was endless. At first, he considered these things examples of deviant behaviour in a few maladjusted people incapable of having a healthy relationship with their partners.

However, as he advanced in his profession as a psychiatrist and talked to his patients, he realised that everyone has an unusual story to tell. His patients would sit down in the comfortable armchair in his office, stare hard at the floor, and begin a long dissertation on what they called 'illnesses' (as if he were not the doctor) or perversions (as if he were not the psychiatrist charged with deciding what was and wasn't perverse).

And one by one, these normal people would describe fantasies that were all to be found in that famous treatise on erotic minorities, a book, in fact, that defended the right of everyone to have the orgasm they chose, as long as it did not violate the rights of their partner.

Women who had studied in convent schools dreamed of being sexually humiliated; men in suits and ties, high-ranking civil servants, told him of the fortunes they spent on Rumanian prostitutes just so that they could lick their feet. Boys in love with boys, girls in love with their fellow schoolgirls. Husbands who wanted to watch their wives having sex with strangers, women who masturbated every time they found some hint that their men had committed adultery. Mothers who had to suppress an impulse to give themselves to the first delivery man who rang the doorbell, fathers who recounted secret adventures with the bizarre transvestites who managed to slip through the strict border controls.

And orgies. It seemed that everyone, at least once in their life, wanted to take part in an orgy.

Dr Igor put down his pen for a moment and thought about himself: what about him? Yes, he would like it too. An orgy, as he imagined it, must be something completely anarchic and joyful, in which the feeling of possession no longer existed, just pleasure and confusion.

Was that one of the main reasons why there were so many people poisoned by Bitterness? Marriages restricted to an enforced monotheism, within which, according to studies that Dr Igor kept safely in his medical library, sexual desire disappeared in the third or fourth year of living together. After that, the wife felt rejected and the man felt trapped, and Vitriol, or Bitterness, began to eat away at everything.

People talked more openly to a psychiatrist than they did to a priest because a doctor couldn't threaten them with Hell. During his long career as a psychiatrist, Dr Igor had heard almost everything they had to tell him.

To *tell* him, for they rarely *did* anything. Even after several years in the profession, he still asked himself why they were so afraid of being different.

When he tried to find out the reason, the most common responses were: 'My husband would think I was behaving like a prostitute', or, when it was a man: 'My wife deserves my respect.'

The conversation usually stopped there. There was no point saying that everyone has a different sexual profile, as individual as their fingerprints, no one wanted to believe that. It was very dangerous being uninhibited in bed; there was always the fear that the other person might still be a slave to their preconceived ideas.

'I'm not going to change the world,' he said, resignedly, asking the nurse to send in the ex-depressive, Zedka, 'but at least I can say what I think in my thesis.'

Eduard saw Veronika leaving Dr Igor's consulting room and making her way to the ward. He felt like telling her his secrets, opening his heart to her, with the same honesty and freedom with which, the previous night, she had opened her body to him.

It had been one of the severest tests he had been through since he had come to Villete as a schizophrenic. But he had managed to resist, and he was pleased, although his desire to return to the world was beginning to unsettle him.

'Everyone knows this young girl isn't going to last until the end of the week. There'd be no point.'

Or perhaps, precisely because of that, it would be good to share his story with her. For three years, he had spoken only to Mari, and even then he wasn't sure she had entirely understood him; as a mother, she was bound to think his parents were right, that they had just wanted the best for him, that his visions of Paradise were the foolish dreams of an adolescent completely out of touch with the real world.

Visions of Paradise. That was exactly what had led him down into hell, into endless arguments with his family, into such a powerful feeling of guilt that he had felt incapable of doing anything and had finally sought refuge in another world. If it hadn't been for Mari, he would still be living in that separate reality.

Then Mari had appeared; she had taken care of him and made him feel loved again. Thanks to her, Eduard was still capable of knowing what was going on around him.

A few days ago, a young woman the same age as him had sat down at the piano to play the *Moonlight Sonata*. Eduard had once more felt troubled by his visions of Paradise and he couldn't have said if it was the fault of the music or the young woman or the moon or the long time he had spent in Villete.

He followed her as far as the women's ward, to find his way barred by a nurse.

'You can't come in here, Eduard. Go into the garden, it's nearly dawn and it's going to be a lovely day.'

Veronika looked back.

'I'm going to sleep for a bit,' she said gently. 'We'll talk when I wake up.'

Veronika didn't know why, but that young man had become part of her world, or the little that remained of it. She was certain that Eduard was capable of understanding her music, of admiring her talent; even if he couldn't utter a word, his eyes said everything, as they did at that moment, at the door of the ward, speaking of things she didn't want to hear about.

Tenderness. Love.

'Living with mental patients is fast making me mad. Schizophrenics don't feel things like that, not for other human beings.'

Veronika felt like turning back and giving him a kiss, but she didn't; the nurse would see and tell Dr Igor, and the doctor would certainly not allow a woman who kissed schizophrenics to leave Villete.

Eduard looked at the nurse. His attraction for the young girl was stronger than he had thought, but he had to control himself. He would go and ask Mari's advice, she was the only person with whom he shared his secrets. She would doubtless tell him what he wanted to hear, that in such a case, love was both dangerous and pointless. Mari would ask Eduard to stop being so foolish and to go back to being a normal schizophrenic (and then she would giggle gleefully at her own nonsensical words).

He joined the other inmates in the refectory, ate what he was given and went outside for the obligatory walk in the garden. While 'taking the sun' (on that day the temperature was below zero), he tried to approach Mari, but she looked as if she wanted to be left alone. She didn't need to say anything, Eduard knew enough about solitude to respect other people's needs.

A new inmate came over to Eduard. He obviously didn't know anyone yet.

'God punished humanity,' he said. 'He punished it with the plague. However, I saw Him in my dreams and He asked me to come and save Slovenia.'

Eduard started to move away, while the man continued shouting:

'Do you think I'm mad? Then read the gospels. God sent His only Son and His Son has risen again.'

But Edward couldn't hear him any more. He was looking at the mountains beyond and wondering what was happening to him. Why did he feel like leaving here if he had finally found the peace he had so longed for? Why risk shaming his parents again, just when all the family problems were resolved? He began to feel agitated, pacing up and down, waiting for Mari to emerge from her silence so that they could talk, but she seemed as remote as ever.

He knew how to escape from Villete. However strict the security might seem, it was actually full of holes, simply because, once people entered Villete, they felt little desire to leave. On the west side, there was a wall that could quite easily be scaled since it was full of footholds; anyone who wanted to climb it would soon find themselves out in the countryside and, five minutes later, on a road heading north to Croatia. The war was over, brothers were once more brothers, the frontiers were no longer guarded as they had been before; with a little luck, he could be in Belgrade in six hours.

Eduard had already been on that road several times, but he had always decided to go back, because he had still not received the signal to go forward. Now things were different: the signal had finally come in the form of a young woman with green eyes, brown hair and the startled look of someone who thinks they know what they want.

Eduard thought of climbing the wall there and then, of leaving and never being seen in Slovenia again. But the girl was sleeping and he needed at least to say goodbye to her.

When everyone had finished 'taking the sun' and the Fraternity had gathered in the lounge, Eduard joined them.

'What's that madman doing here?' asked the oldest member of the group.

'Leave him alone,' said Mari. 'Anyway, we're mad too.'

They all laughed and started talking about the previous day's lecture. The question was this, could Sufi meditation really change the world? Theories were put forward, as were suggestions, methodologies, contrary ideas, criticisms of the lecturer, ways of improving what had been tested over many centuries.

Eduard was sick of this kind of discussion. These people locked themselves up in a mental hospital and set about saving the world without actually taking any risks because they knew that, outside, they would be thought ridiculous, even if some of their ideas were very practical. Everyone had their own theory about everything, and they believed that their truth was the only one that mattered. They spent days, nights, weeks and years talking, never accepting the fact that, good or bad, an idea only exists when someone tries to put it into practice.

What was Sufi meditation? What was God? What was salvation if, that is, the world needed saving? Nothing. If everyone there – and outside Villete too – just lived their lives and let others do the same, God would be in every moment, in every grain of mustard, in the fragment of cloud that is there and then gone the following moment. God was there and yet people believed they still had to go on looking, because it seemed too simple to accept that life was an act of faith.

He remembered the exercise he had heard the Sufi master teaching while he was waiting for Veronika to come back to the piano: simply look at a rose. What more was necessary?

Yet even after the experience of that deep meditation, even after having been brought so close to a vision of Paradise, there they were, discussing, arguing, criticising and constructing theories.

His eyes met Mari's. She looked away, but Eduard was determined to put an end to that situation once and for all; he went over to her and took her by the arm.

'Stop it, Eduard.'

He could say: 'Come with me.' But he didn't want to do so in front of all those people, who would be surprised at his forthright tone. That's why he preferred to kneel down and look beseechingly up at her.

The men and women laughed.

'You've become a saint for him, Mari,' someone said. 'It must have been yesterday's meditation.'

But Eduard's years of silence had taught him to speak with his eyes; he was able to pour all his energies into them. Just as he was absolutely sure that Veronika had understood his tenderness and love, he knew that Mari would understand his despair, because he really needed her.

She resisted a little longer, then she got up and took him by the hand.

'Let's go for a walk,' she said. 'You're upset.'

＊

They went out into the garden again. As soon as they were at a safe distance, certain that no one could hear them, Eduard broke the silence.

'I've been in Villete for years,' he said. 'I've stopped being an embarrassment to my parents, I've set aside all my ambitions, but still the visions of Paradise remain.'

'I know,' said Mari. 'We've often talked about it, and I know what you're leading up to as well: it's time to leave.'

Eduard glanced up at the sky; did Mari feel the same?

'And it's because of the girl,' said Mari. 'We've seen a lot of people die here, always when they least expected it, and usually after they'd entirely given up on life. But this is the first time we've seen it happening to a young, pretty, healthy person with so much to live for. Veronika is the only one who doesn't want to stay in Villete for ever. And that makes us ask ourselves: What about us? What are we doing here?'

He nodded.

'Then, last night, I too asked myself what I was doing in this hospital. And I thought how very interesting to be down in the square, at the Three Bridges, in the market place opposite the theatre, buying apples and talking about the weather. Obviously, I'd be struggling with a lot of other long-forgotten things, like unpaid bills, problems with neighbours, the ironic looks of people who don't understand me, solitude, my children's carping. But all that is just part of life, I think; and the price you pay for having to deal with those minor problems is far less than the price you pay for not recognising they're yours. I'm thinking of going round to my ex-husband's tonight, just to say "Thank you". What do you think?'

'I don't know. Do you think I should go to my parents' house too and say the same thing?'

'Possibly. Basically, everything that happens in our life is our fault and ours alone. A lot of people go through the same difficulties we went through, and they react completely differently. We looked for the easiest way out: a separate reality.'

Eduard knew that Mari was right.

'I feel like starting to live again, Eduard. I feel like making the mistakes I always wanted to make, but never had the courage to, facing up to the feelings of panic that might well come back, but whose presence will merely weary me, since I know I'm not going to die or faint because of them. I can make new friends and teach them how to be mad too in order to be wise. I'll tell them not to follow the manual of good behaviour but to discover their own lives, desires, adventures and to live. I'll quote from Ecclesiastes to the Catholics, from the Koran to the Muslims, from the Torah to the Jews, from Aristotle to the atheists. I never want to be a lawyer again, but I can use my experience to give lectures about men and women who knew the truth about this existence of ours and whose writings can be summed up in one word: Live. If you live, God will live with you. If you refuse to run his risks, He'll retreat to that distant Heaven and be merely a subject for philosophical speculation. Everyone knows this, but no one takes the first step, perhaps for fear of being called mad. At least, we haven't got that fear, Eduard. We've already been inmates of Villete.'

'The only thing we can't do is stand as candidates for President of the Republic. The opposition would be sure to probe into our past.'

Mari laughed and agreed.

'I'm tired of the life here. I don't know if I'll manage to overcome my fear, but I've had enough of the Fraternity, of this garden, of Villete, of pretending to be mad.'

'If I do it, will you?'

'You won't do it.'

'I almost did, just a few moments ago.'

'I don't know. I'm tired of all this, but I'm used to it too.'

'When I came here, diagnosed as a schizophrenic, you spent days, months, talking to me and treating me as a human being. I was getting used to the life I'd decided to lead, to the other reality I'd created, but you wouldn't let me. I hated you and now I love you. I want you to leave Villete, Mari, just as I left my separate universe.'

Mari moved off without answering.

In the small and never used library in Villete, Eduard didn't find the Koran or Aristotle or any of the other philosophers that Mari had mentioned. He found instead the words of a poet:

> *Then I said in my heart, As it happeneth to the fool*
> *so will it happen even to me. . .*
> *Go thy way, eat thy bread with joy,*
> *and drink thy wine with a merry heart;*
> *for God hath already accepted thy works.*
> *Let thy garments be always white;*
> *and let not thy head lack ointment.*
> *Live joyfully with the wife whom thou lovest*
> *all the days of the life of thy vanity,*
> *which he hath given thee under the sun,*
> *all the days of thy vanity:*
> *for that is thy portion in life,*
> *and in thy labour wherein thou labourest under the sun. . .*
> *Walk in the ways of thine heart,*
> *and in the sight of thine eyes:*
> *but know thou, that for all these things*
> *God will bring thee into judgement.*

'God will bring me into judgement,' said Eduard out loud, 'and I will say: "For a time in my life I stood looking at the wind, I forgot to sow, I did not live joyfully, I did not even drink the wine offered me. But one day, I judged myself ready, and I went back to work. I told men about my visions of Paradise, as did Bosch, Van Gogh, Wagner, Beethoven, Einstein and other madmen before me." Fine, let Him say that I left hospital in order to avoid seeing a young girl dying; she will be there in Heaven, and she will intercede for me.'

'What are you saying?' said the man in charge of the library.

'I want to leave Villete,' said Eduard, in a slightly louder voice than normal. 'I've got things to do.'

The librarian rang a bell, and a few moments later, two nurses appeared.

'I want to leave,' said Eduard again, agitated. 'I'm fine, just let me talk to Dr Igor.'

But the two men already had hold of him, one on each arm. Eduard tried to free himself from the arms of the nurses, though he knew it was useless.

'You're having a bit of a crisis, now just keep calm,' said one of them. 'We'll take care of it.'

Eduard started to struggle.

'Let me talk to Dr Igor. I've got a lot to tell him, I'm sure he'll understand.'

The men were already dragging him towards the ward.

'Let me go,' he was yelling. 'Just let me talk for a minute.'

The way to the ward was through the lounge, and all the other inmates were gathered there. Eduard was struggling and things were starting to look ugly.

'Let him go! He's mad!'

Some laughed, others beat with their hands on chairs and tables.

'This is a mental hospital. No one here is obliged to behave the way you do.'

One of the nurses whispered to the other:

'We'd better give them a fright, otherwise the situation will get completely out of control.'

'There's only one way.'

'Dr Igor won't like it.'

'He'll like it still less if this gang of maniacs start smashing up his beloved hospital.'

✳

Veronika woke up with a start, in a cold sweat. There was a terrible noise outside, and she needed silence to go on sleeping. But the racket continued.

Feeling slightly dizzy, she got out of bed and went into the lounge, just in time to see Eduard being dragged off, while other nurses were rushing in, wielding syringes.

'What are you doing?' she screamed.

'Veronika!'

The schizophrenic had spoken to her. He had said her name. With a mixture of surprise and shame, she tried to approach, but one of the nurses stopped her.

'What are you doing? I'm not here because I'm mad. You can't treat me like this.'

She managed to push the nurse away, while the other inmates continued to shout and kick up what seemed to her a terrifying din. Should she go and find Dr Igor and leave there at once?

'Veronika!'

He had said her name again. Making a superhuman effort, Eduard managed to break free from the two male nurses. Instead of running away, though, he stood there, motionless, just as he had the previous night. As if transfixed by a conjuring trick, everyone stopped, waiting for the next move.

One of the nurses came over again, but Eduard looked at him, summoning all his strength.

'I'll go with you, I know where you're taking me, and I know too that you want everyone else to know. Just wait a minute.'

The nurse decided it was worth taking the risk; after all, everything seemed to have returned to normal.

'I think. . . I think you're important to me,' said Eduard to Veronika.

'You can't speak. You don't live in this world, you don't know that my name's Veronika. You weren't with me last night, please, say you weren't there.'

'I was.'

She took his hand. The mad people were shouting, applauding, making obscene remarks.

'Where are they taking you?'

'For some treatment.'

'I'll come with you.'

'It's not worth it. You'd just be frightened, even if I swear to you that it doesn't hurt, that you don't feel anything. And it's much better than sedatives because you recover your lucidity much more quickly.'

Veronika didn't know what he was talking about. She regretted having taken his hand, she wanted to get away from there as soon as possible, to hide her shame, never again to see that man who had witnessed all that was most sordid in her, and who nevertheless continued to treat her with such tenderness.

But again, she remembered Mari's words: she didn't need to explain her life to anyone, not even to that young man standing before her.

'I'll come with you.'

The nurses thought it might be better like that. The schizophrenic no longer needed to be restrained, he was going of his own free will.

When they reached the ward, Eduard lay down on the bed. There were two other men waiting, with a strange machine and a bag containing strips of cloth.

Eduard turned to Veronika and asked her to sit down on the bed.

'In a few minutes, the story will be all round Villete and people will calm down again, because even the maddest of the mad feel fear. Only someone who has experienced this knows that it isn't as terrible as it seems.'

The nurses listened to the conversation and didn't believe a word of what the schizophrenic was saying. It must hurt terribly, but then who knows what goes on inside the head of a madman? The only sensible thing the young man had said was about fear: the story *would* soon be all round Villete and calm would swiftly be restored.

'You lay down too soon,' said one of them.

Eduard got up again, and they spread a kind of rubber sheet beneath him.

'Now you can lie down.'

He obeyed. He was perfectly calm, as if everything that was happening was absolutely routine.

The nurses tied some of the strips of cloth round Eduard's body and placed a piece of rubber in his mouth.

'It's so that he doesn't accidentally bite his tongue,' said one of the men to Veronika, pleased to be able to give some technical information as well as a warning.

They placed the strange machine – not much larger than a shoe box, with a few buttons and three dials on it – on a chair by the bed. Two wires came out of the top part and were connected to what looked like earphones.

One of the nurses placed these 'earphones' on Eduard's temples. The other seemed to be regulating the machine, twiddling some knobs, now to the right, now to the left. Although he couldn't speak because of the piece of rubber in his mouth, Eduard kept his eyes fixed on hers, and seemed to be saying: 'Don't worry, don't be afraid.'

'It's set at 130 volts for 0.3 seconds,' said the nurse controlling the machine. 'Here goes.'

He pressed a button and the machine buzzed. At that moment, Eduard's eyes glazed over, his body thrashed about on the bed with such fury that, but for the straps holding him down, he would have broken his spine.

'Stop it!' shouted Veronika.

'We have,' said the nurse, removing the 'headphones' from Eduard's temples. Even so, Eduard's body continued to writhe about, his head rocking from side to side, so violently that one of the men had to hold it still. The other nurse put the machine in a bag and sat down to smoke a cigarette.

The scene lasted a matter of moments. Eduard's body seemed to return to normal, but then the spasms recommenced, and the nurse had to redouble his efforts to keep Eduard's head still. After a while, the contractions lessened, until they stopped altogether. Eduard's eyes were wide open, and one of the nurses closed them, as one does with the dead.

Then he removed the piece of rubber from Eduard's mouth, untied him and put the strips of cloth in the bag along with the machine.

'The effects of electric shock treatment last about an hour,' he said to the girl, who was no longer shouting and who seemed mesmerised by what she was seeing. 'It's all right, he'll soon be back to normal and he'll be calmer too.'

As soon as the electric charge took effect, Eduard felt what he had experienced before: his normal vision gradually decreased, as if someone were closing a curtain, until everything disappeared. There was no pain or suffering, but he had seen other people being treated with electric shock and he knew how awful it looked.

Eduard was at peace now. If, moments before, he had experienced the stirrings of a new emotion in his heart, if he had begun to understand that love was something other than what his parents gave him, the electric shock treatment – or electroconvulsive therapy (ECT) as the specialists preferred to call it – would certainly restore him to normality.

The main effect of ECT was to destroy short-term memory. There would be no nurturing of impossible dreams for Eduard. He could not continue looking forward to a future that did not exist; his thoughts must remain turned toward the past, or he would again begin wanting to return to life.

✳

An hour later, Zedka went into the ward, almost deserted apart from a bed, where a young man was lying, and a chair, where a young woman was sitting.

When she got closer, she saw that the young woman had been sick again, and that her bent head was lolling slightly to the right.

Zedka turned to call for help, but Veronika looked up.

'It's all right,' she said. 'I had another attack, but it's over now.'

Zedka gently helped her up and led her to the toilet.

'It's a men's toilet,' Veronika said.

'Don't worry, there's no one here.'

She removed Veronika's filthy sweater, washed it and placed it on the radiator. Then, she removed her own woollen top, and gave it to Veronika.

'Keep it. I only came to say goodbye.'

The girl seemed distant, as if she had lost all interest in life. Zedka led her back to the chair where she had been sitting.

'Eduard will wake up soon. He may have difficulty remembering what happened, but his memory will soon come back. Don't be frightened if he doesn't recognise you at first.'

'I won't be,' said Veronika, 'because I don't even recognise myself.'

Zedka pulled up a chair and sat down beside her. She had been in Villete so long, it would cost her nothing to spend a few minutes longer keeping Veronika company.

'Do you remember when we first met? I told you a story to try to explain that the world is exactly as we see it. Everyone thought the king was mad, because he wanted to impose an order that no longer existed in the minds of his subjects.

'There are things in life, though, which, however we look at them, are valid for everyone. Like love, for example.'

Zedka noticed a change in Veronika's eyes. She decided to go on.

'I would say that if someone only has a short time to live and decides to spend that time sitting beside a bed, watching a man sleeping, then that must be love. I'd go further: if, during that time, that person has a heart attack, but sits on in silence, just so as to remain close to the man, I would say that such love had a lot of potential for growth.'

'It might also be despair,' said Veronika. 'An attempt to prove that, after all, there are no reasons to continue battling away beneath the sun. I can't be in love with a man who lives in another world.'

'We all live in our own world. But if you look up at the starry sky, you'll see that all the different worlds up there combine to form constellations, solar systems, galaxies.'

Veronika got up and went over to Eduard. Tenderly, she smoothed his hair. She was glad to have someone to talk to.

'A long time ago, when I was just a child, and my mother was forcing me to learn the piano, I said to myself that I would only be able to play it well when I was in love. Last night, for the first time in my life, I felt the notes leaving my fingers as if I had no control over what I was doing.

'A force was guiding me, constructing melodies and chords that I never even knew I could play. I gave myself to the piano because I had just given myself to this man, without him even touching a hair of my head. I was not myself yesterday, not when I gave myself over to sex or when I played the piano. And yet I think I *was* myself.' Veronika shook her head. 'Nothing of what I'm saying makes any sense.'

Zedka remembered her encounters in space with all those beings floating in different dimensions. She wanted to tell Veronika about it, but was afraid she might just confuse her even more.

'Before you say again that you're going to die, I want to tell you something. There are people who spend their entire lives searching for a moment like the one you had last night, but they never achieve it. That's why, if you were to die now, you would die with your heart full of love.'

Zedka got up.

'You've got nothing to lose. Many people don't allow themselves to love, precisely because of that, because there are a lot of things at risk, a lot of future and a lot of past. In your case, there is only the present.'

She went over and gave Veronika a kiss.

'If I stay here any longer, I won't leave at all. I'm cured of my depression, but in Villete, I've learned that there are other kinds of madness. I want to carry those with me and begin to see life with my own eyes.

'When I came here, I was deeply depressed. Now I'm proud to say I'm mad. Outside, I'll behave exactly like everyone else. I'll go shopping at the supermarket, I'll exchange trivialities with my friends, I'll waste precious time watching television. But I know that my soul is free and that I can dream and talk with other worlds which, before I came here, I didn't even imagine existed.

'I'm going to allow myself to do a few foolish things, just so that people can say: she's just been released from Villete. But I know that my soul is complete, because my life has meaning. I'll be able to look at a sunset and believe that God is behind it. When someone irritates me, I'll tell them what I think of them, and I won't worry what they think of me, because everyone will say: she's just been released from Villete.

'I'll look at men in the street, right in their eyes, and I won't feel guilty about feeling desired. But immediately after that, I'll go into a shop selling imported goods, buy the best wines my money can buy and I'll drink that wine with the husband I adore, because I want to laugh with him again.

'And laughing, he'll say: "You're mad!" And I'll say: "Of course I am, I was in Villete, remember! And madness freed me. Now, my dear husband, you must have a holiday every year, and make me climb some dangerous mountains, because I need to run the risk of being alive."'

'People will say: "She's just been released from Villete and now she's making her husband mad too." And he will realise they're right and he'll thank God because our marriage is starting all over again and because we're both mad, like those who first invented love.'

Zedka left the ward, humming a tune Veronika had never heard before.

The day had proved exhausting, but rewarding. Dr Igor was trying to maintain the *sangfroid* and indifference of a scientist, but he could barely control his enthusiasm. The tests he was carrying out to find a cure for Vitriol poisoning were yielding surprising results.

'You haven't got an appointment today,' he said to Mari, who had come in without knocking.

'It won't take long. I'd just like to ask your opinion about something.'

'Today everyone just wants to ask my opinion,' thought Dr Igor, remembering the young girl's question about sex.

'Eduard has just been given electric shock treatment.'

'Electroconvulsive therapy, please use the correct name, otherwise it will look as if we're a mere band of barbarians.' Dr Igor tried to hide his surprise, but later, he would go and find out who had made that decision. 'And if you want my opinion on the subject, I must make it clear that ECT is not used today as it used to be.'

'But it's dangerous.'

'It used to be *very* dangerous; they didn't know the exact voltage to use, where precisely to place the electrodes, and a lot of people died of brain haemorrhages during treatment. But things have changed: nowadays, ECT is being used with far greater technical precision and it has the advantage of provoking immediate amnesia, avoiding the chemical poisoning that comes with prolonged use of drugs. Read the psychiatric journals and don't confuse ECT with the electric shock treatment used by South American torturers. Right, you've heard my opinion. Now I must get back to my work.'

Mari didn't move.

'That isn't what I came to ask. I want to know if I can leave.'

'You can leave whenever you want and come back whenever you want, because your husband has enough money to keep you in an expensive place like this. Perhaps you should ask me: am I cured? And my reply will be another question: cured of what? You'll say: cured of my fear, of my panic attacks. And I'll say, well, Mari, you haven't actually suffered from that for the last three years.'

'So I'm cured.'

'Of course not. That wasn't what your illness was about. In the thesis I'm writing for the Slovenian Academy of Sciences' (Dr Igor didn't want to go into any detail about Vitriol), 'I'm trying to study so-called normal human behaviour. A lot of doctors before me have made similar studies and reached the conclusion that normality is merely a matter of consensus, that is, a lot of people think something is right, and so that thing becomes right.

'Some things are governed by commonsense: putting buttons on the front of a shirt is a matter of logic, since it would be very difficult to button them up at the side, and impossible if they were at the back.

'Other things, however, become fixed because more and more people believe that's the way they should be. I'll give you two examples. Have you ever wondered why the keys on a typewriter are arranged in that particular order?'

'No, I haven't.'

'We call it the QWERTY keyboard, because that's the order of the letters on the first row of keys. I once wondered why it was like that and I found the answer: the first machine was invented by

Christopher Scholes, in 1873, to improve calligraphy, but there was a problem: if a person typed very fast, the keys got stuck together and stopped the machine working. Then Scholes designed the QWERTY keyboard, *a keyboard that would oblige typists to type more slowly.'*

'I don't believe it.'

'But it's true. It so happened that Remington – who were sewing machine manufacturers at the time – used the QWERTY keyboard for their first typewriters. That meant that more people were forced to learn that particular system, and more companies started to make those keyboards, until it became the only available model. To repeat: the keyboard on typewriters and computers was designed so that people would type more slowly, not more quickly, do you understand? If you changed the letters around, you wouldn't find anyone to buy your product.'

When she saw a keyboard for the first time, Mari had wondered why the letters weren't in alphabetical order, but she had then promptly forgotten about it. She assumed it was simply the best layout in order for people to type quickly.

'Have you ever been to Florence?' asked Dr Igor.

'No.'

'You should go there, it's not far, for that is where you will find my second example. In the cathedral in Florence, there's a beautiful clock designed by Paolo Uccello in 1443. Now the curious thing about this clock is that, although it keeps time like all other clocks, its hands go in the opposite direction to that of normal clocks.'

'What's that got to do with my illness?'

'I'm just coming to that. When he made this clock, Paolo Uccello was not trying to be original: the fact is that, at the time, there were clocks like his as well as others with hands that went in the direction we're familiar with now. For some unknown reason, perhaps because the Duke had a clock with hands that went in the direction we now think of as the 'right' direction, that became the only direction, and Uccello's clock then seemed an aberration, a madness.'

Dr Igor paused, but he knew that Mari was following his reasoning.

'So, let's turn to your illness: each human being is unique, each with their own qualities, instincts, forms of pleasure and desire for adventure. However, society always imposes on us a collective way of behaving, and people never stop to wonder why they should behave like that. They just accept it, the way typists accepted the fact that the QWERTY keyboard was the best possible one. Have you ever met anyone in your entire life who asked why the hands of a clock should go in one particular direction and not in the other?'

'No.'

'If someone were to ask, the response they got would probably be: "You're mad." If they persisted, people would try to come up with a reason, but they'd soon change the subject, because there isn't a reason apart from the one I've just given you. So to go back to your question. What was it again?'

'Am I cured?'

'No. You're someone who is different, but who wants to be the same as everyone else. And that, in my view, is a serious illness.'

'Is wanting to be different a serious illness?'

'It is if you force yourself to be the same as everyone else: it causes neuroses, psychoses and paranoia. It's a distortion of nature, it goes against God's laws, for in all the world's woods and forests, He did not create a single leaf the same as another. But you think it's mad to be different and that's why you chose to live in Villete, because everyone is different here, and so you appear to be the same as everyone else. Do you understand?'

Mari nodded.

'People go against nature because they lack the courage to be different, and then the organism starts to produce Vitriol, or Bitterness as this poison is more commonly known.'

'What's Vitriol?'

Dr Igor realised he had gone too far and decided to change the subject.

'That doesn't matter. What I mean is this: everything indicates that you are not cured.'

Mari had years of experience in law courts and she decided to put it into practice right there and then. Her first tactic was to pretend to be in agreement with her adversary, only to draw him immediately into another line of argument.

'I agree. My reason for coming here was very concrete: I was getting panic attacks. My reason for staying was very abstract: I couldn't face the idea of a different way of life, with no job and no husband. I agree with you that I had lost the will to start a new life, a life I would have to get used to all over again. I'll go further: I agree that in a mental hospital, even with its electric shocks – sorry, ECT, as you prefer to call it – rigid timetables and occasional hysterical outbursts on the part of some inmates, the rules are easier to accept than the rules of a world which, as you say, does everything it can to conform.

'Then last night, I heard a woman playing the piano. She played superbly, in a way I've rarely heard before. As I was listening to the music, I thought of all those who had suffered in order to compose those sonatas, preludes, adagios, how foolish they must have been made to feel when they played their pieces – which were, after all, different – to those who held sway in the world of music then. I thought about the difficulties and humiliations involved in getting someone to fund an orchestra. I thought of the booing public who were not yet used to such harmonies.

'Worse than the composers' suffering, though, was the fact that the girl was playing the music with such soul because she knew she was going to die. And am I not going to die? Where is my soul that I might play the music of my own life with such enthusiasm?'

Dr Igor was listening in silence. It seemed that all his ideas were beginning to bear fruit, but it was still too early to be sure.

'Where is my soul?' Mari asked again. 'In my past. In what I wanted my life to be. I left my soul captive in that moment when I still had a house, a husband, a job I wanted to leave but never had the courage to.

'My soul was in my past. But today it's here, I can feel it again in my body, vibrant with enthusiasm. I don't know what to do. I only know that it's taken me three years to understand that life was pushing me in a direction I didn't want to go in.'

'I think I can see some signs of improvement,' said Dr Igor.

'I don't need to ask if I can leave Villete. I can just walk through the door and never come back. But I needed to say all this to someone, and I'm saying it to you: the death of that young girl made me understand my own life.'

'I think these signs of improvement are turning into something of a miracle cure,' laughed Dr Igor. 'What do you think you'll do?'

'I'll go to El Salvador and work with children there.'

'There's no need to go so far away: Sarajevo is only about two hundred kilometres from here. The war may be over, but the problems continue.'

'Then I'll go to Sarajevo.'

Dr Igor took a form from a drawer and carefully filled it in. Then he got up and accompanied Mari to the door.

'Good luck,' he said, then immediately went back to his office and closed the door. He tried hard not to grow fond of his patients, but he never succeeded. Mari would be much missed in Villete.

When Eduard opened his eyes, the girl was still there. After his first electric shock sessions, he had had to struggle for a long time to remember what had happened; but then the therapeutic effect of the treatment lay precisely in that artificially induced partial amnesia which allowed the patient to forget the problems troubling him and to regain his calm.

However, the more frequently electric shock treatment was given, the less enduring its effects; he recognised the girl at once.

'While you were sleeping, you said something about visions of Paradise,' she said, stroking his hair.

Visions of Paradise? Yes, visions of Paradise. Eduard looked at her. He wanted to tell her everything.

At that moment, however, the nurse came in with a syringe.

'You've got to have this now,' she said to Veronika. 'Dr Igor's orders.'

'I've already had some today and I don't want any more,' she said. 'What's more I've no desire to leave here either. I refuse to obey any orders, any rules and I won't be forced to do anything.'

The nurse seemed used to this kind of reaction.

'Then, I'm afraid, we'll have to sedate you.'

'I need to talk to you,' said Eduard. 'Have the injection.'

Veronika rolled up the sleeve of her sweater, and the nurse injected her with the drug.

'There's a good girl,' she said. 'Now why don't the two of you leave this gloomy ward and go outside for a walk?'

'You're ashamed of what happened last night,' said Eduard, while they were walking in the garden.

'I was, but now I'm proud. I want to know about these visions of Paradise, because I came very close to having one myself.'

'I need to look further, beyond the buildings of Villete,' he said.

'Go on, then.'

Eduard looked behind him, not at the walls of the wards or at the garden where the inmates were walking in silence, but at a street in another continent, in a land where it either rained in torrents or not at all.

Eduard could smell that land. It was the dry season; he could feel the dust in his nostrils and the feeling gave him pleasure, because to smell the earth is to feel alive. He was riding an imported bicycle, he was seventeen, and had just left the American college in Brasília, where all the other diplomats' children studied.

He hated Brasília, but he loved the Brazilians. His father had been appointed Yugoslavian ambassador two years before, at a time when no one even dreamed of the violent division of their country. Milošević was still in power; men and women lived with their differences and tried to find a harmony beyond regional conflicts.

His father's first posting was to Brazil. Eduard dreamed of beaches, carnival, football matches and music, but they ended up in the Brazilian capital, far from the coast – a city created to provide shelter only to politicians, bureaucrats, diplomats and to their children, who didn't quite know what to do, stuck in the middle of all that.

Eduard hated living there. He spent the day immersed in his studies, trying – but failing – to relate to his classmates, trying – but failing – to work up some interest in cars, the latest trainers and designer clothes, the only possible topics of conversation with the other young people.

Now and then, there would be a party, where the boys would get drunk on one side of the room, and the girls would feign indifference on the other. There were always drugs around, and Eduard had already experimented with almost all the possible varieties, not that he could get very excited about any of them; he either got too agitated or too sleepy and immediately lost interest in what was going on around him.

His family were concerned. They had to prepare him to follow in his father's footsteps, and although Eduard had almost all the necessary talents, a desire to study, good artistic taste, a facility with languages, an interest in politics, he lacked one essential quality for a diplomat. He found it difficult to talk to other people.

His parents took him to parties, told him to invite his school friends home and gave him a generous allowance, but Eduard rarely turned up with anyone. One day, his mother asked him why he didn't bring his friends to lunch or supper.

'I know every make of trainer and I know the names of all the girls who are easy to get into bed. After that, there's nothing left to talk to them about.'

Then the Brazilian girl appeared on the scene. The ambassador and his wife felt better when their son began going out on dates and coming home late. No one knew exactly where she had come from, but one night, Eduard invited her home to supper. She was a well-brought-up girl, and his parents felt contented; the boy had finally started to develop his talent for relating to other people. Moreover, they both thought – though neither actually said anything – that the girl's existence removed one great worry from their minds: Eduard clearly wasn't homosexual.

They treated Maria (that was her name) with all the consideration of future in-laws, even though they knew that in two years' time they would be transferred to another post, and they had not the slightest intention of letting their son marry someone from an exotic country. They had plans for him to meet a girl from a good family in France or Germany, who could be a dignified companion in the brilliant diplomatic career the ambassador was preparing for him.

Eduard, however, seemed more and more in love. Concerned, his mother went to talk to her husband.

'The art of diplomacy consists in keeping your opponent waiting,' said the ambassador. 'Whilst you may never get over a first love affair, it always ends.'

But Eduard seemed to have changed completely. He started bringing strange books home, he built a pyramid in his room, and, together with Maria, burned incense every night and spent hours staring at a strange design pinned on the wall. Eduard's marks at school began to get worse.

The mother didn't understand Portuguese, but she could see the book covers: crosses, bonfires, hanged witches, exotic symbols.

'Our son is reading some dangerous stuff.'

'Dangerous? What's happening in the Balkans is dangerous,' said the ambassador. 'There are rumours that Slovenia wants independence, and that could lead us into war.'

The mother, however, didn't care about politics; she wanted to know what was happening to her son.

'What about this mania for burning incense?'

'It's to disguise the smell of marijuana,' said the ambassador. 'Our son has had an excellent education, he can't possibly believe that those perfumed sticks draw down the spirits.'

'My son involved in drugs?'

'It happens. I smoked marijuana too when I was young; people soon get bored with it. I did.'

His wife felt proud and reassured. Her husband was an experienced man, he had entered the world of drugs and emerged unscathed. A man with such strength of will could control any situation.

One day, Eduard asked if he could have a bicycle.

'We've got a chauffeur and a Mercedes Benz. Why do you want a bicycle?'

'To be more in touch with nature. Maria and I are going on a ten-day trip,' he said. 'There's a place near here with huge deposits of crystal, and Maria says they give off really positive energy.'

His father and mother had been brought up under a communist regime: crystals were merely a mineral product composed of certain atoms, and did not give off any kind of energy, either positive or negative. They did some research and discovered that these ideas about 'crystal vibrations' were beginning to be fashionable.

If their son started talking about such things at official parties, he could appear ridiculous in the eyes of others. For the first time, the ambassador acknowledged that the situation was becoming serious. Brasília was a city that lived on rumours, and as soon as his rivals at the embassy learned that Eduard believed in these primitive superstitions, they might think he had picked them up from his parents, and diplomacy, as well as being the art of waiting, was also the art of keeping up a façade of normality whatever the circumstances.

'My boy, this can't go on,' said his father. 'I have friends in the Foreign Office in Yugoslavia. You have a brilliant career as a diplomat ahead of you and you've got to learn to face up to reality.'

Eduard left the house and didn't come back that night. His parents phoned Maria's house, as well as all the mortuaries and hospitals in the city, to no avail. The mother lost her confidence in her husband's abilities as head of the family, however good he might be at negotiating with complete strangers.

The following day, Eduard turned up, hungry and sleepy. He ate and went to his room, lit his incense sticks, said his mantras, and slept for the rest of that evening and night. When he woke up, a brand new bicycle was waiting for him.

'Go and see your crystals,' said his mother. 'I'll explain to your father.'

✳

And so, on that dry, dusty afternoon, Edward cycled happily over to Maria's house. The city was so well designed (in the architects' opinion) or so badly designed (in Eduard's opinion), that there were almost no corners, he just kept straight on down a high speed lane, looking up at the sky full of rainless clouds, then he felt himself rising up at a tremendous speed towards the sky, only to plummet down again and land on the asphalt. Crash!

'I've had an accident.'

He tried to turn over, because his face was pressed against the asphalt, and realised he had no control over his own body. He heard the noise of cars braking, people talking in alarmed voices, someone approaching and trying to touch him, then a shout: 'Don't move him! If anyone moves him, he could be crippled for life!'

The seconds passed slowly and Eduard began to feel afraid. Unlike his parents, he believed in God and in the afterlife, but even so, it seemed grossly unfair to die at seventeen, staring at the asphalt, in a land not his own.

'Are you all right?' he heard someone say.

No, he wasn't all right, he couldn't move, but he couldn't say anything either. The worst thing was that he didn't lose consciousness, he knew exactly what was happening and what his situation was. Why didn't he faint? At precisely the moment when he was looking for God with such intensity, despite everything and everyone, God had no pity on him.

'The doctors are on their way,' someone whispered to him, clutching his hand. 'I don't know if you can hear me, but keep calm. It's nothing serious.'

Yes, he could hear, he would have liked that person – a man – to keep on talking, to promise him that it was nothing serious, even though he was old enough to know that people only say that when the situation is very serious indeed. He thought about Maria, about the place where there were mountains of crystals full of positive energy, unlike Brasília, which had the highest concentration of negativity he had ever encountered in his meditations.

The seconds became minutes, people continued trying to console him, and for the first time since it all happened, he began to feel pain. A sharp pain that came from the centre of his head and seemed to spread throughout his entire body.

'They're here,' said the man who was holding his hand. 'Tomorrow you'll be riding your bike again.'

But the following day, Eduard was in hospital, with both his legs and one arm in plaster, unable to leave for at least a month, and having to listen to his mother's non-stop sobbing, his father's anxious phone calls and the doctor's reassurances, reiterated every five minutes, that the crucial twenty-four hour period had passed, and there was no injury to the brain.

The family phoned the American Embassy, who never believed the diagnoses of the state hospitals and had their own sophisticated emergency service, along with a list of Brazilian doctors they considered capable of attending their own diplomats. Now and again, as part of a 'good neighbour policy', they allowed these services to be used by other diplomats.

The Americans brought along their state-of-the-art machines, carried out a further barrage of tests and examinations and reached the conclusion they always reach: the doctors in the state hospital had correctly evaluated the injuries and had made the right decisions.

The doctors in the state hospital may have been good, but the programmes on Brazilian television were as awful as they are anywhere else in the world, and Eduard had little to do. Maria's visits to the hospital become more and more infrequent; perhaps she had found someone else to go with her to the crystal mountains.

In contrast to his girlfriend's erratic behaviour, the ambassador and his wife went to see him every day, but refused to bring him the

Portuguese books he had at home on the pretext that his father would soon be transferred; so there was no need to learn a language he would never have to use again. Eduard, therefore, contented himself with talking to the other patients, discussing football with the nurses and devouring any magazines that fell into his hands.

Then one day, a nurse brought him a book he had just been given, but which he judged 'much too fat to actually read'. And that was the moment that Eduard's life began to set him on a strange path, one that would lead him to Villete and to his withdrawal from reality and that would distance him completely from all the things that other boys his age would get up to in the years that followed.

The book was about visionaries whose ideas had shaken the world, people with their own vision of an earthly Paradise, people who had spent their lives sharing their ideas with others. Jesus Christ was there, but so was Darwin and his theory that man was descended from the apes; Freud, affirming the importance of dreams; Columbus, pawning the Queen's jewels in order to set off in search of a new continent; Marx, with his belief that everyone deserved the same opportunities.

And there were saints too, like Ignatius Loyola, a Basque soldier who had slept with many women and killed many enemies in numerous battles, until he was wounded at Pamplona and came to understand the universe from the bed where he lay convalescing. Teresa of Ávila, who wanted somehow to find a path to God, and who stumbled across it when she happened to walk down a corridor and pause to look at a painting. Anthony, who, weary of the life he was leading, decided to go into exile in the desert, where he spent ten years in the company of demons and was racked by every conceivable temptation. Francis of Assisi, a young man like himself, who was determined to talk to the birds and to turn his back on everything that his parents had planned for his life.

✳

Having nothing better to do, he began to read the 'fat book' that very afternoon. In the middle of the night, a nurse came in, asking if he needed help, since his was the only room with the light still on. Eduard waved her away, without even looking up from the book.

The men and women who shook the world were ordinary men and women, like him, like his father, like the girlfriend he knew he was losing. They were full of the same doubts and anxieties that all human beings experienced in their daily routine. They were people who had no special interest in religion or God, in expanding their minds or reaching a new level of consciousness, until one day they simply decided to change everything. The most interesting thing about the book was that it told how, in each of those lives, there was a single magical moment that made them set off in search of their own vision of Paradise.

They were people who had not allowed their lives to pass by blankly, and who, to achieve what they wanted, had begged for alms or courted kings, used diplomacy or force, flouted laws or faced the wrath of the powers-that-be, but who had never given up, and were always able to see the advantages in any difficulty that presented itself.

The following day, Eduard handed over his gold watch to the nurse who had given him the book, and asked him to sell it, and, with the money, to buy all the books he could find on the same subject. There weren't any more. He tried reading the biographies of some of those visionaries, but they were always described as if they were someone chosen, inspired, and not an ordinary person who, like everyone else, had to fight to be allowed to say what they thought.

Eduard was so impressed by what he had read, though, that he seriously considered becoming a saint and using the accident as an opportunity to change the direction of his life. But he had two broken legs, he had not had a single vision while in hospital, he hadn't stopped by a painting that shook him to his very soul, he had no friends who would build him a chapel in the middle of the Brazilian plateau, and the deserts were all far away and bristling with political problems. There was, however, something he could do: he could learn to paint and try to show the world the visions those men and women had experienced.

When they removed the plaster and he went back to the Embassy, surrounded by all the care, kindness and attention that the son of an ambassador could hope for from other diplomats, he asked his mother if he could enrol in a course on painting.

His mother said that he had already missed a lot of classes at the American school and that he would have to make up for lost time. Eduard refused. He did not have the slightest desire to go on learning about geography and sciences, he wanted to be a painter. In an unguarded moment, he explained why:

'I want to paint visions of Paradise.'

His mother said nothing, but promised to talk to her women friends and ascertain which was the best painting course available in the city.

When the ambassador came back from work that evening, he found her crying in her bedroom.

'Our son is mad,' she said, her face streaming with tears. 'The accident has affected his brain.'

'Impossible!' the ambassador replied, indignant. 'He was examined by doctors specially selected by the Americans.'

His wife told him what her son had said.

'It's just youthful rebelliousness. Just you wait, everything will go back to normal, you'll see.'

This time, waiting did no good at all, because Eduard was in a hurry to start living. Two days later, tired of marking time while his mother's friends deliberated, he decided to enrol himself on an art course. He started learning about colour and perspective, but he also got to know people who never talked about trainers or makes of car.

'He's living with artists!' said his mother tearfully to the ambassador.

'Oh, leave the boy alone,' said the ambassador. 'He'll soon get sick of it, like he did of his girlfriend, like he did of crystals, pyramids, incense and marijuana.'

But time passed, and Eduard's room became an improvised studio, full of paintings that made no sense at all to his parents: circles, exotic colour combinations and primitive symbols all mixed up with people in attitudes of prayer.

Eduard, the solitary boy, who, in his two years in Brazil, had never once brought friends home, was now filling the house with strange people, all of them badly dressed and with untidy hair, who listened to horrible music at full blast – endlessly drinking and smoking and showing a complete disregard for basic good manners. One day, the director of the American school called his mother.

'I think your son must be involved in drugs,' she said. 'His school marks are well below average, and if he goes on like this, we won't be able to renew his enrolment.'

His mother went straight to the ambassador's office and told him what the director had said.

'You keep saying that, with time, everything will go back to normal,' she screamed hysterically. 'There's your crazy, drug-addict son, obviously suffering from some serious brain injury, and all you care about are cocktail parties and social gatherings.'

'Keep your voice down,' he said.

'No, I won't, and I never will again if you don't do something. The boy needs help, don't you see? Medical help. Do something.'

Concerned that the scene his wife was making might embarrass him in front of his staff, and worried that Eduard's interest in painting was lasting longer than expected, the ambassador, a practical man, who knew all the correct procedures, drew up a plan of attack.

First, he phoned his colleague, the American ambassador, and asked politely if he could again make use of the Embassy's medical facilities. His request was granted.

He went back to the accredited doctors, explained the situation and asked them to go over all the tests they had made at the time. The doctors, fearing a law suit, did exactly as they were asked and concluded that the tests revealed nothing abnormal. Before the ambassador left, they demanded that he sign a document exempting the American Embassy from any responsibility for sending him to them.

The ambassador immediately went to the hospital where Eduard had been a patient. He talked to the director, explained his son's problem and asked that, under the pretext of a routine checkup, a blood test be taken to see if there were any drugs in the boy's system.

They took a blood test and no trace of drugs was found.

There remained the third and final stage of his strategy: talking to Eduard himself and finding out what was going on. Only when he was in possession of all the facts, could he hope to make the correct decision.

Father and son sat down in the living room.

'Your mother's very worried about you,' said the ambassador. 'Your marks have got worse, and there's a danger that your place at the school won't be renewed.'

'But my marks at art school have improved, Dad.'

'I find your interest in art very pleasing, but you have your whole life ahead of you to do that. At the moment, the main thing is to finish your secondary education, so that I can set you on the path to a diplomatic career.'

Eduard thought long and hard before saying anything. He thought about the accident, about the book on visionaries, which had turned out to be only a pretext for finding his true vocation, and he thought about Maria, from whom he had never heard again. He hesitated for some time, but in the end, said:

'Dad, I don't want to be a diplomat. I want to be a painter.'

His father was prepared for that response and knew how to get round it.

'You will be a painter, but first, finish your studies. We'll arrange for exhibitions in Belgrade, Zagreb, Ljubljana and Sarajevo. I've got influence, I can help you a lot, but you must complete your studies.'

'If I do that, I'll be choosing the easy route. I'll enter some faculty or other, get a degree in a subject that doesn't interest me, but which will help me earn a living. Painting will just recede into the background, and I'll end up forgetting my vocation. I'll just have to find a way of earning money through my painting.'

The ambassador was starting to get irritated.

'You've got everything, son, a family which loves you, a house, money, social position, but as you know, our country is going through a difficult time, there are rumours of civil war. Tomorrow I might not even be here to help you.'

'I can help myself. Trust me. One day, I'll paint a series entitled "Visions of Paradise". It'll be a visual history of what men and women have previously only experienced in their hearts.'

The ambassador praised his son's determination, drew the conversation to a close with a smile, and decided to give him another month; after all, diplomacy is also the art of postponing decisions until the problems resolve themselves.

A month passed, and Eduard continued to devote all his time to painting, to his strange friends and to that music apparently expressly designed to induce some psychological disorder. To make matters worse, he had been expelled from the American college for arguing with a teacher about the existence of saints.

Since the decision could be put off no longer, the ambassador made one last attempt and called his son in for a man-to-man talk.

'Eduard, you are now of an age to take responsibility for your own life. We've put up with this for as long as we could, but now you've got to forget all this nonsense about becoming a painter and give some direction to your career.'

'But Dad, being a painter *is* giving a direction to my career.'

'What about our love for you, all our efforts to give you a good education. You never used to be like this, and I can only assume that what's happening is some consequence of the accident.'

'Look, I love you both more than anything or anyone else in the world.'

The ambassador cleared his throat. He wasn't used to such outspoken expressions of affection.

'Then, in the name of the love you have for us, please, do as your mother wants. Just stop all this painting business for a while, get some friends who belong to the same social class as you and go back to your studies.'

'You love me, Dad. You can't ask me to do that, because you've always set me a good example, fighting for the things you cared about. You can't want me to be a man with no will of my own.'

'I said, in the name of love. And I have never said that before, but I'm asking you now. For the love that you bear us, for the love we bear you, come home, and I don't just mean in the physical sense, but really. You're deceiving yourself, running away from reality.

'Ever since you were born, we've built up such dreams of how our lives would be. You're everything to us, our future and our past. Your grandfathers were civil servants and I had to fight like a lion to enter the diplomatic service and make my way up the ladder. And I did all this just to create a space for you, to make things easier for you. I've still got the pen with which I signed my first document as an ambassador, and I lovingly saved it to pass on to you the day you did the same.

'Don't let us down, son. We won't live forever and we want to die in peace, knowing that we've set you on the right path in life.

'If you really love us, do as I ask. If you don't love us, then carry on as you are now.'

*

Eduard sat for long hours staring up at the sky in Brasília, watching the clouds moving across the blue – beautiful clouds, but without a drop of rain in them to moisten the dry earth of the central Brazilian plateau. He was as empty as they were.

If he continued as he was, his mother would fade away with grief, his father would lose all enthusiasm for his career, and both would blame each other for failing in the upbringing of their beloved son. If he gave up his painting, the visions of Paradise would never see the light of day, and nothing else in this world could ever give him the same feelings of joy and pleasure.

He looked around him, he saw his paintings, he remembered the love and meaning he had put into each brushstroke, and he found every one of his paintings mediocre. He was a fraud, he wanted something for which he had not been chosen, and the price of which was his parents' disappointment.

Visions of Paradise were for the chosen few, who appeared in books as heroes and martyrs of the faith in which they believed, people who knew from childhood what the world wanted of them; the so-called facts in that first book he had read were the inventions of a storyteller.

At supper time, he told his parents that they were right; it was just a youthful dream; his enthusiasm for painting had passed. His parents were pleased, his mother wept with joy and embraced her son, and everything went back to normal.

That night, the ambassador secretly commemorated his victory by opening a bottle of champagne which he drank alone. When he went to bed, his wife – for the first time in many months – was already sleeping peacefully.

The following day, they found Eduard's room in confusion, the paintings slashed and the boy sitting in a corner, gazing up at the sky. His mother embraced him, told him how much she loved him, but Eduard didn't respond.

He wanted nothing more to do with love, he was fed up with the whole business. He had thought that he could just give up and follow his father's advice, but he had advanced too far in his work; he had crossed the abyss that separates a man from his dream and now there was no going back.

He couldn't go forwards or back. It was easier just to leave the stage.

Eduard stayed on in Brazil for another five months, being treated by specialists, who diagnosed a rare form of schizophrenia, possibly the result of a bicycle accident. Then war broke out in Yugoslavia and the ambassador was hastily recalled. It was too problematic for the family to look after Eduard, and the only way out was to leave him in the newly opened hospital of Villete.

By the time Eduard had finished telling his story, it was dark and they were both shivering with cold.

'Let's go in,' he said. 'They'll be serving supper.'

'Whenever we went to see my grandmother when I was a child, I was always fascinated by one particular painting in her house. It showed a woman – Our Lady, as Catholics call her – standing poised above the world, with her hands out-stretched to the Earth and with rays of light streaming from her fingertips.

'What most intrigued me about the painting was that this lady was standing on a live snake. I said to my grandmother: "Isn't she afraid of the snake? Won't it bite her on the foot and kill her with its poison?"

'My grandmother said: "According to the Bible, the snake brought Good and Evil to the Earth, and she is keeping both Good and Evil in check with her love."'

'What's that got to do with my story?'

'I've only known you a week, so it would be far too early for me to tell you that I love you, but since I probably won't live through the night, it would also be too late. But then the great madness of men and women is precisely that: love.

'You told me a love story. I honestly believe your parents wanted the best for you, but their love almost destroyed your life. If Our Lady, as she appeared in my grandmother's painting, was treading on a snake, that indicates that love has two faces.'

'I see what you mean,' said Eduard. 'I provoked the nurses into giving me the electric shock treatment, because you get me all mixed up. I can't say for sure what I feel, and love has already destroyed me once.'

'Don't be afraid. Today, I asked Dr Igor for permission to leave here and to choose a place where I can close my eyes for ever. But when I saw you being held down by the nurses, I realised what it was I wanted to be looking at when I left this world: your face. And I decided not to leave.

'While you were sleeping off the effects of the electric shock treatment, I had another heart attack, and I thought my time had come. I looked at your face and I tried to guess what your story was, and I prepared myself to die happy. But death didn't come, my heart survived yet again, perhaps because I'm still young.'

He looked down.

'Don't be embarrassed about being loved. I'm not asking you for anything, just let me love you and play the piano again tonight, just once more, if I still have the strength to do it. In exchange, I ask only one thing, if you hear anyone say that I'm dying, go straight to my ward. Let me have my wish.'

Eduard remained silent for a long time and Veronika thought he must have retreated once more into his separate world, from which he would not return for a long time.

Then, he looked at the mountains beyond the walls of Villete and said:

'If you want to leave, I can take you. Just give me time to grab a couple of jackets and some money. Then we'll go.'

'It won't last long, Eduard. You do know that.'

Eduard didn't reply. He went in and came back at once carrying two jackets.

'It will last an eternity, Veronika, longer than all the identical days and nights I've spent in here, constantly trying to forget those visions of Paradise. And I almost did forget them too, though it seems to me they're coming back.

'Come on, let's go. Mad people do mad things.'

That night, when they were all gathered together for supper, the inmates noticed four people were missing.

Zedka, who everyone knew had been released after a long period of treatment, Mari, who had probably gone to the cinema, as she often did, and Eduard, who had perhaps not recovered from the electric shock treatment. When they thought this, all the inmates felt afraid, and they began their supper in silence.

Finally, the girl with green eyes and brown hair was missing. The one whom they all knew would not see out the week.

No one spoke openly of death in Villete, but absences were noted, although everyone always tried to behave as if nothing had happened.

A rumour started to go from table to table. Some wept, because she had been so full of life and now she would be lying in the small mortuary behind the hospital. Only the most daring ever went there, even during daylight hours. It contained three marble tables and there was generally a new body on one of them, covered with a sheet.

Everyone knew that tonight Veronika would be there. Those who were truly insane soon forgot the presence, during that week, of another guest, who sometimes disturbed everyone's sleep playing the piano. A few, when they heard the news, felt rather sad, especially the nurses who had been with Veronika during her time in the

Intensive Care Unit, but the employees had been trained not to develop strong bonds with the patients, because some left, others died, and the great majority got steadily worse. Their sadness lasted a little longer, and then that too passed.

The vast majority of the inmates, however, heard the news, pretended to be shocked and sad, but actually felt relieved, because once more, the Exterminating Angel had passed over Villete and they had been spared.

When the Fraternity got together after supper, one member of the group gave them a message: Mari had not gone to the cinema, she had left never to return and had given him a note.

No one seemed to attach much importance to the matter: she had always seemed different, rather too mad, incapable of adapting to the ideal situation in which they all lived in Villete.

'Mari never understood how happy we are here,' said one of them. 'We are friends with common interests, we have a routine, sometimes we go out on trips together, invite lecturers here to talk about important matters, then we discuss their ideas. Our life has reached a perfect equilibrium, something that many people outside would love to achieve.'

'Not to mention the fact that, in Villete, we are protected from unemployment, the consequences of the war in Bosnia, from economic problems and violence,' said another. 'We have found harmony.'

'Mari left me this note,' said the one who had given them the news, holding up a sealed envelope. 'She asked me to read it out loud, as if she were saying goodbye to us all.'

The oldest member of the group opened the envelope and did as Mari had asked. He was tempted to stop halfway, but by then, it was too late, and so he read to the end.

'When I was still a young lawyer, I read some poems by an English poet and something he said impressed me greatly: "Be like the fountain that overflows, not like the cistern that merely contains." I always thought he was wrong: it was dangerous to overflow, because we might end up flooding areas occupied by our loved ones and drowning them with our love and enthusiasm. All my life I did my best to be a cistern, never going beyond the limits of my inner walls.

'Then, for some reason I will never understand, I began suffering from panic attacks. I became the kind of person I had fought so hard to avoid becoming: I became a fountain that overflowed and flooded everything around me. The result was my internment in Villete.

'After I was cured, I returned to the cistern and I met all of you. Thank you for your friendship, for your affection and for many happy moments. We lived together like fish in an aquarium, contented because someone threw us food when we needed it, and we could, whenever we wanted to, see the world outside through the glass.

'But yesterday, because of a piano and a young woman who is probably dead by now, I learned something very important: life inside is exactly the same as life outside. Both there and here, people gather together in groups, they build their walls and allow nothing strange to trouble their mediocre existences. They do things because they're used to doing them, they study useless subjects, they have fun because they're supposed to have fun, and the rest of the world can go hang – let them sort themselves out. At the very most, they watch the news on television – as we often did – as confirmation of their happiness, in a world full of problems and injustices.

'What I'm saying is that the life of the Fraternity is exactly the same as the lives of almost everyone outside Villete, carefully avoiding all knowledge of what lies beyond the glass walls of the aquarium. For a long time, it was comforting and useful, but people change, and now I'm off in search of adventure, even though I'm sixty-five and fully aware of all the limitations that age can bring. I'm going to Bosnia. There are people waiting for me there. Although they don't yet know me, and I don't know them. But I'm sure I can be useful, and the danger of an adventure is worth a thousand days of ease and comfort.'

When he had finished reading the note, the members of the Fraternity all went to their rooms and wards, telling themselves that Mari had finally gone mad.

Eduard and Veronika chose the most expensive restaurant in Ljubljana, ordered the finest dishes and got drunk on three bottles of 1988 wine, one of the best vintages of the century. During supper, they did not once mention Villete or the past or the future.

'I like that story about the snake,' he said, filling her glass for the nth time. 'But your grandmother was too old to be able to interpret the story correctly.'

'Have a little respect for my grandmother, please!' roared Veronika drunkenly, making everyone in the restaurant turn round.

'A toast to this young woman's grandmother!' said Eduard, jumping to his feet. 'A toast to the grandmother of this madwoman sitting here before me, who is doubtless some escapee from Villete.'

People turned their attention back to their food, pretending that nothing was happening.

'A toast to my grandmother!' insisted Veronika.

The owner of the restaurant came to their table.

'Will you please behave!'

They went quiet for a few moments, but soon resumed their loud talking, their nonsensical remarks and inappropriate behaviour. The owner of the restaurant went back to their table, told them they didn't need to pay the bill, but they had to leave that instant.

'Think of the money we'll save on that exorbitantly expensive wine,' said Eduard. 'Let's leave before this gentleman changes his mind.'

But the man wasn't about to change his mind. He was already pulling at Veronika's chair, an apparently courteous gesture intended to get her out of the restaurant as quickly as possible.

They walked to the middle of the small square in the centre of the city. Veronika looked up at her convent room and her drunkenness vanished. She remembered that soon she would die.

'Let's buy some more wine!' said Eduard.

There was a bar nearby. Eduard bought two bottles and the two of them sat down and continued drinking.

'What's wrong with my grandmother's interpretation of the painting?' said Veronika.

Eduard was so drunk that he had to make an immense effort to remember what he had said in the restaurant, but he managed it.

'Your grandmother said that the woman was standing on the snake because love must master Good and Evil. It's a nice, romantic interpretation, but it's nothing to do with that. I've seen that image before, it's one of the visions of Paradise I imagined painting. I used to wonder why they always depicted the Virgin like that.'

'And why do they?'

'Because the Virgin equals female energy and is the mistress of the snake, which signifies wisdom. If you look at the ring Dr Igor wears, you'll see that it bears the physician's symbol: two serpents coiled around a stick. Love is above wisdom, just as the Virgin is above the snake. For her, everything is Inspiration. She doesn't bother judging what is Good and what Evil.'

'Do you know something else?' said Veronika. 'The Virgin never took any notice of what others might think of her. Imagine having to explain to everyone that business about the Holy Ghost. She didn't explain anything, she just said: "That's what happened." And do you know what the others must have said?'

'Of course. That she was mad.'

They both laughed. Veronika raised her glass.

'Congratulations. You should paint those visions of Paradise, rather than just talking about them.'

'I'll begin with you,' said Eduard.

Beside the small square there is a small hill. On top of the small hill, there is a small castle. Veronika and Eduard trudged up the steep path, cursing and laughing, slipping on the ice and complaining of exhaustion.

Beside the castle, there is a gigantic yellow crane. For anyone coming to Ljubljana for the first time, the crane gives the impression that the castle is being restored and that work will soon be completed. The inhabitants of Ljubljana, however, know that the crane has been there for many years, although no one knows why. Veronika told Eduard that when children in kindergarten are asked to draw the castle of Ljubljana, they always include the crane in the drawing.

'Besides, the crane is much better preserved than the castle.'

Eduard laughed.

'You should be dead by now,' he said, still under the effects of alcohol, but with a flicker of fear in his voice. 'Your heart shouldn't have survived that climb.'

Veronika gave him a long, lingering kiss.

'Look at my face,' she said. 'Remember it with the eyes of your soul, so that you can reproduce it one day. If you like, that can be your starting point, but you must go back to painting. That is my last request. Do you believe in God?'

'I do.'

'Then you must swear by the God you believe in that you will paint me.'

'I swear.'

'And that after painting me, you will go on painting.'

'I don't know if I can swear that.'

'You can. And I'll go further: thank you for giving meaning to my life. I came into this world in order to go through everything I've gone through, attempted suicide, ruining my heart, meeting you, coming up to this castle, letting you engrave my face on your soul. That is the only reason I came into the world, to make you go back to the path you strayed from. Don't make me feel my life has been in vain.'

'I don't know if it's too early or too late, but, just as you did with me, I want to tell you that I love you. You don't have to believe it, maybe it's just foolishness, a fantasy of mine.'

Veronika put her arms around him and asked the God she did not believe in to take her at that very moment.

She closed her eyes and felt him doing the same. And a deep dreamless sleep came upon her. Death was sweet, it smelled of wine and it stroked her hair.

E duard felt someone prodding him in the shoulder. When he opened his eyes, day was breaking.

'You can go and shelter in the Town Hall, if you like,' said the policeman. 'You'll freeze if you stay here.'

In a second, Eduard remembered everything that had happened the previous night. There was a woman lying curled in his arms.

'She . . . she's dead.'

But the woman moved and opened her eyes.

'What's going on?' asked Veronika.

'Nothing,' said Eduard, helping her to her feet. 'Or rather, a miracle happened: another day of life.'

As soon as Dr Igor went into his consulting room and turned on the light – for daylight still arrived late and winter was dragging on far too long – a nurse knocked at his door.

'Things have started early today,' he said to himself.

It was going to be a difficult day, because of the conversation he would have to have with Veronika. He had been building up to it all week, and had hardly slept a wink the previous night.

'I've got some worrying news,' said the nurse. 'Two of the inmates have disappeared: the ambassador's son and the girl with the heart problem.'

'Honestly, you're a load of incompetents, you are, not that the security in this hospital has ever been up to much.'

'It's just that no one's ever tried to escape before,' said the nurse, frightened. 'We didn't know it was possible.'

'Get out of here! Now I'll have to prepare a report for the owners, notify the police, take steps. Tell everyone I'm not to be disturbed, these things take hours!'

The nurse left, looking pale, knowing that a large part of that major problem would land on his own shoulders, because that is how the powerful deal with the weak. He would doubtless be dismissed before the day was out.

✳

Dr Igor picked up a pad, put it on the table and began making notes; then he changed his mind.

He switched off the light and sat in the office precariously lit by the incipient sunlight, and he smiled. It had worked.

In a while, he would make the necessary notes, describing the only known cure for Vitriol: an awareness of life. And describing the medication he had used in his first major test on patients: an awareness of death.

Perhaps other forms of medication existed, but Dr Igor had decided to centre his thesis round the one he had the opportunity to experiment with scientifically, thanks to a young woman who, quite unwittingly, had become part of his fate. She had been in a terrible state when she arrived, suffering from a severe overdose, nearly in a coma. She had hovered between life and death for nearly a week, just the amount of time he needed to come up with a brilliant idea for his experiment.

Everything depended on one thing: the girl's capacity to survive.

And she had, with no serious consequences, no irreversible health problems; if she looked after herself, she could live as long or longer than him.

But Dr Igor was the only one who knew this, just as he knew that failed suicides tend to repeat the attempt sooner or later. Why not use her as a guinea pig, to see if he could eliminate the Vitriol, or Bitterness, from her organism?

And so Dr Igor had conceived his plan.

Using a drug known as Fenotal, he had managed to simulate the effects of heart attacks. For a week, she had received injections of the drug, and she must have been very frightened, because she had time to think about death and to review her own life. In that way, according to Dr Igor's thesis (the final chapter of his work would be entitled 'An awareness of death encourages us to live more intensely') the girl had gone on to eliminate Vitriol completely from her organism, and would, quite possibly, never repeat her attempt at suicide.

He was supposed to see her today and tell her that, thanks to the injections, he had achieved a total reversal of her heart condition. Veronika's escape saved him the unpleasant experience of lying to her yet again.

What Dr Igor had not counted on was the infectious nature of his cure for Vitriol poisoning. A lot of people in Villete had been frightened by their awareness of that slow, irreparable death. They must all have been thinking about what they were missing, forced to re-evaluate their own lives.

Mari had come to him asking to be discharged. Other patients were asking for their cases to be reviewed. The position of the ambassador's son was more worrying, though, because he had simply disappeared, probably helping Veronika to escape.

'Perhaps they're still together,' he thought.

At any rate, the ambassador's son knew where Villete was, if he wanted to come back. Dr Igor was too excited by the results to pay much attention to minor details.

For a few moments, he was assailed by another doubt: sooner or later, Veronika would realise that she wasn't going to die of a heart attack. She would probably go to a specialist who would tell her that her heart was perfectly normal. She would judge that the doctor who had taken care of her in Villete was a complete incompetent, but then all those who dare to research into forbidden subjects require both a certain amount of courage and a good dose of incomprehension.

But what about the many days that she would have to live with the fear of imminent death?

Dr Igor pondered the arguments long and hard and decided that it didn't really matter. She would consider each day a miracle, which indeed it is, when you consider the number of unexpected things that could happen in each second of our fragile existences.

He noticed that the sun's rays were growing stronger; at that hour, the inmates would be having breakfast. Soon his waiting room would be full, the usual problems would arise, and it was best to start taking notes at once for his thesis.

Meticulously he began to write up his experiment with Veronika; he would leave until later the reports on the building's lack of security.

St Bernadette's Day, 1998

The Devil
and Miss Prym

Hail Mary, conceived without sin,
pray for us who turn to Thee for help.
Amen.

And a certain ruler asked him, saying, 'Good Master,
what shall I do to inherit eternal life?' And Jesus
said unto him, 'Why callest thou me good?
None is good, save one, that is God.'

LUKE 18:18–19

Author's Note

The first story about division comes from ancient Persia: the god of time, having created the universe, sees harmony all around him, but feels that there is still something very important missing – a companion with whom to share all this beauty.

For a thousand years, he prays for a son. The story does not say to whom he prays, given that he is omnipotent, the sole, supreme lord; nevertheless, he prays and, finally, he becomes pregnant.

When he realises he has achieved his heart's desire, the god of time is filled with remorse, suddenly conscious of how fragile the balance of things is. But it is too late and the child is already on its way. All he achieves by his lamentations is to cause the son he is carrying in his belly to divide into two.

The legend recounts that just as Good (Ormuzd) is born out of the god of time's prayers, so Evil (Ahriman) is born out of his remorse – twin brothers.

The concerned father arranges everything so that Ormuzd will emerge first from his belly, to take charge of his brother and to prevent Ahriman from throwing the universe into confusion. However, Evil – being very intelligent and resourceful – manages to push Ormuzd aside at the moment of their birth, and thus is the first to see the light of the stars.

Distraught, the god of time resolves to forge alliances on Ormuzd's behalf: he brings into being the human race so that they can fight alongside Ormuzd and stop Ahriman taking control of everything.

In the Persian legend, the human race is born to be the ally of Good, and, according to tradition, Good will triumph in the end. However, many centuries later, another story about division emerges, this time presenting the opposite view: man as the instrument of Evil.

I imagine that most people will know which story I mean. A man and a woman are in the Garden of Eden, enjoying every imaginable delight. But one thing is forbidden: the couple can never know the meaning of Good and Evil. The Lord God says (Genesis 2:17): '*But of the tree of the knowledge of Good and Evil, thou shalt not eat of it …*'.

And one fine day the serpent appears, swearing that this knowledge is more important than paradise itself and that they should possess that knowledge. The woman refuses, saying that God has threatened her with death, but the serpent assures her that nothing of the kind will happen but quite the contrary, for on the day when they learn what Good and Evil are, they will become God's equals.

Convinced, Eve eats of the forbidden fruit and gives some of it to Adam. From this moment on, the original balance of paradise is destroyed, and the pair are driven out of paradise and cursed. Yet there remain some enigmatic words spoken by God and which confirm what the serpent said: '*Behold, the man is become as one of us, to know Good and Evil …*'.

Here, too (as with the god of time who prays for something even though he himself is the lord of the universe), the Bible fails to explain to whom the one God is speaking, and – assuming he is unique – why he should use the expression '*one of us*'.

Whatever the answer, it is clear that from its very inception the human race has been condemned to exist within the eternal division, always moving between those two opposing poles. So here we are, afflicted by the same doubts as our ancestors. The aim of this book is to tackle this theme, occasionally interpolating into the plot other legends on the subject drawn from the four corners of the earth.

The Devil and Miss Prym concludes the trilogy *And on the Seventh Day*. The first two books were: *By the River Piedra I Sat Down and Wept* (1994) and *Veronika Decides to Die* (1998). Each of the three books is concerned with a week in the life of ordinary people, all of who find themselves suddenly confronted by love, death and power. I have always believed that in the lives of individuals, just as in society at large, the profoundest changes take place within a very reduced time frame. When we least expect it, life sets us a challenge to test our courage and willingness to change; at such a moment, there is no point in pretending that nothing has happened or in saying that we are not yet ready.

The challenge will not wait. Life does not look back. A week is more than enough time for us to decide whether or not to accept our destiny.

Buenos Aires, August 2000

For almost fifteen years, old Berta had spent every day sitting outside her front door. The people of Viscos knew that this was normal behaviour amongst old people: they sit dreaming of the past and of their youth; they look out at a world in which they no longer play a part and try to find something to talk to the neighbours about.

Berta, however, had a reason for being there. And that morning her waiting came to an end when she saw the stranger climbing the steep hill up to the village, heading for its one hotel. He did not look as she had so often imagined he would: his clothes were shabby, he wore his hair unfashionably long, he was unshaven.

And he was accompanied by the Devil.

'My husband's right,' she said to herself. 'If I hadn't been here, no one would have noticed.'

She was hopeless at telling people's ages and put the man's somewhere between forty and fifty. 'A youngster,' she thought, using a scale of values that only old people understand. She wondered how long he would be staying, but reached no conclusion; it might be only a short time, since all he had with him was a small rucksack. He would probably just stay one night before moving on to a fate about which she knew nothing and cared even less.

Even so, all the years she had spent sitting by her front door waiting for his arrival had not been in vain, because they had taught her the beauty of the mountains, something she had never really noticed before, simply because she had been born in that place and had always tended to take the landscape for granted.

As expected, the stranger went into the hotel. Berta wondered if she should go and warn the priest about this undesirable visitor, but she knew he wouldn't listen to her, dismissing the matter as the kind of thing old people like to worry about.

So now she just had to wait and see what happened. It doesn't take a devil much time to bring about destruction; they are like storms, hurricanes or avalanches, which, in a few short hours, can destroy trees planted two hundred years before. Suddenly, Berta realised that the mere fact that Evil had just arrived in Viscos did not change anything: devils come and go all the time without necessarily affecting anything by their presence. They are constantly abroad in the world, some times simply to find out what's going on, at others to put some soul or other to the test. But they are fickle creatures, and there is no logic in their choice of target, being drawn merely by the pleasure of a battle worth fighting. Berta concluded that there was nothing sufficiently interesting or special about Viscos to attract the attention of anyone for more than a day, let alone someone as important and busy as a messenger from the dark.

She tried to turn her mind to something else, but she couldn't get the image of the stranger out of her head. The sky, which had been clear and bright up until then, suddenly clouded over.

'That's normal, it always happens at this time of year,' she thought. It was simply a coincidence and had nothing to do with the stranger's arrival.

Then, in the distance, she heard a clap of thunder, followed by another three. On the one hand, this simply meant that rain was on the way; on the other, if the old superstitions of the village were to be believed, the sound could be interpreted as the voice of an angry God, protesting that mankind had grown indifferent to His presence.

'Perhaps I should do something. After all, what I was waiting for has finally happened.'

She sat for a few minutes, paying close attention to everything going on around her; the clouds had continued to gather above the village, but she heard no other sounds. As a good ex-Catholic, she put no store by traditions and superstitions, especially those of Viscos, which had their roots in the ancient Celtic civilisation that once existed in the place.

'A thunderclap is an entirely natural phenomenon. If God wanted to talk to man, he wouldn't use such roundabout methods.'

She had just thought this when she again heard a peal of thunder accompanied by a flash of lightning – a lot closer this time. Berta got to her feet, picked up her chair and went into her house before the rain started; but this time she felt her heart contract with an indefinable fear.

'What should I do?'

Again she wished that the stranger would simply leave at once; she was too old to help herself or her village, far less assist Almighty God, who, if He needed any help, would surely have chosen someone younger. This was all just some insane dream; her husband clearly had nothing better to do than to invent ways of helping her pass the time.

But of one thing she was sure, she had seen the Devil.

In the flesh and dressed as a pilgrim.

The hotel was, at one and the same time, a shop selling local products, a restaurant serving food typical of the region, and a bar where the people of Viscos could gather to talk about what they always talked about: how the weather was doing, or how young people had no interest in the village. 'Nine months of winter, three months of hell,' they used to say, referring to the fact that each year they had only ninety days to carry out all the work in the fields, fertilising, sowing, waiting, then harvesting the crops, storing the hay and shearing the sheep.

Everyone who lived there knew they were clinging to a world whose days were numbered; even so, it was not easy for them to accept that they would be the last generation of the farmers and shepherds who had lived in those mountains for centuries. Sooner or later the machines would arrive, the livestock would be reared far from there on special food, the village itself might well be sold to a big multinational that would turn it into a ski resort.

That is what had happened to other villages in the region, but Viscos had resisted – because it owed a debt to the past, to the strong traditions of those ancestors who had once chosen to live here, and who had taught them the importance of fighting to the bitter end.

✳

The stranger carefully read the form he was given to fill in at the hotel, deciding what he was going to put. From his accent, they would know he came from some South American country, and he decided it should be Argentina, because he really liked their football team. In the space left for his address, he wrote Colombia Street, knowing that South Americans are in the habit of paying homage to each other by naming important places after neighbouring countries. As his name, he chose that of a famous terrorist from the previous century.

In less than two hours, all the 281 inhabitants of Viscos knew that a stranger named Carlos had arrived in the village, that he had been born in Argentina and now lived in a pleasant street in Buenos Aires. That is the advantage of very small villages: without making the slightest effort, you can learn all there is to know about a person's life.

Which was precisely what the newcomer wanted.

He went up to his room and unpacked his rucksack: it contained a few clothes, a shaving kit, an extra pair of shoes, vitamins to ward off colds, a thick notebook to write in, and eleven bars of gold, each weighing two kilos. Worn out by tension, by the climb and by the weight he had been carrying, the stranger fell asleep almost at once, though not before placing a chair under the door handle, even though he knew he could count on each and every one of Viscos' 281 inhabitants.

The next morning he ate breakfast, left his dirty clothes at reception to be laundered, put the gold bars back in his rucksack, and set off for the mountain to the east of the village. On his way, he saw only one villager, an old woman sitting in front of her house, who was looking at him with great interest.

He plunged into the forest, where he waited until his hearing had become used to the noises made by the insects and birds, and by the wind rattling the leafless branches; he knew that in a place like this someone could easily be observing him without his being aware of it, so he stood there for almost an hour without doing anything.

When he felt sure that any possible observer would have lost interest and moved on without anything to report, he dug a hole close to a rocky outcrop in the shape of a Y and hid one of the bars there. Then he climbed a little higher, spent another hour as if in rapt contemplation of nature, spotted another rocky outcrop – this time in the form of an eagle – and dug another hole, in which he placed the remaining ten gold bars.

The first person he saw as he walked back to the village was a young woman sitting beside one of the many temporary rivers that formed when the ice melted high up in the mountains. She looked up from her book, acknowledged his presence, and resumed her reading; doubtless her mother had told her never to talk to strangers.

Strangers, however, when they arrive in a new place, have the right to try and make friends with people they do not know, and so he went over to her.

'Hello,' he said. 'Very hot for the time of year.'

She nodded in agreement.

The stranger went on: 'I'd like you to come and look at something.'

She politely put down her book, held out her hand, and introduced herself.

'My name's Chantal. I work in the evenings at the bar of the hotel where you're staying, and I was surprised when you didn't come down to dinner, because a hotel doesn't make its money just from renting rooms, you know, but from everything the guests consume. You are Carlos from Argentina and you live in Colombia Street; everyone in the village knows that already, because a man arriving here outside of the hunting season is always an object of curiosity. A man in his fifties, with greying hair, and the look of someone whom has been around a bit.

'And thank you for your invitation, but I've already seen the landscape around Viscos from every possible and imaginable angle; perhaps it would be better if I showed you places you haven't seen, but I suppose you must be very busy.'

'I'm 52, my name isn't Carlos, and everything I wrote on the form at the hotel is false.'

Chantal didn't know what to say. The stranger went on:

'It's not Viscos I want to show you. It's something you've never seen before.'

She had read many stories about young women who decide to go into the forest with a stranger, only to vanish without trace. For a moment she was afraid, but her fear was quickly replaced by a desire for adventure: after all, this man wouldn't dare do anything to her when she had just told him that everyone in the village knew all about him – even if none of the details were actually true.

'Who are you?' she asked. 'If what you say is true, surely you realise I could turn you in to the police for passing yourself off with a false identity?'

'I promise to answer all your questions, but first you have to come with me, because I really do want to show you something. It's about five minutes' walk from here.'

Chantal closed her book, took a deep breath and offered up a silent prayer, while her heart beat in fear and excitement. Then she got up and followed the stranger, convinced that this would prove to be yet another disappointing encounter, one which started out full of promise and turned into yet another dream of impossible love.

The man went over to the Y-shaped rock, indicated the recently dug earth, and suggested she uncover what lay buried there.

'I'll get my hands dirty,' protested Chantal. 'I'll get my dress dirty too.'

The man grabbed a branch, broke it and handed it to her to use as a spade. She found such behaviour distinctly odd, but decided to do as he asked.

344 ON THE SEVENTH DAY

Five minutes later, a grubby, yellowish bar lay before her.

'It looks like gold,' she said.

'It is gold. And it's mine. Now please cover it over again.'

She did as she was told. The man led her to the next hiding place. Again she began digging, and this time was astonished at the quantity of gold she saw before her.

'That's gold too. And it's also mine,' said the stranger.

Chantal was beginning to cover the gold over again with soil, when he asked her to leave the hole as it was. He sat down on one of the rocks, lit a cigarette, and stared at the horizon.

'Why did you want to show me this?' she asked.

He didn't respond.

'Who are you exactly? And what are you doing here? Why did you show me this, knowing I could go and tell everyone what's hidden here on the mountain?'

'So many questions all at once,' the stranger replied, keeping his eyes fixed on the mountains, as if oblivious to her presence. 'As for telling the others, that's precisely what I want you to do.'

'You promised me that, if I came with you, you would answer any questions I asked you.'

'In the first place, you shouldn't believe in promises. The world is full of them: promises of riches, of eternal salvation, of infinite love. Some people think they can promise anything, others accept whatever seems to guarantee better days ahead, as, I suspect, is your case. Those who make promises they don't keep end up powerless and frustrated, and exactly the same fate awaits those who believe those promises.'

He was making things too complicated; he was talking about his own life, about the night that had changed his destiny, about the lies he had been obliged to believe because he could not accept reality. He needed, rather, to use the kind of language the young woman would understand.

Chantal, however, had understood just about everything. Like all older men, he was obsessed with the idea of sex with a younger woman. Like all human beings, he thought money could buy whatever he wanted. Like all strangers, he was sure that young women from remote villages were naïve enough to accept any proposal, real or imaginary, provided it offered a faint chance of escape.

He was not the first and would not, alas, be the last to try and seduce her in that vulgar way. What confused her was the amount of gold he was offering: she had never imagined she could be worth that much, and the thought both pleased her and filled her with a sense of panic.

'I'm too old to believe in promises,' she said, trying to gain time.

'Even though you've always believed in them and still do?'

'You're wrong. I know I live in paradise and I've read the Bible and I'm not going to make the same mistake as Eve, who wasn't contented with her lot.'

This was not, of course, true, and she had already begun to worry that the stranger might lose interest and leave. The truth was that she had spun the web, setting up their meeting in the woods by strategically positioning herself at a spot he would be sure to pass on his way back – just so as to have someone to talk to, another promise to hear, a few days in which to dream of a possible new love and a one-way ticket out of the valley where she was born. Her heart had already been broken many times over, and yet she still believed she was destined to meet the man of her life. At first, she had let many chances slip by, thinking that the right person had not yet arrived, but now she had a sense that time was passing more quickly than she had thought, and she was prepared to leave Viscos with the first man willing to take her, even if she felt nothing for him. Doubtless, she would learn to love him – love, too, was just a question of time.

'That's precisely what I want to find out: are we living in paradise or in hell?' the man said, interrupting her thoughts.

Good, he was falling into her trap.

'In paradise. But if you live somewhere perfect for a long time, you get bored with it in the end.'

She had thrown out the first bait. She had said, though not in so many words: 'I'm free, I'm available.' His next question would be: 'Like you?'

'Like you?' the stranger asked.

She had to be careful, she mustn't seem too eager or she might scare him off.

'I don't know. Sometimes I think that and sometimes I think my destiny is to stay here and that I wouldn't know how to live far from Viscos.'

The next step: to feign indifference.

'Right, then, since you won't tell me anything about the gold you showed me, I'll just thank you for the walk and return to my river and my book.'

'Just a moment!'

The stranger had taken the bait.

'Of course I'll explain about the gold; why else would I have brought you here?'

Sex, money, power, promises. But Chantal decided to pretend that she was expecting some amazing revelation; men take the oddest satisfaction in feeling superior, without knowing that most of the time they are being utterly predictable.

'You're obviously a man with a great deal of experience, someone who could teach me a lot.'

That was it. Gently slacken the rope and then lavish a little light praise on your prey so as not to frighten him off. That was an important rule to follow.

'However, you have a dreadful habit of making long speeches about promises or about how we should behave, instead of replying to a simple question. I'd be delighted to stay if only you'd answer the questions I asked you at the start: who exactly are you? And what are you doing here?'

＊

The stranger turned his gaze from the mountains and looked at the young woman in front of him. He had worked for many years with all kinds of people and he knew – almost for certain – what she must be thinking. She probably thought he had shown her the gold in order to impress her with his wealth, just as now she was trying to impress him with her youth and indifference.

'Who am I? Well, let's say I'm a man who, for some time now, has been searching for a particular truth. I finally discovered the theory, but I've never put it into practice.'

'What sort of truth?'

'About the nature of human beings. I discovered that confronted by temptation, we will always fall. Given the right circumstances, every human being on this earth would be willing to commit evil.'

'I think …'

'It's not a question of what you or I think, or of what we want to believe, but of finding out if my theory is correct. You want to know who I am. Well, I'm an extremely rich and famous industrialist, who held sway over thousands of employees, was ruthless when necessary and kind when I had to be.

'I'm a man who has experienced things that most people never even dream of, and who went beyond all the usual limits in his search for both pleasure and knowledge. A man who found paradise when he thought he was a prisoner to the hell of routine and family, and who found hell when he could at last enjoy paradise and total freedom. That's who I am, a man who has been both good and evil throughout his life, perhaps the person most fitted to reply to my own question about the essence of humanity – and that's why I'm here. I know what you're going to ask next.'

Chantal felt she was losing ground. She needed to regain it rapidly.

'You think I'm going to ask: "Why did you show me the gold?" But what I really want to know is why a rich and famous industrialist would come to Viscos in search of an answer he could find in books, universities, or simply by consulting some illustrious philosopher.'

The stranger was pleased at the girl's intelligence. Good, he had chosen the right person – as ever.

'I came to Viscos because I had a plan. A long time ago, I went to see a play by a writer called Dürrenmatt, whom I'm sure you know …'

His comment was merely intended to provoke her: obviously a young woman like her would never have heard of Dürrenmatt, and he knew that she would again try to appear indifferent, as if she knew who he was talking about.

'Go on,' said Chantal, feigning indifference.

'I'm glad to see you know his work, but let me just remind you about the particular play I mean.' He measured his words carefully so that his remarks would not sound too sarcastic, but would also make it clear that he knew she was lying. 'It's about a woman who makes her fortune and then returns to her home town with the sole intention of humiliating and destroying the man who rejected her in her youth. Her life, her marriage and her financial success have all been motivated by the desire to take revenge on her first love.

'So then I thought up my own game: I would go to some remote place, where everyone looked on life with joy, peace and compassion, and I would see if I could make the people there break a few of the Ten Commandments.'

Chantal looked away and stared at the mountains. She knew the stranger had realised that she had never heard of the author he was talking about and now she was afraid he would ask her about those ten commandments; she had never been very religious and had not the slightest idea what they were.

'Everybody in this village is honest, starting with you,' the stranger went on, 'I showed you a gold bar, which would give you the necessary financial independence to get out of here, to travel the world, to do whatever it is young women from small, out-of-the-way villages dream of doing. The gold is going to stay there; you know it's mine, but you could steal it if you wanted. And then you would be breaking one of the commandments: "Thou shalt not steal".'

The girl turned to look at the stranger.

'As for the other ten gold bars,' he went on, 'they are worth enough to mean that none of the inhabitants of this village would ever need to work again. I didn't ask you to re-bury the gold bars because I'm going to move them to a place only I will know about. When you go back to the village, I want you to say that you saw them and that I am willing to hand them over to the inhabitants of Viscos on condition that they do something they would never ever dream of doing.'

'Like what, for example?'

'It's not an example, it's something very concrete. I want them to break the commandment "Thou shalt not kill".'

'What?'

Her question came out like a yell.

'Exactly what I said. I want them to commit a murder.'

The stranger saw the young woman's body go rigid and realised she might leave at any moment without hearing the rest of the story. He needed to tell her his plan quickly.

'I'm giving them a week. If, at the end of seven days, someone in the village is found dead – it could be a useless old man, or someone with an incurable illness, or a mental defective who requires constant attention, the victim doesn't matter – then the money will go to the other villagers, and I will conclude that we are all evil. If you steal the one gold bar but the village resists temptation, or vice versa, I will conclude that there are good people and evil people – which would put me in a difficult position because it would mean that there's a spiritual struggle going on that could be won by either side. Don't you believe in God and the spiritual world, in battles between devils and angels?'

The young woman said nothing, and this time he realised that he had mistimed his question and ran the risk of her simply turning on her heel and not letting him finish. He had better cut the irony and get to the heart of the matter.

'If I leave the village with my eleven gold bars intact, then everything I wanted to believe in will have proved to be a lie. I will die having received an answer I would rather not have received, because I would find life more acceptable if I was proved right and the world is evil.

'I would continue to suffer, but knowing that everyone else is suffering too would make the pain more bearable. But if only a few of us are condemned to suffer terrible tragedies, then there is something very wrong with Creation.'

Chantal's eyes filled with tears, but she managed to fight them back.

'Why are you doing this? Why did you choose my village?'

'It's nothing to do with you or with your village. I'm simply thinking of myself; the story of one man is the story of all men. I need to know if we are good or evil. If we are good, God is just and will forgive me for all I have done, for the harm I wished on those who tried to destroy me, for the wrong decisions I took at key moments, for the proposition I am putting to you now – for He was the one who drove me towards the dark.

'But if we're evil, then everything is permitted, I never took a wrong decision, we are all condemned from the start, and it doesn't matter what we do in this life, for redemption lies beyond either human thought or deed.'

Before Chantal could leave, he added:

'You may decide not to co-operate, in which case, I'll tell everyone that I gave you the chance to help them, but you refused, and then I'll put my proposition to them myself. If they do decide to kill someone, you will probably be their chosen victim.'

The inhabitants of Viscos soon grew used to the stranger's routine: he woke early, ate a hearty breakfast and went off walking in the mountains, despite the rain that had not stopped falling since his second day in the village and which eventually turned into a near continuous snowstorm. He never ate lunch and generally returned to his hotel early in the afternoon, shut himself in his room and, so everyone supposed, went to sleep.

As soon as night fell, he resumed his walks, this time in the immediate surroundings of the village. He was always the first into the restaurant, he ordered the finest dishes and – never taken in by the prices – always ordered the best wine, which wasn't necessarily the most expensive; then he would smoke a cigarette and go over to the bar, where he had begun to make friends with the regulars.

He enjoyed listening to stories about the region, about the previous generations who had lived in Viscos (someone told him that once it had been a far bigger village than it was today, as you could see from the ruined houses at the far end of the three surviving streets), and about the customs and superstitions that were part of rural life, and about the new techniques in agriculture and animal husbandry.

When the time came for him to talk about himself, he told various contradictory stories, sometimes saying he had been a sailor, at others mentioning the major arms industries he had been in charge of, or talking of a time when he had abandoned everything to spend time in a monastery in search of God.

When they left the bar, the locals argued over whether or not he was telling the truth. The mayor believed that a man could be many different things in his lifetime, although the people of Viscos always knew their fate from childhood onwards; the priest was of a different opinion and regarded the newcomer as someone lost and confused, who had come there to try and find himself.

The only thing they all knew for certain was that he was only going to be there for seven days; the hotel landlady reported that she had heard him phoning the airport in the capital, confirming his departure – interestingly enough, for Africa not South America. Then, after the phone call, he had pulled out a bundle of notes from his pocket to settle the bill for his room as well as to pay for the meals he had taken and those still to come, even though she assured him that she trusted him. When the stranger insisted, the woman suggested he pay by credit card, as most of her guests usually did; that way, he would have cash available for any emergency that might arise during the remainder of his trip. She thought of adding that 'in Africa they might not accept credit cards', but felt it would have been indelicate to reveal that she had listened in on his conversation, or to imply that certain continents were more advanced than others.

The stranger thanked her for her concern, but refused politely.

On the following three nights, he paid – again in cash – for a round of drinks for everyone. Viscos had never seen anything like it, and they soon forgot about the contradictory stories, and the man came to be viewed as friendly, generous and open-minded, prepared to treat country folk as if they were the equals of men and women from the big cities.

By now, the subject of the discussions had changed. When it was closing time in the bar, some of the late drinkers took the mayor's side, saying that the newcomer was a man of the world, capable of understanding the true value of friendship, while others agreed with the priest, with his greater knowledge of the human soul, and said that the stranger was a lonely man in search either of new friends or of a new vision of life. Whatever the truth of the matter, he was an agreeable enough character, and the inhabitants of Viscos were convinced that they would miss him when he left on the following Monday.

Apart from anything else, he was extremely discreet, a quality everyone had noticed because of one particular detail: most travellers, especially those who arrived alone, were always very quick to try and strike up a conversation with the barmaid, Chantal Prym, possibly in hopes of a fleeting romance or whatever. This man, however, only spoke to her when he ordered drinks and never once traded seductive or lecherous looks with the young woman.

Chantal found it virtually impossible to sleep during the three nights following that meeting by the river. The storm – which came and went – shook the metal blinds, making a frightening noise. She awoke repeatedly, bathed in sweat, even though she always switched off the heating at night, due to the high price of electricity.

On the first night, she found herself in the presence of Good. Between nightmares – which she was unable to remember – she prayed to God to help her. It did not once occur to her to tell anyone what she had heard and thus become the messenger of sin and death.

At one point, it seemed to her that God was much too far away to hear her, and so she began praying instead to her grandmother, who had passed away some time ago, and who had brought her up after her mother died in childbirth. She clung with all her strength to the notion that Evil had already touched their lives once and had gone away for ever.

Despite all her personal problems, Chantal knew that she lived in a village of decent men and women who honoured their commitments, people who walked with their heads held high and were respected throughout the region. But it had not always been so. For over two centuries, Viscos had been inhabited by the very dregs of humanity, and everyone took this for granted, saying it was the consequence of a curse put on the village by the Celts when they were vanquished by the Romans.

And so things remained until the silence and courage of a single man – someone who believed not in curses, but in blessings – redeemed its people. Chantal listened to the clattering metal blinds and remembered the voice of her grandmother recounting what had happened.

'Once, many years ago, a hermit – who later came to be known as St Savin – lived in one of the caves hereabouts. At the time, Viscos was little more than a frontier post, populated by bandits fleeing from justice, by smugglers and prostitutes, by confidence tricksters in search of accomplices, even by murderers resting between murders. The wickedest of them all, an Arab called Ahab, controlled the whole village and the surrounding area, imposing extortionate taxes on the local farmers who still insisted on maintaining a dignified way of life.

'One day, Savin came down from his cave, arrived at Ahab's house and asked to spend the night there. Ahab laughed: "You do know that I'm a murderer who has already slit a number of throats, and that your life is worth nothing to me?"

'"Yes, I know that," Savin replied, "but I'm tired of living in a cave and I'd like to spend at least one night here with you."

'Ahab knew the saint's reputation, which was as great as his own, and this made him uneasy, for he did not like having to share his glory with someone so weak. Thus he determined to kill him that very night, to prove to everyone that he was the one true master of the place.

'They chatted for a while. Ahab was impressed by what the saint had to say, but he was a suspicious man who no longer believed in the existence of Good. He showed Savin where he could sleep and then continued menacingly sharpening his knife. After watching him for a few minutes, Savin closed his eyes and went to sleep.

'Ahab spent all night sharpening his knife. Next day, when Savin awoke, he found Ahab in tears at his side.

'"You weren't afraid of me and you didn't judge me. For the first time ever, someone spent a night by my side trusting that I could be a good man, one ready to offer hospitality to those in need. Because you believed I was capable of behaving decently, I did."

'From that moment on, Ahab abandoned his life of crime and set about transforming the region. That was when Viscos ceased being merely a frontier post, inhabited by outcasts, and became an important trading centre on the border between two countries.'

'Exactly.'

Chantal burst into tears, grateful to her grandmother for having reminded her of that story. Her people were good, and she could trust them. While she attempted to go back to sleep, she even toyed with the idea of telling them the stranger's story, if only to see his shocked face as he was driven out of Viscos by its inhabitants.

The next day, she was surprised to see him emerge from the restaurant at the rear of the hotel, go over to the bar-cum-reception-cum-souvenir shop and stand around chatting to the people he met there, just like any other tourist, pretending to be interested in utterly pointless things, such as their methods of shearing sheep or of smoke-curing meat. The people of Viscos always believed that every stranger would be fascinated by their natural, healthy way of life, and they would repeat and expand upon the benefits of life away from modern civilisation, even though, deep in their hearts, every single one of them would have loved to live far from there, among cars that pollute the atmosphere and in neighbourhoods where it was too dangerous to walk, for the simple reason that big cities hold an enormous fascination for country people.

Yet every time a visitor appeared, they would demonstrate by their words – and only by their words – the joys of living in a lost paradise, trying to persuade themselves what a miracle it was to have been born there and forgetting that, so far, not one hotel guest had decided to leave it all behind and come and live in Viscos.

There was a lively atmosphere in the bar that night, until the stranger made one rather unfortunate comment:

'The children here are so well behaved. There's not a squeak out of them in the mornings, not like other places I've visited.'

After an awkward silence – for there were no children in Viscos – someone asked him what he thought of the local dish he had just eaten, and the conversation resumed its normal rhythm, revolving, as usual, around the wonders of the countryside and the problems of life in the big city.

As time passed, Chantal became increasingly nervous, afraid that he might ask her to tell everyone about their meeting in the forest. But the stranger never even glanced at her, and he spoke to her only once, when he ordered – and paid cash for – a round of drinks for everyone present.

As soon as the customers left and the stranger went up to his room, she took off her apron, lit a cigarette from a packet someone had left behind on the table, and told the hotel landlady she would do the clearing up the next morning, since she was worn out after a sleepless night. The landlady agreed, and Chantal put on her coat and went out into the cold night air.

Her room was only two minutes' walk away, and as she let the rain pour down her face, she was thinking that perhaps everything that had happened was just some kind of crazy fantasy, the stranger's macabre way of attracting her attention.

Then she remembered the gold: she had seen it with her own eyes.

Maybe it wasn't gold. But she was too tired to think and – as soon as she got to her room – she took off her clothes and snuggled down under the covers.

On the second night, Chantal found herself in the presence of Good and Evil. She fell into a deep, dreamless sleep, only to wake up less than an hour later. Outside, all was silence; there was no wind banging the metal blinds, not even the sounds made by night creatures; there was nothing, absolutely nothing to indicate that she was still in the world of the living.

She went to the window and looked out at the deserted street, where a fine rain was falling, the mist barely lit by the feeble light of the hotel sign, all of which only made the village seem even more sinister. She was all too familiar with the silence of this remote place, which signified not peace and tranquillity, but a total absence of new things to say.

She looked at the mountains, which lay hidden by low cloud, but she knew that somewhere up there was buried a gold bar or, rather, a yellow object, shaped like a brick, that the stranger had left behind there. He had shown her its exact location, virtually begging her to dig up the bar and keep it for herself.

She went back to bed, tossed and turned for a while, then got up again and went to the bathroom where she examined her naked body in the mirror, spent a few moments worrying that soon she would lose her looks, then returned to bed. She regretted not having picked up the packet of cigarettes left behind on the table, but she knew that its owner was bound to come back for it, and she did not want to incur people's mistrust. That was what Viscos was like: a half-empty cigarette packet had its owner, the button lost off a jacket had to be kept until someone came asking for it, every penny in change had to be handed over, there was never any rounding up the bill. It was a wretched place, in which everything was predictable, organised and reliable.

Realising that she wasn't going to be able to get to sleep, she again attempted to pray and to think of her grandmother, but her thoughts had become fixed on a single scene: the open hole, the earth-smeared metal, the branch in her hand, as though it were the staff of a pilgrim about to set off. She dozed and woke up again several times, but the silence outside continued, and the same scene kept endlessly repeating itself inside her head.

As soon as she noticed the first light of dawn coming in through the window, she dressed and went out.

Although she lived in a place where people normally rose with the sun, it was too early even for that. She walked down the empty street, glancing repeatedly behind her to be sure that the stranger wasn't following her; the mist was so thick, however, that visibility was down to a few yards. She paused from time to time, listening for footsteps, but all she could hear was her own heart beating wildly.

She plunged into the undergrowth, made for the Y-shaped rock – which had always made her nervous because it looked as if it might topple over at any moment – picked up the same branch she had left there the day before, dug at the exact spot the stranger had indicated, stuck her hand into the hole and pulled out the brick-shaped gold bar. She thought she heard something: a silence reigned in the heart of the forest, as though there was a strange presence abroad, frightening the animals and preventing the leaves from stirring.

She was surprised by the weight of the metal in her hands. She wiped it clean, studied the marks on it: two seals and a series of engraved numbers, which she tried in vain to decipher.

How much would it be worth? She couldn't tell with any degree of accuracy, but – as the stranger had said – it would be enough for her not to have to worry about earning another penny for the rest of her life. She was holding her dream in her hands, the thing she had always longed for, and which a miracle had set before her. Here was the opportunity to free herself from all those identical days and nights in Viscos and from the endless going back and forth to the hotel where she had worked since she was eighteen, from the yearly visits of all those friends whose families had sent them away to study and make something of themselves, from all the absences she had long since grown used to, from the men who arrived promising her the world and left the next day without even a goodbye, from all the farewells and non-farewells to which she had long become accustomed. That moment there in the forest was the most important moment of her entire life.

Life had always been so unfair to her: she didn't know who her father was; her mother had died in childbirth, leaving her with a terrible burden of guilt to bear; her grandmother, a countrywoman, had eked out a living as a dressmaker, saving every penny she could so that her granddaughter could at least learn to read and write. Chantal had had so many dreams: she thought she could overcome all obstacles, find a husband, get a job in the big city, be discovered by a talent scout who happened to be visiting that out-of-the-way place in the hope of finding peace, get a career in the theatre, write a best-seller, have photographers calling out to her to pose for them, walk along life's red carpets.

Every day was another day spent waiting. Every night was a night when she might meet someone who would recognise her true worth. Every man she took to her bed was the hope of leaving Viscos the following morning, never again to see those three streets, those stone houses with their slate roofs, the church with its cemetery beside it, the hotel selling local handicrafts that took months to make and were sold for the same price as mass-produced goods.

Occasionally it crossed her mind that the Celts, the ancient inhabitants of her region, might have hidden an amazing cache of treasure there, which one day she would find. Of all her dreams, that had been the most absurd, the most unlikely.

Yet here she was now with a gold bar in her hands, the treasure she had never believed in, her definitive freedom.

She was seized by panic: the one lucky moment in her life could vanish that very afternoon. What if the stranger changed his mind? What if he decided to go in search of another village where he might find another woman more willing to help him in his plans? Why not stand up, go back to her room, put her few possessions into a bag and simply leave?

She imagined herself going down the steep hill, trying to hitch a ride out of the village while the stranger set out on his morning walk and found that his gold had been stolen. She would continue on her way to the nearest town and he would go back to the hotel to call the police.

Chantal would thank the driver who had given her a lift, and then head straight for the bus station and buy a ticket to some far-away place; at that moment, two policemen would approach her, asking her politely to open her suitcase. As soon as they saw its contents, their politeness would vanish: she was the woman they were looking for, following a report filed only three hours earlier.

In the police station, Chantal would have two options: to tell the truth, which no one would believe, or to explain that she had noticed the disturbed soil, had decided to investigate and had found the gold. Once, she had shared her bed with a treasure hunter also intent on unearthing something left by the Celts. He claimed the law of the land was clear: he had the right to keep whatever he found, although any items of historical interest had to be registered with the relevant government department. But the gold bar had no historical value at all, it was brand new, with all its stamps, seals and numbers.

The police would question the man. He would have no way of proving that she had entered his room and stolen his property. It would be his word against hers, but he might prove more influential, have friends in high places, and it would all go his way. Chantal could, of course, always ask the police to examine the gold bar; then they would see that she was telling the truth, for the metal would still bear traces of earth.

By now, the news would have reached Viscos, and its inhabitants – out of envy or jealousy – would start spreading rumours about the girl, saying that there were numerous reports that she often used to go to bed with the hotel guests; perhaps the robbery had taken place while the man was asleep.

It would all end badly: the gold bar would be confiscated until the courts had resolved the matter, she would get another lift back to Viscos, where she would be humiliated, ruined, the target of gossip that would take more than a generation to die down. Later on, she would discover that lawsuits never got anywhere, that lawyers cost much more than she could possibly afford, and she would end up abandoning the case.

The net result: no gold and no reputation.

There was another possible version: the stranger might be telling the truth. If Chantal stole the gold and simply left, wouldn't she be saving the village from a much deeper disgrace?

However, even before leaving home and setting off for the mountain, she had known she would be incapable of taking such a step. Why, at precisely the moment that could change her life forever, was she so afraid? After all, didn't she sleep with whomever she pleased and didn't she sometimes ingratiate herself with visitors just to get a bigger tip? Didn't she lie occasionally? Didn't she envy her former friends who now only came back to the village to visit their families at New Year?

She clutched the gold to her, got to her feet, feeling weak and desperate, then crouched down again, replaced it in the hole and covered it with earth. She couldn't go through with it; this inability, however, had nothing to do with honesty or dishonesty, but with the sheer terror she was feeling. She had just realised there were two things that prevent us from achieving our dreams: believing them to be impossible or seeing those dreams made possible by some sudden turn of the wheel of fortune, when you least expected it. For at that moment, all our fears suddenly surface: the fear of setting off along a road heading who knows where, the fear of a life full of new challenges, the fear of losing for ever everything that is familiar.

People want to change everything and, at the same time, want it all to remain the same. Chantal did not immediately understand why, but that was what was happening to her. Perhaps she was too bound to Viscos, too accustomed to defeat, and any chance of victory was too heavy a burden to bear.

She was convinced that the stranger must now be tired of her silence and that shortly – perhaps that very afternoon – he would decide to choose someone else. But she was too cowardly to change her fate.

The hands that had touched the gold should now be washing the dirty dishes, wielding the sponge and the dishcloth. Chantal turned her back on the treasure and returned to the village, where the hotel landlady was waiting for her, looking vaguely irritated, since Chantal had promised to clean the bar before the one hotel guest was up.

Chantal's fears proved unfounded: the stranger did not leave. She saw him in the bar that night, more seductive than ever, telling tales that might not have been entirely true, but which, at least in his imagination, he had lived intensely. Once again their eyes only met impersonally, when he offered to pay for the regulars' drinks.

Chantal was exhausted. She was praying that they would all leave early, but the stranger seemed particularly inspired, recounting story after story, which his listeners lapped up, with the interest and the hateful respect – or, rather, craven submissiveness – that country people show in the presence of those who come from the big cities, judging them to be more cultivated, educated, intelligent and modern.

'Fools,' she said to herself. 'They don't understand how important they are. They don't understand that whenever someone lifts a forkful of food to their mouth, anywhere in the world, it's thanks to people like the inhabitants of Viscos, who toil from dawn to dusk, working the land with the sweat of their weary bodies, and caring for their livestock with indescribable patience. They are far more necessary to the world than all those city people, yet they behave as if they were inferior beings, uptight and talentless – and they believe it too.'

The stranger, however, seemed determined to show that his culture was worth more than all the labours of the men and women in the bar. He pointed to a print hanging on the wall:

'Do you know what that is? It's one of the most famous paintings in the world: *The Last Supper*, painted by Leonardo da Vinci.'

'It can't be as famous as all that,' said the hotel landlady. 'It was very cheap.'

'That's only a reproduction: the original is in a church a long, long way from here. But there's a story about this picture you might like to hear.'

Everyone nodded, though once again Chantal felt ashamed to be there, listening to a man showing off his pointless knowledge, just to prove that he knew more than anyone else.

'When he was creating this picture, Leonardo da Vinci encountered a serious problem: he had to depict Good – in the person of Jesus – and Evil – in the figure of Judas, the friend who resolves to betray him during the meal. He stopped work on the painting until he could find his ideal models.

'One day, when he was listening to a choir, he saw in one of the boys the perfect image of Christ. He invited him to his studio and made sketches and studies of his face.

'Three years went by. *The Last Supper* was almost complete, but Leonardo had still not found the perfect model for Judas. The cardinal responsible for the church started to put pressure on him to finish the mural.

'After many days spent vainly searching, the artist came across a prematurely aged youth, in rags and lying drunk in the gutter. With some difficulty, he persuaded his assistants to bring the fellow directly to the church, since there was no time left to make preliminary sketches.

'The beggar was taken there, not quite understanding what was going on. He was propped up by Leonardo's assistants, while Leonardo copied the lines of impiety, sin and egotism so clearly etched on his features.

'When he had finished, the beggar, who had sobered up slightly, opened his eyes and saw the picture before him. With a mixture of horror and sadness he said:

'"I've seen that picture before!"

'"When?" asked an astonished Leonardo.

'"Three years ago, before I lost everything I had, at a time when I used to sing in a choir and my life was full of dreams. The artist asked me to pose as the model for the face of Jesus."'

There was a long pause. The stranger was looking at the priest, who was drinking his beer, but Chantal knew his words were directed at her.

'So you see, Good and Evil have the same face; it all depends on when they cross the path of each individual human being.'

He got up, made his excuses, saying he was tired, and went up to his room. Everyone paid what they owed and slowly left the bar, casting a last look at the cheap reproduction of the famous painting, asking themselves at what point in their lives they had been touched by an angel or a devil. Without anyone saying a word to anyone else, each came to the conclusion that this had only happened in Viscos before Ahab brought peace to the region; now, every day was like every other day, each the same as the last.

Exhausted, functioning almost like an automaton, Chantal knew she was the only person to think differently, for she alone had felt the heavy, seductive hand of Evil caressing her cheek. 'Good and Evil have the same face, it all depends on when they cross the path of each individual human being.' Beautiful, possibly true words, but all she really needed now was to sleep, nothing more.

She ended up giving the wrong change to one of the customers, something which almost never happened; she apologised, but did not feel overly guilty. She carried on, inscrutable and dignified, until the priest and the local mayor – generally the last to leave – had departed. Then she shut up the till, gathered her things together, put on her cheap, heavy jacket and went home, just as she had done for years.

On the third night, then, she found herself in the presence of Evil. And Evil came to her in the form of extreme tiredness and a soaring fever, leaving her in a half-conscious state, but incapable of sleep – while outside in the darkness, a wolf kept howling. Sometimes she thought she must be delirious, for it seemed the wolf had come into her room and was talking to her in a language she couldn't understand. In a brief moment of lucidity, she attempted to get up and go to the church, to ask the priest to call a doctor because she was ill, very ill; but when she tried to convert her intentions into actions, her legs gave way beneath her, and she was convinced she would be unable to walk.

Or, if she did manage to walk, she would be unable to reach the church.

Or, if she did reach the church, she would have to wait for the priest to wake up, get dressed and open the door, and meanwhile the cold would cause her fever to rise so rapidly that she would drop dead on the spot, right there outside the house that some considered to be sacred.

'At least they wouldn't have far to take me to the cemetery: I'd be virtually inside it already,' she thought.

Chantal's delirium lasted all night, but she noticed that her fever began to diminish as the morning light came filtering into her room. As her strength returned and she was trying to get to sleep, she heard the familiar sound of a car horn and realised that the baker's van had arrived in Viscos and that it must be time for breakfast.

There was no one there to make her go downstairs to buy bread; she was independent, she could stay in bed for as long as she wanted, since she only began work in the evening. But something had changed in her; she needed contact with the world, before she went completely mad. She wanted to be with the people she knew would now be gathering around the little green van, exchanging their coins for bread, happy because a new day was beginning and they had work to do and food to eat.

She went across to the van, greeting them all, and heard one or two remarks like: 'You look tired' or 'Is anything wrong?'. They were kind and supportive, always ready to help, simple and innocent in their generosity, while her soul was engaged in a bitter struggle for dreams and adventures, fear and power. Much as she would have liked to share her secret, she knew that if she revealed it to a single one of them, the rest of the village would be sure to know it before the morning was over. It was better to thank them for their concern and to carry on alone until her ideas had become a little clearer.

'No, it's nothing. There was a wolf howling all night and I couldn't get to sleep.'

'I didn't hear any wolf,' said the hotel landlady, who was also there buying bread.

'It's been months since any wolves were heard in the area,' confirmed another woman who made conserves to be sold in the hotel shop. 'The hunters must have killed them all, which is bad news for us because the wolves are the main reason the hunters come up here at all, to see who can kill the most elusive animal in the pack. It's a pretty pointless exercise, but they love it.'

'Don't say anything in front of the baker about there being no more wolves in the region,' muttered Chantal's boss. 'If word gets out, no one will come to Viscos at all.'

'But I heard a wolf.'

'Then it must have been the rogue wolf,' said the mayor's wife, who didn't much like Chantal, but who was sufficiently well-bred to hide her feelings.

The hotel landlady got annoyed. There was no rogue wolf. It was just an ordinary wolf, and it was probably dead by now anyway.

The mayor's wife, however, would not give up so easily.

'Regardless of whether or not it exists, we all know that there were no wolves howling last night. You work the poor girl too hard, up until all hours; she's so exhausted she's starting to get hallucinations.'

Chantal left the pair of them to their argument, picked up her bread and went on her way.

'A pointless exercise,' she repeated to herself, recalling the comment made by the woman who made the conserves. That was how they viewed life, as a pointless exercise. She nearly told them about the stranger's proposal there and then, just to see if those smug, narrow-minded people would be willing to take part in a genuinely purposeful exercise: ten gold bars in exchange for a simple murder, one that would guarantee the futures of their children and their grandchildren and return Viscos to its former glory, with or without wolves.

But she held back. She decided instead to tell the story that very night, in front of everyone, in the bar, so that no one could claim not to have heard or understood. Perhaps they would fall on the stranger and march him straight to the police, leaving her free to take her gold bar as a reward for services rendered to the community. Perhaps they simply wouldn't believe her, and the stranger would depart believing that they were all good, which wasn't the case at all.

They were so ignorant, so naïve, so resigned to their lot. They refused to believe anything that didn't fit in with what they were used to believing. They all lived in fear of God. They were all – herself included – cowards when the moment comes to change their fate. But as far as true goodness was concerned, that didn't exist – not in the land of cowardly men, nor in the heaven of Almighty God who sows suffering everywhere, just so that we can spend our whole lives begging him to deliver us from Evil.

The temperature had dropped. Chantal hadn't slept for three nights, but once she was preparing her breakfast, she felt much better. She wasn't the only coward, though she was possibly the only one aware of her own cowardice, because the rest of them thought of life as a 'pointless exercise' and confused fear with generosity.

She remembered a man who used to work in a chemist's in a nearby village and who had been dismissed after twenty years' service. He hadn't asked for his redundancy money because – so he said – he considered his employers to be his friends and didn't want to hurt them, because he knew they had had to dismiss him because of financial difficulties. It was all a lie: the reason the man did not go to court was because he was a coward; he wanted at all costs to be liked; he thought his employers would then always think of him as a generous, friendly sort. Some time later, when he went back to them to ask for a loan, they slammed the door in his face, but by then it was too late, for he had signed a letter of resignation and could make no further demands of them.

Very clever. Playing the part of a charitable soul was only for those who were afraid of taking a stand in life. It is always far easier to have faith in your own goodness than to confront others and fight for your rights. It is always easier to hear an insult and not retaliate than have the courage to fight back against someone stronger than yourself; we can always say we're not hurt by the stones others throw at us, and it's only at night – when we're alone and our wife or our husband or our school friend is asleep – that we can silently grieve over our own cowardice.

Chantal drank her coffee and hoped the day would pass quickly. She would destroy the village, she would bring Viscos to its knees that very night. The village would die within a generation anyway because it was a village without children – young people had their children elsewhere, in places where people went to parties, wore fine clothes, travelled and engaged in 'pointless exercises'.

The day, however, did not pass quickly. On the contrary, the grey weather and the low cloud made the hours drag. The mountains were obscured by mist, and the village seemed cut off from the world, turned in on itself, as if it were the only inhabited place on Earth. From her window, Chantal saw the stranger leave the hotel and, as usual, head for the mountains. She feared for her gold, but immediately calmed herself down – he was sure to come back because he had paid in advance for a week in the hotel, and rich men never waste a penny; only poor people do that.

She tried to read, but couldn't concentrate. She decided to go for a walk round Viscos, and the only person she saw was Berta, the widow, who spent her days sitting outside her house, watching everything that went on.

'It looks like it's finally going to get cold,' said Berta.

Chantal asked herself why people with nothing else to talk about always think the weather is so important. She nodded her agreement.

Then she went on her way, since she had said all she had to say to Berta in the many years she had lived in that village. There was a time when she had considered Berta an interesting, courageous woman, who had managed to continue her life even after the death of her husband in one of the many hunting accidents that happened each year. She had sold some of her few possessions and invested the money – together with the insurance money – in securities, and she now lived off the income.

Over time, however, the widow had ceased to be of interest to her, and had become instead an example of everything she feared *she* might become: ending her life sitting in a chair on her own doorstep, all muffled up in winter, staring at the only landscape she had ever known, watching over what didn't need watching over, since nothing serious, important or valuable ever happened there.

She walked on, unconcerned at the possibility of getting lost in the misty forest, because she knew every track, tree and stone by heart. She imagined how exciting things would be that night and tried out various ways of putting the stranger's proposal – in some versions she simply told them what she had seen and heard, in others she spun a tale that might or might not be true, imitating the style of the man who had not let her sleep now for three nights.

'A highly dangerous man, worse than any hunter I've ever met.'

Walking through the woods, Chantal began to realise that she had discovered another person just as dangerous as the stranger: herself. Up until four days ago, she had been imperceptibly becoming used to who she was, to what she could realistically expect from life, to the fact that living in Viscos wasn't really so bad – after all, the whole area was swamped with tourists in the summer, everyone of whom referred to the place as a 'paradise'.

Now the monsters were emerging from their tombs, darkening her nights, making her feel discontented, put upon, abandoned by God and by fate. Worse than that, they forced her to acknowledge the bitterness she carried around inside her day and night, into the forest and to work, into those rare love affairs and during her many moments of solitude.

'Damn the man. And damn myself too, since I was the one who made him cross my path.'

As she made her way back to the village, she regretted every single minute of her life; she cursed her mother for dying so young, her grandmother for having taught her to be honest and kind, the friends who had abandoned her and the fate that was still with her.

Berta was still at her post.

'You're in a great hurry,' she said. 'Why not sit down beside me and relax a bit?'

Chantal did as she suggested. She would do anything to make the time pass more quickly.

'The village seems to be changing,' Berta said. 'There's something different in the air, and last night I heard the rogue wolf howling.'

The girl felt relieved. She didn't know whether it had been the rogue wolf or not, but she had definitely heard a wolf howling that night, and at least one other person apart from her had heard it too.

'This place never changes,' she replied. 'Only the seasons come and go, and now it's winter's turn.'

'No, it's because the stranger has come.'

Chantal checked herself. Could it be that he had talked to someone else as well?

'What has the arrival of the stranger got to do with Viscos?'

'I spend the whole day looking at nature. Some people think it's a waste of time, but it was the only way I could find to accept the loss of someone I loved very much. I see the seasons pass, see the trees lose their leaves and then grow new ones. But occasionally something unexpected in nature brings about enormous changes. I've been told, for example, that the mountains all around us are the result of an earthquake that happened thousands of years ago.'

Chantal nodded; she had learned the same thing at school.

THE DEVIL AND MISS PRYM

'After that, nothing is ever the same. I'm afraid that is precisely what is going to happen now.'

Chantal was tempted to tell her the story of the gold, but, suspecting that the old woman might know something already, she said nothing.

'I keep thinking about Ahab, our great hero and reformer, the man who was blessed by St Savin.'

'Why Ahab?'

'Because he could see that even the most insignificant of actions, however well intentioned, can destroy everything. They say that after he had brought peace to the village, driven away the remaining outlaws and modernised agriculture and trade in Viscos, he invited his friends to supper and cooked a succulent piece of meat for them. Suddenly he realised there was no salt.

'So Ahab called to his son: "Go to the village and buy some salt, but pay a fair price for it: neither too much nor too little."

'His son was surprised: "I can understand why I shouldn't pay too much for it, father, but if I can bargain them down, why not pay a bit less?"

'"That would be the sensible thing to do in a big city, but in a small village like ours it could spell the beginning of the end."

'The boy left without asking any further questions. However, Ahab's guests, who had overheard their conversation, wanted to know why they should not buy the salt more cheaply if they could. Ahab replied:

'"The only reason anyone would sell salt more cheaply than usual would be because he was desperate for money. And anyone who took advantage of that situation would be showing a lack of respect for the sweat and struggle of the man who laboured to produce it."

'"But such a small thing couldn't possibly destroy a village."

'"In the beginning, there was only a small amount of injustice abroad in the world, but everyone who came afterwards added their portion, always thinking it was very small and unimportant, and look where we have ended up today."'

✳

'Like the stranger, for example,' Chantal said, hoping that Berta would confirm that she too had talked to him. But Berta said nothing.

'I don't know why Ahab was so keen to save Viscos,' Chantal went on. 'It started out as a den of thieves and now it's a village of cowards.'

Chantal was sure the old woman knew something. She only had to find out whether it was the stranger himself who had told her.

'That's true. But I'm not sure that it's cowardice exactly. I think everyone is afraid of change. They want Viscos to be as it always was: a place where you can till the soil and tend your livestock, a place that welcomes hunters and tourists, but where everyone knows exactly what is going to happen from one day to the next, and where the only unpredictable things are nature's storms. Perhaps it's a way of achieving peace, but I agree with you on one point: they all think they have everything under control, when, in fact, they control nothing.'

'Absolutely,' said Chantal.

'Not one jot or one tittle shall be added to what is written,' the old woman said, quoting from the Gospels. 'But we like to live with that illusion because it makes us feel safe. Well, it's a choice like any other, even though it's stupid to believe we can control the world and to allow ourselves to be lulled into a false sense of security that leaves us totally unprepared for life; because then, when you least expect it, an earthquake throws up a range of mountains, a bolt of lightning kills a tree that was preparing for its summer rebirth, or a hunting accident puts paid to the life of an honest man.'

For the hundredth time, Berta launched into the story of her husband's death. He had been one of the most respected guides in the region, a man who saw hunting not as a savage sport, but as a way of respecting local traditions. Thanks to him, Viscos had created a special nature reserve, the mayor had drawn up laws protecting certain near-extinct species, there was a tax per head of each animal killed, and the money collected was used for the good of the community.

Berta's husband tried to see the sport – considered cruel by some and traditional for others – as a way of teaching the hunters something about the art of living. Whenever someone with a lot of money but little hunting experience arrived in Viscos, he would take them out to a piece of waste ground. There, he would place a beer can on top of a stone.

Then he would stand about fifty yards from the can and, with a single shot, send it flying.

'I'm the best shot in the region,' he would say. 'And now you're going to learn how to become as good as me.'

He replaced the can on the same stone, walked back to where he had stood before, took a handkerchief out of his pocket and asked the newcomer to blindfold him. Then he aimed once more in the direction of the target and fired again.

'Did I hit it?' he would ask, removing the blindfold.

'Of course not,' the new arrival would say, pleased to see the proud guide humbled. 'You missed it by a mile. I don't think there's anything you can teach me.'

'I've just taught you the most important lesson in life,' Berta's husband would reply. 'Whenever you want to achieve something, keep your eyes open, concentrate and make sure you know exactly what it is you want. No one can hit their target with their eyes closed.'

Then, one day, while he was replacing the can on the stone after his first shot, the would-be hunter thought it must be his turn to show how good his aim was. Without waiting for Berta's husband to rejoin him, he fired. He missed the target, but hit the guide in the neck. He did not have the chance to learn that important lesson in concentration and objectivity.

✳

'I have to go,' Chantal said. 'There are a few things I need to do before I go to work.'

Berta said goodbye and watched her all the way until she disappeared down the alley beside the church. The years she had spent sitting outside her door, looking up at the mountains and the clouds, and holding conversations in her mind with her dead husband had taught her to 'see' people. Her vocabulary was limited, so she could find no other word to describe all the many sensations that other people aroused in her, but that was what happened: she 'saw through' other people, and could tell what their feelings were.

It had all started at the funeral for her one great love. She was weeping, and a child next to her – the son of an inhabitant of Viscos, who was now a grown man and lived thousands of miles away – asked her why she was sad.

Berta did not want to frighten the child by mentioning death and final farewells, so all she said was that her husband had gone away and might not come back to Viscos for a long time.

'I think he was having you on,' the boy replied. 'I've just seen him hiding behind a grave, all smiles, and with a soup spoon in his hand.'

The boy's mother heard what he said and scolded him for it. 'Children are always seeing things,' she said, apologising to Berta. But Berta immediately stopped crying and looked in the direction the child had indicated; her husband had always had the annoying habit of wanting to eat his soup with a special spoon, however much this irritated her – because all spoons are the same and hold the same amount of soup – yet he had always insisted on using his special spoon. Berta had never told anyone this, for fear people would think him crazy.

So the boy really had seen her husband; the spoon was the proof. Children could 'see' things. From then on, Berta decided that she was going to learn to 'see' as well, because she wanted to talk to her husband, to have him back – if only as a ghost.

At first, she shut herself up at home, rarely going out, waiting for him to appear to her. Then one day, something told her that she should go to the door of her house and start paying attention to other people, that her husband wanted her to have more joy in her life, for her to participate more in what was going on in the village.

She set up her chair outside her house and sat staring at the mountains; there were not many people out and about in the streets of Viscos, but on the very first day of her vigil, a neighbour returned from the next village, saying that they were selling quality cutlery very cheaply at the market there and, as proof, she produced a spoon from her bag.

Berta realised she would never see her husband again, but he was asking her to stay there, watching the village, and that was what she would do. As time went by, she began to perceive a presence beside her, to her left, and she was certain that he was there with her, keeping her company and protecting her from any danger, as well as teaching her to see things that others could not, such as the patterns made by the clouds, which always spelled out messages. She was rather sad that whenever she tried to look at him full on, the presence disappeared, but then she realised that she could talk to him using her intuition, and so they began having long conversations about all kinds of things.

Three years later, she was able to 'see' people's feelings, as well as receive some very useful practical advice from her husband. That was why she refused to be fobbed off with less compensation than she deserved, and why she withdrew her money from the bank just before it crashed, taking with it many local people's hard-earned savings.

One morning – and she could no longer remember exactly when this had happened – her husband told her that Viscos might be destroyed. Berta immediately thought of earthquakes creating whole new ranges of mountains, but he reassured her that nothing of that sort would happen there, at least not for the next few thousand years. He was worried about another sort of destruction, even though he himself was not exactly clear what form it would take. All the same, he asked her to be on her guard, because this was his village, the place he loved most in the whole world, even if he had left it rather sooner than he would have wished.

Berta began to pay more attention to people, to the patterns made by the clouds, to the hunters who came and went, but nothing appeared to indicate that anyone was trying to destroy a village that had never harmed anyone. Yet still her husband insisted that she keep watch, and she had done as he asked.

Then three days ago, she had seen the stranger arrive with a devil by his side and she knew her wait was over. Today, she had noticed that Chantal was accompanied by both a devil and an angel. She immediately linked the two events and understood that something odd was happening in her village.

She smiled to herself, glanced to her left and blew a discreet kiss. She was not a useless old woman; she had something important to do: to save the place where she had been born, even though she had no idea as yet what steps she should take.

Chantal left the old woman immersed in her thoughts, and went back to her room. It was whispered among the inhabitants of Viscos that Berta was a witch. It was said she had shut herself up in her house for almost a year and, during that time, had taught herself the magic arts. When Chantal had asked who could have taught them to Berta, some said it was the devil himself who appeared to her at night, while others swore that she invoked the spirit of a Celtic priest, using words her parents had taught her. But no one was overly concerned: Berta was harmless and she always had good stories to tell.

They were right, although they were always the same stories. Suddenly Chantal paused with her hand on the doorknob. Even though she had heard the story of how Berta's husband had died many times over, it was only now that she realised there was an important lesson in it for her too. She remembered her recent walk in the forest and the pent-up hatred she had felt inside her, a hatred that seemed to fly out all around her, threatening whoever was near, be it herself, the village, the people in it or their children.

But she had only one real target: the stranger. Concentrate, shoot and kill your prey. To do that, she needed a plan – it would be foolish to speak out that night and let the situation run out of control. She decided to put off for another day telling the story of how she had met the stranger, if, that is, she ever did tell the other inhabitants of Viscos.

That night, when she went to collect the money for the round of drinks that the stranger usually bought, Chantal noticed that he had slipped her a note. She put it straight into her pocket, pretending that it was a matter of no importance, even though she was aware of the stranger's eyes occasionally seeking hers, as if silently questioning her. The roles seemed to have been reversed: it was she who was in control of the situation, she who could choose the battlefield and the hour of the fight. That was how all the most successful hunters behaved: they always arranged things so that the prey would come to them.

It was only when she returned to her room, this time confident that she would sleep soundly, that she looked at the note: the stranger was asking her to meet him in the place where they had first met.

He closed by saying that he would prefer to talk to her alone, but added that, if she wanted, they could also speak with everyone else present too.

The threat did not escape her, but she was, in fact, delighted that he had made it. It was proof that he was losing control, because truly dangerous men and women never make threats. Ahab, the man who brought peace to Viscos, always used to say: 'There are two kinds of idiots – those who don't take action because they have received a threat, and those who think they are taking action because they have issued a threat.'

She tore the note into shreds and flushed it down the toilet, then she took a scalding hot bath, slipped into bed and smiled. She had got exactly what she wanted: to meet the stranger again for a conversation alone. If she wanted to find out how to defeat him, she needed to get to know him better.

She fell asleep almost at once – a deep, refreshing, easeful sleep. She had spent one night with Good, one with Good and Evil, and one with Evil. Not one of the three had produced any definite result, but they were all still alive in her soul, and now they were beginning to fight amongst themselves to see who was strongest.

B y the time the stranger arrived, Chantal was drenched – the
storm had recommenced.

'Let's not talk about the weather,' she said. 'As you can see, it's
raining. I know a place where it'll be easier for us to talk.'

She got to her feet and picked up a long canvas bag.

'You've got a shotgun in there,' the stranger said.

'Yes.'

'And you want to kill me.'

'Yes, I do. I don't know if I'll succeed, but that's what I'd like to do. I
brought the weapon here for another reason, though: I might meet the
rogue wolf on the way, and if I could shoot him, I might win some respect
in Viscos. No one believes me, but I heard him howling last night.'

'And what is this rogue wolf?'

At first she doubted whether to share anything more with this man
who was her enemy. But then she remembered a book on Japanese
martial arts – she always read any books left behind by hotel guests,
no matter what the books were about, because she didn't want to
spend her own money buying them. There it was written that the
best way to weaken one's enemy was to get him to believe that you
were on his side.

As they trudged through the wind and the rain, she told him the
story. Two years ago, a man from Viscos – the blacksmith, to be

precise – was out for a walk when, all of a sudden, he came face to face with a wolf and its young. The man was terrified, but he tore off a branch and made to attack the animal. Normally, the wolf would have run away, but as it was with its young, it counter-attacked and bit the man on the leg. The blacksmith, a man whose job requires enormous strength, managed to deal the wolf such a blow that it finally ran back into the forest with its cubs and was never seen again; all anyone knew was that it had a white mark on its left ear.

'But why is it called the rogue wolf?'

'Usually even the fiercest of animals will only attack in exceptional circumstances, in order, for example, to protect its young. However, if an animal does attack and tastes human blood, then it becomes dangerous; it will always want more; it will cease being a wild animal and become a killer. Everyone believes that one day the wolf will attack again.'

'That's my story too,' the stranger thought.

Chantal was walking as fast as she could because she was younger and fitter than him and wanted to gain a psychological advantage over her companion by tiring him out and humiliating him, and yet he managed to keep up with her. He was out of breath, but he never once asked her to slow down.

They reached a small, well-camouflaged, green plastic tent, used by hunters as a hide. They sat inside, rubbing their frozen hands and blowing on them.

'What do you want?' she asked him. 'Why did you give me that note?'

'I'm going to ask you a riddle: of all the days in our life, which is the one that never comes?'

There was no reply.

'Tomorrow,' the stranger said. 'But you seem to believe that tomorrow will come and keep putting off what I asked you to do. We're getting towards the end of the week, and if you don't say something, I'll have to do it myself.'

Chantal left the refuge, stood a safe distance from it, undid the canvas bag, and took out the shotgun. The stranger didn't seem to attach any importance to this.

'You dug up the gold again,' he went on. 'If you had to write a book about your experiences, how do you think most of your readers would react – given all the difficulties they have to face, the injustices dealt to them by life and other people, the struggle they have in order to pay for their children's schooling and to put food on the table – don't you think that those people would be urging you to take the gold and run?'

'I don't know,' she said, loading a cartridge into the gun.

'Nor do I. But that's the answer I'm looking for.'

She inserted the second cartridge.

'You're willing to kill me, despite that reassuring little tale about finding a wolf. But that's all right, because that too provides me with an answer to my question: human beings are essentially evil, even a young woman from a remote village is capable of committing murder for money. I'm going to die, but now I have my answer, so I can die happy.'

'Here, take it,' she said, handing him the gun. 'No one knows that I know you. All the details you gave in the hotel are false. You can leave when you want and, as I understand it, you can go anywhere you want to in the world. You don't need to have a good aim: all you have to do is point the shotgun in my direction and squeeze the trigger. Each cartridge is full of tiny bits of lead; as soon as they leave the barrel, they spread out into a cone shape. They can kill birds or human beings. You can even look the other way if you don't want to see my body being blown apart.'

The man curled his finger round the trigger, and Chantal was surprised to see that he was holding the gun correctly, like a professional. They stood like that for a long while, and she was aware that he had only to slip or be startled by an animal coming on them unexpectedly and his finger could move and the gun go off. She suddenly realised how childish her gesture had been, trying to defy someone merely for the pleasure of provoking him, saying that he was incapable of doing what he was asking others to do.

The stranger was still pointing the gun at her, staring at her unblinking, his hands steady. It was too late now – maybe deep down he thought it wouldn't be such a bad idea to end the life of this young woman who had dared to challenge him. Chantal was on the point of asking him to forgive her, but the stranger lowered the gun before she could say a word.

'I can almost touch your fear,' he said, handing her back the gun. 'I can smell the sweat pouring off you, despite the rain, and even though the wind is shaking the treetops and making an infernal racket, I can hear your heart thumping in your throat.'

'I'm going to do what you asked me to do this evening,' she said, pretending she hadn't heard the truths he was telling her. 'After all, you came to Viscos to learn about your own nature, to find out if you were good or evil. There's one thing I've just shown you: regardless of what I may have felt or stopped feeling just now, you could have pulled the trigger, but you didn't. Do you know why? Because you're a coward. You use others to resolve your own conflicts, but you are incapable of taking certain decisions.'

'A German philosopher once said: "Even God has a hell: his love of mankind". No, I'm not a coward. I've pressed many worse triggers than this one, or, rather, I have made far better guns than this and distributed them around the world. I did it all perfectly legally, got the transactions approved by the government, the export licences, paid all the necessary taxes. I married a woman who loved me, I had two beautiful daughters, I never stole a penny from my company, and always succeeded in recovering any money owed to me.

'Unlike you, who feel persecuted by destiny, I was always a man of action, someone who struggled with the many difficulties in my way, who lost some battles and won others, but always understood that victories and defeats form part of everyone's life – everyone, that is, except cowards, as you call them, because they never lose or win.

'I read a lot. I was a regular churchgoer. I feared God and respected His commandments. I was a highly paid director of a huge firm. Since I was paid commission on every deal we made, I earned more than enough to support my wife, my daughters, and even my grandchildren and my great-grandchildren; because the arms trade is the most profitable business in the world. I knew the value of every item I sold, so I personally checked all our transactions; that way I uncovered several cases of corruption and dismissed those involved and halted the sales. My weapons were made to help defend order, which is the only way to ensure progress and development in this world, or so I thought.'

The stranger came up to Chantal and took her by the shoulders; he wanted her to look him in the eyes and know that he was telling the truth.

'You may consider arms manufacturers to be the lowest of the low. Perhaps you're right, but the fact is that man has used weapons ever since he lived in caves – first to kill animals, then to win power over others. The world has existed without agriculture, without domesticated animals, without religion, without music, but never without weapons.'

He picked up a stone from the ground.

'Here's the first of them, generously donated by Mother Nature to those who had to confront prehistoric animals. A stone like this doubtless saved the life of a man, and that man, after countless generations, led to you and me being born. If he hadn't had that stone, the murderous carnivore would have devoured him, and hundreds of millions of people would not have been born.'

The wind was blowing harder, and the rain was battering them, but neither of them looked away.

'Many people criticise hunters, but Viscos welcomes them with open arms because it lives off them; some people hate seeing a bull in a bullring, but go and buy the meat from the butcher's claiming that the animal had an "honourable" death; a lot of people are critical of arms manufacturers, but they will continue to exist until there's not a single weapon left on the face of the earth. Because as long as one weapon remains, there will always have to be another, to preserve the fragile balance.'

'What has all this got to do with my village?' Chantal demanded. 'What has it got to do with breaking the commandments, with murder, stealing, with the essence of human nature, with Good and Evil?'

At this, the stranger's eyes changed, as if overwhelmed by a deep sadness.

'Remember what I told you at the beginning. I always tried to do my business according to the law; I considered myself what people usually term a "good man". Then one evening I received a phone call in my office: it was a woman's voice, soft but devoid of emotion. She said her terrorist group had kidnapped my wife and daughters. They wanted a large quantity of what they knew I could give them – weapons. They told me to keep quiet about it, they told me that nothing would happen to my family if I followed their instructions.

'The woman rang off saying that she would call again in half an hour and told me to wait for her call in a phone box at the train station. She said not to worry; my family was being well treated and would be freed within a few hours, because all I had to do was send an electronic message to one of our subsidiaries in a certain country. It wasn't even real theft, more like an illegal sale that would go completely unnoticed in the company I worked for.

'Since I was a good citizen, brought up to respect the law and to feel protected by it, the first thing I did was to ring the police. A minute later, I was no longer the master of my own decisions, I was transformed into someone incapable of protecting his own family; my universe was suddenly filled with anonymous voices and frantic phone calls. When I went to the designated phone box, an army of technicians had already hooked up the underground telephone cable to the most modern equipment available, so that they could instantaneously trace exactly where the call was coming from. There were helicopters ready to take off, police cars strategically positioned to block the traffic, trained men, armed to the teeth, on full alert.

'Two different governments, in distant continents, already knew what was going on and they forbade any negotiations; all I had to do was to follow orders, repeat what they told me to say and behave exactly as instructed by the experts.

'Before the day was out, the hiding place where they were keeping the hostages had been discovered, and the kidnappers – two young men and a woman, all apparently inexperienced, simply disposable elements in a powerful political organisation – lay dead, riddled with bullets. Before they died, however, they had time to execute my wife and daughters. If even God has a hell, which is his love for mankind, then any man has his hell within easy reach, and that's his love for his family.'

The stranger fell silent; he was afraid of losing control of his voice and betraying an emotion he preferred to keep hidden. As soon as he had recovered, he went on:

'Both the police and the kidnappers used weapons made by my company. No one knows how the terrorists came to be in possession of them, and that's of no importance: they had them. Despite all my efforts, my struggle to ensure that everything was carried out according to the strictest regulations for their manufacture and sale, my family had been killed by something which I, at some point, had sold – perhaps over a meal at an expensive restaurant, while I chatted about the weather or world politics.'

Another pause. When he spoke again, it was as if he were another person, as if nothing he was saying had anything to do with him.

'I know the weapon and the ammunition used to kill my family well. I know which part of the body they aimed at: the chest. The bullet makes only a small hole on entering – about the size of your little finger. When it hits the first bone, though, it splits into four, and each of the fragments continues in a different direction, brutally destroying everything in its path: kidneys, heart, liver, lungs. Every time it comes up against something solid, like a vertebra, it changes direction again, usually carrying with it sharp bone fragments and bits of torn muscle, until at last it finds a way out. Each of the four exit wounds is almost as big as a fist, and the bullet still has enough force to spatter round the room the bits of tissue, flesh and bone that clung to it during its journey through the body.

'All of this takes less than two seconds; two seconds to die might not seem very long, but time isn't measured like that. You understand, I hope.'

Chantal nodded.

'At the end of that year, I left my job. I travelled to the four corners of the earth, alone with my grief, asking myself how human beings can be capable of such evil. I lost the most precious thing a man can have: my faith in my fellow man. I laughed and I wept at God's irony, at the absurd way he had chosen to demonstrate to me that I was an instrument of Good and Evil.

'All my sense of compassion gradually vanished, and now my heart has entirely shrivelled up; I don't care whether I live or die. But first, for the sake of my wife and daughters, I need to grasp what happened in that hiding place. I can understand how people can kill out of hate or love, but why do it for no particular reason, simply over some business transaction?

'This may seem naïve to you – after all, people kill each other every day for money – but that doesn't interest me, I'm only concerned with my wife and daughters. I want to know what was going on in the minds of those terrorists. I want to know whether, at any point, they might have taken pity on them and let them leave, because their war had nothing to do with my family. I want to know if, when Good and Evil are pitted against each other, there is a fraction of a second when Good might prevail.'

'Why Viscos? Why my village?'

'Why the weapons from my factory, when there are so many armaments factories in the world, some of them with no government controls? The answer is simple: chance. I needed a small place where everyone knew each other and got on together. The moment they learned about the reward, Good and Evil would once again be pitted against each other, and what had happened in that hiding place would happen in your village.

'The terrorists were already surrounded and defeated; nevertheless, they killed my family merely in order to carry out a useless, empty ritual. Your village has what I did not have: it has the possibility to choose. They will be tempted by the desire for money and perhaps believe they have a mission to protect and save their village, but even so, they still retain the ability to decide whether or not to execute the hostage. That's all. I want to see whether other people might have acted differently to those poor, bloodthirsty youngsters.

'As I told you when we first met, the story of one man is the story of all men. If compassion exists, I will accept that fate was harsh with me, but that sometimes it can be gentle with others. That won't change the way I feel in the slightest, it won't bring my family back, but at least it will drive away the devil that's always with me and give me some hope.'

'And why do you want to know whether I am capable of stealing the gold?'

'For the same reason. You may divide the world into trivial crimes and serious ones, but it isn't like that. I think the terrorists did the same. They thought they were killing for a cause, not just for pleasure, love, hate or money. If you took the gold bar, you would have to justify the crime to yourself and to me, and then I would understand how the murderers justified to themselves the killing of my loved ones. As you have seen, I have spent all these years trying to understand what happened. I don't know whether this will bring me peace, but I can't see any alternative.'

'If I did steal the gold, you would never see me again.'

For the first time during the almost thirty minutes they had been talking, the stranger smiled faintly.

'I worked in the arms industry, don't forget. And that included work for the secret service.'

The man asked her to lead him to the river – he was lost, and did not know how to get back. Chantal took the shotgun – she had borrowed it from a friend on the pretext that she was very tense and needed to do a bit of hunting to try and relax – put it back in its bag, and the two of them set off down the hill.

They said nothing to each other on the way down. When they reached the river, the stranger said goodbye.

'I understand why you're delaying, but I can't wait any longer. I can also understand that, in order to struggle with yourself, you needed to get to know me better: now you do.

'I am a man who walks the earth with a devil at his side; in order to drive him away or to accept him once and for all, I need to know the answers to certain questions.'

The fork banged repeatedly against the wineglass. Everyone in the bar, which was packed on that Friday night, turned towards the sound: it was Miss Prym calling for them to be silent.

The effect was immediate: never in all the history of the village had a young woman whose sole duty was to serve the customers acted in such a manner.

'She had better have something important to say,' thought the hotel landlady. 'If not, I'll get rid of her tonight, despite the promise I made to her grandmother never to abandon her.'

'I'd like you all to listen,' Chantal said. 'I'm going to tell you a story that everyone here, apart from our visitor, will know,' she said, pointing to the stranger. 'After that, I'll tell you another story that no one here, apart from our visitor, will know. When I've finished, it will be up to you to judge whether or not it was wrong of me to interrupt your well-earned Friday evening rest, after an exhausting week's work.'

'She's taking a terrible risk,' the priest thought. 'She doesn't know anything we don't know. She may be a poor orphan with few possibilities in life, but it's going to be difficult to persuade the hotel landlady to keep her on after this.'

But, when he thought about it again, perhaps it wouldn't. We all commit sins, which are generally followed by two or three days of anger, after which all is forgiven; besides, he couldn't think of anyone else in the village who could do her job. It was a young person's job, and there were no other young people in Viscos.

'Viscos has three streets, a small square with a cross in it, a few ruined houses and a church with a cemetery beside it,' Chantal began.

'Just a moment,' the stranger said.

He took a small cassette recorder out of his pocket, switched it on, and placed it on his table.

'I'm interested in everything to do with the history of Viscos. I don't want to miss a single word, so I hope you don't mind if I record you.'

Chantal did not know whether she minded or not, but there was no time to lose. She had been battling with her fears for hours, and now that she had finally found the courage to begin, she did not want any interruptions.

'Viscos has three streets, a small square with a cross in it, a few ruined houses and a few well-preserved ones, a hotel, a post box, and a church with a cemetery next to it.'

Her description this time was a little more complete. She was not so nervous now.

'As we all know, it used to be a haven for outlaws until our great lawmaker, Ahab, after his conversion by St Savin, succeeded in transforming it into the village we know today, home only to men and women of good will.

'What the stranger doesn't know, and as I am going to explain now, is how Ahab managed to achieve that transformation. At no point did he try to convince anyone, because he knew what people were like; they would confuse honesty with weakness, and his authority would immediately be placed in doubt.

What he did was to send for some carpenters from a neighbouring village, give them a piece of paper with a drawing on it, and order them to build something on the spot where the cross now stands. Day and night throughout the next ten days, the inhabitants of the village heard the sound of hammers and watched men sawing up planks of wood, fitting them together and screwing one piece to another. At the end of the ten days, this giant jigsaw puzzle was erected in the middle of the square, covered with a cloth. Ahab called all the villagers together for the inauguration of the monument.

'Solemnly, without any speeches, he removed the cloth: there stood a gallows, complete with rope, trap door, everything, brand new and greased with beeswax to withstand the ravages of the weather for many years. Then, taking advantage of the fact that everyone was there, Ahab read out a series of new laws that protected farmers, encouraged the raising of livestock and rewarded anyone bringing new trade to Viscos. He added that, from then on, everyone would either have to find honest work or leave the village. That was all he said; not once did he mention the "monument" he had just inaugurated. Ahab did not believe in making threats.

'When the ceremony was over, people gathered together in various groups. Most of them believed that Ahab had been duped by the saint, that he had lost his nerve, and that he should be killed. During the days that followed, many plans were made with that objective in mind. But the plotters could not avoid the sight of the gallows in the middle of the square, and they thought: What is that doing there? Was it erected in order to deal with anyone who goes against the new laws? Who is on Ahab's side and who isn't? Are there spies in our midst?

'The gallows looked at the villagers, and the villagers looked at the gallows. Gradually, the rebels' initial defiance gave way to fear; they all knew Ahab's reputation and they knew he never went back on a decision. Some of them left the village, others decided to try the new jobs that had been suggested, simply because they had nowhere else to go or because they were conscious of the shadow cast by that instrument of death in the middle of the square. Before long, Viscos had been pacified and it became a large trading centre near the frontier, exporting the finest wool and producing top-quality wheat.

'The gallows remained in place for ten years. The wood withstood the weather well, but the rope occasionally had to be replaced with a new one. The gallows was never used. Ahab never once mentioned it. The mere sight of the gallows was enough to turn courage into fear, trust into suspicion, bravado into whispers of submission. When ten years had passed and the rule of law had finally been established in Viscos, Ahab had the gallows dismantled and used the wood to build a cross instead.'

Chantal paused. The bar was completely silent apart from the sound of the stranger clapping.

'That's an excellent story,' he said. 'Ahab really understood human nature: it isn't the desire to abide by the law that makes everyone behave as society requires, but the fear of punishment. Each one of us carries a gallows inside us.'

'Today, at the stranger's request, I am pulling down the cross and erecting another gallows in the middle of the square,' Chantal went on.

'Carlos,' someone said, 'his name is Carlos, and it would be more polite to call him by his name than to keep referring to him as "the stranger".'

'I don't know his real name. All the details he gave on the hotel form are false. He's never paid for anything with a credit card. We have no idea where he came from or where he's going to; even the phone call to the airport could be a lie.'

They all turned to look at the man, who kept his eyes fixed on Chantal.

'Yet, when he did tell you the truth, none of you believed him. He really did work for an armaments factory, he really has had all kinds of adventures and been all kinds of different people, from loving father to ruthless businessman. But because you live here in Viscos, you cannot comprehend how much richer and more complex life can be.'

'That girl had better explain herself,' thought the hotel landlady. And that's just what Chantal did:

'Four days ago, he showed me ten large gold bars. They are worth enough to guarantee the future of all the inhabitants of Viscos for the next thirty years, to provide for major improvements to the village, a children's playground, for example, in the hope that one day children will live here again. He then immediately hid them in the forest, and I don't know where they are.'

Everyone again turned towards the stranger, who, this time, looked back at them and nodded his head.

'That gold will belong to Viscos if, in the next three days, someone in the village is murdered. If no one dies, the stranger will leave, taking his gold with him.

'And that's it. I've said all I had to say, and I've re-erected the gallows in the square. Except that this time, it is not there to prevent a crime, but so that an innocent person can be hanged, so that the sacrifice of that innocent person will bring prosperity to the village.'

For the third time, all the people in the bar turned towards the stranger. Once again, he nodded.

'The girl tells a good story,' he said, switching off the recorder and putting it back in his pocket.

Chantal turned away and began washing glasses in the sink. It was as if time had stopped in Viscos; no one said a word. The only sound that could be heard was that of running water, of a glass being put down on a marble surface, of the distant wind shaking the branches of leafless trees.

The mayor broke the silence:

'Let's call the police.'

'Go ahead,' the stranger said. 'I've got a recording here, and my only comment was: "The girl tells a good story."'

'Please, go up to your room, pack your things, and leave here at once,' said the hotel landlady.

'I've paid for a week and I'm going to stay a week. Even if you have to call the police.'

'Has it occurred to you that you might be the person to be murdered?'

'Of course. And it really doesn't matter to me. But if you did murder me, then you would have committed the crime, but you would never receive the promised reward.'

One by one, the regulars in the bar filed out, the younger ones first and the older people last. Soon only Chantal and the stranger were left.

She picked up her bag, put on her coat, went to the door and then turned to him.

'You're a man who has suffered and wants revenge,' she said. 'Your heart is dead, your soul is in darkness. The devil by your side is smiling because you are playing the game he invented.'

'Thank you for doing as I asked. And for telling me the true and very interesting story of the gallows.'

'In the forest, you told me that you wanted answers to certain questions, but from the way you have constructed your plan, only Evil will be rewarded; if no one is murdered, Good will earn nothing but praise. And as you know, praise cannot feed hungry mouths or help to restore dying villages. You're not trying to find the answer to a question, you're simply trying to confirm something you desperately want to believe: that everyone is evil.'

A change came over the stranger's face, and Chantal noticed it.

'If the whole world is evil, then the tragedy that befell you is justified,' she went on. 'That would make it easier for you to accept the deaths of your wife and daughters. But if good people do exist, then, however much you deny it, your life will be unbearable; because fate set a trap for you, and you know you didn't deserve it.

It isn't the light you want to recover, it's the certainty that there is only darkness.'

'What exactly are you driving at?' he said, a slight tremor in his voice.

'The wager should be fairer. If, after three days, no one is murdered, the village should get the ten gold bars anyway. As a reward for the integrity of its inhabitants.'

The stranger laughed.

'And I will receive my gold bar, as a reward for my participation in this sordid game.'

'I'm not a fool, you know. If I agreed to that, the first thing you would do is to go outside and tell everyone.'

'Possibly. But I won't; I swear by my grandmother and by my eternal salvation.'

'That's not enough. No one knows whether God listens to vows, or if eternal salvation exists.'

'You'll know I haven't told them, because the gallows is there now in the middle of the village. It will be clear if there's been any kind of trickery. And anyway, even if I went out there now and told everyone what we've just been talking about, no one would believe me; it would be the same as arriving in Viscos and saying: "Look, all this is yours, regardless of whether or not you do what the stranger is asking." These men and women are used to working hard, to earning every penny with the sweat of their brow; they would never even admit the possibility of gold just falling from heaven like that.'

The stranger lit a cigarette, finished off his drink and got up from the table. Chantal awaited his reply standing by the open door, letting the cold air into the room.

'I'll know if there's been any cheating,' he said. 'I'm used to dealing with people, just like your Ahab.'

'I'm sure you are. So that means "yes", then.'

Again he nodded his agreement.

'And one more thing: you still believe that man can be good. If that weren't the case, you wouldn't have invented all this nonsense to convince yourself otherwise.'

Chantal closed the door and walked down the main street in the village – completely deserted at that hour – sobbing uncontrollably. Without wanting to, she had become caught up in the game; she was betting on the fact that people were basically good, despite all the Evil in the world. She would never tell anyone what she and the stranger had just been talking about because, now, she too wanted to know the answer.

She was aware that, although the street was empty, from behind the curtains in darkened rooms, the eyes of Viscos were watching as she walked back home. It didn't matter; it was far too dark for anyone to see her tears.

The man opened the window of his room, hoping that the cold would silence the voice of his devil for a few moments.

As expected, it did not work, because the devil was even more agitated than usual after what the girl had just said. For the first time in many years, the stranger noticed that the devil seemed weaker, and there were moments when he even appeared rather distant; however, he soon reappeared, no stronger or weaker than usual, but much as he always was. He lived in the left-hand side of the man's brain, in the part that governs logic and reasoning, but he never allowed himself to be seen, so that the man was forced to imagine what he must be like. He tried to picture him in a thousand different ways, from the conventional devil with horns and a tail to a young woman with blonde curls. The image he finally settled on was that of a young man in his twenties, with black trousers, a blue shirt, and a green beret perched nonchalantly on his dark hair.

He had first heard the devil's voice on an island, where he had travelled after resigning from his job; he was on the beach, in terrible emotional pain, trying desperately to believe that his suffering must have an end, when he saw the most beautiful sunset he had ever seen. It was then that his despair came back in force, and he plumbed the depths of the deepest abyss in his soul precisely because such a sunset should also have been seen by his wife and children. He broke into uncontrollable sobs and felt that he would never climb up from the bottom of that pit.

At that moment, a friendly, companionable voice told him that he was not alone, that everything that had happened to him had a purpose, which was to show that each person's destiny is pre-ordained. Tragedy always happens, and nothing we do can alter by one jot the evil that awaits us.

'There is no such thing as Good: virtue is simply one of the many faces of terror,' the voice said. 'When man understands that, he will realise that this world is just a little joke played on him by God.'

Then the voice – which identified itself as the prince of this world, the only being who really knows what happens on Earth – began to show him the people all around him on the beach. The wonderful father who was busy packing things up and helping his children put on some warm clothes and who would love to have an affair with his secretary, but was terrified of his wife's response. His wife who would like to work and have her independence, but who was terrified of her husband's response. The children who behaved themselves because they were terrified of being punished. The girl who was reading a book all on her own beneath a sunshade, pretending she didn't care, but inside was terrified of spending the rest of her life alone. The boy running around with a tennis racquet, terrified of having to live up to his parents' expectations. The waiter serving tropical drinks to the rich customers and terrified that he could be sacked at any moment. The young girl who wanted to be a dancer, but who was studying law instead because she was terrified of what the neighbours might say. The old man who didn't smoke or drink and said he felt much better for it, when in truth it was the terror of death that whispered in his ears like the wind. The married couple who ran by, splashing through the surf, with a smile on their face but with a terror in their hearts telling them that they would soon be old, boring and useless. The man with the suntan who swept up in his launch in front of everybody and waved and smiled, but was terrified because he could lose all his money from one moment to the next. The hotel owner, watching the whole idyllic scene from his office, trying to keep everyone happy and cheerful, urging his accountants to ever greater vigilance, and terrified because he knew that however honest he was government officials would still find mistakes in his accounts if they wanted to.

There was terror in each and every one of the people on that beautiful beach and on that breathtakingly beautiful evening. Terror of being alone, terror of the darkness filling their imaginations with devils, terror of doing anything not in the manuals of good behaviour, terror of God's judgement, of what other people would say, of the law punishing any mistake, terror of trying and failing, terror of succeeding and having to live with the envy of other people, terror of loving and being rejected, terror of asking for a rise in salary, of accepting an invitation, of going somewhere new, of not being able to speak a foreign language, of not making the right impression, of growing old, of dying, of being pointed out because of one's defects, of not being pointed out because of one's merits, of not being noticed either for one's defects or one's merits.

Terror, terror, terror. Life was a reign of terror, in the shadow of the guillotine. 'I hope this consoles you a little,' he heard the devil say. 'They're all terrified; you're not alone. The only difference is that you have already been through the most difficult part; your worst fear became reality. You have nothing to lose, whereas these people on the beach live with their terror all the time; some are aware of it, others try to ignore it, but all of them know that it exists and will get them in the end.'

Incredible though it may seem, these words did console him somewhat, as if the suffering of others alleviated his own. From that moment on, the devil had become a more and more frequent companion. He had lived with him for two years now, and he felt neither happy nor sad to know that the devil had completely taken over his soul.

As he became accustomed to the devil's company, he tried to find out more about the origin of Evil, but none of his questions received precise answers.

'There's no point trying to discover why I exist. If you really want an explanation, you can tell yourself that I am God's way of punishing himself for having decided, in an idle moment, to create the Universe.'

Since the devil was reluctant to talk about himself, the man decided to look up every reference he could find to hell. He discovered that most religions have something called 'a place of punishment', where the immortal soul goes after committing certain crimes against society (everything seemed to be seen in terms of society, rather than of the individual). Some religions said that once the spirit was separated from the body, it crossed a river, met a dog and entered hell by a gate of no return. Since the body was laid in a tomb, the place of punishment was generally described as being dark and situated inside the earth; thanks to volcanoes, it was known that the centre of the earth was full of fire, and so the human imagination came up with the idea of flames torturing sinners.

He found one of the most interesting descriptions of this punishment in an Arabian book: there it was written that once the soul had left the body, it had to walk across a bridge as narrow as a knife edge, with paradise on the right and, on the left, a series of circles that led down into the darkness inside the earth. Before crossing the bridge (the book did not explain where it led to), each person had to place all his virtues in his right hand and all his sins in his left, and the imbalance between the two meant that the person always fell towards the side to which his actions on Earth had inclined him.

Christianity spoke of a place where there would be weeping and gnashing of teeth. Judaism described a cave with only room enough for a finite number of souls – when this hell was full, the world would end. Islam spoke of the fire in which we would all burn 'unless God desires otherwise'. For Hindus, hell was never a place of eternal torment, since they believed that the soul would be reincarnated after a certain period of time in order to pay for its sins in the same place where they had been committed – in other words, in this world. Even so, there were no fewer than twenty-one of these places of punishment in what was usually referred to as 'the lower depths'.

The Buddhists also distinguished between the different kinds of punishment a soul might face; eight fiery hells and eight freezing ones, as well as a kingdom where the condemned soul felt neither heat nor cold, only infinite hunger and thirst.

Nothing though could compare to the huge variety that the Chinese had thought up; unlike everyone else – who placed hell deep down inside the earth – the Chinese believed that the souls of sinners went to a mountain range known as the Little Wall of Iron and surrounded by another mountain range known as the Great Wall. In the space between these two ranges, there were no less than eight large hells one on top of the other, each of which controlled sixteen smaller hells, which in turn controlled ten million hells beneath them. The Chinese also said that devils were made up of the souls of those who had already completed their punishment.

The Chinese were also the only ones to offer a convincing explanation of the origin of devils – they were evil because they had personal experience of evil, and now they wanted to pass it on to others, in an eternal cycle of vengeance.

'Which is perhaps what is happening to me,' the stranger said to himself, remembering Miss Prym's words. The devil had heard those words too and felt he had lost some of his hard-won ground. The only way he could regain it was to leave no room for doubt in the stranger's mind.

'All right, so you had a moment of doubt,' the devil said, 'but the terror remains. The story of the gallows was a good one, because it clearly shows that mankind is virtuous only because terror exists, but that men are still essentially bad, my true descendants.'

The stranger was shivering now, but decided to leave the window open a while longer.

'God, I did not deserve what happened to me. If you did that to me, I can do the same to others. That is justice.'

The devil was worried, but resolved to keep quiet – he could not show that he too was terrified. The man was blaspheming against God and trying to justify his actions, but this was the first time in two years he had heard him addressing the heavens.

It was a bad sign.

'It's a good sign,' was Chantal's first thought when she heard the baker's van sounding its horn. Life in Viscos was going on as usual, the bread was being delivered, people were leaving their houses, they would have the whole of Saturday and Sunday to discuss the insane proposition put before them, and then, with some regret, they would watch the stranger depart on Monday morning. Later that evening, she would tell them about the wager she had made, announcing that they had won the battle and were rich.

She would never become a saint like St Savin, but for many generations to come she would be remembered as the woman who saved the village from Evil's second visitation. Maybe they would make up legends about her; the village's future inhabitants might refer to her as a lovely young woman, the only one who had not abandoned Viscos because she knew she had a mission to fulfil. Pious ladies would light candles to her, and young men would sigh passionately over the heroine they had never known.

She was proud of herself, but was aware that she should watch what she said and make no mention of the gold bar that belonged to her, otherwise they would end up convincing her that, in order to be considered a saint, she should also divide up her share.

In her own way she was helping the stranger to save his soul, and God would take this into account when he made a final reckoning of her deeds. The fate of the stranger mattered little to her, however; what she had to do now was to hope that the next two days passed as quickly as possible, for it was hard to keep a secret like that locked up in her heart.

The inhabitants of Viscos were neither better nor worse than those of neighbouring villages, but there was no way they would be capable of committing a murder for money – of that she was sure. Now that the story was out in the open, no man or woman could take the initiative alone. First, because the reward would have to be divided up equally, and she knew that no one would want to risk themselves purely so that others might gain. Second, because, if they were thinking what she deemed to be the unthinkable, they needed to be able to count on the full co-operation of all the others – with the exception, perhaps, of the chosen victim. If a single individual was against the idea – and if need be, she would be that person – the men and women of Viscos all ran the risk of being denounced and imprisoned. Better to be poor and honourable than rich and in jail.

Chantal went downstairs remembering that hitherto even the election of a mayor to govern this village with its three streets had provoked heated arguments and internal divisions. When they wanted to make a children's playground in the lower part of the village, there was such a fuss that the building works were never begun – some said that the village had no children anyway, others roared that a playground would be just the thing to bring them back when their parents came to the village on holiday and saw that things were changing. In Viscos they debated everything: the quality of the bread, the hunting regulations, the existence (or not) of the rogue wolf, Berta's strange behaviour and, possibly, Miss Prym's secret meetings with some of the hotel guests, although no one would ever dare mention it to her face.

She approached the van with the air of someone who, for the first time in her life, was playing a leading role in the history of her village. Until then she had been the helpless orphan, the girl who had never managed to find a husband, a poor night-worker, a lonely wretch in search of company; they were losing nothing by waiting. In two days' time, they would come and kiss her feet and thank her for her generosity and for their affluence, they would perhaps insist upon her running for mayor in the coming elections (thinking it through, it might be good to stick around for a while longer and enjoy her newly won glory).

The group of people gathered around the van were buying their bread in silence. Everyone turned to look at her, but no one said a word.

'What's going on in this place?' asked the lad selling the bread. 'Did someone die?'

'No,' replied the blacksmith, who was there too, despite it being a Saturday morning when he could sleep until late. 'Someone's having a bad time and we're all rather worried.'

Chantal couldn't understand what was happening.

'Go ahead and buy what you came to buy,' she heard someone say. 'The lad has to get going.'

Mechanically, she held out her money and took the bread. The baker's lad shrugged his shoulders – as if abandoning any attempt to understand what was going on – gave her the change, wished everyone good day and drove off.

'Now it's my turn to ask what's going on in this village,' she said, and fear made her speak more loudly than good manners usually permitted.

'You know what's going on,' the blacksmith said. 'You want us to commit a murder in return for money.'

'I don't want anything! I just did what the guy told me to! Have you all gone mad?'

'You're the one who's gone mad. You should never have allowed yourself to become that madman's mouthpiece! What on earth do you want? What are you getting out of it? Do you want to turn this place into a hell, just like it was in the Ahab stories. Have you lost all sense of honour and dignity?'

Chantal began to tremble.

'You really have gone mad! Did you actually take the wager seriously?'

'Just leave her,' said the hotel landlady. 'Let's go home and have breakfast.'

The group gradually dispersed. Chantal was still trembling, clutching her bread, rooted to the spot. Those people who had never agreed about anything in their lives before were, for the first time ever, in complete accord: she was the guilty one. Not the stranger, not the wager, but her, Chantal Prym, the instigator of the crime. Had the world turned upside down?

She left the bread by her door and set off towards the mountain; she wasn't hungry or thirsty, she didn't want anything. She had just understood something very important, something that filled her with fear, horror and utter terror.

No one had said anything to the baker's boy.

Something like this would normally be talked about, either with indignation or amusement, but the lad with the van, who delivered bread and gossip to the various villages in the region, had left with no idea of what was going on. It was clear that everyone in Viscos was gathered there together for the first time that day, and no one had had time to discuss what had taken place the previous night, although everyone knew what had happened in the bar. And yet, unconsciously, they had all made a pact of silence.

In other words, each one of those people, in their heart of hearts, was thinking the unthinkable, imagining the unimaginable.

Berta called to her. She was still at her post, watching over the village, though to no avail, since the danger was already there and was far greater than anyone could possibly have envisaged.

'I don't want to talk,' said Chantal. 'I can't think, react or say anything.'

'You can at least listen. Sit down here.'

Of all the people she had known, Berta was the only one who had ever treated her with any kindness. Chantal did not just sit down, she flung her arms around Berta. They stayed like that for a long while, until Berta broke the silence.

'Now go off into the forest and clear your head; you know you're not the problem. The rest of them know that too, but they need someone to blame.'

'It's the stranger who's to blame!'

'You and I know that, but no one else does. They all want to believe they've been betrayed, that you should have told them sooner, that you didn't trust them.'

'Betrayed?'

'Yes.'

'Why would they want to believe that?'

'Think about it.'

Chantal thought. Because they needed someone to blame. A victim.

'I don't know how this story will end,' said Berta. 'Viscos is a village of good people, although, as you yourself once said, they are a bit cowardly. Even so, it might be a good idea if you were to go somewhere far away from here for a while.'

She must be joking. No one could possibly take the stranger's bet seriously. No one. And anyway, she didn't have any money and she had nowhere to go.

But that wasn't true. A gold bar awaited her and it could take her anywhere in the world. But she didn't want to think about that.

At that very moment, as if by some quirk of fate, the stranger walked past them and set off for his walk in the mountains, as he did every morning. He nodded and continued on his way. Berta followed him with her eyes, while Chantal tried to spot whether anyone in the village had noticed his greeting. They would say she was his accomplice. They would say there was a secret code between the two of them.

'He looks worried,' said Berta. 'There's something odd about him.'

'Perhaps he's realised that his little game has become reality.'

'No, it's something more than that. I don't know what, but … it's as if … no, no, I don't know what it is.'

'I bet my husband would know,' Berta thought, aware of a nervous fidgeting to her left, but now was not the time to talk to him.

'It reminds me of Ahab,' she said to Chantal.

'I don't want to think about Ahab, about legends, about anything! All I want is for the world to go back to how it was, and for Viscos – for all its faults – not to be destroyed by one man's madness!'

'It seems you love this place more than you think.'

Chantal was trembling. Berta hugged her again, placing her head on her shoulder, as if she were the daughter she had never had.

'As I was saying, Ahab told a story about heaven and hell that used to be passed from parent to child, but has been forgotten now. Once upon a time, a man, his horse and his dog were travelling along a road. As they passed by a huge tree, it was struck by lightning, and they all died. But the man failed to notice that he was no longer of this world and so he continued walking along with his two animal companions. Sometimes the dead take a while to register their new situation …'

Berta thought of her husband, who kept insisting that she get rid of Chantal because he had something important to say. Maybe it was time to explain to him that he was dead, so that he would stop interrupting her story.

'It was a long, uphill walk, the sun was beating down on them and they were all sweating and thirsty. At a bend in the road they saw a magnificent marble gateway that led into a gold-paved square, in the centre of which was a fountain overflowing with crystal-clear water. The man went over to the guard at the entrance.

"'Good morning."

"'Good morning," the guard replied.

"'What is this lovely place?"

"'It's Heaven."

"'Well, I'm very glad to see it, because we're very thirsty."

"'You're welcome to come in and drink all the water you want." And the guard indicated the fountain.

"'My horse and dog are also thirsty."

"'I'm terribly sorry," said the guard, "but animals are not allowed in here."

'The man was deeply disappointed for he really was very thirsty, but he was not prepared to drink alone, so he thanked the guard and went on his way. Exhausted after more trudging uphill, they reached an old gateway that opened on to a dirt road flanked by trees. A man, his hat pulled down over his face, was stretched out in the shade of one of the trees, apparently asleep.

"'Good morning," said the traveller.

'The other man greeted him with a nod.

"'We're very thirsty – me, my horse and my dog."

"'There's a spring over there amongst those rocks," said the man indicating the spot. "You can drink all you want."

'The man, his horse and his dog went to the spring and quenched their thirst.

'The traveller returned to thank the man.

"'Come back whenever you want," he was told.

"'By the way, what's this place called?"

"'Heaven."

"'Heaven? But the guard at the marble gateway told me that was Heaven!"

"'That's not Heaven, that's Hell."

'The traveller was puzzled.

"'You shouldn't let others take your name in vain, you know! False information can lead to all kinds of confusion!"

"'On the contrary, they do us a great favour, because the ones who stay there are those who have proved themselves capable of abandoning their dearest friends.'"

Berta stroked the girl's head. She could feel that inside that head Good and Evil were waging a pitiless battle, and she told her to go for a walk in the forest and ask nature which village she should go to.

'Because I have the feeling that our little mountain paradise is about to desert its friends.'

'You're wrong, Berta. You belong to a different generation; the blood of the outlaws who once populated Viscos runs thicker in your veins than in mine. The men and women here still have their dignity, or if they don't, they at least have a healthy mistrust of one another. And if they don't even have that, then at least they have fear.'

'OK, maybe I'm wrong. Even so, do as I tell you, and go and listen to what nature has to say.'

Chantal left. And Berta turned towards the ghost of her husband, asking him to keep quiet; after all, she was a grown woman, indeed, she was an elderly woman, who shouldn't be interrupted when she was trying to give advice to someone much younger. She had learned to look after herself, and now she was looking after the village.

Her husband begged her to take care. She should be wary of offering advice to the young woman because nobody knew where matters might end.

Berta was taken aback because she thought the dead knew everything – hadn't he been the one to warn her of the dangers to come? Perhaps he was getting too old and was beginning to get obsessive about other things besides always eating his soup with the same spoon.

Her husband retorted that she was the old one, for the dead never age, and that, although the dead knew things of which the living had no knowledge, it would take a long time before he gained admittance to the realm of the archangels. He, being only recently dead (having left Earth a mere fifteen years before), still had a lot to learn, even though he knew he could offer substantial help.

Berta enquired whether the realm of the archangels was more attractive and comfortable. Her husband told her not to be facetious and to concentrate her energies on saving Viscos. Not that this was a source of particular interest to him – he was, after all, dead, and no one had touched on the subject of reincarnation (although he had heard a few conversations concerning this eventuality), and if reincarnation did exist, he was hoping to be reborn somewhere new. But he also wanted his wife to enjoy some peace and comfort during the days still remaining to her in this world.

'So, stop worrying,' thought Berta. Her husband wouldn't take her advice; he wanted her to do something, anything. If Evil triumphed, even if it was in some small, forgotten place with only three streets, a square and a church, it could nevertheless go on to contaminate the valley, the region, the country, the continent, the seas, the whole world.

Although Viscos had 281 inhabitants, Chantal being the youngest and Berta the oldest, it was controlled by a mere half-dozen individuals: the hotel landlady, responsible for the wellbeing of tourists; the priest, responsible for the care of souls; the mayor, responsible for the hunting regulations; the mayor's wife, responsible for the mayor and his decisions; the blacksmith, who had survived being bitten by the rogue wolf; and the owner of most of the lands around the village. It was he who had vetoed the idea of building a children's playground in the vague belief that Viscos would one day start growing again, and besides the site would be perfect for a luxury home.

It mattered little to the rest of the villagers what did or didn't happen to the place, for they had their sheep, their wheat and their families to take care of. They visited the hotel bar, attended Mass, obeyed the laws, had their tools repaired at the blacksmith's forge and, from time to time, acquired some land.

The landowner never went to the bar. He had learned of the story through his maid, who had been there on the night in question and had left in high excitement, telling her friends and him that the hotel guest was a very rich man; who knows, perhaps she could have a child by him and force him to give her part of his fortune. Concerned about the future, or, rather, about the fact that Miss

Prym's story might spread and drive away hunters and tourists alike, he decided to call an emergency meeting. The group were gathering in the sacristy of the small church, just as Chantal was heading for the forest, the stranger was off on one of his mysterious walks and Berta was chatting with her husband about whether or not to try and save the village.

'The first thing we have to do is call the police,' said the landowner. 'It's obvious the gold doesn't exist; and besides, I suspect the man of trying to seduce my maid.'

'You don't know what you're talking about, because you weren't there,' the mayor insisted. 'The gold does exist. Miss Prym wouldn't risk her reputation without concrete proof. Not that that alters things, of course, we should still call the police. The stranger must be a bandit, a fellow with a price on his head, trying to conceal his ill-gotten gains here.'

'Don't be idiotic!' the mayor's wife said. 'If he was, surely he'd be more discreet about it.'

'All this is completely relevant. We must call the police straightaway.'

Everyone agreed. The priest served a little wine to calm everyone's nerves. They began to discuss what they would say to the police, given that they had no actual proof that the stranger had done anything; it might all end with Miss Prym being arrested for inciting a murder.

'The only proof is the gold. Without the gold, we can't do anything.'

Of course. But where was the gold? Only one person had ever seen it, and she didn't know where it was hidden.

The priest suggested they form search parties. The hotel landlady drew back the curtain of the sacristy window that looked out over the cemetery; she pointed to the mountains on one side, to the valley below, and to the mountains on the other side.

'We would need a hundred men searching for a hundred years to do that.'

The landowner silently bemoaned the fact that the cemetery had been constructed on that particular spot; it had a lovely view, and the dead had no use for it.

'On another occasion, I'd like to talk to you about the cemetery,' he said to the priest. 'I could offer you a far bigger plot for the dead, just near here, in exchange for this piece of land next to the church.'

'Nobody would want to buy that and live on the same spot where the dead used to lie.'

'Maybe no one from the village would, but there are tourists desperate to buy a summer home; it would just be a matter of asking the villagers to keep their mouths shut. It would mean more income for the village and more taxes for the town hall.'

'You're right. We just have to ask the villagers to keep their mouths shut. That wouldn't be so hard.'

A sudden silence fell. A long silence, which nobody dared to break. The two women admired the view; the priest started polishing a small bronze statue; the landowner took another sip of wine; the blacksmith tied and untied the laces on both boots; and the mayor kept glancing at his watch, as if to suggest that he had other pressing engagements.

But nobody said a word; everyone knew that the people of Viscos would never say a word if someone were to express an interest in purchasing what had once been the cemetery; they would keep quiet purely for the pleasure of seeing another person coming to live in that village on the verge of disappearing. Even if they didn't earn a penny by their silence.

Imagine if they did though.

Imagine if they earned enough money for the rest of their lives.

Imagine if they earned enough money for the rest of their lives and their children's lives.

At that precise moment, a hot and wholly unexpected wind blew through the sacristy.

'What exactly are you proposing?' asked the priest after a long five minutes.

Everyone turned to look at him.

'If the inhabitants really can be relied on to say nothing, I think we can proceed with negotiations,' replied the landowner, choosing his words carefully in case they were misinterpreted – or correctly interpreted, depending on your point of view.

'They're good, hardworking, discreet people,' the hotel landlady said, adopting the same strategy. 'Today, for example, when the driver of the baker's van wanted to know what was going on, nobody said a thing. I think we can trust them.'

Another silence. Only this time it was an unmistakably oppressive silence. Eventually, the game began again, and the blacksmith said:

'It isn't just a question of the villagers' discretion, the fact is that it's both immoral and unacceptable.'

'What is?'

'Selling off hallowed ground.'

A sigh of relief ran round the room; now that they had dealt satisfactorily with the practical aspects, they could proceed with the moral debate.

'What's immoral is sitting back and watching the demise of our beloved Viscos,' said the mayor's wife. 'Knowing that we are the last people to live here, and that the dream of our grandparents, our ancestors, Ahab and the Celts, will be over in a few years' time. Soon, we'll all be leaving the village, either for an old people's home or to beg our children to take in their strange, ailing parents, who are unable to adapt to life in the big city and spend all their time longing for what they've left behind, sad because they could not pass on to the next generation the gift they received from their parents.'

'You're right,' the blacksmith said. 'The life we lead is an immoral one. When Viscos does finally fall into ruin, these fields will be abandoned or else bought up for next to nothing; then machines will arrive and open up bigger and better roads. The houses will be demolished, steel warehouses will replace what was built with the sweat of our ancestors. Agriculture will become entirely mechanised, and people will come in to work during the day and return at night to their homes, far from here. How shaming for our generation; we let our children leave, we failed to keep them here with us.'

'One way or another, we have to save this village,' said the landowner, who was possibly the only one who stood to profit from Viscos' demise, since he was in a position to buy up everything, then sell it on to a large industrial company. But of course he certainly didn't want to hand over, for a price below market value, lands that might contain buried treasure.

'What do you think, Father?' asked the hotel landlady.

'The only thing I know well is my religion, in which the sacrifice of one individual saved all humanity.'

Silence descended for a third time, but only for a moment.

'I need to start preparing for Saturday Mass,' he went on. 'Why don't we meet up later this evening?'

Everyone immediately agreed, setting a time late in the day, as if they were all immensely busy people with important matters to deal with.

Only the mayor managed to remain calm.

'What you've just been saying is very interesting, an excellent subject for a sermon. I think we should all attend Mass today.'

Chantal hesitated no longer. She headed straight for the Y-shaped rock, thinking of what she would do with the gold as soon as she got it. Go home, get the money she kept hidden there, put on some more sensible clothes, go down the road to the valley and hitch a lift. No more wagers: those people didn't deserve the fortune within their grasp. No suitcase: she didn't want them to know she was leaving Viscos for good – Viscos with its beautiful but pointless stories, its kind but cowardly inhabitants, the bar always crammed with people talking about the same things, the church she never attended. Naturally there was always the chance that she would find the police waiting for her at the bus station, the stranger accusing her of theft etc., etc. But now she was prepared to run any risk.

The hatred she had felt only half an hour before had been transformed into a far more agreeable emotion: vengeance.

She was glad to have been the first to reveal to those people the evil hidden in the depths of their false, ingenuous souls. They were all dreaming of the chance to commit a murder – only dreaming, mind you, because they would never actually do anything. They would spend the rest of their lives asleep, endlessly telling themselves how noble they were, how incapable of committing an injustice, ready to defend the village's dignity at whatever cost, yet aware that terror alone had prevented them from killing an innocent. They would congratulate themselves every morning on keeping their integrity, and blame themselves each night for that missed opportunity.

For the next three months, the only topic of conversation in the bar would be the honesty of the generous men and women of the village. Then the hunting season would arrive and the subject wouldn't be touched upon – there was no need for visitors to know anything about it, they liked to think they were in a remote spot, where everyone was friends, where good always prevailed, where nature was bountiful, and that the local products lined up for sale on a single shelf in the hotel reception – which the hotel landlady called her 'little shop' – were steeped in this disinterested love.

But the hunting season would come to an end, and then the villagers would be free to return to the topic. This time around, after many evenings spent dreaming about the riches they had let slip through their fingers, they would start inventing hypotheses to fit the situation: why did nobody have the courage, at dead of night, to kill useless old Berta in return for ten gold bars? Why did no hunting accident befall the shepherd Santiago, who drove his flock up the mountainside each morning? All kinds of hypotheses would be weighed up, first timidly and then angrily.

One year on and they would be consumed with mutual hatred – the village had been given its opportunity and had let it slip. They would ask after Miss Prym, who had vanished without trace, perhaps taking with her the gold she had watched the stranger hide. They would say terrible things about her, the ungrateful orphan, the poor girl whom they had all struggled to help after her grandmother's death, who had got a job in the bar when she had proved incapable of getting herself a husband and leaving, who used to sleep with the hotel guests, usually men much older than herself, and who made eyes at all the tourists just to get a bigger tip.

They would spend the rest of their lives caught between self-pity and loathing; Chantal would be happy, that was her revenge. She would never forget the looks those people around the van gave her, imploring her silence regarding a murder they would never dare to commit, then rounding on her as if she was to blame for all the cowardice that was finally rising to the surface.

'A jacket. My leather trousers. I can wear two tee shirts and strap the gold bar around my waist. A jacket. My leather trousers. A jacket.'

There she was, in front of the Y-shaped rock. Beside her lay the stick she had used two days before to dig up the gold. For a moment she savoured the gesture that would transform her from an honest woman into a thief.

No, that wasn't right. The stranger had provoked her, and he also stood to gain from the deal. She wasn't so much stealing as claiming her wages for her role as narrator in this tasteless comedy. She deserved not only the gold but much, much more for having endured the stares of the victimless murderers standing round the baker's van, for having spent her entire life there, for those three sleepless nights, for the soul she had now lost – assuming she had ever had a soul to lose.

She dug down into the soft earth and saw the gold bar. When she saw it, she heard a noise.

Someone had followed her. Automatically, she began pushing the earth back into the hole, realising as she did so the futility of the gesture. Then she turned, ready to explain that she was looking for the treasure, that she knew the stranger walked regularly along this path, and that she had happened to notice that the soil had been recently disturbed.

What she saw, however, robbed her of her voice – for it had no interest in treasure, in village crises, justice or injustice, only in blood.

The white mark on its left ear. The rogue wolf.

It was standing between her and the nearest tree; it would be impossible to get past the animal. Chantal stood rooted to the spot, hypnotised by the animal's blue eyes. Her mind was working frantically, wondering what would be her next step – the branch would be far too flimsy to counter the beast's attack. She could climb onto the Y-shaped rock, but that still wasn't high enough. She could choose not to believe the legend and scare off the wolf as she would any other lone wolf, but that was too risky, it would be wisest to recognise that all legends contain a hidden truth.

'Punishment.'

Unfair punishment, just like everything else that had happened in her life; God seemed to have singled her out purely to demonstrate his hatred of the world.

Instinctively she let the branch fall to the ground and, in a movement that seemed to her interminably slow, brought her arms up to her throat: she couldn't let him sink his teeth in there. She regretted not wearing her leather trousers; the next most vulnerable part were her legs and the vein there, which, once pierced, would see you bleed to death in ten minutes – at least that was what the hunters always said, to explain why they wore those high boots.

The wolf opened its mouth and snarled. The dangerous, pent-up growl of an animal who gives no warning, but attacks on the instant. She kept her eyes glued to his, even though her heart was pounding, for now his fangs were bared.

It was all a question of time; he would either attack or run off, but Chantal knew he was going to attack. She glanced down at the ground, looking for any loose stones she might slip on, but found none. She decided to launch herself at the animal; she would be bitten and would have to run towards the tree with the wolf's teeth sunk into her. She would have to ignore the pain.

She thought about the gold. She would soon be back to look for it. She clung to every shred of hope, anything that might give her the strength to confront the prospect of her flesh being ripped by those sharp teeth, of one of her bones poking through, of possibly stumbling and falling and having her throat torn out.

She prepared to run.

Just then, as if in a movie, she saw a figure appear behind the wolf, although still a fair distance away.

The beast sensed another presence too, but did not look away, and she continued to fix him with her stare. It seemed to be only the force of that stare that was averting the attack, and she didn't want to run any further risks; if someone else was there, her chances of survival were increased – even if, in the end, it cost her the gold bar.

The presence behind the wolf silently crouched down and moved to the left. Chantal knew there was another tree on that side, easy to climb. At that moment, a stone arced across the sky and landed near the wolf, which turned with phenomenal speed and hurtled off in the direction of this new threat.

'Run!' yelled the stranger.

She ran in the direction of her only refuge, while the man likewise clambered lithely up the other tree. By the time the rogue wolf reached him, he was safe.

The wolf began snarling and leaping, occasionally managing to get partway up the trunk, only to slip back down again.

'Tear off some branches!' shouted Chantal.

But the stranger seemed to be in a kind of trance. She repeated her instruction twice, then three times, until he registered what she was saying. He began tearing off branches and throwing them down at the wolf.

'No, don't do that! Pull off the branches, bundle them up, and set fire to them! I don't have a lighter, so do as I say!'

Her voice had the desperate edge of someone in real peril. The stranger grabbed some branches and took an eternity to light them; the previous day's storm had soaked everything and, at that time of the year, the sun didn't penetrate into that part of the forest.

Chantal waited until the flames of the improvised torch had begun to burn fiercely. She would have been quite happy to have him spend the rest of the day in the tree, confronting the fear he wanted to inflict on the rest of the world, but she had to get away and so was obliged to help him.

'Now show me you're a man!' she yelled. 'Get down from the tree, keep a firm hold on the torch and walk towards the wolf!'

The stranger could not move.

'Do it!' she yelled again and, when he heard her voice, the man understood the force of authority behind her words – an authority derived from terror, from the ability to react quickly, leaving fear and suffering for later.

He climbed down with the burning torch in his hands, ignoring the sparks that occasionally singed his cheeks. When he saw the animal's foam-flecked teeth close to, his fear increased, but he had to do something – something he should have done when his wife was abducted, his daughters murdered.

'Remember, keep looking him in the eye!' he heard the girl say.

He did as she said. Things were becoming easier with each passing moment; he was no longer looking at the enemy's weapons but at the enemy himself. They were equals, both capable of provoking fear in each other.

His feet touched the ground. The wolf recoiled, frightened by the fire: it continued snarling and leaping, but did not come near.

'Attack him!'

He advanced on the beast, which snarled more loudly than ever, showing his teeth, but still retreating.

'Chase him! Get him away from here!'

The flames were burning more fiercely now, and the stranger realised that they would soon be burning his hands; he did not have much time. Almost without thinking, keeping his eyes fixed on those sinister blue ones, he ran at the wolf, which stopped snarling and leaping, spun round and disappeared back into the forest.

In the twinkling of an eye, Chantal had scrambled down from her tree. She had soon gathered up a handful of kindling from the ground and made her own torch.

'Let's get out of here. Now.'

'And go where?'

Where? To Viscos, where everyone would see them arriving together? Into another trap where the fire would no longer produce the desired effect? She slumped to the ground, her back suddenly wracked with pain, her heart pounding.

'Make a bonfire,' she said to the stranger, 'and let me think.'

She attempted to move and let out a cry – it was as if someone had stuck a dagger in her shoulder. The stranger collected leaves and branches and built a fire. Every time she moved Chantal contorted with pain and let out a dull groan; she must have really hurt herself when she was climbing up the tree.

'Don't worry, you haven't broken anything,' the stranger said, hearing her cry out in pain. 'I've had the same thing. When your body reaches an extreme of tension, all the muscles contract and make you pay the price. Let me give you a massage.'

'Don't touch me. Don't come near me. Don't talk to me.'

Pain, fear, shame. He must have been there when she was digging up the gold; he knew – for the devil was his companion and devils can see into the human soul – that this time Chantal had intended to steal it.

By now, he also knew that the whole village was dreaming of committing a murder. He knew that they were too frightened actually to carry out the crime, but their intention was enough to answer his question: human beings are essentially bad. And since he knew she was about to flee, the wager the two of them had made the previous evening meant nothing, and he could return from whence he came (wherever that was) with his treasure intact and his suspicions confirmed.

She tried to find the most comfortable position to sit in, but there wasn't one; she would have to stay put. The fire would keep the wolf at bay, but it would be bound to attract the attention of some passing shepherds. And the two of them would be seen together.

She remembered that it was a Saturday. People would be in their homes full of ugly knick-knacks, plaster saints and reproductions of famous paintings, all trying to have a good time – and this weekend, of course, they had the best opportunity to do that since the end of the Second World War.

'Don't talk to me.'

'I didn't say a word.'

Chantal considered crying, but didn't want to do so in front of him. She bit back her tears.

'I saved your life. I deserve the gold.'

'I saved your life. The wolf was about to attack you.'

It was true.

'On the other hand, I believe you saved something else deep inside me,' the stranger went on.

A trick. She would pretend she hadn't understood; that was like giving her permission to take his fortune, to get out of there for good, end of story.

'About last night's wager. I was in so much pain myself that I needed to make everyone suffer as much as I was suffering; that was my one source of consolation. You were right.'

The stranger's devil didn't like what he was hearing at all. He asked Chantal's devil to help him out, but her devil was new and hadn't yet asserted total control.

'Does that change anything?'

'Nothing. The bet's still on, and I know I'll win. But I also know how wretched I am and how I became that way: because I feel I didn't deserve what happened to me.'

Chantal asked herself how they were going to get out of there; even though it was still only morning, they couldn't stay in the forest forever.

'Well, I think I deserve my gold, and I'm going to take it, assuming you don't stop me,' she said. 'I'd advise you to do the same. Neither of us needs to go back to Viscos; we can head straight for the valley, hitch a ride, and then each of us can follow our own destiny.'

'You can go, if you like. But at this very moment the villagers are deciding who should die.'

'That's as maybe. They'll devote a couple of days to it, until the deadline is up; then they'll devote a couple of years to arguing about who should have been the victim. They are hopelessly indecisive when it comes to doing anything, and implacable when it comes to apportioning blame – I know my village. If you don't go back, they won't even trouble themselves to discuss it. They'll dismiss it as something I made up.'

'Viscos is just like any other village in the world, and whatever happens there happens in every continent, city, camp, convent, wherever. That's something you don't understand, just as you don't understand that this time fate has worked in my favour: I chose exactly the right person to help me. Someone who, behind the mask of a hardworking, honest young woman, also wants revenge. Since we can never see the enemy – because if we take this tale to its logical conclusion, our real enemy is God for putting us through everything we've suffered – we vent our frustrations on everything around us. It's a desire for vengeance that can never be satisfied, because it's directed against life itself.'

'What are we doing sitting around here talking?' asked Chantal, irritated because this man, whom she hated more than anyone else in the world, could see so clearly into her soul. 'Why don't we just take the money and leave?'

'Because yesterday I realised that by proposing the very thing that most revolts me – a senseless murder, just like that inflicted on my wife and daughters – the truth is I was trying to save myself. Do you remember the philosopher I mentioned in our second conversation? The one who said that God's hell is His love for humanity, because human behaviour makes every second of His eternal life a torment?

'Well, that same philosopher said something else too, he said: *Man needs what's worst in him in order to achieve what's best in him.*'

'I don't understand.'

'Until now, I used to think solely in terms of revenge. Like the inhabitants of your village, I used to dream and plan day and night, but never do anything. For a while, I used to scour the newspapers for articles about other people who had lost their loved ones in similar situations, but who had ended up behaving in exactly the opposite way to myself: they formed victim support groups, organisations to denounce injustice, campaigns to demonstrate how the pain of loss can never be replaced by the burden of vengeance.

'I too tried to look at matters from a more generous perspective: I didn't succeed. But now I've gained courage; I've reached the depths and discovered that there is light at the bottom.'

'Go on,' said Chantal, for she too was beginning to see a kind of light.

'I'm not trying to prove that humanity is perverse. What I'm trying to do is to prove that I unconsciously asked for the things that happened to me. Because I'm evil, a total degenerate and I deserved the punishment that life gave me.'

'You're trying to prove that God is just.'

The stranger thought for a moment.

'Maybe.'

'I don't know if God is just. He hasn't treated me particularly fairly, and it's that sense of powerlessness that has destroyed my soul. I cannot be as good as I would like to be, nor as bad as I think I need to be. A few minutes ago, I thought He had chosen me to avenge Himself for all the sadness men cause Him. I think you have the same doubts, albeit on a much larger scale, because your goodness was not rewarded.'

Chantal was surprised at her own words. The man's devil noticed that her angel was beginning to shine with greater intensity, and everything was beginning to be turned inside out.

'Resist!' he said to the other demon.

'I am resisting,' he replied. 'But it's an uphill struggle.'

'Your problem isn't to do with God's justice exactly,' the man said. 'It's more the fact that you always chose to be a victim of circumstance. I know a lot of people in your situation.'

'Like you, for example.'

'No. I rebelled against something that happened to me and I don't care whether others like my attitude or not. You, on the other hand, believed in your role as helpless orphan, someone who wants to be accepted at all costs. Since that doesn't always happen, your need to be loved was transformed into a stubborn desire for revenge. At heart, you wish you were like the rest of Viscos' inhabitants – in other words, deep down, we'd all like to be the same as everyone else. But destiny accorded you a different fate.'

Chantal shook her head.

'Do something,' said Chantal's devil to his colleague. 'Even though she's saying no, her soul understands and is saying yes.'

The stranger's devil was feeling humiliated because the new arrival had noticed that he wasn't strong enough to get the man to shut up.

'Words don't matter in the end,' the devil said. 'Let them talk, and life will see to it that they act differently.'

'I didn't mean to interrupt you,' the stranger said. 'Please, go on with what you were saying about God's justice.'

Chantal was pleased not to have to listen any more to things she didn't want to hear.

'I don't know if it makes sense. But you must have noticed that Viscos isn't a particularly religious place, even though it has a church, like all the villages in this region. That's because Ahab, even though he was converted to Christianity by St Savin, had serious reservations about the influence of priests. Since the majority of the early inhabitants were bandits, he thought that all the priests would do, with their threats of eternal damnation, would be to send them back to their criminal ways. Men who have nothing to lose never give a thought for eternal life.

'Naturally, the first priest duly appeared, and Ahab understood what the real threat was. To compensate for it, he instituted something he had learned from the Jews – a Day of Atonement – except that he determined to establish a ritual of his own making.

'Once a year, the inhabitants shut themselves up in their houses, made two lists, turned to face the highest mountain and then raised their first list to the heavens.

'"Here, Lord, are all the sins I have committed against you," they said, reading the account of all the sins they had committed. Business swindles, adulteries, injustices, things of that sort. "I have sinned and beg forgiveness for having offended You so greatly."

'Then – and here lay Ahab's originality – the residents immediately pulled the second list out of their pocket and, still facing the same mountain, they held that one up to the skies too. And they said something like: "And here, Lord, is a list of all Your sins against me: You made me work harder than necessary, my daughter fell ill despite all my prayers, I was robbed when I was trying to be honest, I suffered more than was fair."

'After reading out the second list, they ended the ritual with: "I have been unjust towards You and You have been unjust towards me. However, since today is the Day of Atonement, You will forget my faults and I will forget Yours, and we can carry on together for another year."'

'Forgive God!' said the stranger. 'Forgive an implacable God who is constantly creating and destroying!'

'This conversation is getting too personal for my taste,' said Chantal, looking away. 'I haven't learned enough from life to be able to teach you anything.'

The stranger said nothing.

✳

'I don't like this at all,' thought the stranger's devil, beginning to see a bright light shining beside him, a presence he was certainly not going to allow. He had banished that light two years ago, on one of the world's many beaches.

Given the large number of legends, of Celtic and Protestant influences, of certain unfortunate examples set by the Arab who had eventually brought peace to the village, and given the constant presence of saints and bandits in the surrounding area, the priest knew that Viscos was not exactly a religious place, even though its residents still attended baptisms and weddings (although nowadays these were merely a distant memory), funerals (which, on the contrary, occurred with ever increasing frequency) and Christmas Mass. For the most part, few troubled to make the effort to attend the two weekly Masses – one on Saturday and one on Sunday, both at eleven o'clock in the morning; even so, he made sure to celebrate them, if only to justify his presence there. He wished to give the impression of being a busy, saintly man.

To his surprise, that day the church was so crowded that he had to allow some of the congregation up on to the altar steps, otherwise they could not have fitted everyone in. Instead of turning on the electric heaters suspended from the ceiling, he had to ask members of the congregation to open the two small side windows, as everyone was sweating; the priest wondered to himself whether the sweat was due to the heat or to the general tension.

The entire village was there, apart from Miss Prym – possibly ashamed of what she had said the previous day – and old Berta, whom everyone suspected of being a witch and therefore allergic to religion.

'In the Name of the Father, and of the Son, and of the Holy Ghost.'

A loud 'Amen' rang out. The priest began the liturgy, said the introit, had the usual faithful church member read the lesson, solemnly intoned the responsory, and recited the Gospel in slow, grave tones. After which, he asked all those in the pews to be seated, whilst the rest remained standing.

It was time for the sermon.

'In the Gospel according to Luke, there is a moment when an important man approaches Jesus and asks: *'Good Master, what shall I do to inherit eternal life?'* And, to our surprise, Jesus responds: *'Why callest thou me good? None is good, save one, that is, God.'*

'For many years, I pondered over this little fragment of text, trying to understand what Our Lord was saying: That He was not good? That the whole of Christianity, with its concept of charity, is based on the teachings of someone who considered Himself to be bad? Finally, I saw what he meant: Christ, at that moment, is referring to His human nature. As man, He is bad, as God, He is good.'

The priest paused, hoping that the congregation understood his message. He was lying to himself: he still couldn't grasp what Christ was saying, since if his human nature was bad, then his words and actions would also be bad. But this was a theological discussion of no relevance just then; what mattered was that his explanation should be convincing.

'I am not going to run on too long today. I want all of you to understand that part of being human is to accept our baser, perverse nature and know that the only reason that we were not condemned to eternal damnation because of this base nature was that Jesus sacrificed himself to save humanity. I repeat: the sacrifice of the Son of God saved us all. The sacrifice of a single person.

'I wish to close this sermon by mentioning the beginning of one of the sacred books that together comprise the Bible, the Book of Job.

God is sitting upon His celestial throne, when the Devil comes to speak to Him. God asks where he has been and the Devil replies that he has been "going to and fro on Earth".

'"Did you see my servant Job? Did you see how he worships me, and performs all his sacrifices?"

'The Devil laughs and replies: "Well, Job does, after all, have everything, so why wouldn't he worship God and make sacrifices? Take away the good You gave him, and see if he worships You then."

'God accepts the challenge. Year after year he punishes the man who most loved Him. Job is in the presence of a power he cannot comprehend, whom he believed to be the Supreme Judge, but who is destroying his animals, killing his children and afflicting his body with boils. Then, after great suffering, Job rebels and blasphemes against the Lord. Only then does God restore to him that which He had taken away.

'For years now we have witnessed the decay of our village. I wonder now whether this might not be a divine punishment for our uncomplaining acceptance of whatever was dealt out to us, as if we deserved to lose the place we live in, the fields where we cultivate our crops and graze our sheep, the houses built by the dreams of our ancestors. Has not the moment come for us to rebel? If God forced Job to do as much, might He not be requiring us to do likewise?

'Why did God force Job to behave in that way? To show that he was by nature bad, and that everything that came to him was by grace and grace alone, and not as a reward for good behaviour. We have committed the sin of pride in believing ourselves to be better than we are – and that is why we are suffering.

'God accepted the Devil's wager and – so it seems – committed an injustice. Remember that: God accepted the Devil's wager. And Job learned his lesson for, like us, he too was committing the sin of pride in believing that he was a good man.

'*None is good*, says the Lord. No one. We should stop pretending to a goodness that offends God and accept our faults: if one day we have to accept a wager with the Devil, let us remember that our Father who is in heaven did exactly the same in order to save the soul of His servant Job.'

The sermon was at an end. The priest asked everyone to stand up, and continued the Mass. He was sure that the message had been fully understood.

'L et each of us just go our own way, me with my gold bar and you ...'

'You mean my gold bar,' the stranger broke in.

'All you have to do is pack up your things and disappear. If I don't take the gold, I'll have to go back to Viscos. I'll be sacked from my job or stigmatised by the whole population. They'll think I lied to them. You can't, you simply can't do that to me. Let's say I deserve it as payment for all my work.'

The stranger rose to his feet and picked up some of the branches from the fire.

'The wolf will run away from the flames, won't it? Well, then, I'm off to Viscos. You do what you think best, steal the gold and run away if you want, I really don't care any more. I've got something more important to do.'

'Just a minute! Don't leave me here alone!'

'Come with me, then.'

Chantal looked at the fire before her, at the Y-shaped rock, at the stranger who was already moving off, taking some of the fire with him. She could do likewise: take some wood from the fire, dig up the gold and head straight down to the valley; there wasn't any need for to her go home and get the little money she had so carefully scraped together. When she reached the town in the valley, she would ask the bank to value the gold, she would then sell it, buy clothes and suitcases, and she would be free.

'Wait!' she called after the stranger, but he was still walking towards Viscos and would soon be lost to view.

'Think fast,' she told herself.

She didn't have much time. She too took some burning twigs from the fire, went over to the rock and once again dug up the gold. She picked it up, cleaned it off on her dress and studied it for the third time.

Then she was seized with panic. She took her handful of burning wood and, hatred oozing from her every pore, ran after the stranger, down the path he must have taken. She had met two wolves that day, one who could be scared off with fire, and another who wasn't scared of anything any more because he had already lost everything he valued and was now moving blindly forward, intent on destroying everything in his path.

She ran as fast as she could, but she didn't find him. His torch would have burned out by now, but he must still be in the forest, defying the rogue wolf, wanting to die as fiercely as he wanted to kill.

She reached the village, pretended not to hear Berta calling to her and met up with the congregation leaving Mass, amazed that virtually the entire population had gone to church. The stranger had wanted to provoke a murder and had ended up filling the priest's diary; it would be a week of confessions and penances – as if God could be hoodwinked.

Everyone stared at her, but no one spoke to her. She met each of their stares because she knew that she was not to blame in any way. She had no need of confession, she was merely a pawn in an evil game, one that she was slowly beginning to understand – and she didn't at all like what she saw.

She locked herself in her room and peeped through the window. The crowd had now dispersed, and again something strange was going on; the village was unusually empty for a sunny Saturday. As a rule, people stood about chatting in small groups in the square where once there had been a gallows and where now there was a cross.

She stood for a while gazing at the empty street, feeling the sun on her face, though it no longer warmed her, for winter was beginning. If people had been out in the square, that would have been their topic of conversation – the weather. The temperature. The threat of rain or drought. But today they were all in their houses, and Chantal did not know why.

The longer she gazed at the street, the more she felt she was the same as all those other people – she, who had always believed herself to be different, daring, full of plans that would never even occur to those peasant brains.

How embarrassing. And yet, what a relief too; she was no longer in Viscos by some cruel whim of destiny, but because she deserved to be there. She had always considered herself to be different, and now she saw that she was just the same as them. She had dug up the gold bar three times, but had been incapable of actually running off with it. She had committed the crime in her soul, but had been unable to carry it out in the real world.

Now she knew that there was no way she could commit the crime, for it wasn't a temptation, it was a trap.

'Why a trap?' she wondered. Something told her that the gold bar she had seen was the solution to the problem the stranger had created. But, however hard she tried, she could not work out what that solution might be.

Her newly arrived devil glanced to one side and saw that Miss Prym's light, which before had seemed to be growing, was now almost disappearing again; what a shame his colleague wasn't there with him to celebrate the victory.

What he didn't know was that angels also have their strategies: at that moment, Miss Prym's light was hiding so as not to awaken a response in its enemy. All that the angel required was for Chantal to rest a little so that he could converse with her soul without interference from the fear and guilt that human beings love to load themselves down with every day of their lives.

Chantal slept. And she heard what she needed to hear and understood what she needed to understand.

'Let's drop all this talk of land and cemeteries,' the mayor's wife said, as soon as they were all gathered again in the sacristy. 'Let's talk plainly.'

The other five agreed.

'Father, you convinced me,' said the landowner. 'God justifies certain acts.'

'Don't be cynical,' replied the priest. 'When we looked through that window, we all knew what we meant. That's why that hot wind blew through here; it was the Devil come to keep us company.'

'Of course,' agreed the mayor, who did not believe in devils. 'We're all convinced. We'd better talk plainly, or we'll lose precious time.'

'I'll speak for all of us,' said the hotel landlady. 'We are thinking of accepting the stranger's proposal. To commit a murder.'

'To offer up a sacrifice,' said the priest, more accustomed to the rites of religion.

The silence that followed showed that everyone was in agreement.

'Only cowards hide behind silence. Let us pray in a loud voice so that God may hear us and know that we are doing this for the good of Viscos. Let us kneel.'

They all reluctantly kneeled down, knowing that it was useless begging forgiveness from God for a sin committed in full consciousness of the evil they were doing. Then they remembered

Ahab's Day of Atonement; soon, when that day came around again, they would accuse God of having placed them in terrible temptation.

The priest suggested that they pray together.

'Lord, You once said that no one is good; accept us then with all our imperfections and forgive us in Your infinite generosity and Your infinite love. For as You pardoned the Crusaders who killed the Muslims in order to re-conquer the holy land of Jerusalem, as You pardoned the Inquisitors who sought to preserve the purity of Your Church, as You pardoned those who insulted You and nailed You to the cross, so pardon us who must offer up a sacrifice in order to save our village.'

'Let's get down to practicalities,' said the mayor's wife, rising to her feet. 'Who should be sacrificed? And who should carry it out?'

'The person who brought the Devil here was a young woman whom we have all always helped and supported,' commented the landowner, who in the not-too-distant past had himself slept with the girl he was referring to and had ever since been tormented by the idea that she might tell his wife about it. 'Evil must fight Evil, and she deserves to be punished.'

Two of the others agreed, arguing that, in addition, Miss Prym was the one person in the village who could not be trusted because she thought she was different from everyone else and was always saying that one day she would leave.

'Her mother's dead. Her grandmother's dead. Nobody would miss her,' the mayor agreed, thus becoming the third to approve the suggestion.

His wife, however, opposed it.

'What if she knows where the treasure is hidden? After all, she was the only one who saw it. Moreover, we can trust her precisely because of what has just been said – she was the one who brought Evil here and led a whole community into considering committing a murder. She can say what she likes, but if the rest of the village says nothing, it will be the word of one neurotic young woman against us, people who have all achieved something in life.'

The mayor was undecided, as always when his wife had expressed her opinion:

'Why do you want to save her, if you don't even like her?'

'I understand,' the priest responded. 'That way the guilt falls on the head of the one who precipitated the tragedy. She will bear that burden for the rest of her days and nights. She might even end up like Judas, who betrayed Jesus and then committed suicide, in a gesture of despair and futility, because she created all the necessary preconditions for the crime.'

The mayor's wife was surprised by the priest's reasoning – it was exactly what she had been thinking. The young woman was beautiful, she led men into temptation, and she refused to be contented with the typical life of an inhabitant of Viscos. She was forever bemoaning the fact that she had to stay in the village, which, for all its faults, was nevertheless made up of honest, hardworking people, a place where many people would love to spend their days (strangers, naturally, who would leave after discovering how boring it is to live constantly at peace).

'I can't think of anyone else,' the hotel landlady said, aware of how difficult it would be to find someone else to work in the bar, but realising that, with the gold she would receive, she could close the hotel and move far away. 'The peasants and shepherds form a closed group, some are married, many have children a long way from here, who might become suspicious should anything happen to their parents. Miss Prym is the only one who could disappear without trace.'

For religious reasons – after all, Jesus cursed those who condemned an innocent person – the priest had no wish to nominate anyone. But he knew who the victim should be; he just had to ensure that the others came to the same conclusion.

'The people of Viscos work from dawn to dusk, come rain or shine. Each one has a task to fulfil, even that poor wretch of a girl whom the Devil decided to use for his own evil ends. There are only a few of us left, and we can't afford the luxury of losing another pair of hands.'

'So, Father, we have no victim. All we can hope is that another stranger turns up tonight, yet even that would prove risky, because he would inevitably have a family who would seek him out to the ends of the earth. In Viscos everyone works hard to earn the bread brought to us by the baker's van.'

'You're right,' said the priest. 'Perhaps everything we have been through since last night has been mere illusion. Everyone in this village has someone who would miss them, and none of us would want anything to happen to one of our own loved ones. Only three people in this village sleep alone: myself, Berta and Miss Prym.'

'Are you offering yourself up for sacrifice, Father?'

'If it's for the good of the community.'

The other five felt greatly relieved, suddenly aware that it was a sunny Saturday, that there would be no murder, only a martyrdom. The tension in the sacristy evaporated as if by magic, and the hotel landlady felt so moved she could have kissed the feet of that saintly man.

'There's only one thing,' the priest went on. 'You would need to convince everyone that it is not a mortal sin to kill a minister of God.'

'You can explain it to Viscos yourself!' exclaimed the mayor enthusiastically, already planning the various reforms he could put in place once he had the money, the advertisements he could take out in the regional newspapers, attracting fresh investment because of the tax cuts he could make, drawing in tourists with the changes to the hotel he intended to fund, and having a new telephone line installed that would prove less problematic than the current one.

'I can't do that,' said the priest. 'Martyrs offer themselves up when the people want to kill them. They never incite their own death, for the Church has always said that life is a gift from God. You'll have to do the explaining.'

'Nobody will believe us. They'll consider us to be the very worst kind of murderer if we kill a holy man for money, just as Judas did to Christ.'

The priest shrugged. It felt as if the sun had once again gone in, and tension returned to the sacristy.

'Well, that only leaves Berta,' the landowner concluded.

After a lengthy pause, it was the priest's turn to speak.

'That woman must suffer greatly with her husband gone. She's done nothing but sit outside her house all these years, alone with the elements and her own boredom. All she does is long for the past. And I'm afraid the poor woman may slowly be going mad: I've often passed by that way and seen her talking to herself.'

Again a gust of wind blew through the sacristy, startling the people inside because all the windows were closed.

'She's certainly had a very sad life,' the hotel landlady went on. 'I think she would give anything to join her beloved. They were married for forty years, you know.'

They all knew that, but it was hardly relevant now.

'She's an old woman, near the end of her life,' added the landowner. 'She's the only person in the village who does nothing of note. I once asked her why she always sat outside her house, even in winter, and do you know what she told me? She said she was watching over our village, so that she could see when Evil arrived.'

'Well, she hasn't done very well on that score.'

'On the contrary,' said the priest, 'from what I understand of your conversation, the person who let Evil enter in should also be the one who should drive it out.'

Another silence, and everyone knew that a victim had been chosen.

'There's just one thing,' the mayor's wife commented. 'We know when the sacrifice will be offered up in the interests of the well being of the village. We know who it will be. Thanks to this sacrifice, a good soul will go to heaven and find eternal joy, rather than remain suffering here on earth. All we need to know now is how.'

'Try to speak to all the men in the village,' the priest said to the mayor, 'and call a meeting in the square for nine o'clock tonight. I think I know how. Drop by here shortly before nine, and the two of us can talk it over.'

Before they left, he asked that, while the meeting that night was in progress, the two women should go to Berta's house and keep her talking. Although she never went out at night, it would be best not to take any risks.

C hantal arrived at the bar in time for work. No one was there.

'There's a meeting in the square tonight at nine,' the hotel landlady said. 'Just for the men.'

She didn't need to say anything more. Chantal knew what was going on.

'Did you actually see the gold?'

'Yes, I did, but you should ask the stranger to bring it here. You never know, once he's got what he wants, he might simply decide to disappear.'

'He's not mad.'

'He is.'

The hotel landlady thought that this might indeed be a good idea. She went up to the stranger's room and came down a few minutes later.

'He's agreed. He says it's hidden in the forest and that he'll bring it here tomorrow.'

'I guess I don't need to work today, then.'

'You certainly do. It's in your contract.'

She didn't know how to broach the subject she and the others had spent the afternoon discussing, but it was important to gauge the girl's reaction.

'I'm really shocked by all this,' she said. 'At the same time, I realise that people need to think twice or even ten times before they decide what they should do.'

'They could think it over twenty or two hundred times and they still wouldn't have the courage to do anything.'

'You may be right,' the hotel landlady agreed, 'but if they do decide to make a move, what would you do?'

The woman needed to know what Chantal's reaction would be, and Chantal realised that the stranger was far closer to the truth than she was, despite her having lived in Viscos all those years. A meeting in the square! What a pity the gallows had been dismantled.

'So what would you do?' the landlady insisted.

'I won't answer that question,' she said, even though she knew exactly what she would do. 'I'll only say that Evil never brings Good. I discovered that for myself this afternoon.'

The hotel landlady didn't like having her authority flouted, but thought it prudent not to argue with the young woman and risk an enmity that could bring problems in the future. On the pretext that she needed to bring the accounts up to date (an absurd excuse, she thought later, since there was only one guest in the hotel), she left Miss Prym alone in the bar. She felt reassured; Miss Prym showed no signs of rebellion, even after she had mentioned the meeting in the square, which showed that something unusual was happening in Viscos. Besides, Miss Prym also had a great need for money, she had her whole life ahead of her, and would almost certainly like to follow in the footsteps of her childhood friends who had already left the village. And, even if she wasn't willing to co-operate, at least she didn't seem to want to interfere.

The priest dined frugally then sat down alone on one of the church pews. The mayor would be there in a few minutes.

He contemplated the whitewashed walls, the altar unadorned by any important work of art, decorated instead with cheap reproductions of paintings of the saints who – in the dim and distant past – had lived in the region. The people of Viscos had never been very religious, despite the important role St Savin had played in resurrecting the fortunes of the place. But the people forgot this and preferred to concentrate on Ahab, on the Celts, on the peasants' centuries-old superstitions, failing to understand that it took only a gesture, a simple gesture, to achieve redemption: that of accepting Jesus as the sole Saviour of humanity.

Only hours earlier, he had offered himself up for martyrdom. It had been a risky move, but he had been prepared to see it through and deliver himself over for sacrifice, had the others not been so frivolous and so easily manipulated.

'No, that's not true. They may be frivolous, but they're not that easily manipulated.' Indeed, through silence or clever words, they had made him say what they wanted to hear: the sacrifice that redeems, the victim who saves, decay transformed anew into glory. He had pretended to let himself be used by the others, but had only said what he himself believed.

He had been prepared for the priesthood from an early age, and that was his true vocation. By the time he was twenty-one, he had already been ordained a priest, and had impressed everyone with his gifts as a preacher and his skill as a parish administrator. He said prayers every evening, visited the sick and those in prison, gave food to the hungry – just as the holy scriptures commanded. His fame soon spread throughout the region and reached the ears of the bishop, a man known for his wisdom and fairness.

The bishop invited him, together with other young priests, for an evening meal. They ate and talked about various matters until, at the end, the bishop, who was getting old and had difficulties walking, got up and offered each of them some water. The priest had been the only one not to refuse, asking for his glass to be filled to the brim.

One of the other priests whispered, loud enough for the bishop to hear: 'We all refused the water because we know we are not worthy to drink from the hands of this saintly man. Only one among us cannot see the sacrifice our superior is making in carrying that heavy bottle.'

When the bishop returned to his seat, he said:

'You, who think you are holy men, were not humble enough to receive and so denied me the pleasure of giving. Only this man allowed Good to be made manifest.'

He immediately appointed him to a more important parish.

The two men became friends and continued to see each other often. Whenever he had any doubts, the priest would turn to the person he called 'my spiritual father', and he usually left satisfied with the answers he got. One evening, for example, he was troubled because he could no longer tell whether or not his actions were pleasing to God. He went to see the bishop and asked what he should do.

'Abraham took in strangers, and God was happy,' came the reply. 'Elijah disliked strangers, and God was happy. David was proud of what he was doing, and God was happy. The publican before the altar was ashamed of what he did, and God was happy. John the

Baptist went out into the desert, and God was happy. Paul went to the great cities of the Roman Empire, and God was happy. How can one know what will please the Almighty? Do what your heart commands, and God will be happy.'

The day after this conversation, the bishop, his great spiritual mentor, died from a massive heart attack. The priest saw the bishop's death as a sign, and began to do exactly what he had recommended; he followed the commands of his heart. Sometimes he gave alms, sometimes he told the person to go and find work. Sometimes he gave a very serious sermon, at others he sang along with his congregation. His behaviour reached the ears of the new bishop, and he was summoned to see him.

He was astonished to find that the new bishop was the same person who, a few years earlier, had made the comment about the water served by his predecessor.

'I know that today you're in charge of an important parish,' the new bishop said, an ironic look in his eye, 'and that over the years you became a great friend of my predecessor, perhaps even aspiring to this position yourself.'

'No,' the priest replied, 'aspiring only to wisdom.'

'Well, you must be a very wise man by now, but I've heard strange stories about you, that sometimes you give alms and that sometimes you refuse the aid that our Church says we should offer.'

'I have two pockets, each contains a piece of paper with writing on it, but I only put money in my left pocket,' he said in reply.

The new bishop was intrigued by the story: what did the two pieces of paper say?

'On the piece of paper in my right pocket, I wrote: *I am nothing but dust and ashes*. The piece of paper in my left pocket, where I keep my money, says: *I am the manifestation of God on Earth*. Whenever I see misery and injustice, I put my hand in my left pocket and try to help. Whenever I come up against laziness and indolence, I put my hand in my right pocket and find I have nothing to give. In this way, I manage to balance the material and the spiritual worlds.'

The new bishop thanked him for this fine image of charity and said he could return to his parish, but warned him that he was in the process of restructuring the whole region. Shortly afterwards, the priest received news that he was being transferred to Viscos.

He understood the message at once: envy. But he had made a vow to serve God wherever it might be, and so he set off for Viscos full of humility and fervour: it was a new challenge for him to meet.

A year went by. And another. By the end of five years, despite all his efforts, he had not succeeded in bringing any new believers into the church; the village was haunted by a ghost from the past called Ahab, and nothing the priest said could be more important than the legends that still circulated about him.

Ten years passed. At the end of the tenth year, the priest realised his mistake: his search for wisdom had become pride. He was so convinced of divine justice that he had failed to balance it with the art of diplomacy. He thought he was living in a world where God was everywhere, only to find himself amongst people who often would not even let God enter their lives.

After fifteen years, he knew that he would never leave Viscos: by then, the former bishop was an important cardinal working in the Vatican and quite likely to be named Pope – and he could never allow an obscure country priest to spread the story that he had been exiled out of envy and greed.

By then, the priest had allowed himself to be infected by the lack of stimulus – no one could withstand all those years of indifference. He thought that had he left the priesthood at the right moment, he could have served God better; but he had kept putting off the decision, always thinking that the situation would change, and by then it was too late, he had lost all contact with the world.

After twenty years, he woke up one night in despair: his life had been completely useless. He knew how much he was capable of and how little he had achieved. He remembered the two pieces of paper he used to keep in his pockets, and realised that now he always reached into his right-hand pocket. He had wanted to be wise, but had been lacking in political skills. He had wanted to be just, but had lacked wisdom. He had wanted to be a politician, but had lacked courage.

'Where is Your generosity, Lord? Why did You do to me what You did to Job? Will I never have another chance in this life? Give me one more opportunity!'

He got up, opened the Bible at random, as he usually did when he was searching for an answer, and he came upon the passage during the Last Supper when Christ tells the traitor to hand him over to the Roman soldiers looking for him.

The priest spent hours thinking about what he had just read: why did Jesus ask the traitor to commit a sin?

'So that the scriptures would be fulfilled,' the wise men of the Church would say. Even so, why was Jesus asking someone to commit a sin and thus leading him into eternal damnation?'

Jesus would never do that; in truth, the traitor was merely a victim, as Jesus himself was. Evil had to manifest itself and fulfil its role, so that ultimately Good could prevail. If there was no betrayal, there could be no cross, the words of the scriptures would not be fulfilled, and Jesus' sacrifice could not serve as an example.

The next day, a stranger arrived in the village, as so many others had before. The priest gave the matter no importance, nor did he connect it to the request he had made to Jesus, or to the passage he had read in the Bible. When he heard the story of the models Leonardo da Vinci had used in his *Last Supper*, he remembered reading the corresponding text in the Bible, but dismissed it as a coincidence.

It was only when Miss Prym told them about the wager that he realised his prayers had been answered.

Evil needed to manifest itself if Good was finally to move the hearts of these people. For the first time since he had come to the parish, he had seen his church full to overflowing. For the first time, the most important people in the village had visited him in the sacristy.

'Evil needs to manifest itself, for them to understand the value of Good.' Just as the traitor in the Bible, soon after betraying Jesus, understood what he had done, so the people in the village would realise what they had done and be so overwhelmed by remorse that their only refuge would be the Church. And Viscos – after all these years – would once again become a Christian village.

His role was to be the instrument of Evil; that was the greatest act of humility he could offer to God.

The mayor arrived as arranged.

'I want to know what I should say, Father.'

'Let me take charge of the meeting,' the priest replied.

The mayor hesitated; after all, he was the highest authority in Viscos, and he did not want to see an outsider dealing in public with such an important topic. The priest, it was true, had been in the village now for more than twenty years, but he had not been born there, he did not know all the old stories and he did not have the blood of Ahab in his veins.

'In matters as grave as this, I think I should be the one to speak directly to the people,' he said.

'Yes, you're right. It would probably be better if you did; things might go wrong, and I don't want the Church involved. I'll tell you my plan, and you can take on the task of making it public.'

'On second thoughts, if the plan is yours, it might be fairer and more honest for you to share it with everyone.'

'Fear again,' thought the priest. 'If you want to control someone, all you have to do is to make them feel afraid.'

The two women reached Berta's house shortly before nine and found her doing some crochet-work in her tiny living room.

'There's something different about the village tonight,' the old woman said. 'I heard lots of people walking around, lots of footsteps going past. The bar isn't big enough to hold them all.'

'It's the men in the village,' the hotel landlady replied. 'They're going to the square, to discuss what to do about the stranger.'

'I see. I shouldn't think there's much to discuss though, is there? Either they accept his proposal or they allow him to leave in two days' time.'

'We would never even consider accepting his proposal,' the mayor's wife said indignantly.

'Why not? I heard that the priest gave a wonderful sermon today, explaining how the sacrifice of one man saved humanity, and how God accepted a wager with the Devil and punished his most faithful servant. Would it be so wrong if the people of Viscos decided to accept the stranger's proposal as – let's say – a business deal?'

'You can't be serious.'

'I am. It's you who are trying to pull the wool over my eyes.'

The two women considered getting up, there and then, and leaving at once, but it was too risky.

'Apart from that, to what do I owe the honour of this visit? It's never happened before.'

'Two days ago, Miss Prym said she heard the rogue wolf howling.'

'Now we all know that the rogue wolf is just a stupid story dreamed up by the blacksmith,' the hotel landlady said. 'He probably went into the forest with a woman from another village, and when he tried to grab her, she fought back, and that's why he came up with the story of the wolf. But even so, we decided we'd better come over here to make sure everything was all right.'

'Everything's fine. I'm busy crocheting a tablecloth, although I can't guarantee I'll finish it; who knows, I might die tomorrow.'

There was a moment of general embarrassment.

'Well, you know, old people can die at any time,' Berta went on.

Things had returned to normal. Or almost.

'It's far too soon for you to be talking like that.'

'Maybe you're right; tomorrow is another day, as they say. But I don't mind telling you that it's been on my mind a lot today.'

'For any particular reason?'

'Do you think there should be?'

The hotel landlady wanted to change the subject, but she had to do so very carefully. By now, the meeting in the square must have begun and it would be over in a few minutes.

'I think that, with age, people come to realise that death is inevitable. And we need to learn to face it with serenity, wisdom and resignation. Death often frees us from a lot of senseless suffering.'

'You're quite right,' Berta replied. 'That's exactly what I was thinking this afternoon. And do you know what conclusion I came to? I'm very, very afraid of dying. I don't think my time has quite come.'

The atmosphere in the room was getting tenser and tenser, and the mayor's wife remembered the discussion in the sacristy about the land beside the church; they were talking about one thing, but meaning something else entirely.

Neither of the two women knew how the meeting in the square was going; neither of them knew what the priest's plan was, or what the reaction of the men of Viscos would be. It was pointless trying to talk more openly with Berta; after all, no one accepts being killed without putting up a fight. She made a mental note of the problem: if they wanted to kill the old woman, they would have to find a way of doing so that would avoid a violent struggle that might leave clues for any future investigation.

Disappear. The old woman would simply have to disappear. Her body couldn't be buried in the cemetery or left on the mountainside; once the stranger had ascertained that his wishes had been met, they would have to burn the corpse and scatter the ashes in the mountains. So in both theory and in practice, Berta would be helping their land become fertile again.

'What are you thinking?' Berta asked, interrupting her thoughts.

'About a bonfire,' the mayor's wife replied. 'A lovely bonfire that would warm our bodies and our hearts.'

'It's just as well we're no longer in the Middle Ages, because, you know, there are some people in the village who say I'm a witch.'

There was no point in lying, the old woman would only become suspicious, so the two women nodded their agreement.

'If we were in the Middle Ages, they might want to burn me alive, just like that, just because someone decided I must be guilty of something.'

'What's going on here?' the hotel landlady was wondering to herself. 'Could someone have betrayed us? Could it be that the mayor's wife, who's here with me now, came over earlier and told her everything? Or could it be that the priest suddenly repented and came to confess himself to this sinner?'

'Thank you so much for your visit, but I'm fine, really, in perfect health, ready to make every necessary sacrifice, including being on one of those stupid diets to lower my cholesterol levels, because I want to go on living for a long while yet.'

458 AND ON THE SEVENTH DAY

Berta got up and opened the door. The two women said goodbye to her. The meeting in the square had still not finished.

'I'm so pleased you came. I'm going to stop my crocheting now and go to bed. And to tell you the truth, I believe in the rogue wolf. Now since you two are so much younger than me, would you mind hanging around until the meeting finishes and make quite sure that the wolf doesn't come to my door?'

The two women agreed, bade her goodnight, and Berta went in.

'She knows!' the hotel landlady whispered. 'Someone has told her! Didn't you notice the ironic tone in her voice? She knows we're here to keep an eye on her.'

The mayor's wife was confused.

'But how can she know? No one would be so crazy as to tell her. Unless …'

'Unless she really is a witch. Do you remember the hot wind that suddenly blew into the sacristy while we were talking?'

'Even though the windows were shut.'

The hearts of the two women contracted and centuries of superstitions rose to the surface. If Berta really was a witch, then her death, far from saving the village, would destroy it completely.

Or so the legends said.

Berta switched off the light and stood watching the two women in the street out of a corner of her window. She didn't know whether to laugh or cry, or simply to accept her fate. She was sure of one thing, though, she had been marked out to die.

Her husband had appeared earlier that evening, and to her surprise, he was accompanied by Miss Prym's grandmother. Berta's first reaction was one of jealousy: what was he doing with that woman? But then she saw the worried look on both of their faces, and became even more troubled when she heard what they had to say about what had gone on in the sacristy.

The two of them told her to run away at once.

'You must be joking,' Berta replied. 'How am I supposed to run away? My legs can barely carry me the hundred yards to church, so how could I possibly walk all the way down the road and out of the village? Please, sort this problem out up in heaven and do something to protect me! After all, why else do I spend my time praying to all the saints?'

It was a much more complicated situation than Berta could imagine, they explained: Good and Evil were locked in combat, and no one could interfere. Angels and devils were in the midst of one of the periodic battles that decide whether whole regions of the earth are to be condemned for a while or saved.

'I'm not interested; I have no way of defending myself, this isn't my fight, I didn't ask to be caught up in it.'

Nobody had. It had all begun two years earlier with a mistake made by a guardian angel. During a kidnapping, two women were marked out to die, but a little three-year-old girl was supposed to be saved. This girl, it was said, would be a consolation to her father and help him to maintain some hope in life and overcome the tremendous suffering he would undergo. He was a good man, and although he would have to endure terrible suffering (no one knew why, that was all part of God's plan, which had never been fully explained), he would recover in the end. The girl would grow up marked by the tragedy and, when she was twenty, would use her own suffering to help alleviate that of others. She would eventually do work of such vital importance that it would have an impact all over the world.

That had been the original plan. And everything was going well: the police stormed the hideout, shots started flying and the people chosen to die began to fall. At that moment, the child's guardian angel – as Berta knew, all three-year-olds can see and talk to their guardian angels all the time – signalled to her to crouch down by the wall. But the child did not understand and ran towards him so that she could hear better.

She moved barely a matter of inches, just enough to be struck by a fatal bullet. From then on, the story took a new twist. What was meant to become an edifying story of redemption, turned into a merciless struggle. The devil made his appearance, claiming that the man's soul should be his, being as it was full of hatred, impotence and a desire for vengeance. The angels could not accept this; he was a good man and had been chosen to help his daughter make great changes in the world, even though his profession was hardly ideal.

But the angels' arguments no longer rang true to him. Bit by bit, the devil took over his soul, until now he controlled him almost completely.

'Almost completely,' Berta repeated. 'You said "almost".'

They agreed. There was still a tiny chink of light left, because one of the angels had refused to give up the fight. But he had never been listened to until the previous night, when he had managed briefly to speak out. And his instrument had been none other than Miss Prym.

Chantal's grandmother explained that this was why she was there; because if anyone could change the situation, it was her granddaughter. Even so, the struggle was more ferocious than ever, and the stranger's angel had again been silenced by the presence of the devil.

Berta tried to calm them down, because they both seemed very upset. They, after all, were already dead; she was the one who should be worried. Couldn't they help Chantal change the course of things?

Chantal's devil was also winning the battle, they replied. When Chantal was in the forest, her grandmother had sent the rogue wolf to find her – the wolf did, in fact, exist, and the blacksmith had been telling the truth. She had wanted to awaken the stranger's good side and had done so. But apparently the argument between the two of them had got them nowhere; they were both too stubborn. There was only one hope left: that Chantal had seen what they wanted her to see. Or rather, they knew she had seen it, but what they wanted was for her to understand what she had seen.

'What's that?' Berta asked.

They refused to say. Their contact with human beings had its limits, there were devils listening in to their conversation who could spoil everything if they knew of the plan in advance. But they insisted it was something very simple, and if Chantal was as intelligent as her grandmother said she was, she would know how to deal with the situation.

Berta accepted this answer; the last thing she wanted was an indiscretion that might cost her her life, even though she loved hearing secrets. But there was something she still wanted explained and so she turned to her husband:

'You told me to stay here, sitting on this chair all these years, watching over the village in case Evil entered it. You asked that of me long before that guardian angel made a mistake and the child was killed. Why?'

Her husband replied that, one way or another, Evil was bound to pass through Viscos, because the Devil was always abroad in the Earth, trying to catch people unawares.

'I'm not convinced.'

Her husband was not convinced either, but it was true. Perhaps the fight between Good and Evil is raging all the time in every individual's heart, which is the battleground for all angels and devils; they would fight inch by inch for thousands of millennia in order to gain ground, until one of them finally vanquished the other. Yet even though he now existed on a spiritual plane, there were still many things he did not understand – many more, in fact, than on Earth.

'You've convinced me. Go and rest; if I have to die, it will be because my hour has come.'

Berta did not say that she felt slightly jealous and would like to be with her husband again; Chantal's grandmother had always been one of the most sought-after women in the village.

They left, claiming that they had to make sure the girl had understood what she had seen. Berta felt even more jealous, but she managed to calm herself, even though she suspected that her husband only wanted to see her live a little longer so that he could enjoy the company of Chantal's grandmother undisturbed.

Besides, the independence he thought he was enjoying might well come to an end the very next day. Berta considered a little and changed her mind: the poor man deserved a few years' rest, it was no hardship to let him go on thinking he was free to do as he liked – she was sure he missed her dreadfully.

Seeing the two women still on guard outside her house, she thought it wouldn't be so bad to be able to stay a while longer in that valley, staring up at the mountains, watching the eternal conflicts between men and women, the trees and the wind, between angels and devils. Then she began to feel afraid and tried to concentrate on something else – perhaps tomorrow she would change the colour of the ball of yarn she was using; the tablecloth was beginning to look distinctly drab.

Before the meeting in the square had finished, she was fast asleep, sure in her mind that Miss Prym would eventually understand the message, even if she did not have the gift of speaking with spirits.

'I n church, on hallowed ground, I spoke of the need for sacrifice,' the priest said. 'Here, on unhallowed land, I ask you to be prepared for martyrdom.'

The small, dimly lit square – there was still only one street lamp, despite the mayor's pre-election promises to install more – was full to overflowing. Peasants and shepherds, drowsy-eyed because they were used to going to bed and rising with the sun, stood in respectful, awed silence. The priest had placed a chair next to the cross and was standing on it so that everyone could see him.

'For centuries, the Church has been accused of fighting unjust battles, when, in reality, all we were doing was trying to survive threats to our existence.'

'We didn't come here to hear about the Church, Father,' a voice shouted. 'We came to find out about Viscos.'

'I don't need to tell you that Viscos risks disappearing off the map, taking with it you, your lands and your flocks. Nor did I come here to talk about the Church, but there is one thing I must say: only by sacrifice and penitence can we find salvation. And before I'm interrupted again, I mean the sacrifice of one person, the penitence of all and the salvation of this village.'

'It might all be a lie,' another voice cried out.

'The stranger is going to show us the gold tomorrow,' the mayor said, pleased to be able to give a piece of information of which even the priest was unaware. 'Miss Prym does not wish to bear the responsibility alone, so the hotel landlady persuaded the stranger to bring the gold bars here. We will act only after receiving that guarantee.'

The mayor took over and began telling them about the improvements that would be made to life in the village: the rebuilding work, the children's playground, the reduced taxes and the planned redistribution of their newly acquired wealth.

'In equal shares,' someone shouted.

It was time for the mayor to take on a commitment he hated to make; as if suddenly awoken from their somnolent state, all eyes were turned in his direction.

'In equal shares,' the priest said, before the mayor could respond. There was no other choice: everyone had to take part and bear the same responsibility and receive the same reward, otherwise it would not be long before someone denounced the crime – either out of jealousy or vengeance. The priest was all too familiar with both those words.

'Who is going to die?'

The mayor explained the fair process by which Berta had been chosen: she suffered greatly from the loss of her husband, she was old, had no friends, and seemed slightly mad, sitting outside her house from dawn to dusk, making absolutely no contribution to the growth of the village. Instead of her money being invested in lands or sheep, it was earning interest in some far-off bank; the only ones who benefited from it were the traders who, like the baker, came every week to sell their produce in the village.

Not a single voice in the crowd was raised against the choice. The mayor was glad because they had accepted his authority; but the priest knew that this could be a good or a bad sign, because silence does not always mean consent – usually all it meant was that people were incapable of coming up with an immediate response. If someone did not agree, they would later torture themselves with the idea that they had accepted without really wanting to, and the consequences of that could be grave.

'I need everyone here to agree,' the priest said. 'I need everyone to say out loud whether they agree or disagree, so that God can hear you and know that He has valiant men in His army. If you don't believe in God, I ask you all the same to say out loud whether you agree or disagree, so that we will all know exactly what everyone here thinks.'

The mayor did not like the way the priest had used the verb 'need': 'I need' he had said, when it would have been more appropriate to say: 'we need', or 'the mayor needs'. When this business was over, he would have to re-impose his authority in whatever way was necessary. Now, like a good politician, he would let the priest take the lead and expose himself to risk. 'I want you all to say that you agree.'

The first 'yes' came from the blacksmith. Then the mayor, to show his courage, also said 'yes' in a loud voice. One by one, every man present declared out loud that they agreed with the choice – until they had all committed themselves. Some of them did so because they wanted to get the meeting over and done with so that they could go home; some were thinking about the gold and about the quickest way they could leave the village with their newly acquired wealth; others were planning to send money to their children so that they would no longer have to feel ashamed in front of their friends in the big city. Almost no one in the crowd believed that Viscos would regain its former glory; all they wanted were the riches they had always deserved, but had never had.

But no one said 'no'.

'108 women and 173 men live in this village,' the priest went on. 'Since it is the tradition here for everyone to learn how to hunt, every-one owns at least one shotgun. Tomorrow morning, I want you each to leave a shotgun in the sacristy, with a single cartridge in it. I'm asking the mayor, who has more than one gun, to bring one for me as well.'

'We never leave our weapons with strangers,' a hunting guide shouted. 'Guns are sacred, temperamental, personal. They should never be fired by other people.'

'Let me finish. I'm going to explain how a firing squad works. Seven soldiers are chosen to shoot the condemned man. Seven rifles are handed out to the squad, but only six of them are loaded with real bullets, the seventh contains a blank. The gunpowder explodes in exactly the same way, the noise is identical, but there's no lead to be fired into the victim's body.

'None of the soldiers knows which rifle contains the blank. In that way, each of them thinks that his gun contained the blank and that his friends were responsible for the death of the man or woman none of them knew, but whom they were forced to shoot in the line of duty.'

'So all of them believe they are innocent,' the landowner chimed in, speaking for the first time.

'Exactly. Tomorrow I will do the same: I'll take the lead out of eighty-seven of the cartridges and leave the other shotguns with live ammunition in them. All the weapons will go off at the same time, but no one will know which of them has pellets inside; in that way, all of you can consider yourselves innocent.'

Tired though the men were, they greeted the priest's idea with a huge sigh of relief. A different kind of energy spread through the crowd as if, from one hour to the next, the entire situation had lost its tragic air and had been transformed into a simple treasure hunt. Every man was convinced that his gun would carry the blank ammunition, and that he would not therefore be guilty; he was simply showing solidarity with his fellows, who wanted to change their lives and where they lived. Everyone was excited now; at last, Viscos had become a place where different, important things happened.

'The only weapon you can be sure will be loaded is mine, because I can't choose for myself. Nor will I keep my share of the gold. I'm doing this for other reasons.'

Again, the mayor did not like the way the priest spoke. He was trying to impress on the people of Viscos what a courageous man he was, a generous leader capable of any sacrifice. If the mayor's wife had been there, she would doubtless have said that the priest was preparing to launch himself as a candidate for the next elections.

'Wait until Monday,' he told himself. He would publish a decree announcing such a steep increase in tax on the church that it would be impossible for the priest to stay on in the village. After all, he was the only one who claimed he didn't want to be rich.

'What about the victim?' the blacksmith asked.

'She'll be there,' the priest said. 'I'll take care of that. But I need three men to come with me.'

When no one volunteered, the priest chose three strong men. One of them tried to say 'no', but his friends stared him down, and he quickly changed his mind.

'Where will the sacrifice take place?' the landowner asked, addressing the priest. The mayor again sensed authority slipping away from him; he needed to regain it at once.

'I'm the one who decides that,' he said, shooting a furious look at the landowner. 'I don't want the earth of Viscos to be stained with blood. We'll do it at this same time tomorrow night up by the Celtic monolith. Bring your lanterns, lamps and torches, so that everyone can see clearly where they are pointing their shotgun, and nobody misses.'

The priest got down from his chair – the meeting was over. The women of Viscos once again heard footsteps in the street, the men returning to their houses, having a drink, staring out of the window, or simply collapsing into bed, exhausted. The mayor returned to his wife, who told him what had happened in Berta's house, and how frightened she had been. But after they – together with the hotel landlady – had analysed every single word that had been said, the two women concluded that the old woman knew nothing; it was merely their sense of guilt making them think like that.

'Make-believe ghosts, like the rogue wolf,' the mayor said.

The priest went back to the church and spent the whole night in prayer.

Chantal breakfasted on the bread she had bought the day before, since the baker's van didn't come on Sundays. She looked out of her window and saw the men of Viscos leaving their houses, each carrying a weapon. She prepared herself to die, as there was still a possibility that she would be the chosen victim; but no one knocked on her door – instead, they carried on down the street, went into the sacristy, and emerged again, empty-handed.

She left her house and went down to the hotel, where the hotel landlady told her about everything that had happened the previous night: the choice of victim, what the priest had proposed and the preparations for the sacrifice. Her hostile tone had vanished, and things seemed to be changing in Chantal's favour.

'There's something I want to tell you; one day, Viscos will realise all that you did for its people.'

'But the stranger still has to show us the gold,' Chantal insisted.

'Of course. He just went out carrying an empty rucksack.'

Chantal decided not to go to the forest, because that would mean passing by Berta's house, and she was too ashamed to look at her. She went back to her room and remembered her dream of the previous night.

For she had had a strange dream in which an angel handed her the eleven gold bars and asked her to keep them.

Chantal told the angel that, for this to happen, someone had to be killed. But the angel said that this wasn't the case: on the contrary, the bars were proof that the gold did not exist.

That was why she had insisted to the hotel landlady that the stranger should show everyone the gold; she had a plan. However, since she had always lost every other battle in her life, she had her doubts as to whether she would be able to win this one.

Berta was watching the sun setting behind the mountains when she saw the priest and three other men coming towards her. She felt sad for three reasons: she knew her time had come; her husband had not appeared to console her (perhaps because he was afraid of what he would hear, or ashamed of his own inability to save her); and she realised that the money she had saved would end up in the hands of the shareholders of the bank where she had deposited it, since she had not had time to withdraw it and burn it.

She felt happy for two reasons: she was finally going to be reunited with her husband, who was doubtless, at that moment, out and about with Miss Prym's grandmother; and although the last day of her life had been cold, it had been filled with sunlight – not everyone had the good fortune to leave the world with such a beautiful memory of it.

The priest signalled to the other men to stay back, and he went forward on his own to greet her.

'Good evening,' she said. 'See how great God is to have made the world so beautiful.'

'They're going to take me away,' she told herself, 'but I will leave them with all the world's guilt to carry on their shoulders.'

'Think, then, how beautiful paradise must be,' the priest said, but Berta could see her arrow had struck home, and that now he was struggling to remain calm.

'I'm not sure about that, I'm not even sure it exists. Have you been there yourself, Father?'

'Not yet. But I've been in hell and I know how terrible that is, however attractive it might appear from the outside.'

Berta understood him to mean Viscos.

'You're mistaken, Father. You were in paradise, but you didn't recognise it. It's the same with most people in this world; they seek suffering in the most joyous of places because they think they are unworthy of happiness.'

'It appears that all your years spent sitting out here have brought you some wisdom.'

'It's been a long time since anyone bothered to come and chat with me, and now, oddly enough, everyone has discovered that I still exist. Just imagine, Father, last night, the hotel landlady and the mayor's wife honoured me with a visit; and now here's the parish priest doing the same – have I suddenly become such an important person?'

'Very much so,' the priest replied. 'The most important person in the village.'

'Have I come into money or something?'

'Ten gold bars. Future generations of men, women and children will give thanks to you. It's even possible they'll put up a statue in your honour.'

'I'd prefer a fountain, because as well as being decorative, it quenches people's thirst and soothes those who are worried.'

'A fountain it will be then. You have my word on it.'

Berta thought it was time to put an end to this farce and come straight to the point.

'I know everything, Father. You are condemning an innocent woman who cannot fight for her life. Damn you, sir, and damn this village and all who live in it.'

'Damned indeed,' the priest said. 'For more than twenty years, I've tried to bless this village, but no one heard my calls. For the same twenty years, I've tried to inculcate Good into men's hearts, until I finally realised that God had chosen me to be his left arm, and to show the evil of which men are capable. Perhaps in this way they will become afraid and accept the faith.'

Berta felt like crying, but controlled the impulse.

'Fine words, Father, but empty. They're just an excuse for cruelty and injustice.'

'Unlike all the others, I'm not doing this for the money. I know that the gold is cursed, like this whole place, and that it won't bring happiness to anyone. I am simply doing as God has asked me. Or rather, as he commanded me, in answer to my prayers.'

'There's no point arguing further,' Berta thought, as the priest put his hand in his pocket and brought out some pills.

'You won't feel a thing,' he said. 'Let's go inside.'

'Neither you nor anyone else in this village will set foot in my house while I'm still alive. Perhaps later tonight the door will stand wide open, but not now.'

The priest gestured to one of the men, who approached carrying a plastic bottle.

'Take these pills. You'll soon fall asleep and when you wake up, you'll be in heaven, with your husband.'

'I've always been with my husband and, despite suffering from insomnia, I never take pills to get to sleep.'

'So much the better; they'll take effect at once.'

The sun had disappeared, and darkness was beginning to fall on the valley, the church, and on the entire village.

'And what if I don't want to take them?'

'You'll take them just the same.'

Berta looked at the three men and saw that the priest was right. She took the pills from him, placed them in her mouth and drank the entire bottle of water. Water: it has no taste, no smell, no colour and yet it is the most important thing in the world. Just like her at that moment.

She looked once more at the mountains, now covered in darkness. She saw the first star come out and thought that she had had a good life; she had been born and would die in a place she loved, even though it seemed that her love was unrequited, but what did that matter? Anyone who loves in the expectation of being loved in return is wasting their time.

She had been blessed. She had never been to another country, but she knew that here in Viscos the same things happened as everywhere else. She had lost the husband she loved, but God had granted her the joy of continuing at his side, even after his death. She had seen the village at its height, had witnessed the beginning of its decline, and was leaving before it was completely destroyed. She had known mankind with all its faults and virtues, and she believed that, despite all that was happening to her now, despite the struggles her husband swore were going on the invisible world, human goodness would triumph in the end.

She felt sorry for the priest, for the mayor, for Miss Prym, for the stranger, for every one of the inhabitants of Viscos: Evil would never bring Good, however much they wanted to believe that it would. By the time they discovered the truth, it would be too late.

She had only one regret: never having seen the sea. She knew it existed, that it was vast and simultaneously wild and calm, but she had never been to see it or tasted the salt water on her tongue or felt the sand beneath her bare feet or dived into the cold water like someone returning to the womb of the Great Mother (she remembered that this was an expression favoured by the Celts).

Apart from that, she did not have much to complain about. She was sad, very sad, to have to leave like this, but she did not want to feel she was a victim: doubtless God had chosen this role for her, and it was far better than the one He had chosen for the priest.

'I want to talk to you about Good and Evil,' she heard him say, just as she began to feel a kind of numbness in her hands and feet.

'There's no need. You don't know what goodness is. You were poisoned by the evil done to you, and now you're spreading that plague throughout our land. You're no different from the stranger who came to visit us and destroy us.'

Her last words were barely audible. She looked up at the one star, then closed her eyes.

The stranger went into the bathroom in his hotel room, carefully washed each of the gold bars and replaced them in his shabby, old rucksack. Two days ago he had left the stage, and now he was returning for the final act – he had to make a last appearance.

Everything had been carefully planned: from the choice of a small, remote village with few inhabitants down to the fact of having an accomplice, so that if things did not work out, no one could ever accuse him of inciting people to murder. The tape recorder, the reward, the careful steps he had taken, first making friends with the people in the village and then spreading terror and confusion. Just as God had done to him, so he would do unto others. Just as God had given him all that was good only to cast him into the abyss, so he would do the same.

He had taken care of every detail, except one: he had never thought his plan would work. He had been sure that when the moment came to choose, a simple 'no' would change the story; at least one person would refuse to take part, and that person would be enough to prove that not everything was lost. If one person saved the village, the world itself would be saved, hope would still be possible, goodness would be strengthened, the terrorists would not have truly known the evil they were doing, there could be forgiveness, and his days of suffering would be but a sad memory that he could learn to live with and he could perhaps even seek happiness again. For that 'no' he would have liked to have heard, the village would have received its reward of ten gold bars, independently of the wager he had made with Chantal.

But his plan had failed. And now it was too late, he couldn't change his mind.

Someone knocked at his door.

'Let's go,' he heard the hotel landlady say. 'It's time.'

'I'll be right down.'

He picked up his jacket, put it on and met the landlady downstairs in the bar.

'I've got the gold,' he said. 'But, just so there's no misunderstanding, you should be aware that there are several people who know where I am. If you decide to change your victim, you can be sure that the police will come looking for me; you yourself saw me making all those phone calls.'

The hotel landlady merely nodded.

The Celtic monolith was half an hour's walk from Viscos. For many centuries, people had thought it was merely an unusually large stone, polished by the wind and the ice, which had once stood upright, but that had been toppled by a bolt of lightning. Ahab used to hold the village council there because the rock served as a natural open-air table.

Then one day the Government sent a team to write a survey of the Celtic settlements in the valley, and someone noticed the monument. Then came the archaeologists, who measured, calculated, argued, excavated and reached the conclusion that a Celtic tribe had chosen the spot as some kind of sacred place, even though they had no idea what rituals had been performed there. Some said it was a sort of observatory, others said that fertility rites – in which young virgins were possessed by priests – had taken place there. The experts discussed it for a whole week, but then left to look at something more interesting, without reaching any definite conclusions about their findings.

When he was elected, the mayor tried to attract tourism to Viscos by getting an article published in the regional press about the Celtic heritage of the village. But the paths through the forest were difficult, and the few intrepid visitors who came found only a fallen stone at the end of them, whereas other villages could boast sculptures, inscriptions and other far more interesting things. The idea came to nothing, and the monolith soon resumed its usual function as a weekend picnic table.

That evening, there were arguments in several households in Viscos all over the same thing: the men wanted to go alone, but their wives insisted on taking part in the 'ritual sacrifice', as the inhabitants had come to call the murder they were about to commit. The husbands argued that it was dangerous, a shotgun might go off by accident; their wives said that the men were just being selfish and that they should respect the women's rights, the world was no longer as they thought it was. In the end, the husbands yielded, and the wives rejoiced.

Now the procession was heading for the monolith, a chain of 281 points of light in the darkness, for the stranger was carrying a torch, and Berta was not carrying anything, so the number of inhabitants of the village was still exactly represented. Each of the men had a torch or lantern in one hand and, in the other, a shotgun, its breech open so that it would not go off by accident.

Berta was the only one who did not need to walk. She was sleeping peacefully on a kind of improvised stretcher that two woodcutters were struggling along with. 'I'm glad we won't have to carry this great weight back,' one of them was thinking, 'because by then, with all the buckshot in her, she'll weigh three times as much.'

He calculated that each cartridge would contain, on average, at least six small balls of lead. If all the loaded shotguns hit their target, the old woman's body would be riddled with 522 pellets, and would end up containing more metal than blood.

The man could feel his stomach churning. He resolved not to think any more about it until Monday.

No one said a word during the walk. No one looked at anyone else, as if this was a kind of nightmare they wanted to forget as quickly as possible. They arrived out of breath – more from tension than from exhaustion – and formed a huge semicircle of lights in the clearing where the Celtic monument lay.

The mayor gave a signal, and the woodcutters untied Berta from the stretcher and laid her on the monolith.

'That's no good,' the blacksmith protested, remembering the war films he'd seen, with soldiers crawling along the ground. 'It's hard to shoot someone when they're lying down.'

The woodcutters shifted Berta into a sitting position with her back against the stone. It seemed ideal, but then a sudden sob was heard and a woman's voice said:

'She's looking at us. She can see what we're doing.'

Berta could not, of course, see a thing, but it was unbearable to look at that kindly lady, asleep, with a contented smile on her lips, and to think that in a short while she would be torn apart by all those tiny pellets.

'Turn her round,' ordered the mayor, who was also troubled by the sight.

Grumbling, the woodcutters returned once more to the monolith and turned the body round, so that this time she was kneeling on the ground, with her face and chest resting on the stone. It was impossible to keep her upright in this position, so they had to tie a rope round her wrists, throw it over the top of the monument, and fasten it on the other side.

Berta's position was now utterly grotesque: kneeling, with her back to them, her arms stretched out over the stone, as if she were praying or begging for something. Someone protested again, but the mayor said it was time to do what they had come to do.

And the quicker the better. With no speeches or justifications; that could wait until tomorrow – in the bar, on the streets, in conversations between shepherds and farmers. It was likely that one of the three roads out of Viscos would not be used for a long while, since they were all so accustomed to seeing Berta sitting there, looking up at the mountains and talking to herself. Luckily, the village had two other exits, as well as a narrow short cut, with some improvised steps down to the road below.

'Let's get this over with,' said the mayor, pleased that the priest was now saying nothing, and that his own authority had been re-established. 'Someone in the valley might see these lights and decide to find out what's going on. Prepare your shotguns, fire, and then we can leave.'

Without ceremony. Doing their duty, like good soldiers defending their village. With no doubts in their minds. This was an order, and it would be obeyed.

And suddenly, the mayor not only understood the priest's silence, he realised that he had fallen into a trap. If one day the story of what had happened got out, all the others could claim, as all murderers did in wartime, that they were merely obeying orders. But what was going on at that moment in their hearts? Did they see him as a villain or as their saviour?

He could not weaken now, at the very moment when he heard the shotguns being snapped shut, the barrels fitting perfectly into the breech blocks. He imagined the noise that 174 guns would make, but by the time anyone arrived to see what was going on, they would be far away. Shortly before they had begun the climb up to the monolith, he had ordered them to extinguish all lights on the way back. They knew the route by heart, and the lights were simply to avoid any accidents when they opened fire.

Instinctively, the women stepped back, and the men took aim at the inert body, some fifty yards away. They could not possibly miss, having been trained since childhood to shoot fleeing animals and birds in flight.

The mayor prepared to give the order to fire.

'Just a moment,' shouted a female voice.

It was Miss Prym.

'What about the gold? Have you seen it yet?'

The shotguns were lowered, but still ready to be fired; no, no one had seen the gold. They all turned towards the stranger.

He walked slowly in front of the shotguns. He put his rucksack down on the ground and one by one took out the bars of gold.

'There it is,' he said, before returning to his place at one end of the semicircle.

Miss Prym went over to the gold bars and picked one up.

'It's gold,' she said. 'But I want you to check it. Let nine women come up here and examine each of the bars still on the ground.'

The mayor began to get worried: they would be in the line of fire, and someone of a nervous disposition might set off a gun by accident; but nine women – including his wife – went over to join Miss Prym and did as she asked.

'Yes, it's gold,' the mayor's wife said, carefully checking the bar she had in her hands, and comparing it to the few pieces of gold jewellery she possessed. 'I can see it has a hallmark and what must be a serial number, as well as the date it was cast and its weight. It's the real thing all right.'

'Well, hang on to that gold and listen to what I have to say.'

'This is no time for speeches, Miss Prym,' the mayor said. 'All of you get away from there so that we can finish the job.'

'Shut up, you idiot!'

These words from Chantal startled everyone. None of them dreamed that anyone in Viscos could say what they had just heard.

'Have you gone mad?'

'I said shut up!' Chantal shouted even more loudly, trembling from head to foot, her eyes wide with hatred. 'You're the one who's mad, for falling into this trap that has led us all to condemnation and death! You are the irresponsible one!'

The mayor moved towards her, but was held back by two men.

'We want to hear what the girl has to say,' a voice in the crowd shouted. 'Ten minutes won't make any difference!'

Ten or even five minutes would make a huge difference, and everyone there, men and women, knew it. As they became more aware of the situation, their fear was growing, the sense of guilt was spreading, shame was beginning to take hold, their hands were starting to shake, and they were all looking for an excuse to change their minds. On the walk there, each man had been convinced that he was carrying a weapon containing blank ammunition and that soon it would all be over. Now they were starting to fear that their shotguns would fire real pellets, and that the ghost of the old woman – who was reputed to be a witch – would come back at night to haunt them.

Or that someone would talk. Or that the priest had not done as he had promised, and they would all be guilty.

'Five minutes,' the mayor said, trying to get them to believe that it was he who was giving permission, when in fact it was the young woman who was setting the rules.

'I'll talk for as long as I like,' said Chantal, who appeared to have regained her composure and to be determined not to give an inch; she spoke now with an authority no one had ever seen before. 'But it won't take long. It's strange to see what's going on here, especially when, as we all know, in the days of Ahab, men often used to come to the village claiming to have a special powder that could turn lead into gold. They called themselves alchemists, and at least one of them proved he was telling the truth when Ahab threatened to kill him.

'Today you are trying to do the same thing: mixing lead with blood, certain that this will be transformed into the gold we women are holding. On the one hand, you're absolutely right. On the other, the gold will slip through your fingers as quickly as it came.'

The stranger could not grasp what the young girl was saying, but he willed her to go on; he had noticed that, in a dark corner of his soul, the forgotten light was once again shining brightly.

'At school, we were all told the famous legend of King Midas, who met a god who offered to grant him anything he wished for. Midas was already very rich, but he wanted more money, and he asked to have the power to turn everything he touched into gold.

'Let me remind you what happened: first, Midas transformed his furniture, his palace and everything around him into gold. He worked away for a whole morning, and soon had a golden garden, golden trees and golden staircases. At noon, he felt hungry and wanted to eat. But as soon as he touched the succulent leg of lamb that his servants had prepared, that too was turned into gold. He raised a glass of wine to his lips, and it was instantly turned into gold. In despair, he ran to his wife to ask her to help him, for he was beginning to understand his mistake, but as soon as he touched her arm, she turned into a golden statue.

'The servants fled the palace, terrified that the same thing would happen to them. In less than a week, Midas had died of hunger and thirst, surrounded by gold on all sides.'

'Why are you telling us this story?' the mayor's wife wanted to know, putting her gold bar back on the ground and returning to her husband's side. 'Has some god come to Viscos and given us this power?'

'I'm telling you the story for one simple reason: gold itself has no value. Absolutely none. We cannot eat it or drink it or use it to buy more animals or land. It's money that's valuable, and how are we going to turn this gold into money?

'We can do one of two things: we can ask the blacksmith to melt the bars down into 280 equal pieces, and then each one of you can go to the city to exchange it for money. But that would immediately arouse the suspicions of the authorities, because there is no gold in this valley, so it would seem very odd if every Viscos inhabitant were suddenly to turn up bearing a small gold bar. The authorities would become suspicious. We would have to say we had unearthed an ancient Celtic treasure. But a quick check would show that the gold had been made recently, that the area round here had already been excavated, that the Celts never had this amount of gold – if they had, they would have built a large and splendid city on this site.'

'You're just an ignorant young woman,' the landowner said. 'We'll take in the bars exactly as they are, with the government hallmark and everything. We'll exchange them at a bank and divide the money between us.'

'That's the second thing. The mayor takes the ten gold bars, goes to the bank, and asks them to exchange them for money. The bank cashier wouldn't ask the same questions as if each of us were to turn up with our own gold bar; since the mayor is a figure of authority, they would simply ask him for the purchase documents for the gold. The mayor would say he didn't have them, but would point out – as his wife says – that each bar bears a government hallmark, and that it's genuine. There's a date and a serial number on each one.

'By this time, the man who gave us the gold will be far from here. The cashier will ask for more time because, although he knows the mayor and knows he is an honest man, he needs authorisation to hand over such a large amount of money. Questions will be asked about where the gold came from. The mayor will say it was a present from a stranger – after all, our mayor is an intelligent man and has an answer for everything.

'Once the cashier has spoken to his manager, the manager – who suspects nothing, but he is nevertheless a paid employee and doesn't want to run any risks – will phone the bank headquarters. Nobody there knows the mayor, and any large withdrawal is regarded as suspicious; they will ask the mayor to wait for two days, while they confirm the origin of the gold bars. What might they discover? That the gold had been stolen perhaps. Or that it was purchased by a group suspected of dealing in drugs.'

Chantal paused. The fear she had felt when she first tried to take her gold bar with her was now being shared by all of them. The story of one person is the story of all of humanity.

'This gold has serial numbers on it. And a date. This gold is easy to identify.'

Everyone looked at the stranger, who remained impassive.

'There's no point asking him anything,' Chantal said. 'We would have to take it on trust that he's telling the truth, and a man who calls for a murder to be committed is hardly to be trusted.'

'We could keep him here until the gold has been changed into money,' the blacksmith said.

The stranger nodded in the direction of the hotel landlady.

'We can't touch him. He's got powerful friends. I overheard him phoning various people, and he's reserved his plane tickets; if he disappears, they'll know he's been kidnapped and come looking for him in Viscos.'

Chantal put the gold bar down on the ground and moved out of the line of fire. The other women did the same.

'You can shoot if you like, but since I know this is a trap set by the stranger, I want nothing to do with this murder.'

'You don't know anything!' the landowner cried.

'But if I'm right, the mayor would soon be behind bars, and people would come to Viscos to find out who he stole this treasure from. Someone would have to explain, and it's not going to be me.

'But I promise to keep quiet. I'll simply plead ignorance. And besides, the mayor is someone we know, not like the stranger who is leaving Viscos tomorrow. He might take all the blame on himself and say that he stole the gold from a man who came to spend a week in Viscos. Then we would all see him as a hero, the crime would go undiscovered, and we could all go on living our lives – somehow or other – but without the gold.'

'I'll do it,' the mayor said, knowing that this was all pure invention on the part of this madwoman.

Meanwhile, the noise of the first shotgun being disarmed was heard.

'Trust me!' the mayor shouted. 'I'll take the risk!'

But the only response was that same noise, then another, and the noises seemed to spread by contagion, until almost all the shotguns had been disarmed: since when could anyone believe in the promises of a politician? Only the mayor and the priest still had their shotguns at the ready; one was pointing at Miss Prym, the other at Berta. But the woodcutter – the one who, earlier on, had worked out the number of pellets that would penetrate the old woman's body – saw what was happening, went over to the two men and took their weapons from them: the mayor was not mad enough to commit a murder purely out of revenge, and the priest had no experience of weapons and might miss.

Miss Prym was right: it is very dangerous to believe in other people. It was as if everyone there had suddenly become aware of that, because they began to drift away from the clearing, the older people first, then the younger ones.

Silently, they all filed down the hillside, trying to think about the weather, the sheep they had to shear, the land that would soon need ploughing again, the hunting season that was about to start. None of this had happened, because Viscos is a village lost in time, where every day is the same.

They were all saying to themselves that this weekend had been a dream.

Or a nightmare.

Only three people and two torches remained in the clearing – and one of those people was fast asleep, still tied to the stone.

'There's the village gold,' the stranger said to Chantal. 'It looks like I end up without the gold and without an answer.'

'The gold doesn't belong to the village, it belongs to me. As does the bar buried beside the Y-shaped rock. And you're going to come with me to make sure it gets changed into money; I don't trust a word you say.'

'You know I wasn't going to do what you said I would do. And as for the contempt you feel for me, it's nothing more than the contempt you feel for yourself. You should be grateful for all that's happened, because by showing you the gold, I gave you much more than the possibility of simply becoming rich. I forced you to act, to stop complaining about everything and to take a stand.'

'Very generous of you, I'm sure,' said Chantal with a touch of irony in her voice. 'From the very start, I could have told you something about human nature; even though Viscos is a village in decline, it once had a wise and glorious past. I could have given you the answer you were looking for, if only I had thought of it.'

Chantal went over to untie Berta; she saw that Berta had a cut on her forehead, perhaps because of the way her head had been positioned on the stone, but it was nothing serious. Now they just had to wait there until morning for Berta to wake up.

'Can you give me that answer now?' the stranger asked.

'Someone must already have told you about the meeting between St Savin and Ahab.'

'Of course. The saint came, talked to him briefly, and the Arab converted to Christianity because he realised that the saint was much braver than him.'

'That's right. Except that, before going to sleep, the two of them talked together for a while. Even though Ahab had begun to sharpen his knife the moment the saint set foot in his house, safe in the knowledge that the world was a reflection of himself, he was determined to challenge the saint and so he asked him:

'"If, tonight, the most beautiful prostitute in the village came in here, would you be able to see her as neither beautiful nor seductive?"

'"No, but I would be able to control myself," the saint replied.

'"And if I offered you a pile of gold coins to leave your cave in the mountain and come and join us, would you be able to look on that gold and see only pebbles?"

'"No, but I would be able to control myself."

'"And if you were sought by two brothers, one of whom hated you, and the other who saw you as a saint, would you be able to feel the same towards them both?"

'"It would be very hard, but I would be able to control myself sufficiently to treat them both the same."

Chantal paused.

'They say this dialogue was important in Ahab's conversion to Christianity.'

The stranger did not need Chantal to explain the story. Savin and Ahab had the same instincts – Good and Evil struggled in both of them, just as they did in every soul on the face of the earth. When Ahab realised that Savin was the same as him, he realised too that he was the same as Savin.

It was all a matter of control. And choice.

Nothing more and nothing less.

Chantal looked for the last time at the valley, the mountains and the woods where she used to walk as a child, and she felt in her mouth the taste of the crystal-clear water, of the freshly-picked vegetables and the local wine made from the best grapes in the region, jealously guarded by the villagers so that no visiting tourist would ever discover it – given that the harvest was too small to be exported elsewhere, and that money might change the wine producer's mind on the subject.

She had only returned to say goodbye to Berta. She was wearing the same clothes she usually wore, so that nobody there would know that, in her short visit to the city, she had become a wealthy woman. The stranger had arranged everything, signing all the papers necessary for the transfer in ownership of the gold bars, so that they could be sold and the money deposited in Miss Prym's newly opened account. The bank clerk had been exaggeratedly discreet and had asked no questions beyond those necessary for the transactions. But Chantal was sure she knew what he was thinking: he assumed he was looking at the young mistress of an older man.

'What a wonderful feeling!' she thought. In the bank clerk's estimation, she must be extremely good in bed to be worth that immense amount of money.

✳

She passed some of the local residents: none of them knew that she was about to leave, and they greeted her as if nothing had happened, as if Viscos had never received a visit from the Devil. She returned the greeting, also pretending that that day was exactly the same as every other day in her life.

She did not know how much she had changed thanks to all she had discovered about herself, but she had time to find out. Berta was sitting outside her house – not because she was still on the watch for Evil, but because she didn't know what else to do with her life.

'They're going to build a fountain in my honour,' she announced. 'It's the price for my silence. But I know the fountain won't last long or quench many people's thirst, because Viscos is doomed whichever way you look at it: not because of a devil who appeared in these parts, but because of the times we live in.'

Chantal asked what the fountain would look like. Berta had decided that it should be a sun spouting water into the mouth of a frog. She was the sun and the priest was the frog.

'I'm quenching his thirst for light and will continue to do so for as long as the fountain remains.'

The mayor had complained about the cost, but Berta would not listen, and so they had no choice. Building work was due to start the following week.

'And now you are finally going to do as I suggested, my girl. One thing I can tell you with absolute certainty: life can seem either very long or very short, according to how you live it.'

Chantal smiled, gave her a kiss, and turned her back on Viscos for the last time. The old woman was right: there was no time to lose, though she hoped that her life would be very long indeed.